The Police Agent

BY THE SAME AUTHOR

Rocambole (2006) (stage plays)
The Vampire and the Devil's Son (2007)
The Immortal Woman (2013)

The Police Agent

by
Pierre-Alexis Ponson du Terrail

Translated, annotated and introduced by
Brian Stableford

A Black Coat Press Book

Visit our website at www.blackcoatpress.com

TABLE OF CONTENTS

PONSON DU TERRAIL

L'AUBERGE
DE LA RUE DES ENFANTS-ROUGES

ÉDITION ILLUSTRÉE DE VIGNETTES SUR BOIS

Prix : 2 francs

PARIS
VICTOR BENOIST ET Cie, ÉDITEURS, RUE GIT-LE-CŒUR, 10, A PARIS
ANCIENNE MAISON CHARLIEU ET BUILLERY

Introduction

L'Auberge de la rue des Enfants Rouges by Vicomte Pierre-Alexis Ponson du Terrail was first published as a feuilleton serial in *La Patrie* in 1867, and was subsequently reprinted in book form in 1868 by Dentu. It is here translated as *The Police Agent*. The original title must have been attached to the story when the only part of it that Ponson had so far imagined was the prologue, in which the inn to which it refers is featured; in the main body of the story, as the author improvised it by degrees, the inn plays no part, and the narrative becomes increasingly focused on the activities of the police agent whose actions determine all of its twists and turns.

Ponson once informed an interviewer that his method of composition consisted of devising an interesting narrative hook and offering it to a newspaper editor, saying that if the first five episodes developing that beginning did not please the public, he would end the story in a further three, and if it did, he would continue it indefinitely. All his longer works, therefore, tend to be rambling, often changing genre as well as direction; a few, like the present example, do have an ultimate destination in mind before the end actually arrives, and thus the merest hint of a plot, but even when the author had some such end in mind, he never had a plan of how to get there, the story growing as he simply added more segments to it, making them up as he went.

Given that the publication in daily episodes of between one and two thousand words required the continual insertion of further narrative hooks to maintain sufficient eagerness on the part of readers to buy the following day's newspaper, the pace of the resultant narrative had to be both rapid and relentless. When reproduced in book form, inevitably, such narratives often seem confused and incoherent, full of trivial continuity errors, with some plot threads and characters being abandoned or forgotten while new ones are continually introduced, and it is only in rare cases that they form an esthetically satisfactory whole. The closest modern equivalent of the narrative method is that of TV soap operas, but they always remain in serial form, having no further phase of collation to highlight the eccentricities of the ensemble.

Most *feuilletonistes* employed a narrative method akin to Ponson's, but he was the most extreme, and, during his brief heyday in the 1860s, the most prolific. In the interview in which he explained his method he affirmed that he got up at four o'clock in the morning and worked relentlessly until he had competed all the episodes due for delivery that day—he sometimes worked on as many as five serials simultaneously—in order that he could be finished by lunch-time and spend the afternoon in leisure pursuits. He was probably exaggerating, if not actually lying—the implication that he actually wrote his work rather than dictating it to an amanuensis, as most *feuilletonistes* did, might be reckoned dubious—but the fact remains that he did produce the work with a truly remarkable fluency.

That kind of fluency is impossible to achieve without a certain amount of formularization: the continual reuse of similar narrative hooks and devices, of tried and tested effect. In all of Ponson's stories, therefore, the same melodramatic clichés recur time and time again, but precisely because of their eternal recurrence, the need for variety and innovation inevitably became pressing, and increasingly difficult to meet. When *feuilleton* fiction first became an important element in the marketing of French newspapers, in the 1840s, the scope for such innovation was still vast, and the great pioneers of the genre, Alexandre Dumas and Eugène Sue, were easily able to produce work that seemed spectacularly unprecedented, even though they borrowed most of the motifs they adapted to the new form from pre-existing works of fiction designed in a very different fashion. By 1867, however, more than two decades of incessant borrowing and copying by *feuilletonistes* had made the quest for further invention very difficult, although not impossible.

Ponson, along with his great rival as the Second Empire's leading *feuilletoniste*, Paul Féval, pioneered a number of important new trends that were to become vital foundation-stones not only for their immediate successors but for all future writers of popular fiction, of which by far the most important was the early development of crime fiction and initial exploration of its dramatic possibilities. The crime fiction they wrote seems eccentric to 21st century eyes because the various genres of modern crime fiction have undergone elaborate and spectacular refinement in the interim, but their work remains fascinating as an exemplification as the first groping steps in that process of evolution. *L'Auberge de la rue des Enfants Rouges* clearly did not set out to be one of the key works in that process of origination, but in the process of its organic growth it became one. Its narrative contains some of early examples of deductive detection applied to matters of criminal investigation, as well as containing primitive foreshadowings of what ultimately became the "police procedural" genre of crime fiction.

Before considering those aspects of the story, however, it is also worth considering some of the things that feuilleton fiction in the 1860s was not able to do, even though several of its leading authors, including Ponson and Féval, were obviously very ardent to do it. That might seem paradoxical, but it must be remembered that *feuilletonistes* were far more vulnerable than other writers during their process of composition to the pressure exerted by their editors, partly—but not entirely—reacting to the pressure exerted by their readers. When *feuilletonistes* introduced elements into their plots that their editors did not like, or about which some readers complained, they were quickly told to get rid of them, or to transform them into something more acceptable, thus sometimes engendering awkward narrative shifts.

The pattern of their careers suggests very strongly that both Féval and Ponson were intensely interested in the materials of the Gothic fiction that had become briefly popular at the end of the 18th century, some of whose elements were incorporated into the standard tropes of feuilleton fiction, although others, especially the supernatural elements, had been deliberately sidelined because of an apparently commonsensical assumption that they were "obsolete" in a positivistic era in which belief in the supernatural no longer seemed intellectually respectable.

Féval and Ponson were both particularly interested in the motif of the vampire and they both tried continually to write vampires into their fiction, but were continually frustrated by negative editorial pressure demanding that they should get rid of it or, at the very least, rationalize its apparently supernatural manifestations. None of the rationalizations that either author applied as patches came remotely close to plausibility, and many were utterly incoherent, but the very fact that they kept trying in such hostile circumstances is interesting in itself as an aspect of the continual war that writers have always fought against editorial pig-headedness and the mercuriality of the portion of reader response that takes the form of vocal complaint.

At the very beginning of his career, on which he embarked in his twenties, having been born in 1829, Ponson produced *La Baronne trépassée* (1852),[1] a Gothic extravaganza that attempted in exuberant fashion to renew and reinvigorate a number of supernatural motifs, centrally and most spectacularly the vampire *femme fatale*. Its effects were so extravagant that no reductive "explanation" was rationally possible but that did not prevent the author, presumably under pressure, from being continually forced to make token efforts in that direction. The similarly extravagant "Le Castel du diable," (tr. as "The Devil's Manse" in *The Chambrion and Other Stories*) which began serialization in 1852 was rapidly aborted after similarly drastic rationalizing moves reduced it to nonsensicality.

For some time thereafter, Ponson appears to have taken the lesson to heart, a policy probably reinforced when his next attempt at a supernatural extravaganza, "Le Revenant," which began as a serial in *Le Constitutionnel* in 1859, was also swiftly aborted. When he became a very popular writer in the 1860s, however, mainly due to the success of his flamboyant picaresque adventure stories featuring the spectacular character of Rocambole, he returned to the assault again, in three serials he began in 1867-69, *L'Auberge de la rue des Enfants Rouges* was the first, the other two were *La Messe noire* [The Black Mass] and

---

[1] tr. as *The Vampire and the Devil's Son*, Black Coat Press, ISBN 978-1-932983-55-5.

La Femme immortelle (1869).[2] He was forced to capitulate in all three instances, elements introduced as supernatural being partly or wholly rationalized, sometimes implausibly.

In the specific case of *L'Auberge de la rue des Enfants Rouges*, that process of capitulation produced some interesting results. The retention within the plot of the vampires introduced in the prologue is achieved by a strategy that does not dismiss their predation as mere illusion—always the cheapest strategy of writers subject to this kind of pressure—but changes its significance and credits it with real effects that are not without fascination in themselves. More importantly, however, when the author was forces to change the focus of his story, substituting a crime story for the supernatural romance he originally imagined, the retention of the vampiric villain as a particularly gruesome example of a repetitive murderer gave the story a significant precursory role in the development of what is nowadays an entire subgenre of "serial killer fiction" that focuses on the fetishistic aspects of hypothetical crimes of that sort.

By far the most striking aspect of that compulsory adaptation on the author's part, however, is the context in which the police agent who becomes the novel's central character by default has to operate. Set in the 1750s, the story unfolds in an era in which the role of the French police was very different from the role of police forces in later eras. Put crudely, the mission of the police under what was soon to become the *Ancien Régime* was not to protect members of society in general but to protect the aristocracy, and to uphold the law only insofar as it had that purpose. The result of that, in the specific context of the narrative, is that the police agent at the center of the plot does not employ his cunning ingenuity and his detective skills to pursue the princely serial killer intent on exsanguinating his multiple victims, but rather to protect him and preserve him from potential vengeance, while simultaneously serving other predatory aristocratic interests—specifically and most essentially, providing the lecherous King Louis XV with a steady supply of virgins to despoil.

The result of this recontextualization is that the police and the arch-criminals featured in the plot are on the same side, possessed of all the power and legal authority, which leaves something of a vacuum where the story's heroes might be located, and something of a puzzle for the author to address. Who can possibly play a heroic role in such circumstances, in which all virtue seems destined to be cruelly and savagely victimized? How can they possibly prevail? How can they even escape torture, murder and annihilation? Such narrative problems are not easy to solve, and whether the particular solutions that the author eventually adopted, after subjecting his sympathetic characters to a relentless barrage of threats and persecutions, are plausible or morally satisfactory is a matter of opinion. Nevertheless, his attempts to grapple with them are intriguing, and their chief corollary—the gradual development and refinement of the

---

[2] tr. as *The Immortal Woman*, Black Coat Press, ISBN 978-1-61227-175-0.

strange character of the police agent Porion, who becomes the story's overwhelming ominous presence—has a peculiar magnificence.

It is difficult to be sure, given the drastic lack of information provided by the story's abrupt conclusion, but it seems likely that when Ponson eventually wrote *Fin* at the end of the serial, that he planned to feature Porion in further works, perhaps building him into a series character analogous to Rocambole. In the event, the author's career was decisively interrupted by the Franco-Prussian War in 1870s, when he took up arms against the invading Prussians, who devastated his estate and burned his château, and he died in 1871 from the after-effects of wounds sustained in the conflict, so he never got the opportunity to employ Porion again—a circumstance that might be reckoned regrettable, if only because it would have been interesting to see the further projects to which his detective skills and ingenious scheming might have been applied.

What makes that unfulfilled possibility even more intriguing is that Porion is not the only detective featured in the plot; the Maréchal Duc de Richelieu similarly indulges in an ingenious piece of detective work, which nearly thwarts one of Porion's most daring schemes, before Porion turn the tables on him and they end up as allies in infamy. Had Ponson ever managed to write a sequel, it might well have featured the same duo teamed up again in Machiavellian alliance, with or without the assistance of Porion's other employer and protector, Madame de Pompadour. The possibilities were not endless, of course, all historical fiction having the dire inconvenience of being confined by what actually happened—or is said to have happened—in recorded history. Nevertheless, there was interesting scope for further chicanery, and one can only regret the abortion of that potential. Historical fiction was all the rage in the 1860s for the simple reason that Napoléon III's censors placed severe restrictions on contemporary fiction; the corrupt aristocracy of the *ancien régime* was both fair game and an easy target, as well as one offering abundant scope for stigmatization of the evil abuses of power.

In the event, *L'Auberge de la rue des Enfants Rouges* was reprinted in 1872, following Ponson's death, and again in 1876 in a cheaper edition, always retaining its misleading and uninspiring title, and was then virtually forgotten for well over a century. Ironically, it eventually came back into historical view by virtue of the element that had been suppressed, as an early example of vampire fiction, in an era when vampire fiction became a genre in its own right and its prehistory acquired a new academic interest.

It still retains some interest in that context, not only because of the stirring melodrama of the inciting incident, but also because of the strategy by which the vampirism of the Tartar Prince is "rationalized." It is, however, even more interesting as an early contribution to the development of crime fiction, by virtue of the highly equivocal role played by its central character—another narrative strategy that has come back into fashion in no uncertain terms in the modern subgenre of crime thrillers in which all the most powerful and most evil villains are deeply embedded in one or other of the "security services."

This translation was made from the copy of the novel reproduced on the Bibliothèque Nationale website, which is a cheap single-volume edition issued by Victor Benoist et Cie.

Brian Stableford

THE POLICE AGENT

PROLOGUE: THE VAMPIRE

I

One October evening in 175*, at half past five in the afternoon, one young man of about twenty-five years-old and another who was scarcely fifteen, both mounted on vigorous roan horses, were riding through the heart of the forest of Sénart, along the road from Melun to Paris. One glance sufficed to see that they were two brothers.

The child resembled the man; like him, he was dressed in a good doublet of thick blue fabric decorated with silver braid, shod in riding boots, coiffed with a small triangular felt hat, and gloved in leather, like provincial gentlemen going to Paris for the first time, and as yet unaware of the latest fashions and manners of high society.

They were trotting side by side, each with a small saddlebag, and chatting as they went.

"We'll soon be in Paris, André," said the elder. "If the information given to us by the woodcutter we met on the road a quarter of an hour ago is accurate, we have less than five leagues to go."

"And we'll be in Paris?" said the child, in a joyful tone.

"Yes, my dear André. We're going to stay in the Rue des Enfants Rouges, in the home of a former servant of our family, whom you didn't know, because he left our service before you were born."

"And he keeps an inn?"

"Yes, at the sign of the Blue Dragon."

The elder of the two horsemen gave his mount a slap with his riding-crop, and continued: "We'll have covered fifteen leagues today, my dear André. It's rather a long stage for someone your age, so we'll go to bed early, in order that you'll be ready to set out for Versailles tomorrow. There I'll introduce you to the King, who, in memory of the services of our venerable father, will admit you to the company of his pages."

The child was radiant when his brother spoke thus. "It appears," he said, "that the king's pages have beautiful embroidered clothes."

"Yes, replied the elder brother, smiling.

"And you, Hector, what will be your uniform in the gray musketeers?"

"It will be red."

"Well," said young André, naively, "why are they called the gray musketeers, then?"

"Because of the color of their horses."

"Oh! That's different." Then, becoming slightly melancholy, the child added: "So you won't keep your horse, Hector?"

"No, my friend."

"What will you do with it?"

"What I'll do with yours. We'll sell both of them when we arrive in Paris."

"Poor Coco!" said the child, passing an affectionate hand over the horse's neck.

"My dear André," said the big brother, "We're not rich, as you know. When he died, our father left us a poor manor in which the wind blows under the doors, surrounded by a little stone land in which oats and rye grow better than wheat. Our great aunts and our mother bled themselves white for our modest equipment, and you can imagine that, with the best will in the world, we can't keep our old hunting companions."

The child sighed again. "Poor Coco," he repeated. "As long as he falls into good hands! He's a valiant horse, Hector, and you know that ten hours at free rein haven't tired him out."

As young André mentioned free rein the two horses stopped abruptly, pricking their ears, snorting loudly, and one of them started to whinny joyfully. That was because, in the distant depths of the forest, a sound familiar to them rang out: a joyful fanfare, enthusiastically blown.

"Oh, my dear brother," exclaimed André, "what fine music. Let's pause for a moment."

"And what a full-throated pack," said Hector, who was leaning over the neck of his horse in order to listen more attentively to the baying of some thirty dogs, urged on vigorously by the sound of the horn.

"It's a ten-pointer, without a doubt!" said the child.

"I believe so," replied the big brother.

And as he spoke, the stag passed by, as rapid as lightning, crossing the highway in two bounds two or three hundred paces in front of the two young men. Then, after the stag cane the pack, and after the pack, huntsmen in red coats, and behind the huntsmen, three riders, two men and a woman.

All that was rapid, and almost fantastic; the two young men were dazed by it.

André sighed. Hector pressed the shoulder of his quivering horse with his knee, and they resumed their route, to the sounds of the horn and the pack, which faded away in the forest.

The road curved to the right a little beyond the place where the stag had crossed, and reached a crossroads, in the middle of which stood a signpost bearing the indication: *Carrefour du Roi.*

Eight forest paths radiated around that signpost.

When they had arrived there, the two young men stopped again, in the hope that they might see the hunt traversing one of the eight paths.

While they were waiting they heard the sound of small bells and whip-cracks, the hoof-beats of horses on the hard and sonorous ground, and, at the same time, they saw one of the large carriages appear that the end of the last reign had made fashionable, King Louis XIV having liked to follow hunts in a vehicle toward the end of his life. It was harnessed to four vigorous horses covered in tinkling bells, mounted by postillions in red coats.

The carriage came straight toward the crossroads. If they had wanted to continue on their route, the two young men would have been obliged to cross its path, but they did not think of that, dominated as they were by a somewhat provincial curiosity.

In fact, the carriage, in addition to its opulent and bizarre team in harness, was flanked to either side by two riders whose costume was even more bizarre. They were clad in furs, shod in funnel-topped boots, which had not been fashionable in France for a long time, and coiffed in small pointed bonnets that were also covered in animal-hide.

As the carriage was coming toward them, a man on horseback emerged from a thicket and approached them. He was wearing a blue uniform with silver braid—that of the king's huntsmen, for Sénart was a royal domain. Looking at Hector, he said: "I can see that your Lordship is surprised to see those savages of a sort?"

"Indeed," replied Hector. "Who are those men?"

"Cossacks."

"Indeed?"

"And in that carriage there's an eccentric of whom there has been much talk for the last two years."

"Oh," said the two brothers, with an increasing curiosity. "Who is that person, then?"

"A great Tartar lord."

"Truly?"

"He's almost six feet tall," the huntsman continued, "and is proportionately rich."

"What does that mean?"

"It's said that he has more than six thousand livres a day to consume."

"Damn!" murmured Hector. "The king surely doesn't have as much."

"That's quite possible," replied the huntsman.

"And he goes about thus, with those men clad in bearskins and horses overloaded with bells?"

"He's following the hunt."

"What? That pack..."

"Is his."

"And he follows it in a carriage?"

"It's not what amuses him the most, but what means has he of doing otherwise? He can no longer walk."

"He's an old man, then?"

"Now, yes—but six months ago, he was a young one. One wouldn't have thought him any older than thirty. He went hunting every week in the company of Monsieur de Clermont, who is, as you know, the king's cousin,[3] and they went to supper in the home of the young Marquis de Brunoy,[4] whom they drove mad by striving to make him drink." The huntsman continued, obligingly: "He was a solid fellow then, the Tartar, and it appears that all the women at court and elsewhere were fighting over him, and that he put them all in accord. It's no bad thing, moreover, to have so much money, and when one gives away diamonds by the handful as one might hand out beans." He smiled as he concluded.

"What happened to him, then?" asked Hector, seriously.

"No one knows, exactly."

"In truth!"

"But one morning, he woke up with his body covered by a kind of black crust, his lips swollen and his eyes bloodshot, horrible to behold."

"And since then?"

"Since then, he can no longer walk. But he says that he'll be cured, and ladies continue to flock to his door."

While the valet was speaking, the carriage arrived at the crossroads.

The two Cossacks dismounted; two valets got down from the seat and started unpacking an immense wooden hamper.

"That's milord's snack," said the huntsman, and drew away.

---

[3] Louis de Bourbon, Comte de Clermont (1709-1771), one of the "Princes of the Blood" fathered by Louis XIV on his mistresses, acquired a distinctly equivocal reputation, partly because of his scandalous abuses of his aristocratic authority and partly because he was said to be the Grand Master of French Freemasonry.

[4] Marquis de Brunoy was one of the titles of Jean-Pâris de Marmontel (1690-1766), which was popularized long after his death by the anonymous satire *Les Folies du Marquis de Brunoy, ou Ses Mille et Une Extravagances* (1804), and was also featured in an 1836 play credited to Alexandre Dumas and two collaborators, based on an article by Léon Gozlan, with which the author was undoubtedly familiar. The real Marmontel was, of course, not young in the 1750s.

Hector and his brother, as surprised by what they could see as by what they had just heard, did not think of continuing on their way. Both of them were staring at the carriage, which was scarcely ten paces away, and they would have liked to see the singular person of whom mention had just been made to them. The curtains of the carriage were hermetically closed at the front, however, and in order to glimpse the Tartar it would have been necessary for them to go to the side-doors, which would have been extremely impolite.

While they were hesitating, the Cossacks removed successively from the hamper a cloth, which they spread on the grass next to the signpost, and venerable bottles covered with cobwebs, which they placed on the cloth, along with an enormous venison pâté, smoked meat, a wild boar ham and various delicacies that fascinated the gaze of the two travelers. They were young, well mounted, and had made a long journey; their last meal had been eaten in Fontainebleau five or six hours before, and they were not expecting to eat supper until Paris, still five leagues distant.

Young André said to his brother, naively: "Since this Tartar's rich, he might invite us to dinner."

Hector smiled. "We'll dine as well in the Rue des Enfants Rouges," he said. "Let's go, little brother."

But before he had pressed the shoulder of his horse with his knee, Hector was obliged to focus his gaze on the carriage, one of the doors having just opened.

A man got down.

If the huntsman had told the truth, it was not the Tartar, for, apart from the fact that the man appeared to the two young men to be short rather than tall, he had no dark wounds on his face. He was a middle-aged man, paltry in appearance, going bald, with russet side-whiskers, clad in a long brown robe edged with fur, and coiffed in a conical astrakhan bonnet.

The man advanced toward Hector and bowed courteously.

Hector returned the salute, increasingly astonished.

The unknown man addressed him in French, but with a strong German accent.

"Gentleman, my name is Hermann Schutzberg, and I'm a physician of the Faculty of Heidelberg."

Hector bowed again.

The short man went on: "I'm attached to the personnel of the Russian Prince Trespatky, to whom that carriage belongs, and the pack that you might have seen passing by just now."

The young gentleman nodded his head, and waited

"Listen—one can hear the halloo out there, in the distance, and the hunt must be over," Hermann Schutzberg went on. "Monsieur le Comte de Clermont, Prince of the Blood, and the beautiful Princess Woïna, the prince's sister, will come to share this meal."

At the final words, young André, who was dying of hunger, shivered with a secret joy."

"Prince Trespatky," Herman Schutzberg concluded, "has asked me to invite you both to dinner."

Hector did not have time to respond. A man put his head out of the carriage window, and the two young men uttered a gasp of alarm. They had just perceived a kind of monster covered in leprosy, who shouted: "Well, Hermann, do the messieurs accept my invitation?"

At the same time, the Tartar set for on the ground and advanced painfully, on crutches, to meet Hector. That latter, like his brother, was mute with horror. The monster perceived that, and his ulcerated lips grimaced an odious smile.

"I frighten you," he said, "but don't worry. Hermann will cure me, and in six months, I'll appear to you as beautiful as daylight.

At the same time he darted a glance at young André of singular covetousness.

In spite of the assurance he gave the young people of his imminent cure, they were nevertheless about to draw away when a newcomer arrived at the signpost.

It was a woman: the amazon that they had perceived at a distance following the hunt. And, on seeing her, Hector no longer had the strength to flee; he remained there, as if petrified by admiration. Princess Woïna was as beautiful and as radiant as her brother was horrible and repulsive.

"Oh, how beautiful she is!" murmured Hector, dazzled.

II

Hector de Pierrefeu—that was the young gentleman's name—was fascinated by the woman, while his brother, too young as yet to experience emotions of that sort, was subject to a different attraction. He had turned his eyes away from the monster to watch the preparations for the picnic. His fifteen-year-old stomach was speaking as loudly as the inflammable heart of his big brother.

The beautiful Woïna dismounted, and threw her bridle to one of the Cossacks. Then she went to her brother, to whom she extended her hand.

There was a ten-second conversation between the horrible Tartar and the woman as beautiful as an angel—a conversation of which Hector did not hear a word, for it took place in the Russian language, but which, he divined, concerned the two of them.

Then the beautiful Woïna, turning her head, looked at Hector and his brother. She advanced toward them and said to them, in a voice as harmonious as a caress: "You won't refuse, will you, Messieurs?"

Hector, dazzled, stammered a few scarcely intelligible words, and dismounted. His brother imitated him.

At that moment, another rider arrived at the signpost. It was the Comte de Clermont—the king's cousin, as the huntsman had said.

The curiosity excited in them by that young lord, who was still young and handsome, finished reconciling the two young men to the repulsive face of the Tartar. The latter, in any case, was careful to place his sister beside Hector.

Young André marveled at the amber yellow wines that the Cossacks poured into sculpted gold goblets. Hector only had eyes for the beautiful Woïna; he only heard the celestial music of her voice.

The Comte de Clermont and the Tartars were in a very good mood. The hunt provided the first topic of conversation; then they progressed to intimate details.

Young André babbled like a warbler in a bush, with the aid of the wine. Thus, while his brother was admiring the beautiful Tartar woman, he confessed that his name was André de Pierrefeu, that he was the son of a Burgundian gentleman who had died in the king's service, that he was going to Paris with his brother, he to enter into the company of pages and his brother to the gray musketeers. He added that they would both be staying at the Blue Dragon Inn in the Rue des Enfants Rouges.

The Tartar and Monsieur de Clermont listened, smiling.

An hour went by.

It was a delightful hour for Hector, who could not weary of admiring Woïna, and a charming hour for the child, to whom Monsieur de Clermont promised mountains and marvels. In the end, however, it was necessary to separate, and it was not without regret on the part of the two young men. The beautiful Woïna had darted Hector a tender glance.

The Comte de Clermont, passing his hand over young André's rosy cheek, said to him: "I'm going to Versailles next week; I shall see the king, and you'll be well treated, on my recommendation."

A few minutes later, the two brothers were in the saddle and drawing away from their hosts at the Carrefour du Roi.

Hector sighed. When one is twenty-five and has a little imagination, the heart beats rapidly, and it is easy to dream of adventures. In the year of grace 175*, every gentleman quitting his province to come and seek his fortune in Paris immediately dreamed about some beautiful lady, who would hold him in high esteem and enable him make rapid progress.

Hector had solicited humbly, in a tremulous voice—and discreetly, to be sure—permission to present himself at the Tartar's town house on the Quai des Tournelles. Woïna had replied with a smile, and that smile was an acquiescence. So, during the rest of the journey, Hector said little, replying distractedly to the questions multiplied by his little brother, and they entered Paris at eight o'clock in the evening, André slightly sobered up and Hector half-crazy with amour for the beautiful Woïna.

They went in via the Faubourg Saint-Antoine and followed the street of that name as far as that of the Temple. There, they were within a short distance of the Rue des Enfants Rouges.[5] They were obliged nevertheless to ask the way.

"The second street on the left," an honest bourgeois sitting on his doorstep told them.

"Thank you," said Hector.

"Are you going to the Blue Dragon?" asked the bourgeois.

"Yes."

The bourgeois shook his head. "There are better inns in the quarter," he said.

"But we know the innkeeper," said Hector, and he continued on his way.

The bourgeois watched the draw away. "Those are handsome young fellows," he murmured, leaning toward his wife, who had joined him on the doorstep, "who don't appear to be anxious about the Blue Dragon's sinister reputation."

"Shut up, fool," his wife replied. "Why get mixed up in things that don't concern you?"

---

[5] There is no Rue des Enfants Rouges in Paris, but there is a Marché des Enfants Rouges—i.e., a market—in the Marais, founded in the 17th century, which still exists today. Red was the color of charity in 17th century Paris, so the children in a nearby orphanage were dressed in that color, and the market took its name from them.

And, as if she were afraid that the husband's words might be overheard by someone, she swiftly dragged him back into the house and closed the door.

In the meantime, Hector and André were going into the courtyard of the Blue Dragon. It was a veritable inn, such as there were in Paris then but which no longer exist today, except perhaps in one of the remoter outlying districts. There was a stable for the horses, a large table for their riders, a well-furnished cellar, and a kitchen as vast as a guard-room, in which a fire was blazing joyously before a Homeric spit placed on large wrought-iron forks.

Who, then, would have said that it was not a good inn? The bourgeois, to whom his wife had reprimanded him sharply, had to be a simple calumniator. The Blue Dragon was surely the best hostelry in the whole Saint-Martin quarter. And what service for travelers! Scarcely had the hooves of the horses struck the cobblestones of the courtyard than maidservants, scullions and stable-hands came running—and in their midst, the hotelier himself.

He was a short stout man with graying hair and a majestic appearance, who answered to the name of Master Boniface, and was the churchwarden of the Église Saint Martin-des-Champs. He had a jovial face when visitors of a certain age arrived, but his face darkened if, perchance, instead of mature men, the newcomers were young. He therefore frowned on seeing Hector and his brother dismount and hand their bridles to the stable-hands.

Hector ran toward him, and held out his hand.

"Bonjour, my good friend Boniface," he said. "Don't you recognize me?"

Master Boniface shuddered and took a step back. "It seems to me," he stammered, "yes…in fact…no…it's not possible!"

"What!" said the young man, "You don't recognize your little Hector, then?

"Lord God! Is it really true?"

"Yes, it's really me, Hector de Pierrefeu!"

"Ah!" said the landlord, who went very pale.

"How distraught you are!"

"Excuse me, Monsieur le Comte—you were only ten years old when I left the château. The emotion of seeing you again…the joy…you understand…"

"Yes, yes, my good friend."

Boniface wiped away large drops of sweat that were pearling on his brow.

"This is my brother," said Hector, taking André by the hand.

Boniface went even paler. "Are you going to stay here?" he asked, in a strangled voice.

"Of course—you wouldn't want us to go elsewhere?"

"That's true…you're right…it's a great honor for me…"

Master Boniface's emotion was increasing rather than calming down.

"We've come to ask you for supper and a bed," said Hector. "Then, tomorrow…"

"Tomorrow?" said Boniface, anxiously.

"We're going to Versailles."

The hotelier appeared to breathe out, and his anguish calmed down slightly. He took the two young men into the main room of the inn, which was also the kitchen. A woman was sitting by the foreside in front of the spit, which was rotating, garnished with an enormous quarter of beef. The woman, who was tall and thin, of sinister aspect in spite of a certain vulgar beauty, darted a strange gaze at the young men.

"Look, wife," said Boniface, whose voice resumed trembling slightly, "this is the son of my former master, the Comte de Pierrefeu."

"Handsome young men," she said, with a smile that made the hotelier shiver.

Hector and his brother were installed by the fireside.

Boniface leaned toward his wife, and whispered: "You'll answer for these two with your head!"

The woman shrugged her shoulders. Then, with a pitying smile, she said: "Are we the masters?"

"This time, we shall be..."

"Imbecile!"

Boniface consulted the large walnut-framed clock in the corner of the room with his gaze. "Eight o'clock," he said. "The man won't come."

"I hope so, for your sake," his wife replied, in a muted and ironic tone.

Boniface bowed his head, and did not say another word. He turned his inn upside down in order to give the sons of his former master an appropriate welcome, but he did not want the table in the kitchen to be laid.

"Where are you going to give us supper, then?" asked Hector.

"In your room, Monsieur le Comte."

"Why?"

"Because you'll be more tranquil there."

"As you wish," said the young man, who was still thinking about the beautiful Woïna.

While Boniface conducted the young men to their lodgings, the stable-lad said in a loud voice: "These gentlemen are doubtless leaving early in the morning. At what time is it necessary to have the horses ready?"

The hotelier looked at him askance. "The gentlemen are leaving in broad daylight, after breakfast," he replied. "You can go to bed."

Hector and his brother ate moderately. André was not hungry, but he was tired. Hector was thinking about the beautiful Tartar woman.

Doubtless to do them honor, Boniface had wanted to serve them personally. When they had finished their meal he said to Hector: "You'd do well to lock your doors carefully, Monsieur le Comte."

"Bah! There are thieves in Paris, then?" asked Hector, laughing.

"Which is to say," Boniface replied, "that for seven or eight months, there's been talk of nothing but murders and thefts in the quarter. Only last week, someone tried to force the doors of the stable to steal the horses of a Norman gentleman who was lodging here."

"Well, I'll lock my door carefully," Hector replied.

"It wouldn't do any harm to put your sword under your bolster."

"Bah!"

"And a good pair of pistols on your night-stand."

"You're frightening me!"

The hotelier did not have time to justify his fears, for the door opened and his wife came in.

"Don't listen to my husband, Monsieur le Comte," she said, pulverizing the unfortunate Boniface with a glance. "He's a little mad...since the evening when he was beaten crossing the Pont Neuf, he sees nothing but thieves, assassins and prowlers everywhere. That was as well once, but today, thank God, the Lieutenant de Police mounts a good guard."

At the same time, she dismissed Boniface with an imperious gesture. The man must have feared his wife at least as much as thieves, for he went out, uttering deep sighs, without even turning his head.

Then Madame Boniface said to Hector: "Here's a letter for you."

"A letter!" said the young man, astonished.

The innkeeper's wife had taken a small folded sheet of paper from beneath her apron, sealed with blue wax that exhaled a mysterious perfume.

"It's a woman who brought it," added Madame Boniface.

Hector took the letter, tremulously, and cast his eyes over the address, which read: *To Monsieur le Comte Hector de Pierrefeu, at the Blue Dragon.*

The letter really was for him. Who, then, could be writing to him?

The writing revealed a woman's hand. And what other woman that the beautiful Woïna could know that young Hector de Pierrefeu was staying at the Blue Dragon in the Rue des Enfants Rouges?

The young man, seized by a violent heartbeat, broke the seal on the letter with a tremulous hand.

III

The mysterious letter was conceived as follows:

If Hector de Pierrefeu is as brave as he is handsome, as tender as he is witty, and does not disdain an amorous adventure, he will quit the Blue Dragon Inn at ten o'clock and go along the Rue du Temple as far as the riverbank.
There we will find a person who will take him to one who is dying of love for him.

There was no signature—but every line, every word, was ablaze in Hector's eyes in letters of fire, and seemed to trace the name of Woïna.

He had the strength to hide his emotion, however, and to maintain an almost impassive face.

"Thank you," she said to Madame Boniface, "That's all." And he put the letter in his pocket.

Young André was asleep on his feet, and paid no attention to the letter that his brother had just received.

The innkeeper's wife left, after having expected that the young man might indicate by a word what he intended to do.

A sand-glass placed on the mantelpiece of the room was, however, the sole motive for his apparent calm. It marked nine o'clock. In order to conform to the indications of the letter, Hector had a full hour to wait.

In any case, as a true chevalier, he saw no need to impart the secret of his good fortune to anyone, especially the innkeeper and his wife.

He therefore put on an appearance of going to bed, and following Master Boniface's recommendation, he placed his pistols on a night-table and his sword under the bolster. Then he waited, first for his little brother to go to sleep, and then for the hour of the rendezvous to arrive.

In the meantime, the hotelier's wife had gone back to the main room of the inn.

The innkeeper was sitting by the fire at that moment, with his head in his hands and his elbows on his knees, with an expression of sinister dolor, almost of despair.

His wife whose name was Catherine, tapped him on the shoulder. "What are you doing here?" she said.

"Nothing," he replied, in a sullen tone.

The scullions, the kitchen-maids and everyone else had gone to bed.

"Are you going to feel sorry for yourself all night?" said Catherine, in a mocking tone.

Boniface raised his eyes to the heavens,

"What are you doing here, instead of taking care of our business?"

"We don't have any business this evening."

"You're mistaken..."

He shivered from head to toe, and murmured dully: "At least, I hope not." Then, looking at the clock, which marked some time after nine o'clock, he said, vehemently: "No, no! We won't have..."

"Oh, you think so?"

"*The man* always comes at nightfall. Since he hasn't come, it's because he isn't coming..."

"I hope so, for your sake," said Madame Boniface, with muted irony. "You're always so frightened, when we have work to do, that it really is a great pity to see you in this state."

"Wife, wife!" murmured Master Boniface, in a somber and despairing tone, "you'll see...the punishment will be terrible..."

Catherine shrugged her shoulders, and replied: "It's necessary to earn one's poor living...and then..."

"And then what?"

"You know full well that we belong to them body and soul, and that we're forced to obey."

"Oh, woe, woe!" murmured Master Boniface, covering his face with both hands.

"Imbecile," said his wife.

"Don't you understand, then," he went on, with a sudden vehemence, "that those two young men are the sons of my former master?"

"Of course I understand. So what?"

"Well, no, it shall not be...it cannot be...even if I have to denounce the truth to the Lieutenant de Police."

"You wouldn't have time," said his wife, coldly.

He got to his feet abruptly. "Why not?" he said.

"Because you'd be dead before you reached the threshold of his house."

"Woe!" repeated Master Boniface, in a despairing tone.

"But I think you're getting all upset for no reason," Catherine added.

He looked at her anxiously.

"Undoubtedly," she went on. "The man hasn't come; he won't."

"Oh, may God hear you!"

"Aren't those handsome messieurs leaving for Versailles in the morning?"

"Yes, that's what they said."

"Well, go to sleep tranquilly...or rather..." Catherine appeared to reflect. "Damn!" she said, after a momentary silence, "I wasn't mistaken just now, when I told you that instead of lamenting, you'd do better to occupy yourself with our affairs."

"What do you mean?"

"Didn't the draper from the Rue du Chantre, Master Loyseau, come here today?"

"Of course."

"And didn't he say that he was ready to pay, this evening, the annual rent he owes us for the shop we lease to him?"

"That's true."

"Then go get your money."

"But I can as easily go tomorrow."

"No, it's better to have it than to have it owing. Money's always better in the home of the person to whom it belongs than that of the man who owes it."

"But what if the man comes…?"

"He won't come, I tell you."

"My God!" said Boniface, putting his hands together. "May that woman be telling the truth!"

"Go fetch your money, then!" exclaimed Catherine, impatiently.

Boniface got to his feet, unsteadily. Catherine, who was a megaera before whom the unfortunate Boniface was trembling like a child, took him by the shoulders and shoved him toward the door, repeating: "Go on, then."

He uttered a sigh that would have moved a tiger to compassion; then, taking his hat and cloak, he opened the door to the street and went out, not wanting to go through the courtyard.

Then Catherine went to the door, which he had left open. The moon was shining brightly, illuminating the least object. The innkeeper's wife followed her husband with her eyes until he turned the corner of the Rue du Temple. She listened until the noise of his footsteps had faded away in the distance.

Then she closed the door again, saying to herself in a mocking tone: "If one listened to that imbecile with his sentiments, we'd be ruined. At a hundred écus per head is six hundred livres that will fall to us from the sky; it's always the same.

As she said it, Catherine pricked up her ears again. Footsteps were audible in the street.

"It's *him!*" she said.

And she ran to open the door.

Indeed, a man enveloped in a vast cloak slid rather than stepped into the inn.

Catherine closed the door again.

"Bonjour, Madame Boniface," he said, taking off his cloak, which he threw on to a chair, but without taking off the small velvet mask that he wore over his face.

"Bonjour, Monseigneur," replied Catherine, in a respectful tone.

He was a short man with red hair, graying at the temples, entirely clad in black, whose eyes were shining through the mask like ardent coals.

He sat down.

"Hee hee," he said. "We have fresh prey this evening."

"That's true," said Catherine.

"Has anyone brought a letter?"

"Yes, a young man that I recognized as one of yours, Monseigneur."

"And has that letter reached its destination?"

"Certainly. I handed it to him myself."

"He'll go to the rendezvous then?"

"I don't know."

"What?"

"Well he's still up there, in his room..."

"Ah!"

"And I can't hear any sound," Catherine retorted. "I'm afraid that he might be in bed, asleep."

The little man made an ill-humored gesture. "That would upset all our plans," he said. Fortunately, at that moment he heard some movement above his head. "What's that?" he said.

"I think it's him," said Catherine.

"Truly!"

"Their room is directly overhead." The innkeeper's wife raised a finger vertically, toward the ceiling.

Someone was walking about up there.

Catherine put out the lamp that was burning on the table. She had already covered the fire. Then she took the man she had addressed as Monseigneur by the hand. "Come," she said.

The little man allowed himself to be drawn into the parlor that was adjacent to the main room, separated from it by a small glazed door fitted with curtains. She closed that door behind them, and they both waited.

Footsteps were heard on the staircase. The man coming down was moving cautiously. He opened the door separating the staircase from the main room quietly. Then he crossed the room on tiptoe, heading through the darkness to the door to the street. He opened it, and paused momentarily on the threshold.

The night was clear and the moon bright.

Hidden behind the glazed door of the small room, Catherine and the mysterious visitor she called Monseigneur saw Hector de Pierrefeu, illuminated by the moon's rays, dart a furtive glance into the street.

"It's him," said the man in the mask.

Hector closed the door, and the sound of footsteps soon died away in the distance.

Then Catherine and the man came out of their hiding-place. The innkeeper's wife lit the lamp again.

"Where's your husband?" asked the unknown man.

"He's gone out."

"Why?"

"I sent him away, for fear that he might prevent the young man from going to the rendezvous."

"But we need him."

"He'll come back."

As she said that, the door opened and Boniface appeared on the threshold.

At the sight of the man in the mask, he uttered a cry, and recoiled, pale and shivering.

"You weren't expecting me so late, were you?" said the little man, with a mocking expression.

Boniface did not reply. It was as if he were petrified. Suddenly, however, he took a step toward the man in the mask and dropped to his knees.

"Mercy, Monseigneur, mercy!" he stammered.

"What?" said the little man, in a haughty tone.

"Mercy!" repeated Boniface, whose teeth were chattering in terror.

"Mercy for whom?"

"For the two children."

Dry and mocking laughter resounded beneath the unknown man's mask.

Boniface put his hands together and went on: "They're the sons of my former master…I knew them when they were very small."

"Well," said the unknown man, sniggering, "let's share."

A frisson ran through Boniface's body.

"The elder one's gone," said Catherine.

"Gone!"

"Yes, he's gone to an amorous rendezvous." At the same time, she opened the drawer in a dresser and took out a black mask.

"Let's go!" said the little man. "If the Prince knew you needed so much persuasion, you might well have to repent if it tomorrow. To work!"

Boniface bowed his head, and two hot tears trickled down his cheeks.

IV

Meanwhile, Hector de Pierrefeu had turned the corner of the Rue des Enfants Rouges and was now going down the Rue du Temple.

The moonlight was bright and, in spite of the late hour, the edicts and the curfew, which was still in force, there were quite a few bourgeois and common people in the streets.

No lights could be seen in the windows, but the casements were open here and there, the Parisians, deeming, since the moon could not be extinguished as they had blown out their candles, they had every right to take advantage of its light.

Hector did not know Paris at all, so, when he had taken a hundred steps along the Rue du Temple, he felt a need to ask for directions.

The same bourgeois that he had addressed a few hours before to ask him the way to the Rue des Enfants Rouges, was still on his threshold. Thanks to the moonlight, Hector recognized him and went toward him. The bourgeois also recognized him, and saluted him.

"My dear Monsieur," said Hector, "Am I really in the Rue du Temple?"

"Yes, my gentleman."

"And this street goes down to the river, does it not?"

"It terminates in the Place de Grève, which is beside the river," the bourgeois replied.

"Which is the same thing," said Hector. "Thank you, and *au revoir*."

But the bourgeois retained him with a gesture. "Pardon me, my gentleman, but wasn't it you who asked me for directions earlier today?"

"Yes, that was me," said Hector.

"You're not staying at the Blue Dragon?"

"Yes."

"Ah!" said the bourgeois, "and you're here?"

"Of course. What's extraordinary about that?"

"It's just that...just that," stammered the bourgeois, "as true as my name's Onésime Morel, and I'm a furrier by trade, when a handsome young gentleman like you stays at the Blue Dragon..."

"Well?"

"He doesn't come out again."

"Well, you can see that I've come out."

The bourgeois was about to reply, but someone else emerged from the depths of the shop on to the threshold. "Shut up, wretch!" she said, in a shrill and sharp voice. "You're always getting mixed up in things that don't concern you."

And, taking her husband by the arm, the megaera pulled him violently into the house, leaving Hector bewildered.

What if the furrier were telling the truth and there was danger in staying at the Blue Dragon? But an idea occurred to him suddenly. *But isn't Boniface an old family servant?* he thought. *What can I have to fear from him?*

The mysterious letter that he had slipped into his doublet was burning his breast. After a hesitating for a few seconds, therefore Hector resumed his route. As he was about to reach the Place de Grève, however, his hesitation gripped him again. A woman was sitting on the single step that served as a perron to a low door.

"My good woman," said Hector, going up to her. "Do you know the Blue Dragon inn?"

At that name the old woman shuddered, stood up swiftly and took a step backwards. "Why are you asking me that?" she said. "Are you one of the Lieutenant de Police's sergeants?"

"Not at all!" said Hector, laughing.

"Go on your way," said the old woman. "I'm a poor woman who only minds her own business and not that of others. Go on, go on…I don't know what you want me to say."

She went inside precipitately, with those last words, and closed her door.

"Too bad!" murmured Hector. "Let it not be said that a Pierrefeu kept a pretty woman waiting."

And he continued on his way.

The Place de Grève, ordinarily deserted, was animated that evening. A red glow was visible in the center, and men were moving back and forth all around it.

Curiosity took hold of Hector, and he approached.

The light was coming from a fire; the men surrounding it, who numbered seven or eight, had a sinister and criminal appearance.

When he got closer, our hero perceived a wooden beam rising above the fire. It was a gallows. The men warming themselves were none other than the assistants of Monsieur de Paris, as the executioner was known in those days. The men were chatting in low voices. Hector lent an ear, and this is the conversation he overheard:

"What time are we going to hang the two men?" said one.

"At daybreak."

"They're thieves aren't they?"

"I don't know, but I think so."

"Perhaps from Cartouche's gang?"[6]

"I don't know."

---

[6] The famous bandit known as Cartouche (Louis-Dominique Garthausen, 1693-1721) was long dead by the 1750s.

The questioner began to laugh. "Well, Canuche, on seeing you sad and in a bad mood like this, one might think that these two men that we've never seen—for we never make the acquaintance of our clients until it's time I send them to the next world—were of interest to you."

"No," said Canuche.

"But it was with an ill grace that you helped us set up the gallows!"

Canuche replied: "That's because I have an idea."

"What?"

"I think we're hanging too many poor people."

Those words were greeted with a noisy burst of laughter.

"And not enough gentlemen!" added Canuche, in a sullen tone.

Hector was ten paces from the brazier, and the faces of the executioner's valets seemed livid to him in the firelight. The man named Canuche, who appeared to be in command of the others, was still young, with a forehead covered in yellow hair and a pale, sad face.

"You're laughing," the man went on, "but there's nothing to laugh at."

"Good," said the first interlocutor, "now Canuche is getting sick of the work."

"Does our métier disgust you?"

"No, but I'd rather hang other people."

"Which?"

"I just told you—gentlemen."

"Why?"

"Because they're the ones committing all these crimes that have been putting Paris in turmoil for some time."

"What crimes?"

"You don't know that children are being stolen?"

"So it's said, but it's not true."

"I know what I'm talking about," murmured Canuche, "but what I know isn't anyone's business."

Children are being stolen! thought Hector de Pierrefeu. *What does that mean?*

Another of the valets added: "And murdered men are being found in the nets at Saint-Cloud."

"Bah!"

Canuche added, in an irritated tone: "But it's none of our business, after all. Let's not talk about it."

"Why?"

"It brings bad luck."

Hector had not been noticed by any of the valets. He drew closer still. The conversation piqued his curiosity to the highest degree.

"So, Canuche," one of the men continued, "you think that these fine things are the work of gentlemen?"

"I believe so."

"But..."

"I won't tell you why I believe it...that's none of my business, it yours either. And let's be careful, after having hanged so many people, not to be hanged in our turn."

With those words, Canuche lay down beside the brazier, rounded one of his arms, put his head on it, and adopted the attitude of a man who would not be sorry to sleep for a while.

Hector drew away. Once again he was on the point of retracing his steps and going back to the Blue Dragon, to watch over his brother. Had not Canuche said that children were being stolen? But what children? Undoubtedly, infants three or four years old, whom acrobats took away in order to train them for their infernal métier. Hector's brother was not yet a man, but he was no longer a child. Then again, was Boniface not there to watch over him?

While making these reflections, Hector caressed the cherished love-letter with his hand. Could that unsigned letter have come from anyone other than the beautiful Woïna?

Our hero went on all the way to the river.

There was no quay in those days and no parapet; the Place de Grève descended in a shallow slope to the water's edge. The shore was deserted; one could not see beyond the black silhouettes of the edifices that rose up on the left bank. No other sound could be heard but the dull splashing of the water.

Where, then, was the person who was supposed to serve as Hector de Pierrefeu's guide?

A suspicion crossed his mind: a terrible suspicion that brought drops of sweat to his brow. Might he not be the victim of a ruse, and this rendezvous he had been given nothing but a means of causing him to abandon his brother André for a while? Canuche's words with regard to stolen children came back to his mind.

But he did not have time to form a resolution. Suddenly, he perceived a black dot in the middle of the river; he distinctly heard the curt and rhythmic sound of two oars striking the water. A boat seemed to be heading toward him.

Hector waited. Soon, the boat was so close to the bank that, with the aid of the moonlight, Hector was able to see them people manning it. He saw a man and a woman. The man was rowing the boat, the woman standing up at the prow. Adroitly removed from the current, the boat came to dig the tip of its keel into the sand, ten paces from the place where Hector was standing, motionless and mute.

The woman leapt lightly to the shore, and then marched straight toward Hector, who waited for her, standing still. She was enveloped in a large cloak, and her face was covered by a small black velvet mask.

In that epoch, the usage of masks was frequent, and a woman of quality traveling abroad n the streets of Paris in broad daylight with her face masked did not attract attention or excite curiosity. But Hector was from the provinces, and it was with a certain astonishment that he saw the masked woman coming toward him. Was it Woïna, then? No, if Hector believed in the tenor of the note he had received. Yes, if he paid attention to the mask.

The woman came to him and put her hand on his shoulder. "Are you not the man who is waiting?" she said.

"What is your name?"

"Hector de Pierrefeu."

"It is indeed you."

As soon as the unknown woman spoke, Hector had understood that it was not the Tartar beauty. Prince Trespatky's sister had a harmonious and youthful voice. This woman, on the contrary, had the slightly shrill and quavering voice of a duenna.

"I've been instructed to take you to the woman who is waiting for you," she said.

"I'm ready to go with you," Hector replied. "But one word, please."

"Speak."

"Is it not Princess Woïna who sent you?"

"I can't tell you anything."

"Oh!"

"And if you cannot comply with all the conditions that I'm instructed to impose upon you," the unknown woman said, "you may return whence you came."

"What must I do?"

"Firstly, climb into this boat."

"Very well."

"When you are there, I shall blindfold your eyes with a scarf."

"I'm not to know where you're taking me, then?"

"No."

"You can blindfold me," said Hector. "Is that all?"

"No. The person who is waiting for her is masked, like me."

"Yes, but she will take off her mask?"

"I don't believe so."

"It's not the Princess, then?"

"I can't tell you anything."

After all, Hector thought, *I can understand that. The Princess doesn't want to be compromised. It's her, it's really her.*

"Do you accept?" the duenna asked.

"Yes."

"I have one more condition to impose on you."

"What is it?"

"Whatever you see and hear tonight, and however strange what you see or hear appears, you will give me your word as a gentleman never to reveal any of it."

"You have it."

"So you've decided to go with me?"

"Yes."

"Come, then." She took him by the hand and made him get into the boat.

Hector perceived them that the man lying the oars was also masked.

The unknown woman sat Hector down beside her, at the rear of the boat. Then she took a large piece of silk from her bosom, and made a blindfold, placed it over the young man's eyes and knotted it solidly behind his head.

Then, plunged in darkness, Hector sensed by the movement imprinted on the boat that it was moving into open water. Where was he being taken? He could not tell. By the freshness of the air current, and the rapidity that the boat seemed to have acquired, and the time that each stroke of their oars took, however, he deduced that instead of going upriver, they were heading downstream.

Then he also remembered the other words spoken by Canuche, the executioner's valet: "Don't you know that murdered men have been found in the nets at Saint-Cloud?" But Hector was brave, and it was, in any case, too late to renounce the adventure.

The journey lasted half an hour. At the end of that time the boat experienced a violent jolt, and then became immobile.

"We've arrived," said the duenna.

"Take off my blindfold, then," Hector replied.

"No, not yet." She took his hand. "Get up and step over the edge. Here…good."

Hector's foot trod on the sand of the bank.

"Now, come," the duenna concluded.

Scarcely had they taken two steps, however, than Hector de Pierrefeu stopped.

"What is it?" asked his mysterious guide.

Hector had just perceived that his sword was no longer at his side. "My sword," he said. "Where's my sword?"

"I've taken it away."

"Why?"

"Because one does not go armed into the house to which I'm taking you."

"But…however…"

The duenna's tone was mocking. "Are you afraid?"

"No, certainly not."

"Come, then." And she added, in a dryer tone; "There's still time. If you want to go back, I'll take you back to the place where I picked you up."

"No," said Hector, his pride wounded. "Ever if you're taking me to the devil, I'll go with you."

The duenna did not reply, but she continued to draw Hector along.

Hector thought about Woïna, and said to himself: *Truly, to pay for an hour of that woman's amour with all one's blood and one's life wouldn't be too dear. Let's go!*

And, once he had quit the bank, he felt the pavement of a street resonating beneath his feet.

V

Still plunged in the most profound obscurity, Hector marched, guided by the duenna, for about a quarter of an hour.

Then the duenna stopped.

At the same time, the young man heard a muffled sound. It was the knocker of a door, lifting and falling back on to an iron striking-pad.

The door opened. The duenna pushed Hector in front of her, and another sound informed him that the door had just closed again. The cobblestones that he had had underfoot a short while before were succeeded by a uniform and resonant surface, doubtless formed by flagstones, and his spurred boots resounded, awakening distant echoes.

"You're not taking off my blindfold?" he said.

"No, not yet," replied the duenna.

The sound of his footfalls informed Hector that he was traversing a vestibule as sonorous as the corridors of a cloister. Fresh, almost damp air whipped his face.

Finally, the duenna stopped again, pushed a door, and made Hector cross the threshold. He suddenly experienced a tripe sensation. A warmer atmosphere enveloped him; his sense of smell was charmed by a mysterious and penetrating perfume, and he had certainly come into an illuminated place, for an imperceptible light traversed his blindfold.

"We've arrived," said the duenna. At the same time, she untied the blindfold. Hector could not retain an exclamation, so dazzling did the light that struck his eyes seem. For a moment, that dazzle prevented him from seeing where he was, Eventually, however, he adapted to the light that, for him, had succeeded a profound obscurity, and looked at the objects surrounding him.

The duenna was standing before him. He was in a small room whose walls were hung with brightly-colored oriental fabrics. The floor was covered by a soft carpet. Tall candelabras, placed on the mantelpiece, to either side of a rococo clock, supported ten candles, whose glare had struck Hector. Next to the fire, a winged chair with cushions awaited the visitor. The duenna made him sit down, and placed herself beside him.

"Where am I, then?" asked the poor gentleman, who had never seen furniture so elegant, wall-hangings so sparkling, luxurious and stunning. "What is this palace?"

"This palace is yours, if you wish," replied the duenna, smiling.

"But, where is she?" And he paraded his gaze around, seeing no one except the duenna, beneath whose mask and headdress a few white hairs were protruding.

"Wait...she'll come..."

36

Hector breathed out. For a moment, he was afraid that the old woman had brought him to this place on her own account.

"You'll be faithful to your word?" she said.

"Of course."

"You won't ask her to take off her mask?"

"Certainly not."

"And when you leave here, whatever you've seen and heard..."

"Madame," said Hector, proudly, "as true as my name is Pierrefeu, Seigneur de Charmeuse, I swear to you..."

"Charmeuse!" exclaimed the duenna.

"Yes, that's the name of one of my family's estates."

"Charmeuse!" she repeated, in a singular tone. And she got up from the wing-chair where she was sitting beside Hector.

"Yes, Madame," said Hector, slightly astonished. "We're called by our name, Pierrefeu de Charmeuse."

"Are you Burgundian, then?"

"Yes."

"And have you not a relative, perhaps an uncle, who was a captain in the Royal-Cravates, and whose name was...Raoul?"

The duenna's voice had begun to tremble as she asked those questions, and she as agitated by a singular emotion.

"Raoul de Charmeuse was my father," Hector said. "As he had an older brother, who has since died without issue, he only bore the same Charmeuse then."

"And you're his son?"

"Yes."

"Oh!" said the old woman, wringing her hands. "My God!"

She pronounced the last word in a veritable tone of despair. Hector gazed at her, stupefied.

"My God!" she repeated, as if terrified. And she took him by the hand, saying: "Come, come with me!"

But as she said it, the clock struck midnight.

The duenna uttered a muffled cry.

At the same time, a curtain lifted and a door opened.

"Too late!" murmured the distraught duenna.

But Hector did not hear those words, so violent was the emotion that had suddenly gripped him.

The door that had opened gave passage to a woman—and that woman, who marched straight toward Hector, had to be her! She was masked, but her neck, her arms and shoulders were bare, and dazzlingly white, and she had luxuriant loose blonde tresses that could only belong to the beautiful Woïna. Her gaze, humid with sensuality, shone through the black velvet mask like a star in the celestial vault after a rainstorm.

Hector fell to his knees, palpitating, voiceless, his hands joined.

And yet, the duenna did not budge. She was still there, mute and shivering, gazing with somber despair at the young man who could no longer see her.

The blonde-haired woman made an imperious gesture. "Well," she said, "what are you doing here?"

The duenna stammered a few words.

"Get out, then!" ordered the newcomer.

Oh, thought Hector, in ecstasy, *it's really her...I recognize her voice!*

The duenna headed slowly toward the door. Just as she was about to cross the threshold, she turned round and darted one last glance at Hector: a desperate glance. Then she disappeared.

The blonde-haired woman had brought Hector to his feet. "Come and sit down here, next to me," she said. She curled up graciously in her wing-chair as she spoke, and Hector was not longer capable of being mistaken. It really was Woïna's voice he could hear.

So, as she abandoned her hand to him, and he raised it to his lips in order to cover it with kisses, he cried: "Oh, dear Woïna!"

She shivered at that name. "Shut up!" she said. "That name is not mine."

"Oh!"

"I have never borne it," she said, in a voice that seemed tremulous.

"But it's really you, though!" said Hector.

"Who?"

"The Prince's sister?"

"What Prince?" she said. But her voice, increasingly tremulous, made it obvious enough that she was lying.

Then Hector remembered the oath he had sworn to the duenna not to demand that the woman awaiting him unmask herself, and he said to himself: *What does it matter to me, since it's definitely Woïna?*

Then he knelt down before her again. "Pardon me!" he said.

She resumed smiling through her mask. "Child," she said, "will you listen to me?"

"Yes," he said, "speak..." And he hung on her lips, so to speak.

"An abyss separates us," she said. "That abyss, I have filled in. Know that I am not free. Know that I have a husband."

Hector made a gesture that betrayed a surge of jealousy.

"A husband that I hate!" she went on.

"Ah!" he said, as a sigh of relief swelled his breast.

"But a husband who would kill me if he found me here, with my hand in yours."

"Oh! I would defend you!" said Hector, with a chivalrous enthusiasm

"Dear child!"

"He would not succeed in reaching you without treading upon my cadaver," the young man added, with a proud smile.

38

"But he won't find us," the blonde-haired woman added. "We are in my house here, lost in a distant quarter of Paris…the people who surround us are devoted to me…"

She spoke, and Hector listened to that soft and harmonious voice; she gazed at him, and he was intoxicated by that gaze; she smiled at him, and that smile fell upon his soul and electrified it.

"Tel me," she continued, "Would you like us to enjoy a mysterious and endless happiness? Would you like that?"

"I love you!" he stammered.

"You'll come here every night…but you'll be discreet, won't you?"

"Oh," he said, "can you ask me that?"

"And if ever your encounter me without this mask, which I have sworn an oath never to take off in your presence, if you happen to encounter me in society, swear to me that not a gesture will give you away, that not a muscle of your face will twitch?"

"I swear to you."

"That's good," she said. "I love you too."

And she kissed him on the forehead.

Then, extending her hand toward a side-table on which here was an ebony wand, she picked it up and used it to rap on a bell.

At that sound, the door through which the duenna had gone out opened again. Hector then saw two valets who were rolling a small table in front of them, already laid.

"I'm inviting you to supper," said the blonde-haired woman.

Like their mistress, and like the duenna, the two lackeys were masked.

They brought the table to the fireside, in front of the wing-chair, without saying a word, and they left.

The table was laid with a delicious cold supper; amber yellow wines sparkled in glasses of Bohemian crystal. The bitter and penetrating perfume of Perigord truffles embalmed the air, already charged with warm and mysterious emanations.

After the dazzlement of his eyes, after the voluptuous fascination, Hector found himself gripped by gastronomic seductions.

The woman in the mask served him with her beautiful hands; she poured him long draughts of the topaz-colored wine, and while they supped they united their lips a thousand times in a thousand kisses.

They had sampled all the dishes, and they had tasted all the wines, except for one. That one was a pale green, and the bottle that contained it as bizarre in its form; one might have thought it the sacred vase of some Far Eastern religion.

"What's that?" asked Hector, finally, becoming increasingly dazed, warmed by the generous wines that she had poured incessantly. He had put one of the arms around her flexible and slender waist, and he was kissing her neck as he asked the question.

"That," she said, "is the wine of Cyprus."

"Why haven't you poured me any?"

"It's the forbidden wine."

"Pardon?"

"The wine of knowledge," she added, alluding to the famous tree in the terrestrial paradise that was, it is said, the first cause of all the evils of humankind.

"And if I drank some, what would happen to me?"

"Perhaps a great misfortune."

"What?"

"You'd love me for all your life."

"Oh, pour, then, pour it quickly." And he held out his glass, avidly.

"You're absolutely sure?"

"Yes."

"You'll drink it all in a single draught?"

"Yes, pour."

She extended her hand, took the bottle, poured two fingers into Hector's goblet, and said to him, smiling: "It's you who wanted it."

Hector put the glass to his lips and drank.

Suddenly, an unusual warmth ran through his entire body; a shower of sparks seemed to emerge from his eyes; his forehead was bathed by an abundant sweat; his swollen heart suddenly ceased to beat.

"Oh, my God!" he stammered. And he fell backwards abruptly, closed his eyes and sprawled on the wing-chair, inert.

One might have thought that he was dead.

Then Woïna struck the bell again.

The valets came in. They did not testify any surprise on seeing Hector in that strange state. Doubtless, a similar scene was renewed every night for them, and they were accustomed to it. They took away the table, and withdrew.

The blonde woman extended Hector on the wing-chair, lying on his back, and unfastened his doublet. Then she opened his shirt and laid his chest bare.

But Hector was not dead, or even unconscious. He had been struck by an attack of devastating catalepsy. His rigid limbs could not make any movement, and his heart was scarcely beating; he would have made efforts in vain to open his eyes. However, he could hear, and he had not lost either his intelligence or consciousness of what was happening to him. The sense of hearing even seemed to have been enhanced in him, to the detriment of all the others.

So he could hear! He heard the door, which opened again, and the footfalls of a man on the floor. Then a dialogue was established between the newcomer and the blonde woman.

"It's a pity."

"You found him handsome, then?"

"He's nice enough to eat."

"I'll eat him!" said the man, with a ferocious smile. "I need to cure myself!"

"Yes, but I want my share!" answered the blonde woman. "I want my share of the pink fresh blood that's flowing in his blue veins."

"Coquette!"

"I too want to be beautiful!"

Hector made futile efforts to vanquish the lethargy that was gripping him.

He could not see the man who had just come in, but he guessed who it was. He guessed that it was a matter of the monster covered in leprosy that he had encountered in the forest of Sénart. He understood now that he had fallen into a trap and that his life was at stake. Although his heart leapt in his breast, however, and his thought awakened proud and full of life, his body refused him all service. One might have thought that his soul was imprisoned henceforth in a stone or marble envelope. He tried to cry out, but his throat would not let any sound pass.

At the same time, he felt a slight pain. It was doubtless the female vampire who had plunged into his bosom a golden pin detached from her hair.

There was a silence. Then Hector felt another sensation. To the same place that he had felt a prick, it seemed to him that the blonde woman's lips were applied with a bitter voluptuousness.

The vampire was tranquilly drinking his blood.

That lasted five minutes in reality, but for Hector it as a century of agony. Then the burning contact of lips suddenly ceased.

"My turn," said the man's voice."

"Are we going to dispatch him tonight?" asked the blonde woman.

"No."

"Why not?"

"Because I have to take a bath in an hour."

"Oh, that's true; I wasn't thinking. It'll be tomorrow, then?"

"Yes."

Hector would have consented wholeheartedly to dying immediately if he had been able to triumph over his lethargy, to get up and rush upon those two wretches who drank human blood.

"My turn," repeated the male vampire.

And Hector felt other lips applied to the puncture-wound, and his entire being revolted. It was certainly the hideous Tartar, covered with leprosy, who was drinking his blood now! But that revolt was entirely internal. The perfidious liquor had made his body an inert mass, delivered without defense to his enemies.

I'm doomed! thought the unfortunate young man. *Who will watch over my brother now?*

VI

Hector de Pierrefeu felt that his life was ebbing away through the imperceptible wound that had just been made in his breast. His mind, vivacious until then and with all its force, was gradually weakening. Perhaps even the thought that survived alone in his inert body would have been completely extinguished had the vampire not interrupted his horrible suction suddenly.

"That's enough, brother," said the blonde vampire. "If you take it all today, you'll have none left for tomorrow."

"That's true," said the male vampire.

"Then again," the blonde woman continued, "it's necessary not to forget that Hermann, our honored doctor, requires absolutely that the blood be warm when you take your bath. If you kill him tonight, tomorrow..."

"You're right, my sister," the vampire interrupted.

Hector heard all that, and his body even refused a shiver. One might have thought that he was a watch, all of whose pieces remained intact, but in which the mainspring was broken.

Bizarrely enough, just as he could hear, he was sensible to touch. The lips of the blonde woman, and then those of the male vampire, had given him an impression of horror. He had felt the prick. He felt perfectly clearly the vampire's sister place a small apparatus over his wound designed to close it.

"Are we going to leave him here until tomorrow?" asked the man.

"Of course."

"Do you think the dose of the narcotic was strong enough for him not to come out of his lethargy?

"He'll never come out of it," said the blonde woman, coldly.

"Oh! You think so?"

"He'll pass from life to death without ever opening his eyes again."

"My sister," said the male vampire, "do you know Hermann's opinion of the narcotic of which you've just made use?"

"Yes; he claims that only the body is nearly dead, but that the mind is awake and the ears can hear."

"So the young man can hear us."

"So Herman says—but as the people we've put to sleep have never woken up, we'll never know whether Hermann is mistaken or whether he's divined the truth.

"How many does this one make?"

"He's the forty-seventh."

"In two months?"

"Yes."

There was a silence; then the blonde woman went on: "In spite of the amity and the protection of the Comte, in spite of your fortune and in spite of all the precautions we've taken, I believe, my brother, that we're playing a terrible game."

"Bah! It's necessary that I be cured, and Hermann claims that I only need to take another dozen baths in order for my leprosy to fall away and for me to become as handsome as the day again."

"You know that all the mysterious disappearances are causing a great rumor in Paris?"

"Pooh! What can that do to us?"

"My brother," the young woman continued, "If you ask me, we should leave..."

"Get away!

"We should go back to our lands in southern Russia; there, the people belong to us and we can do as we like."

"But my dear," said the vampire "you're mad. Can you and I quit Paris?"

"Why not?"

"For one thing, the Comte is infatuated with you."

"Which means that he'll go with us."

"So be it. But what about the Duchesse de Villepinte, who adores me...and who doesn't know our little secrets, like the Comte, and won't go with us?"

"That's true. But are you sure that the Duchesse adores you?"

"Oh!" said the vampire, conceitedly

"In spite of your leprosy?"

"I put a mask on when I go to see her."

"And you take care to drop a large diamond on the carpet of her boudoir," added the young woman, in a mocking tone.

"Naughty!" said the vampire, laughing.

Hector did not miss a word of that cynical conversation. *Oh*, he thought, *if only I could revive for an hour, escape from here and run to Versailles; I know enough now to provide work for Monsieur de Paris—and Canuche was right; the executioner is beginning to have a thirst for gentlemen.*

"So we're staying in Paris?" said the blonde woman.

"Yes, certainly."

"And if we're discovered?"

"My dear," said the vampire, coldly, "When one has a Prince of the Blood for an accomplice, one has no fear of the King's wrath."

"In fact, you're right...and since it's thus, remember that the night's advancing, and that it would be good to sleep for a few hours. Our boat is waiting for us..."

"And the Comte will be there when you get up tomorrow," sniggered the vampire. "You wouldn't want to have rings around your eyes."

"I want to be beautiful." With those words, she struck the bell.

The duenna reappeared.

"Watch over this boy," she said to her. "Monseigneur will come back to-morrow evening, with Dr. Hermann."

The duenna bowed, but a ray of hope was gleaming in her eyes.

Hector heard the footsteps of the vampire and his sister drawing away, and the noise of the door closing. He had twenty hours to live.

The duenna went to the window and opened it. Then she leaned out. The window overlooked the street. A dull sound that reached the duenna told her that the main door of the house had just closed again. The vampire and his sister, walking side by side, drew away and went along the street, at the end of which the river could be seen.

The duenna followed them with her eyes; she saw them climb into the boat that had brought her and Hector, and when the boat moved away she closed the window again,

Then Hector heard these words distinctly: "My God, if I could save him!"

In fact, the duenna approached him and began to contemplate him. "Oh, wretch that I am," she murmured, "miserable venal woman, whom the love of gold has led to crime! I know full well that they'll kill me…but what does that matter to me, if I can save him!"

Hector, still inert and paralyzed, wondered now why that woman was taking an interest in him after having lured him into the trap in which he would find the most horrible of deaths.

She had knelt down next to him and her lips brushed his forehead.

"Oh," she said, again, "how he resembles his father! And I didn't recognize him…and nothing told me that I was the son of my beloved Raoul! Oh, wretch, wretch that I am!"

In her turn she struck the bell.

Almost immediately, a man came in. "What do you want, Lénore?" The man who had entered was one of the valets who had taken away the table, but he was no longer wearing his mask. He was a man of about forty, with hair that was almost white, and a face ravaged by passions. By his sly, hesitant, almost savage gaze, one divined that the wretch must have suffered for a long time before becoming the servant of great villains.

The duenna had also taken off her mask. She was a woman more than fifty years old, but whose face conserved the traces of a beauty that must have been marvelous.

She looked at the valet and said: "Robert, are all human sentiments extinct in you?"

"Why are you asking me that?" he replied, astonished.

"Robert," she continued, "don't you feel horrified by the abominable work we do?"

He shivered, bowed his head and murmured in a strangled voice: "It's necessary to live."

"To live by killing others, though?"

The valet did not reply.

"Say rather," the duenna continued, "that it's fear of death that enchains you here."

"That's possible," he replied. "You know full well, Lénore, that the day when we refuse to obey will be the last day of our life."

"Well, what does that matter to me?" she cried, suddenly

The valet took a step back, and looked at her with a gaze full of stupor. "What?" he said. "It's you who are speaking like that?"

"It's me."

"You!" he said, with a savage irony. "Who have been luring the unfortunate victims of this accursed house with an infernal skill?"

"Well, I'm renouncing my frightful métier."

"You?"

"I want to save this young man." And she pointed at Hector, still inert, who might have been thought to be dead.

"That young man?" said the valet, his curiosity and astonishment redoubled.

"Yes." And the duenna suddenly seized the hand of the valet Robert. "Listen," she said, "listen to me. Lénore is a pseudonym. It's under that name that, having fallen to the utmost depths of debauchery, I went further, to fall lower still and become the accomplice of crime. But before being a vile prostitute, I was once a woman, a beautiful woman, young and loving...and I was loved. I remember my youth. I sold flowers in public squares in those days. I was beautiful. Louis poured into my apron. All the gentlemen who passed through the Palais-Royal looked at me, smiling, offering me their fortune and their heart. But one alone had the gift of making me shudder; one alone pleased me; one alone was beloved. That was the father of this young man. Do you understand, now?"

"Yes," said Robert.

"Do you understand why I want to save him?"

"Yes, but..."

"But what?" said the duenna, recklessly.

"You know full well, Lénore, that it isn't possible."

"Why?"

"Because saving him," said Robert, "is exposing us to death."

"What does it matter?"

"And then...in the state he's in..." Robert pointed at Hector, still in lethargy. He continued: "Where could we take him? Where could we hide him?"

"I don't know—but it's necessary to save him."

Robert shook his head and repeated: "It's impossible."

"Oh!" said Lénore, despairingly. "All the same, it's necessary."

"You know that downstairs on the ground floor of the house there are two men on watch who belong body and soul to the wretches we obey ourselves. How do you expect us to get out? How do you expect us to get through?"

"That's true," said Lénore. "Does the house have a terrace?"

"Yes."

"Does that terrace give access to the roofs of the house next door?"

"No," he said. "Lénore, renounce saving this young man."

"And if I don't want to?"

"But it's death for you, fool!"

"I shall die!"

"What about me?" The voice of the man became pleading. "I want to live."

"Coward."

"Oh, don't accuse me, Lénore, don't accuse me of cowardice," the valet went on. "If you knew...but no, you don't...you can't know. Well, I'll tell you everything. I have a daughter! A beautiful and pure daughter—me, infamous and soiled! A daughter who knows nothing about our horrible life...a daughter who looks at me with love and respect...me, the complaisant valet of these drinkers of human blood. If I die, what will become of her?"

He had tears in his eyes as he spoke thus.

But Lénore cried: "You have a daughter! And you hesitate to save this child! You're a father, and you don't understand? And while your daughter, happy, ignorant, has faith in you, you make yourself an executioner...oh, wretch!"

And Lénore looked at the valet Robert with an indignation mingled with scorn.

"But what do you want us to do?" cried the valet.

"I want us to save him."

"How?"

"I don't know." But suddenly, she slapped her forehead. "Ah!" she said.

"What?" asked Robert

"Do you remember that the Prince had supper here one day?"

"Yes."

"When he got drunk?"

"Perfectly. It was about two months ago."

"That's right."

"When he was drunk, he touched the green bottle."

"Yes, I remember."

"And he fell backwards, and stayed for more than an hour in the condition of this young man."

"Well?"

"Well, Madame came and opened that dresser you see there."

"Good."

"She took a flask out of it."

"And then?"

"She poured two drops from its contents on to a handkerchief, and rubbed the prince's temples with the handkerchief."

"And he came round?"

"Immediately."

"Well, what do you want to do?"

"How many are there downstairs?"

"Two."

"Well, then—two against two."

"What do you mean?"

"If I can find the flask that the prince's sister used, I'll return the young man to life."

"And then?"

"Then" the duenna concluded, "you and he will open a passage, sword in hand."

And she approached the dresser where the precious flask was to be found.

VII

The duenna opened the dresser, rummaged through various objects momentarily, and suddenly said, in a joyful tone: "I have it!"

In fact, she had just put her hand on a small pot about an inch long, which contained a reddish liquid.

She leaned over the young man and, removing the stopper from the phial, poured a few drops of its contents into the palm of her hand. Then she began to rub Hector's lips, eyelids and temples.

Full of anxiety, the valet Robert watched her do it. "He won't come back," he said, shaking his head.

"Yes, yes," said Lénore. "You'll see."

"But when he comes round, if he comes round," said Robert, "how will we explain to him?"

"We won't explain anything. We'll put a sword in his hand and we'll say to him: 'It's necessary to get out of here or die.'"

"But where will you get a sword? You know full well that you took his away from him."

"Yes, but there are some here."

"Really?"

"There are at least three, perhaps four, in the next room. Monseigneur left them, one after another. He arrives on an empty stomach; he goes away dead drunk..."

"Drunk on human blood," Robert murmured.

"And he leaves his sword, which I'm careful to lock up." The duenna added: "Look—open that door...good...you'll see a cupboard."

"I see it. The key is in the door."

"Open it—they're in there."

While speaking, Lénore continued rubbing Hector's lips and temples. Afterwards, she put her ear to his breast.

Suddenly, she quivered with joy. The heartbeats, which had seemed extinct, were beginning to make themselves heard distinctly. At the same time, the lips parted and delivered passage to a sigh. Then, little by little, the limbs lost their marmoreal rigidity, and the two arms, dangling alongside the body, began to twitch.

"He's coming to! He's coming to!" Lénore murmured, with a feverish joy.

Then the eyes opened.

The gaze, vague and indecisive at first, gradually became intelligent, and fixed itself on Lénore with an indescribable expression of gratitude. Finally, the entire body was gripped by convulsive tremors, agitated by spasms, and suddenly, Hector, who succeeded by degrees in breaking the bonds of the lethargy, found himself on his feet. He took two steps forward, waved his arms, and looked at Lénore again. Only his tongue was still in default.

The valet Robert came back carrying swords. Hector extended his hand and seized one. Then, presumably, the satisfaction that he felt delivered the *coup de grâce* to the paralysis, and his tongue was loosened.

"Give it to me!" he said. "We shall soon see..." And, as Lénore tried to explain the situation, he said: "No need...I was as if dead, but I heard everything, so I know everything. Let's go!"

He had thrown away the leather scabbard of the sword, whose blade was not glinting in the candlelight.

But Lénore put a finger over her mouth. "Shh!" she said. "It's necessary to take them by surprise and not give them time to put themselves on the defensive."

The valet Robert was one of those men of somber humor and concentrated character who pass suddenly, without any transition, from extreme weakness to unbreakable resolution. Lénore had spoken to him about his daughter; she had invoked an affection that had remained pure in the depths of that debased soul, and a cord, mute until then, had suddenly vibrated. Now, he was resolved to save Hector, even if he had to perish himself. He had seized a sword and was brandishing it.

"Let's go," he repeated, after Hector.

Lénore picked up a candle and opened the door.

The door opened to a long and vast corridor, which ended in a staircase.

Robert leaned toward her ear and said: "If there were only the two of them downstairs, we could go out very quietly, on tiptoe, and perhaps they wouldn't wake up, for they've drunk more than usual this evening, and I think they're drunk—but there's Minos."

"Oh, if I could poison him!" murmured Lénore.

Minos was a dog, an enormous dog with bristling hair, bloodshot eyes, and an ever-gaping maw, armed with terrible jaws. The Tartar had brought him from the Caucasus; the animal only knew two men, and only obeyed them: the Tartar and a muzjik, who was one of the two men that Lénore had mentioned.

That muzjik, when the house contained a victim destined for his master's barbaric pleasures, had the custom of sleeping across the doorway. Minos slept at his feet. At the slightest noise, the dog leapt up. It was not one of those mongrels that make more noise than action, which howl extravagantly but with which a blow with a stick reckons. Minos growled for the space of a second—just the time required to wake the muzjik—and then bounded forward and leapt at the throat of whoever appeared to be an enemy.

The muzjik was always armed with a long spear with a triangular iron head. The valet who slept next to him, who was French, possessed a pair of pistols. Both of them, moreover, were devoted body and soul to the vampire, and had the mission not only keeping watch on the duenna, who had served him for a long time, but the valet Robert, who was a more recent recruit than them.

Lénore wanted to snuff out her candle.

"No," said Robert.

"Why not?"

"It's necessary to be able to see to confront the dog,"

Indeed, scarcely had they arrived at the top step of the stairway than Minos, who was lying at the bottom, growled dully.

"Peace, Minos!" said the muzjik, waking up with a start.

The dog continued to growl.

Then the muzjik got up, and, approaching the staircase, saw the light.

"Is that you, Lénore?" he said.

Lénore did not reply.

"What do you want, Robert?" he repeated.

Lénore made a sign to Robert, who did not reply.

"Go, Minos, go!" cried the muzjik, who, not receiving any response, scented danger.

The dog launched itself up the stairs, gave voice to one last roar, and charged Robert, who was descending first. The muzjik, spear in hand, followed the dog.

Suddenly, the dog uttered a howl of pain, agitated momentarily in the middle of the stairway, like an uprooted tree on the side of a hill, and came to roll heavily into the legs of the muzjik, whom he covered with his blood. At the moment when the dog leapt at Robert's throat, Hector de Pierrefeu, who had recovered all his energy and all his strength, had plunged his sword into its maw. The weapon had traversed the tongue and then the throat, and the ferocious animal had been mortally wounded.

"To me! Help me!" cried the muzjik, who, while the writhing dog was expiring at his feet, had perceived the silhouettes of Lénore, Robert and Hector at the top of the stairs.

Then the duenna blew out the candle.

"Ready!" cried Robert.

"Ready!" repeated Hector.

But the other valet, already woken up by the dog's howls, came running, and fired one of his pistols at hazard. The candle being extinct, the stairway was plunged in darkness. The flash of the gunshot illuminated it momentarily.

By that glimmer, the valet perceived Hector and understood everything. *He's won over Lénore and Robert*, he thought. And, taking the second pistol from his belt, he fired again, this time in the direction in which he had perceived the young man.

A cry of pain was heard, and then cries of rage. In the darkness, a frightful battle began.

The muzjik's spear, Robert's sword and Hector's blade clashed and struck sparks reciprocally.

The other valet, armed with a sword defended the stairs one step at a time.

Lénore, immobile and mute, kept her distance.

The combat was long, furious and terrible. The adversaries could not see one another, but they sensed one another and encountered one another.

Finally, the muzjik dropped his spear. Hector's blade had traversed his breast, and he fell heavily across the stairway.

The other valet had given up and run away. At the moment when the muzjik fell they heard him open the door to the street and launch himself outside.

"We're saved!" cried Lénore, who had lit the candle again and could now see the dying muzjik lying on his dead dog.

"We're doomed!" said Robert.

"Doomed!"

"Yes—listen!"

The heavy and measured tread of a police patrol was, indeed, audible in the street.

Murders, the mysterious disappearances and the abductions had multiplied so greatly in recent times that the Lieutenant de Police, Monsieur de Sartine,[7] had given the strictest orders. Any nocturnal racket was severely repressed, and anyone who was going abroad with a weapon in hand was arrested pitilessly. The valet Robert had understood that the other lackey, on going out, had encountered a police patrol and was bringing them in all haste.

In fact, almost immediately someone knocked on the door.

"Don't open it!" said Robert, seeing Lénore descending the stairway.

"But the police will be for us!"

"No, fool! Don't open it!"

"Why not?"

---

[7] Antoine Gabriel de Sartine, Comte d'Alby (1729-1801) was appointed Lieutenant General of the Parisian Police in 1759, holding that post until 1774. The substitution of an asterisk for the last digit of the story's date might be an attempt to blur the anachronism of this element of the story, which later events prove to be set considerably earlier than 1759. Many of the Lieutenant's responsibilities were not concerned with policing as it would now be understood; he was in charge of public hygiene and food supply, and many his actual political achievements were in that context—he pioneered the organization of the city's army of street-sweepers and well as the system of police commissariats. Sartine became a quasi-legendary figure in the historical crime fiction written in the latter part of the 19th century, largely thanks to the success of the agents and spies of his secret police

"Because this house belongs to the Comte de Clermont, and whatever we might say, we'll still be in the wrong."

"Perhaps you're right," said Lénore. "But what can we do, then? What's going to happen?"

The butts of rifles hammered the door, and an imperious voice, doubtless that of an officer, cried: "In the name of Monseigneur le Lieutenant de Police, open up!"

"The terrace," Robert murmured.

"That's true," said Lénore—and she took Hector de Pierrefeu by the hand. "Come," she said. "Come on—there's not a moment to lose."

They both went back upstairs.

The house, whose construction dated back two centuries, had three stories, and it had been built in the Italian style—which is to say that that its roof was in the form of a terrace. It was reached by way of a kind of trapdoor located at the top of the stairs.

Lénore, who seemed to have recovered the legs of her youth, went up first, opened the trapdoor and continued to draw Hector along

Robert, meanwhile, had sealed the main door of the house as best he could, closing all the bolts and piling behind it everything that came to hand. As the door was thick and had solid iron fittings, it was able to resist for more than an hour that blows of the policemen's rifle-butts—for, having obtained no response, the officer had ordered that it be broken down.

Lénore dragged Hector over the terrace. The first light of dawn was infiltrating the sky, and the moon was about to disappear over the horizon, but its oblique rays still permitted them to see distinctly.

"Look—there," said Lénore. And she showed him the roof of a nearby house. Between that roof and the terrace there was a gap of only four or five feet, for the street that separated them was exceedingly narrow.

Lénore would not have been able to cross it, but Hector ought to have the agility of youth. And then, his life depended on it...

"Go," said Lénore, "and may God protect you."

Hector took a run-up, and leapt.

He reached the edge of the roof. In spite of its extreme declivity, he succeeded in hanging on to it, maintaining his equilibrium there, and, holding on to the chimney-pots, he went straight ahead.

"Keep going!" Lénore shouted to him. "Go! You're sure to find an open window somewhere."

Then a strange voyage commenced for the young man, from roof to roof. He continued going forward, but as he went on, he felt his strength ebbing away. During the few minutes of the battle that had taken place in the dark, the valet who had then run away had fired two pistol shots. One bullet had missed, but the other had attained Hector, who had thought at first that he had received a violent punch. It was, therefore, not until he was on the roof that he perceived that his blood was flowing abundantly.

Already, however, the police were arriving on the terrace, and were getting ready, on seeing a man fleeing, to pursue him.

Hector took a few more paces, his hand on his wound, as if he were trying to stem the blood that was flowing from it. As he took those paces, a vertigo took possession of him; a cloud passed before his eyes.

"My brother!" he murmured.

Just as he was about to collapse, however, he perceived an open window, and through that window a lamp, and he rallied his forces. The window, a hinged skylight, was that of a mansard. In that mansard there was a table, on that table a lamp, and next to the lamp was a young woman, who was doing needle-work.

Making a desperate effort, Hector went to fall, bloody and half dead, at the feet of that terrified young woman...

PART ONE: THE KING SUFFERS ENNUI

I

One morning, between nine and ten o'clock, the carriage of Gabriel de Sartine, the Lieutenant General of the kingdom's police, entered the courtyard of the Château de Versailles.

At the same moment, a man who had been waiting for a long time at the top of the perron, and who appeared to be prey to a keen impatience, descended in a hurry and opened the carriage door himself.

The Lieutenant de Police stepped down to the ground and bowed to the man who had just rendered him that small, entirely obsequious, service with a deference that immediately excluded any idea of inferiority on his part.

"Bonjour, my dear Monsieur Lebel," said Monsieur de Sartine, taking the arm of the man who had me to meet him, in a familiar fashion.[8]

"Bonjour, Monsieur Lieutenant," replied Lebel, who was none other than the valet de chambre of His Majesty Louis XV. "We're waiting for you."

"Really?"

"And with impatience, I swear to you!"

"Oh!" said Monsieur de Sartine. "Has something new happened here, then?"

"The King is suffering ennui."

A smile glided over the lips of the young Lieutenant de Police—for Monsieur de Sartine, newly appointed to that post, thanks to the protection of Madame de Pompadour, was scarcely thirty years-old.[9] "But what you're telling me there, my dear Monsieur Lebel, isn't new at all."

"Alas, no."

"The King suffers ennui every day, or very nearly."

"Which desolates us, Monsieur Lieutenant," said Lebel,

---

[8] François Lebel (1716-1781), whose forename is sometimes rendered as Dominique, was Louis XV's senior valet de chamber for many years.

[9] Jeanne Poisson (1721-1764), later Madame de Pompadour, was Louis XV's official chief mistress from 1745-51, but she remained close to him thereafter as a confidante and took charge of the king's schedule, thus acquiring great influence, although she was probably not the omnipotent schemer depicted in many 19th century historical melodramas. In 1756, she was appointed the Queen's lady-in-waiting, but Queen Marie (1703-1768) played no part in Court life, hence allowing her to be airbrushed out of the backcloth of the present novel.

"The Marquise, however..."

"The Marquise de Pompadour, with all her wit, can no longer succeed in distracting the King."

"The Maréchal..."

"Monsieur de Richelieu comes every day to tell him a story, to bring the King up to date with the intrigues of the court and the city, but when he has gone the King yawns and says: 'Poor Richelieu, he's beginning to drivel on somewhat...he's always telling me the same stories.'"

Monsieur de Sartine winked. "And...the Parc-des-Cerfs?" he said.[10]

"It's more than a month since the King set foot there."

Hmm!" murmured the Lieutenant General. "All that might be very serious, my dear Monsieur Lebel, if..."

"Well?" said Lebel, anxiously.

"If I hadn't brought His Majesty a great subject of distraction."

"Really?"

"You'll see. Never will my humble reports have interested him to such a degree."

"May God hear you!" murmured the consternated Lebel.

"Where is the King?"

"In his study."

"Alone?"

"With the Marquise."

What King Louis XV called, in summer, his "study," was a vast room adjacent to the orangery, in which there was a billiard-table, a game of skittles, a cup-and-ball and a swing. All those things had amused the King for a few days, especially the billiard-table. Then the King had resumed yawning extravagantly.

When Monsieur de Sartine, announced by Lebel, came in, the King, who was trying to distract himself by playing cup-and-ball, but only succeeding in relaxing his jaw, suddenly became more cheerful.

"Bonjour, Sartine," he said.

"You've arrived in a timely fashion, Monsieur le Lieutenant," said the Marquise.

Monsieur de Sartine had a voluminous portfolio under his arm.

"What's happening in Paris?" asked the King.

"Horrors, Sire."

At that word, the blasé features of the King became animated, and a smile glided over the beautiful lips of Madame de Pompadour.

"Tell us about them, Monsieur de Sartine," she said.

The Lieutenant hesitated.

"What is it, then?" said the King, with a hint of curiosity.

---

[10] The Parc-des-Cerfs [Deer Park] was a mansion used by Louis XV for amorous liaisons, which acquired a legendary reputation as a kind of seraglio.

"It's just that," Monsieur de Sartine stammered, "Your Majesty alone..." And he directed a rapid glance at Madame de Pompadour, which could translated as: "It's a manner of piquing the curiosity of the King even further."

The redoubtable favorite doubtless understood that, for she said to Monsieur de Sartine: "Is it a State Secret?"

"Yes, Madame."

The King smiled disdainfully. "What does that matter?" he said.

"No, no," said the Marquise. "I'll withdraw."

"Stay, my beauty."

"No, Sire, no," And she stood up.

Lebel had remained on the threshold.

"Go away, Lebel," said the King. Then, looking at his Lieutenant de Police: "What you have to tell me is very extraordinary, then?"

"Horrible," said Monsieur de Sartine, whose face took on an almost lugubrious expression.

In the meantime, the Marquise and Lebel left. Then Monsieur de Sartine placed his immense portfolio on a table and took out a wad of papers.

"Oh, not all that, Sartine," said the King. "Sit down and tell me the things simply. You tell stories so well!"

The Lieutenant General bowed. Then, pushing away his portfolio, he said: "Has Your Majesty ever heard of mention of vampires?"

"What are they?"

"Vampires are beings that nourish themselves on human blood."

"Bah! And do they exist?"

"A monk who died recently," Monsieur de Sartine went on, "Dom Calmet, has written very interesting things about them."[11]

"Oh! Really?"

"He claims that in Hungary, dead men emerge from their tombs by night to go forth and prick the living in the neck while they sleep, and feed on their blood."

"What nonsense!" said the King, whose curiosity suddenly died down. "And it's to tell me that nonsense that you've come from Paris, Sartine?"

"No, Sire."

"Get to the point, then."

"For that, it's necessary for me to talk to Your Majesty about the vampires of Hungary."

"But why?"

---

[11] The reference to the recent death of Dom Antoine Augustine Calmet (1672-1757) implies that at this point in the story Ponson still considered it to be set in 1759. Calmet's 1746 treatise popularizing the vampire folklore of Eastern Europe became the standard source for subsequent legendry and literature dealing with the theme.

"Because there are some of them in Paris."

"What?" said the King.

"I said, Sire, that there are vampires in Paris."

The King shrugged his shoulders. "Sartine," he said, "if Monsieur de Voltaire, who is a philosopher, and doesn't believe in anything, could hear you..."

"Well, Sire?"

"He'd laugh out loud."

"Does Your Majesty think so?"

"Well," said the King, naively, "how can you expect a man who has all the difficulty in the world believing in the existence of God to be able to believe that the dead resuscitate?"

"Ah!" said Monsieur de Sartine. "That's exactly where the difference commences, Sire."

"Between what?"

"Between the vampires of Hungary and those of Paris."

"Which is?"

"Those of whom Dom Calmet speaks emerge from a cemetery..."

"And those of Paris?"

"Emerge from a town house, or even a palace, and are very much alive."

"What are you telling me, Sartine?"

The Lieutenant General had maintained a cool and severe expression.

"Sire," he said, "the throats of children are being cut in Paris, and there are men taking baths in blood."

"Get away!" said the King.

"And," Sartine added, coolly, "I have come to obtain Your Majesty' orders."

This time, the King ceased yawning. He dropped his cup-and-ball, and waited for Sartine to explain.

Sartine continued: "For some time, Sire, a quarter of Paris known as the Carré Saint-Martin, which comprises the street of that name, the Rue du Temple and all those perpendicular to them, has been prey to a forceful rumor; the poor people are very agitated, and sinister stories have been circulating from street to street and house to house."

"About what?" said the King, interested in spite of himself.

"Children disappearing at dead of night, and never seen again."

"Oh!"

"Several murdered young men have been found in the nets at Saint-Cloud."

"You've already told me that, Sartine.

"Yes, Sire, but what I couldn't tell Your Majesty, because it hadn't struck me then, was that the traces borne by those men were always identical."

"What were they?"

"They had the carotid artery half-severed.

"Bah!"

"And, in addition, a small puncture-wound above the breast that seemed to have been made by a pin."

"Bizarre," said the King, lowering his head again.

"Public rumor accused an innkeeper by the name of Boniface of the disappearance of the children. I had searches carried out, which had no result. The identity of the last two cadavers found in the nets at Saint-Cloud was established; they were recognized as two young clerks in a shop in the Rue du Temple, who were seen going out one evening in the company of equivocal women."

"So?" said the King.

"That last circumstance," Sartine went on, "let me reluctantly to think that the same hand might be making the children disappear and striking down the men. But with what end? My most skillful agents, sent on campaign, were unable to discover anything. However, more and more accusations accumulated against the landlord of the Blue Dragon, Master Boniface, and a month ago, a new event gave more weight to those accusations. Two young gentlemen, two brothers, arriving from the provinces, the Sires de Pierrefeu..."

"Pierrefeu?" said the King.

"Yes, Sire."

"It seems to me that I know that name, Sartine. Wait a moment..."

The King appeared to assemble distant memories, scattered and confused. Then, suddenly, he slapped his forehead. "Of course!" he said. "There was a Pierrefeu in my company at Fontenoy. I think he was wounded close beside me."

"That's possible," replied the Lieutenant de Police.

"Well, Sartine, what happened to them?"

"They disappeared, Sire."

"Both of them?"

"Both of them. They entered Paris one evening at dusk, and went to stay at the Blue Dragon. A bourgeois of the Rue du Temple named Onésime Morel, a furrier, tried to dissuade them from going to the inn."

"But they stayed there anyway?"

"Yes, Sire."

"And then?"

"Then the elder one went out; the same bourgeois saw him heading for the Place de Grève."

"A singular stroll!" said the King.

"The other remained in bed at the inn."

"God! And the elder?"

"He was not seen to come back."

"And the younger?"

"Also disappeared. The innkeeper, whom I've had arrested, claims that the young man asked for his horse and left for Versailles before daybreak."

"All this is quite extraordinary, Sartine," said the King, who had picked up his cup-and-ball again, "but it doesn't appear to have any connection with the vampires you were talking about."

"Quite the contrary, as Your Majesty will see."

"Go on."

"Yesterday morning, I received this letter."

And the Lieutenant de Police took from the stack of papers that he had brought a letter folded in four, which he set before the King's eyes.

The letter read as follows:

If, as people believe, Monsieur le Lieutenant de Police is a man of honor, and if he is interested in knowing what becomes of the children who have been disappearing frequently for some time, he will accept the following conditions:

A man will present himself in the evening at the home of Monsieur le Lieutenant. That man will be masked, but Monsieur le Lieutenant will not ask him to remove his mask.

That man will then make revelations of the greatest importance to Monsieur le Lieutenant, and he will be allowed to leave freely thereafter, without his face having been seen.

If Monsieur le Lieutenant accepts these conditions, it will be easy for him to make it known to the person who is writing to him. One day, at about two o'clock, His Lordship will go by carriage to the Châtelet. He has only to lower one of the windows of the carriage while passing over the bridge and put his head out of the window. That will be proof of his acceptance.

"And did you do that, Sartine?"

"Yes, Sire."

"And did the masked man come?"

"At eight o'clock precisely; he was introduced to my study."

"Well, what did he tell you?"

"There is in Paris," Sartine continued, "a foreigner who created a stir last year at court and in the city, a great Russian lord by the name of Trespatky."

"The Marquise has mentioned him to me," observed Louis XV.

"That man, who is tall, and possessed of colossal strength, had a rugged and savage beauty that turned the heads of many women."

"Really?"

"In addition, he is immensely rich, and sows pearls and diamonds as one might sow peach-stones."

"That's worth more than a pretty face," said the King, smiling.

"But he doesn't have that any longer, Sire."

"The pretty face?"

"His has become an object of horror."

"Ah! The Marquise mentioned that to me too! A leper..."

"Precisely. Now, the Tartar wants to be cured."

"Let him see Fagon, my physician; he's a clever man."[12]

"Oh," said Sartine, "he has an excellent physician, Sire, as you shall see."

"I'm listening, Sartine."

"The physician said to him: 'Whence does leprosy come? From a vice you have in the blood. How can it be cured? It's quite simple: it's necessary to replace your corrupted blood by purer blood.'"

"It seems to me that the physician speaks very casually," said the King.

"You shall see that he was not, Sire. Every day he bleeds his patient."

"Good."

"The corrupted blood runs out drop by drop, and is replaced by another."

"But where is that obtained?"

"It's the blood of the children and the men who disappear."

"What horror!" said the King. "But how can the substitution be effected?"

"In three ways."

"Ah."

"By means of a discreet suction. The unfortunate whose blood is destined for the Tartar's veins is put to sleep with the aid of a narcotic, and the latter sucks that blood, directly, so to speak, after having pricked the breast with a pin."

"What else?"

"Sometimes, with the aid of a apparatus that resembles a bellows, the physician insufflates his master with the fresh blood is the vein he has opened, and through which the vitiated blood is allowed to flow out."

"And the third measure?"

"Oh, that's the most hideous, Sire. The wretch takes a bath in the blood, while still warm."

"And that's what the masked man told you, Sartine?"

"Yes, Sire."

"And do you believe it?"

"Yes, Sire."

"Well, there's a simple action to take."

"I await Your Majesty's orders."

"Have the Tartar arrested; the Parliament will judge him, and he'll be broken on the wheel on the Place de Grève.

"But sire, the Tartar has accomplices."

"They'll be hanged."

"He has a young and beautiful sister."

---

[12] Guy-Crescent Fagon, who died in 1718, had famously been Louis XIV's physician. The error appears to have been pointed out to the author, who subsequently includes a note suggesting that the Fagon to which this line refers is the son of the famous one.

The King shivered, but it was only for the duration of a lightning-flash. "Pooh!" he said. "If I believed everything I was told, my kingdom would be paved with young and beautiful women, but people exaggerated greatly, alas." And the King, appearing to forget everything that the King had just told him, sighed, and continued, after a pause: "It's a long time since I saw a pretty woman!" Then, suddenly: "But, in fact, you're the Lieutenant de Police, are you not, Sartine?"

"By your Majesty, pleasure, yes, Sire."

"Then the police ought to be useful for something?" the King continued.

Sartine waited. "Can you imagine," Louis XV went on, "that I'm in love...in love with a woman that it's necessary for you to find for me." And while playing with his cup-and-ball, Louis XV added: "It's very boring being King."

Sartine awaited the confidences of his august interlocutor, and the King said: "You shall see, Sartine, how unfortunate I am!" And he threw away his cup-and-ball, crossed his legs and told his Lieutenant de Police the following story.

II

"My poor Sartine, it really isn't amusing to be King."

"However," observed the Lieutenant de Police, "Your Majesty would be able to exchange his condition whenever he wishes."

That sally brought a smile to Louis XV's lips. "Pooh!" he said. "I believe that anyone who exchanged places with me would end up repenting of it. But you'll see..."

"I'm listening, Sire.

"On morning, when I was suffering from ennui even more than usual, Richelieu[13] said to me: 'Your Majesty ought to go shoot quail in the Parc de Marly.'

"The diversion pleased me, and I said to Richelieu: 'Let's go! But it will be just the two of us, won't it?'

"It was a Sunday. The Marquise was at mass, my daughters were at confession; the dauphin was doing I know not what, and the members of my household where spread out all over the place. That day, the Palace of Versailles, resembled the house of a Parisian bourgeois.

"Richelieu asked for a carriage without armories, and we left for Marly without an escort, without any guards, only taking with us two valets charged with carrying the game we shot, and two fine dogs, pointers, that the English ambassador had given me.

"We arrived in Marly, we were hunting, I was having a good time, and we reached the extremity of the park, which, as you know, descends from the heights all the way to the water's edge.

"An ardent sun was beating down on our heads. I'd killed three dozen quail and I was tired. Furthermore, I was dying of hunger and I'd have given a province for an orange.

"Richelieu and I sat down near the limit of the park, under a tree, to shelter from the sun's rays. 'I'm dying of thirst,' I said.

"Richelieu said: 'It's the same in hunting as in war, Sire. Let Your Majesty look through the hedge.'

---

[13] The Maréchal Duc de Richelieu in question is Armand de Vignerot du Plessis (1696-1788), the great nephew of the famous Cardinal and Statesman who had been all-powerful for a period in early 17th century France. The Maréchal had known Louis XV as a child and became a close friend of the King when he returned to the Court on the 1750s after a brilliant military career, although his position became precarious when he opposed Madame de Pompadour. He was a notorious womanizer, and that determined the reputation attributed to him in 19th century literary melodrama.

"'Well?'

"'Does he not see a small white house on the river bank?'

"'Yes, certainly.'

"'Well, it's a tavern.'

"'A tavern!'

"'Yes, Sire, and Your Majesty, since he is thirsty, and we're more than a league from the château, he can easily have a drink there.'

"The adventure pleased me. The boundary hedge had a gap in it, and by ducking down we could get through it. On the other side of the hedge there was a ditch.

"Richelieu set me an example, and I rediscovered the agility I had when I was twenty years-old, and crossed it.

"Five minutes later, we went into the tavern.

"It was deserted, and a worthy fellow with a rubicund face, who was sitting sadly behind a tin-plate counter, took us for local gentlemen. He hastened to serve us a very clear white wine, which I can still remember, Sartine, and I'm quite certain that one couldn't find a better one in the cellars of Versailles."

"Oh, Sire!"

"When we had slaked our thirst, Richelieu and I, sitting under the arbor located at the door of the tavern, we heard bursts of laughter, songs and joyful cries coming from the water's edge.

"Then, a whole band of shop assistants and girls irrupted into the tavern.

"Oh, those young folk amused me, my poor Sartine, and I felt very sorry then about my métier of kingship. The men had roses in the buttonholes of their coarse brown jackets; the girls had put them in their hair. And they were all laughing, singing and making mischief, which was a delight to behold.

"The girls were pretty…but there was one of them…one above all..."

The King stopped, in order to sigh deeply. Then he resumed:

"I nudged Richelieu's elbow and I said to him: 'I'd trade the Marquise, her hooped skirts and her beauty-spots, and my entire Parc-aux-Cerfs, for that pretty sprig of a girl.'"

"'Your Majesty has only to desire it,' replied the Maréchal.

"'Well, I desire it,' I retorted.

"But the worthy Richelieu, who has been credited with a great reputation for intelligence, is a trifle silly, as you shall see, Sartine."

"What did he do, then, Sire?"

"Nothing that I wanted him to do, There was a very simple thing to be done, in my opinion, and that was to mingle with the merry band, incognito, and flirt with the girls. But the Maréchal talked to me about etiquette, propriety, the scandal that would ensue if I happened to be recognized, and he promised me that the girl would be at Versailles that very evening."

"And doubtless," said Sartine, smiling, "the Maréchal failed to keep his word?"

"Which is to say that he instructed one of the valets who were with us to follow the shop-workers and the girls to Paris, where they would not fail to return by coach, and…you understand the rest, don't you?"

"Yes, Sire."

"The valet that had received the instruction to follow the young folk, to approach the girl and inform her that her beauty had the admiration of her sovereign, came back two hours later with a black eye, a broken arm and two or three fewer teeth."

"Oh!"

"The shop-assistants had given him a beating, and left him half dead on the road."

"And what did the Maréchal say, Sire?"

"The Maréchal, who was furious, departed for Paris, swearing that he would find the girl and bring her to me."

"And he hasn't come back?"

"Yes, but without the girl." And the King uttered a sigh that might have moved a mountain.

"Your Majesty would, therefore, be glad to find that young woman again?"

"Which is to say," said the King, naively, "that since that day I've been suffering from twice as much ennui as usual. And if you don't find her for me…"

"I'll find her, Sire."

The King's face lit up. "Truly?" he said.

"Am I not Your Majesty's Lieutenant de Police?"

"That's true," said Louis XV. "Well, then, go on, Sartine, and put everyone to work."

"Yes, Sire, but…"

"But what?"

"Your Majesty has no orders to give me?"

"I've ordered you to find that young woman."

"I understand that. But the Tartar…"

"Oh, that's true," said the King. "I'd completely forgotten him."

"I'm awaiting Your Majesty's orders."

"Well, do whatever you wish."

"Your Majesty is giving me full authority, then?"

"Of course."

"Not only regarding the Tartar, but his sister?"

"Yes."

Sartine had put is portfolio under his arm again, but he did not leave.

"Go on, then, Sartine," said the King, impatiently

"It's just that I haven't told Your Majesty everything."

"What more is there?" said Louis XV, frowning.

"The Tartar has an accomplice."

"His sister…you told me."

"No, another."

"Ah! Someone at Court?"

"Yes, Sire."

"Damn!" said the King.

"A great Lord, Sire."

"Well," said the King, "We'll talk about it again tomorrow, Find the girl for me, Sartine."

And the King dismissed his Lieutenant de Police with a gesture.

III

Monsieur de Sartine left the King's study.

Lebel was waiting for him in the antechamber. "Well?" he asked, anxiously. "The King...?"

"The King has just furnished me with a means of distracting him."

"Oh! Really?"

"I believe so," said Sartine, "and I'm returning to Paris without losing a minute."

"But Monsieur," said Lebel, "Madame la Marquise has instructed me not to allow you to leave immediately."

"The Marquise wishes to see me?"

"Yes."

Sartine was not a man to treat such a desire lightly. He therefore went to see Madame de Pompadour.

"Now," said the Marquise, "tell me the story that you've just told the King."

Sartine did not have to be begged. He recommenced his story, and did not leave out any detail.

"But that's abominable!" exclaimed the Marquise, finally.

"All the more abominable," replied Sartine, "because very highly-placed individuals are implicated in all these crimes."

"Bah!"

"The King didn't want to hear me out, but you, Madame..."

"I'm listening."

"And the highly-placed individual is a Prince of the Blood."

"And might that Prince," said Madame de Pompadour, "be the Comte de Clermont?"

Sartine nodded his head affirmatively.

Madame de Pompadour was no longer smiling, and had become very pensive. "In sum," she said, "what has the King ordered you to do?"

"Nothing."

"What are you going to do?"

"Await orders."

"You're right, Monsieur de Sartine. We already have a host of awkward affairs on our hands."

"But Madame," Sartine observed, "all Paris is murmuring."

"Let it murmur." And as if Madame de Pompadour wanted to imitate the King's reserve, she added: "In the meantime, what are you going to do to amuse the King?"

"I'll try to find the girl."

"What girl?"

"The one for whom the King is amorous." And Sartine recounted to Madame de Pompadour the confidence the King had made him.

The favorite shrugged her shoulders. "When you've found her," she said, "the King won't think about her any longer. It's of no importance—find her."

"That's what I'm going to do."

"However," said Madame de Pompadour, as Sartine took his leave, "Lieutenant de Police as you are, it appears to me to be difficult for you to put your hand on a girl with the sole indication that the King thinks her pretty."

"I hope that Monsieur de Richelieu will be able to give me some information."

"So be it."

"And then, the valet who was beaten must recall her face."

"Good. Is that all?"

"Finally," said Sartine, "I have at hand a precious man."

"Really?"

"A pearl, a jewel, for affairs of this sort."

"What is the name of this phoenix?"

"His name is Porion, Madame."

"He's one of your agents?"

"Yes."

"And you'll send him on campaign?"

"This very day."

With that final word, Sartine made the customary three bows and headed for the door—but the Marquise called him back.

"My dear Lieutenant," she said, "it's agreed, is it not, that we'll let the people of Paris murmur, until further notice?"

"Yes, Madame."

"It wouldn't displease me," the Marquise added, with a cruel smile, "to see Monsieur de Clermont's head fall on the Grève, but there are heads, like certain fruits, for which it is necessary to wait for them to be ripe. Let's wait."

Sartine climbed back into his carriage, and had himself taken back to Paris at top speed. When he reached his house, he gave the order for the police agent Porion to be summoned.

A quarter of an hour later, Porion arrived.

He was a middle-aged man, gray haired, his long face provided with a long nose, carefully shaven, wearing a pigtail over his shoulder. When the bourgeois of the Rue Saint-Denis saw him pass by, with his cinnamon-covered coat, his pale brown waistcoat, his gray trousers and his orange stockings, with a cane under his arm and his eyes sheltered behind gold-rimmed spectacles, they said, laughing; "There goes Père Cinnamon."[14]

At the Châtelet, in the study of the Lieutenant de Police, the man called himself Porion; everywhere else, he was known by the nickname of Père Cinnamon.

What was his profession? No one knew, exactly. According to some, he was a former furrier; according to others he had been a clerk in the army catering corps. For some, he had been a steward in a good house, who had retired with substantial savings.

"A worthy fellow, though!" everyone said.

He smiled at young women, took treats for children out of his pockets, complimented the parents, and passed for being exceedingly obliging.

He lived in the Rue aux Ours, above the shop of a druggist named Jarnodet whose sign bore the legend: *At the Golden Pestle*. Every evening, he went to play tric-trac in a tavern celebrated among the bourgeois of the quarter, the Pied-de-Mouton in the Rue des Lombards.

That establishment, which dated back more than a century, had had a placid destiny for a long time. The regulars were sober, economical, settled, God-fearing folk who loved the King and conformed scrupulously with his edicts. However, it had happened that one year, when bread as dear and people were dying of hunger and cold, a few notable bourgeois had expressed a little too loudly their opinion of the poor administration of public affairs. Two of them had even proffered words insulting to the King, which constituted a clear case of the crime of *lèse majesté*.

Père Cinnamon, who happened to be in the tavern at the time, had manifested a violet alarm, reprimanded the two bourgeois and expressed the hope that the impious words would not have grave consequences. He had even given the two of them imprudent advice so affectionate that they had thanked him warmly—which did not alter the fact that, during the following night, all the troublemakers were arrested and the two unfortunates who had spoken too loudly were hanged a fortnight later.

But no one suspected Père Cinnamon of having denounced them.

Another time, there was a riot in the Rue des Lombards. The watchmen arrived and dispersed the crowd, arresting the most turbulent, but could not lay hands on the person who had fomented the riot, and who was none other than the druggist Jarnodet. The following day, Jarnodet was arrested, dragged before the Parliament and sentenced to be hanged. When the poor devil was taken to execution, he perceived Père Cinnamon, who, mopping his eyes with his handkerchief, was in the front rank as he passed by. He threw himself into his arms,

---

[14] This nickname is rendered in the original as "Père Cannelle," but as it refers specifically to the color of his coat, I thought it best to translate it in order to preserve the implication.

washed him with his tears, and asked him to look after his children. Père Cinnamon promised to do so, and the druggist's widow—who, while remaining inconsolable, continued his trade—had no friend more devoted.

If anyone had said to the good people of the Rue Saint-Denis and the neighboring streets that Père Cinnamon was a policeman, they would have split their sides laughing, and sworn to heaven that the worthy fellow was being horribly slandered.

Such was the man that Monsieur de Sartine summoned, and in whom he had limitless confidence, for he knew full well that he was his most energetic and most skillful agent.

IV

"Porion," said Monsieur de Sartine, "It's necessary for you to set out on campaign right away."

"Yes, Monseigneur," replied Père Cinnamon, but added, with a smile, "although it's necessary for me to know what it's about."

"I'll tell you. It's necessary to find a young woman who has had the honor of pleasing the King."

"Ah!" said Porion, and appeared to be waiting for further details.

"As to her name," Sartine went on, "I don't know it. What she looks like, I don't know either."

Porion did not blink.

"In sum," the Lieutenant de Police, concluded, "I'm absolutely ignorant as to exactly when the King saw her, for the simple reason that I forgot to ask him."

Porion remained impassive. "However," he observed, respectfully, "your Lordship can surely give me one slight detail?"

"What?"

"Is the young woman at Court?"

"No."

"Of the gentry?"

"No."

"Of the bourgeoisie?"

"I don't know. It appears that the King encountered her in the company of several other girls."

"Ah! Very good."

"With shop assistants."

"Marvelous. Where?"

"In a tavern on the bank of the Seine, under the walls of the Parc de Marly."

"And the king found her beautiful?"

"So beautiful that he's lost his appetite." Sartine interrupted himself: "Oh, I forgot one important detail."

Porion waited.

"Monsieur de Richelieu has seen the young woman."

"Good."

"And one of the King's lackeys, who followed her on Monsieur de Richelieu's orders, and was beaten by the shop-workers."

"If that is the case," said Porion, "Your Lordship can be certain that I shall find the young woman." And he took a step toward the door.

Sartine added: "Call in on my treasurer and collect the money of which you might have need."

Porion bowed, but as he was about to cross the threshold of the study he turned round.

"What is it?" Sartine asked.

"Your Lordship had instructed me..."

"Oh, yes!" the Lieutenant de Police interrupted. "I'd ordered you to investigate the affair of the mysterious disappearances."

"Yes, Monseigneur, and I'm already on the track...."

"Of whom?"

"Of one of the young men who was staying at the Blue Dragon."

"The younger?"

"No, the elder."

"What became of him?"

"I believe he's alive. But..."

Sartine interrupted his agent. "Porion," he said, "for reasons that I can't reveal to you, don't involve yourself in that affair any longer. I'll talk to you about it again when the time comes."

"As you wish, Monseigneur."

"Find me the young woman."

And the Lieutenant dismissed Porion.

The latter left. As one might imagine, he was careful not to forget the recommendation Monsieur de Sartine had made and to call on the treasurer, from whom he obtained fifty pistoles, for which he gave a receipt. Then he left the Châtelet and went down as far as the Pont au Change. There he stopped, leaned over the parapet and gazed at the water, with the naïve expression of a bourgeois following the stupid evolutions of a fisherman who had stationed himself under a bridge.

Père Cinnamon—for Porion had resumed the latter's debonair manner and physiognomy—needed to reflect a little.

The Lieutenant, he said to himself, *always gives me such missions. Go find a young woman who pleases the King, but about whom absolutely nothing is known, neither her name, nor her hair-color, nor her age. It's true that Monsieur de Richelieu has seen her, but he has seen so many women, Monsieur de Richelieu! And then, Monsieur de Sartine can talk about him casually. Go present yourself to Monsieur de Richelieu! He'd give me a fine reception.*

While Père Cinnamon was making these reflections, a hand touched his shoulder.

The newcomer was a man of twenty-five or twenty-six, tall and lanky, his head ornamented by yellow hair and a face augmented by a nose like a trunk. He was wearing a waistcoat as yellow as his hair, with a broad white strip of cloth around his tricorn hat, which was the distinctive mark of the honorable corporation of grocers.

Porion suppressed a gesture of ill-humor that might have been translated as "To the devil with the nuisance!" and Père Cinnamon matched his interlocutor's smile.

"Bonjour, Merluche, my lad," he said. "Where are you coming from like this?"

"I've been to make a delivery of sugar at the Café de Chandelle in the Rue Saint-André-des-Arts," the grocer's boy replied.

"Oh, very good."

"And you, Père Cinnamon, what are you doing here? We haven't seen you at the Pied-de-Mouton for some time."

"I've been ill, my lad. The evenings are damp. At my age, it's necessary to look after oneself and go to bed early," Père Cinnamon replied, in a single breath. "You ask me what I'm doing here—as you can see, I'm watching the water flow."

"It's an unhealthy distraction, Père Cinnamon," replied the grocer's boy.

"Why is that, my lad?"

"Because it gives one the urge to drown oneself."

"You think so?"

"As proves poor Agénor Chapuzot, one of my comrades."

"He drowned himself?"

"No later than yesterday."

"And why is that, my lad?"

"No one knows, exactly," said Merluchet.

"Really?"

"He drowned himself yesterday morning; he was fished out downstream of the Louvre two hours later."

"But perhaps he drowned by accident?" said Porion.

"No, as proof of which, there was a stone suspended around his neck."

"Was he in love?"

"It's quite possible." And the grocer's apprentice, showing his beautiful teeth in a Homeric laughter, exclaimed: "Now that you make me think of it, Père Cinnamon, I believe that Agénor *was* in love."

"With whom?"

"His cousin."

"A pretty girl?"

"Oh, very pretty."

Good, thought Porion. *It's always a question of a pretty girl.* Aloud he said: "His cousin made him unhappy, then?"

"She made fun of him a little; to such an extent that one Sunday, when we all went together to eat a fry-up in Marly..."

Porion shivered.

"She said that she'd never seen a man as ugly as him," the grocer's boy finished, still laughing.

"Oh, you went to Marly?"

"We go there every Sunday."

"Several of you?"

"Sometimes fifteen or twenty, each with his fiancée or his promise."

"And you have a good time out there?"

"We go on boating the river to give us an appetite."

"Really?"

"Then sometimes we go dancing in Bougival village."

"Poor Agénor," said Père Cinnamon.

"You know him?"

"Slightly..." Porion was lying; it was the first time he had head the name pronounced. To give weight to his assertion, he added: "Wasn't he in drapery?"

"No," said the grocer, "he was a druggist."

"Oh yes...that's right."

"At the Silver Mortar in the Rue de Vinaigriers."

"You're right." Porion engraved the indication on his memory. Then he asked another question: "So his cousin wasn't his fiancée?"

"Which is to say that he certainly wanted her, but she didn't want him."

"It's a fact that he wasn't handsome."

"Frightful," murmured the grocer, who believed himself to be an Adonis.

"Are you sure his cousin is pretty?"

"Oh, stunningly beautiful."

"What's her name?"

"Cécile."

"She doesn't have another name?"

"I only know that one."

"And where does she live?"

"I don't know. Agénor was very jealous."

"Poor fellow!" And, adopting an indifferent expression, Père Cinnamon leaned on the parapet of the bridge again, saying to the grocer: "Don't be late back, my lad, or your boss will scold you."

"You're right. *Bonsoir*, Père Cinnamon."

"*Bonsoir*, my lad."

Porion watched the young man draw away, and murmured: "And there are imbeciles who think that the police know everything! It's a grave error; the police only know what they've been told!"

73

V

After that philosophical reflection, Père Cinnamon leaned his elbows on the parapet of the bridge again and started counting on his fingers while spitting into the water. At times, he willingly occupied himself with statistics.

This is what he was counting: in a quarter of an hour he had received three precious items of information. The first was that the grocer's apprentice belonged to one of the joyful bands that went to spend Sunday on the bank of the Seine at Marly or thereabouts. The second was that there was an exceptionally beautiful girl whose cousin had drowned himself in despair. And finally, the aforesaid cousin, whose name was Agénor Chapuzot, made his living as a druggist in the Rue des Vinaigriers, at the Silver Mortar.

Three items of information in less than a quarter of an hour!

"The hunt is beginning well," murmured Porion. "I have a vague idea that, if I stay here for another quarter of an hour, I might see the girl herself pass by: a manner of hunting like any other. Instead of running after the prey, you wait for the prey to come to you."

And, while watching the water flow, Porion made a brief plan of campaign.

Nothing simpler, he thought. *There's a tavern in the Rue de Vinaigriers where I'm known. I'll go there shortly; they'll welcome me. Where, in any case, isn't Père Cinnamon welcome? Such a worthy fellow!*

And Porion smiled, in a fashion to make one quiver.

I'll shed a few tears, he went on, *over the fate of poor Agénor Chapuzot. They'll chatter about him again. After ten minutes, I'll know how he lived, his habits, his frequentations the name of his cousin and her address. Then, still departing from the supposition that she's the young woman the King likes, once the young woman is discovered, I'll go to see Monsieur de Richelieu. The Maréchal will consent to go with me, or he'll send the valet who was beaten to accompany me...and the rest will go like clockwork.*

On that last thought, Porion quit his immobility and started striding back and forth along the bridge. He wanted to go away, but something was holding him back. What? It would have been impossible for him to explain it.

The mysterious bond that held him on the bridge was so strong that he stayed there for more than an hour, repeatedly plunging into the two currents of the crowd that was increasing around him the investigative gaze of the police agent "in plain clothes," as people say nowadays.

Suddenly, Porion shivered. "Good," he murmured. "It's the day for my acquaintances to cross this bridge."

In fact, a young man who was describing slight zigzags as he walked, coming from the Latin Quarter, came toward him, saying: "Why, *bonjour*, Père Cinnamon. How are you?"

"*Bonjour*, Monsieur Mardochée," replied Porion.

The person to whom he gave that name was a young man of between twenty-five and twenty-eight, tall and lithe, with a friendly, slightly rounded face, but sparkling with humor and intelligence. His long and unkempt hair, devoid of powder and naturally curly, hung down over his shoulders and was completing the greasing of an old gray coat with nacre buttons. His tricorn was dented, deprived of its plume and stained by a few splashes of mud, which proved that it had fallen off in the street and that its owner had put it back on his head afterwards without even brushing it with his elbow.

He was carrying a folder under his arm and a small square box. An old sword with a cockleshell guard, a "cabage-cleaver" from another era, was beating his calf gallantly. For the young man that Porion had addressed simply as Mardochée was a gentleman, or at least genteel, and he was enormously proud of the privilege of wearing a sword.

"Where are young going like this, Monsieur Mardochée?" asked Porion.

"Mardochée de Mardoche, Papa Cinnamon," rectified the punctilious gentleman.

"That's true," said Porion, smiling.

"The terrain of Mardoche," the young man continued, with a slight Gascon accent, "is situated in Angoumois."

"Oh, really?"

"Excellent wine is harvested there..." With that, Messire Mardochée de Mardoche uttered a sigh. "Unfortunately," he added, "my grandfather sold it and ate the price—which means that, such as you see me, Père Cinnamon, I'm reduced to making a living by utilizing the talents that nature has given me, painting frightful bourgeois individuals like yourself for three écus." And he tapped Porion's abdomen joyfully. "Ah!" he went on, "when shall I paint your portrait, old Papa?"

"Whenever you wish," said Porion, "as long as it's not today."

"You don't have time to pose?"

"It's not that."

"What is it, then?"

"I fear that you might be seeing double."

"Bah! Am I slightly emotional?"

"I think so. And then," Porion continued, "if you were seeing double and painted me the same way, you'd give me two heads, which would make me resemble the phenomenal calf that was show to us last year at the Saint-Germain fair."

"Always a quip to make people laugh, Père Cinnamon," murmured the painter, in a melancholy fashion. Then, placing his free hand on Porion's shoulder, he said: "All the same, you ought to let me make your portrait today: two écus of six livres, that wouldn't kill a man, after all..."

"Certainly not," said Porion.

"It would save me from going as far as the Rue des Vinaigriers.."

"Oh, that's where you're going?"

"Yes, to the Pomme Verte tavern. There's always some bourgeois there who'll allow himself to be portrayed."

"But do you think, Porion said, "that in the state you're in..."

A melancholy smile came to Mardochée's lips.

"I'll make you a confidence, Père Cinnamon."

"Go on."

"Times are hard…"

"To whom are you talking, Monsieur Mardochée?"

"It's nearly two months since two sous met up in my pocket."

Porion waited for the sequel to that confidence.

"I've exhausted my credit," the artist went in. "The rôtisseur in the Rue de Buci, from whom I get my meals, sent me away yesterday morning, which means..."

"Which means," said Porion, "that you're probably hungry."

"Since yesterday morning..."

"You had a singular fashion of walking just now, though."

The poor artist had a melancholy smile. "That," he said, "is because I still have credit with Mère Lazare, the tavern-keeper on the Pont Saint-Michel, but she only serves drinks. So, as my stomach felt hollow, I filled it by drinking. Let's see, Père Cinnamon," the painter concluded, "come with me as far as my studio; it's only a short distance away in the Rue Saint-André-des-Arts. I'll sketch you in a quarter of an hour…you give me two écus…and we'll dine together joyfully. It's my treat."

All that was said in a good-humored tone, without obsequiousness or baseness.

"Listen," said Porion "I'll make you another proposition."

"Ah!"

"Let's go to dinner first."

"But…your portrait…"

"You'll make it tomorrow. It's me who's inviting you today……"

"But you'll come tomorrow?"

"I promise."

"It's just that," Mardochée said, simply, "I have the double pride of a gentleman and an artist, and I don't accept alms. I want my salary, nothing more."

"Well, you'll have your salary in advance," said Porion.

"So be it. Where are we going?"

"To the Pomme Verte in the Rue des Vinaigriers."

And Porion led Messire Mardochée de Mardoche, painter and gentleman, away, saying to himself: *I've got an idea...and if I can put it into execution, I won't need Monsieur de Richelieu in order to find the girl that pleases the King.*

VI

Messire Mardochée de Mardoche, painter and gentleman, had installed his innocent batteries in the Pomme Verte tavern—which is to say that it was there that he went to indoctrinate, here and there, a meager clientele, and make portraits at two, three or four écus of six livres.

Furthermore, Mardochée was full of talent, and if he had lived in a less ingrate epoch, his canvases would have been covered in gold.

Père Cinnamon gave him his arm and seemed to have rediscovered his youthful legs. While going along the Rue Saint-Martin, which was very similar then to what it is today, he developed in his mind the famous idea that he had just had.

Let's suppose for a moment, he said to himself, *that I find the young woman whom I believe to the one who has had the honor of pleasing the King; instead of going to find Monsieur de Richelieu, I'll have her portrait made by Mardochée, and I'll take it to the King myself. If the King cries; "That's her!" I'll abduct the girl and take her to Versailles.*

Mardochée had had hunger pangs that the lure of a god meal augmented increasingly as they walked. So, the man who normally walked slowly, like a true Paris idler, stopping here and there, sometimes to eye a young woman, sometimes to look at a mason on a roof, did not deign to pay the slightest attention to an acrobats' booth set up next to the Porte Saint-Martin, in front of which a clown clad in rags was reeling off his hilarious patter without laughing.

Nor did Père Cinnamon manifest the slightest desire to listen to the performer's gibes, and they continued on their way. Less than a quarter of an hour later, they arrived in the Rue des Vinaigriers.

The Pomme Verte tavern was a worthy rival of Ramponneau's Porcherons.[15] The aristocrats of the court went to Ramponneau's in fine parties; high-ranking bourgeois preferred the establishment in the Rue des Vinaigriers. There was a big garden there, with trellises and an arbor, and an apple-tree in the middle whose fruits never ripened, and which served the tavern as a sign.

The society was numerous when Père Cinnamon and Mardochée arrived.

A dozen drinkers were established under one of the arbors, forming a circle around a man of about forty-five, who was reputed to be a good talker and a frank bad lot. That individual was known as Master Pépin, and he was the richest jeweler in the Saint-Martin quarter. A widower, with no children, at the head

---

[15] In fact, the famous cabaret owed by Jean Ramponneau did not acquire the name of Les Porcherons until 1771, and his celebrity was still in the making when the present story is set, not really taking off until 1760, when his previous tavern was renamed Le Tambour Royal.

of an important business, Master Pépin would have given half his wealth to be a gentleman. Bourgeois mores were not made for him. He mocked his neighbors who led regular lives, and was reputed in the quarter to be a true Don Juan. The husbands he had deceived and the wives he had seduced were counted in hundreds. But as he was rich he was an object of admiration rather than reprobation.

"Yes, my friends," he was saying, at the moment when Mardochée and Père Cinnamon came in, "I've never seen a prettier girl."

"What's that?" said Père Cinnamon, who had pricked up his ears at the mention of a pretty girl.

"Yes, Père Cinnamon," Master Pépin went on, "I was saying that I've discovered a pearl of beauty."

"Oh, really?" said Porion.

"There's isn't a woman at Court in Versailles who's worth s much."

"Damn, Master Pépin! And what do you count on doing about it?" asked Père Cinnamon.

The jeweler winked. "A fine question!" he said.

"But perhaps the girl has a lover?" said Porion.

"I don't think so."

"A father?"

"Again, I don't think so. She's always alone."

"Well?"

"No later than this evening, when she takes her needlework back to the Rue Saint-Denis, I'll accost her."

"Bad lot!" said Père Cinnamon.

Mardochée had sat down at table and was eating voraciously. Between mouthfuls, however, he asked: "Is she truly pretty?"

"An angel!" said the amorous jeweler.

"And good?"

"I'm sure of it."

"Brunette or blonde?"

"Blonde."

"Hmm," said Mardochée, pouring himself a glass of wine, which he swallowed in a single draught. "I'd prefer it is she were brunette."

"Why?"

"Because I'm in love with a blonde."

"Bah!"

"But there are so many blonde women," said Père Cinnamon, "that..."

"Where does she live?" asked Mardochée then, his eyes gleaming.

"I don't know exactly."

"Ah!"

"But she lives in the Latin Quarter, that's certain."

"Like mine," said Mardochée. "I can see her mansard from the window of my studio."

"All that I can tell you," continued the conquering jeweler, obligingly, "is that she passes over the Pont au Change every evening at six o'clock."

Good, thought Porion. *It's necessary that I see that. Who knows?*

Mardochée, as we have said, was carrying a small box in his hand and a folder under his arm when he encountered Père Cinnamon. The box, as you will have guessed, was his box of paints. As for the folder, it contained sketches, charcoal drawings and two unfinished portraits in pastels.

As the jeweler said that the girl passed over the Pont au Change every day at six o'clock, Mardochée stood up, his mouth still full, and said to Master Pépin: "For my personal tranquility, let me carry out an experiment."

"What?"

"I've begun a portrait of the woman I love."

"Aha!"

"I'll show it to you." And he opened his folder and set one of the two pastels before the jeweler's eyes.

Master Pépin uttered an exclamation: "That's her!"

At that exclamation, Mardochée, who was somewhat the worse for wine, uttered a roar. "Ah! That's her!" he said.

"Yes," stammered the jeweler.

Mardochée leapt over the table and seized him by the throat. "Wretch!" he shouted.

"Help!" cried the jeweler, half-strangled.

Mardochée, who was as strong as a Turk, knocked the Don Juan down beneath him, disdained to draw his sword, but took possession of a knife and cried: "If you don't swear to me, on your share of paradise, that you'll respect that young woman," he cried, "I'll kill you!"

The jeweler was a coward. He swore all the oaths that Mardochée demanded.

"That's good," said the latter, "but I have my eye on you, fellow!" And he let the jeweler get up.

During the struggle, Père Cinnamon had examined the pastel, and admitted that the woman represented therein was veritably very beautiful.

Suddenly, one of the drinkers approached in his turn, and said: "But I know her!"

"Oh, you know her!" roared Mardochée, still brandishing his knife.

"That's Cécile," said the drinker, who was a merchant's clerk.

"Cécile?"

"Yes, the cousin of poor Agénor Chapuzot, who drowned himself."

At those words, Père Cinnamon swallowed two glasses of wine in order to master his emotion. Then he set about trying to calm Mardochée down, which as all the easier because the shop assistant protested his respect for Mademoiselle Cécile Robert. After which he sat down again, and Mardochée sat down with him.

At ten o'clock in the evening, everyone had left the Pomme Verte except Père Cinnamon and Mardochée. The painter, dead drunk, was asleep under the table.

The police agent called the landlord and recommended that he put his guest to bed and get him sleep off his wine in peace.

While the landlord obeyed, thanks to the two écus that Père Cinnamon put into his hand, the latter took possession of the folder containing the pastel and went out, murmuring: "Now let's make a round trip to Versailles. I've got time to come back before Mardochée wakes up."

VII

In 175* to go from the Rue des Vinaigriers to Versailles at ten o'clock in the evening, in a hurry, was not an easy matter. The road was a good four leagues long, and carriages were scarce. Then again, one did not get into the palace as easily as an ordinary house.

On the threshold of the tavern, Porion said that to himself, and many other things besides. He consulted the distance to be traveled, counted the number of doormen he would find standing guard under the walls of the palace, the guardsmen lined up in the courtyards, the musketeers stacked on the staircases and the gentlemen of service spaced out in the antechambers.

To get as far as His Majesty, he thought, *I'd have to say to all and sundry: "I've brought the portrait of the woman with whom the King is smitten." Now, for a start, the King might not like that, and might have me whipped with stirrup-leathers by way of recompense. Secondly, before I reach him it's very probable that Madame de Pompadour would be alerted to it. In that case, I'd be sent to the Bastille by way of a* lettre de cachet.

Hmm! Hmm! Hmm!

Porion, alias Père Cinnamon, made these reflections in less than ten minutes—which did not prevent him from continuing his route in the direction of the Porte Saint-Martin.

Carriages for hire were rare in those days; one found them here and there, at street-corners. Twenty years earlier, a Parisian had had the fortunate idea of the omnibus, and the King had authorized their establishment, but the Court had recriminated loudly, declaring the idea absurd, and the poor inventor had been ruined.

At first sight, however, there was one simple thing that Porion could do: that was to go to the Châtelet, where he could go in night and day, thanks to a little yellow card that Monsieur de Sartine had delivered to a few of his senior police employees, have the Lieutenant General woken up, confide the result of his investigations to him, and await his orders.

But he did not even give that a thought.

That man, who had been given the nickname of Père Cinnamon because of his coat and his debonair manner, who sheltered a soul of iron beneath a kindly and slightly sly smile, was ambitious. He had formulated a dream a long time ago—a dream that might appear to be absurd, at first—which was that of replacing Monsieur Sartine himself some day.

That would have seemed absurd to anyone else, but it appeared quite natural to Porion. And after all, Porion might have been right. In his opinion, it was necessary to have a hare to make jugged hare, and it was necessary to have a policeman to make a Lieutenant de Police.

Now, Monsieur de Sartine was an aristocrat.

So, in consequence, Porion said to himself: *If I find the girl, the King will take me in consideration, and if I can simply chat with him for half an hour, I'll be able to prove to him that Monsieur de Sartine is a pitiful Lieutenant de Police, whereas I would be a better one.*

Papa Cinnamon said all that to himself during the journey from the Rue des Vinaigriers to the Porte Saint-Martin. There, he stopped. The Opéra, which was then close to where the Théâtre de la Porte Saint-Martin is today, was giving a gala performance that evening. There would certainly be a considerable number of gentlemen there who had come from Versailles, and who would not fail to return there after the play.

Two dozen armoried carriages, harnessed to excellent horses, were stationed in the vicinity of the theater. Porion inspected them from the corner of his eye, and thought: *There'll surely be a place for me in one of them.*

As we have said, the fellow lived in the Rue aux Ours, in a modest house above a druggist's shop. But one does not follow his métier without having the need for occasional disguises and modifications of costume. Now, Porion had, very close to the Porte Saint-Martin, in the Rue Vertbois, a good friend who exercised the profession of second-hand clothes dealer. That man, whose name was Concelot, had sometimes seen his old friend Porion come into his shop in the middle of the night, to ask him for some garment or other, and subject himself to a complete metamorphosis. As he was in on the secret of Porion's mysterious profession, he had given him a key to his shop.

Porion therefore went into it, without making any noise, and without even waking up the clothes-dealer, who slept upstairs in a cupboard. He lit a candle, took off is clothes, searched for others among the stock, and in less than half an hour later he would have been unrecognizable even for those who saw him every day at the Pomme Verte, and even for Monsieur de Sartine, who had assisted him with more than one transformation of that sort.

A quarter of an hour later, an elegant gentleman, showing his calves, and wearing a powdered peruke, went into the Opéra, installed himself in a forestage box, and became the focus of all the lorgnettes. Porion had been rejuvenated by twenty years at a stroke, and the fake diamonds by which he was covered were worthy of the kind of ovation that had been given to him. The performance was, however, nearing its end, and if Porion wanted to find a traveling companion bound for Versailles he had no time to lose.

Among the lorgnettes aimed at him, there was one that fixed obstinately upon the enormous diamond buttons that he was bore on his shirt. It was in the hands of a woman seated in the box opposite. Porion recognized her immediately. In fact, Porion, whom no one recognized, knew everyone.

Good! he thought. *It's the Maréchale d'H***. In the evening, paste shines as brightly as diamonds, and the Maréchale, who is heaped with debts, is wondering what opulent stranger I might be. She'll take me back in her carriage.*

The Maréchale was a woman of about forty-five, still very beautiful, especially by candlelight, a trifle extravagant, who had generated as much talk about her as anyone. She was very witty, and the King sometimes deigned to be amused by her sallies. On days when Louis XV's ennui assumed such proportions that Madame de Pompadour lost patience with it, they sent, in despair of the cause, for the Maréchale. At the Château of Versailles she was known as the Crackpot. The King sometimes laughed at her eccentricities, but never got annoyed with her.

Porion knew all that.

The difficulty for him was to make contact with the Maréchale. Fortunately, the paste with which he was covered had begun the overtures. *I'll wager*, he thought, *that the Maréchale is being tormented by a few discourteous creditors; it must be easy to approach her.* And Porion took out ostentatiously, a beautiful notepad with silver claps, and a pencil, and scribbled a note on one sheet, which he tore off:

The Dutch banker Van Roëk would be glad to lay his homages at the feet of Madame la Maréchale d'H*** and to place himself under her protection, having a difference with His Majesty's government with regard to a considerable sum that is owed to him by the Ministry of War.

If Madame la Maréchale d'H*** would deign to accord a quarter of a hour of conversation this evening to Monsieur Van Roëk the latter would be only too glad to show his appreciation.

That note written, the pretended financier quit his box and went to the foyer, where Mademoiselle Louison, who had succeeded Nanette Lolier, displayed the most beautiful flowers, bought a two-louis bouquet, slipped his note inside and charged the pretty flower-seller with taking the whole to the Maréchale.

Then he waited.

Five minutes later, the florist returned.

"Madame la Maréchale," she said, "will wait for Monsieur at the exit from the Opéra."

"Where?"

"In her carriage."

"Very good."

"Madame la Maréchale," Mademoiselle Louison continued, "is returning to Versailles this evening, and she invites Monsieur to accompany her."

That response pleased Porion so greatly that he gave Louison a third louis and asked her to go tell the Maréchale that he would be certain not to miss the rendezvous.

Then he went back to his box, saying to himself: *I'll promise the poor Maréchale a hundred thousand livres, and I'll be very unfortunate if I don't get in to see the King tomorrow even before the gentlemen of the bedchamber.**

VIII

"Madame," said the pretended financier to the Maréchale, while both of them were rolling at top speed along the road to Versailles, "my case is quite simple. When the army last entered into campaign against the Imperials, I made loans totaling three millions, on which I would make a profit of slightly more than a million if I were repaid."

"Really," said the Maréchale, to whom the word "million" seemed more harmonious than all the music she had ever heard.

"The Minister of War," Porion went on, "has raised that figure to three millions and a quarter, and he only wants to give me two."

"What do you mean by that, Monsieur?" asked the Maréchale, who did not understand, or pretended not to understand.

"It's quite simple," Porion continued, naively. "Suppose that things turn out as the Minister of War wishes."

"All right."

"I'll be regulated at four millions."

"Perfect!"

"But I'll only be given two."

"Oh?"

"The State will nevertheless pay four millions."

"Where will the other two millions go, then?"

"That's what I advise you to ask, Madame, of those who do not want to allow me to reach the King."

"But that's an infamy!" exclaimed the Maréchale.

"So great," said Porion, "that I would gladly give a hundred thousand écus to be able to talk to the King, face to face, for an hour."

The figure of a hundred thousand écus vibrated in the skull of the poor indebted Maréchale like a veritable drum-roll.

A hundred thousand écus! She only owed scarcely half that sum. Her debts paid, she would be rich, if such a windfall reached her!

Porion was playing the role of a Dutch banker marvelously. He had been able to pose the affair of three millions like a man who sees things from above; he had mentioned giving a hundred thousand écus as if it were a matter of ten pistoles. How could the Maréchale have doubted him?

So she said, swiftly: "You've done well, Monsieur to address yourself to me."

"That's what I was advised to do, Madame."

"In Paris?"

"No, in Holland."

And Porion, the best-informed man in France and Navarre, leaned toward the Maréchale's ear, and pronounced a name that made her quiver: "Ruisdalher." It was the name of another financier who had loved the Maréchale, during his sojourn in Paris, at a handsome cash price.

"Well, Monsieur Van Roëk," she said, "I swear to you that the King will receive you tomorrow morning."

"Tomorrow will be too late, Madame."

"Too late!"

"Undoubtedly. At this very moment the police must know that I am in France, and the Minister of War, who has an interest in my not seeing the king, will already have taken his precautions. It's necessary that I be introduced to the king's presence before his *petit lever*."

"I'll take charge of that," said the Maréchale.

"But for that," Porion continued, "it would be necessary for me to get into the Château de Versailles tonight."

"Nothing simpler," said the Maréchale, who was intent on her hundred thousand écus.

"In truth!" exclaimed the fake financier, in a naïve fashion.

"I lodge in the château."

"Ah!

"And I offer you hospitality in my apartment."

Damn! thought Porion. *The Maréchale does things well. She's offering herself, into the bargain.* "But Madame," he said. "What would people say if I were seen to enter your apartment? For, after all, the guards on duty open the door of every carriage as it goes through the gate of the court of honor."

The Maréchale uttered a burst of laughter. "I've just had a ludicrous idea," she said, "but I'll wager that it will please you."

"Go on."

"I have two lackeys hanging from my carriage-straps."

"Good."

"Shortly before we reach Versailles, you'll put on the livery of one of them and take his place.

"Perfect!" said Porion. "But your servants…what will they think?"

"Oh," said the Maréchale, laughing more loudly, "they've seen many other things!"

A quarter of a league from Versailles the Maréchale called a halt. One of the lackeys gave his ample fur-lined pelisse and his plumed and braided hat to Monsieur Van Roëk, who retained beneath them the garments with the paste buttons that had dazzled the Maréchale. Then the lackeys were given permission to go womanizing in Versailles until the following day.

The carriage entered the courtyard of the palace without any hindrance.

The Maréchale, on getting down at the foot of the perron, gave the fake lackey her lorgnette, her fan and delightful little Havana lap-dog from which she was never separated, and he followed her.

The guards and sentinels had no suspicions, but the two chambermaids who were waiting to undress their mistress opened their eyes wide at first. The Maréchale sent them away and shut herself with the pretended financier in a boudoir where a delightful half-light reigned, procured by lamps with alabaster globes.

As he took off the lackey's pelisse, Porion detached one of the buttons of his costume, which fell on to the floor. That button, which was pure paste, had the effect on the Maréchale of the elder brother of the famous regent diamond.

"Oh, my God," she said, on seeing it fall. "What are you doing, Monsieur? You're sowing your buttons."

"It's necessary to sow to harvest," the impudent fellow replied. Making himself comfortable, he did not pick up the fake diamond.

But it was written that Porion would not have all the advantages of which he had dreamed, for while he was casually raising the Maréchale's hand to his lips, someone rapped gently on the door, and a voice, youthful and soft, although masculine, made itself heard, saying: "Are you asleep, Madame la Maréchale? Your women don't want to let me in."

"Oh, my God!" murmured the Maréchale. "It's the young Chevalier d'O***, one of the King's pages." And she took Porion by the hand and hid him behind a screen. Then she opened the door and the page came in.

"Madame," he said, "the King can't sleep. He sent for the Marquise to converse with him, but the Marquise has a violent migraine and compresses on her head. Then the King said: 'Go find me Madame la Maréchale d'H***.'"

"That's fine, my darling. Tell the King that I'm coming."

She sent the page away, and while she hastily readjusted her clothing, Porion came out from behind his screen. "The King can't sleep, then?"

"It appears so. I'll take advantage of it to talk to him about you."

Porion winked. "Madame la Maréchale," he said, "I've just had an excellent idea."

"Oh, really?"

"The King has his police; the Minister of War has his own."

"Well?"

"I also have mine."

"In truth!"

"And my police inform me that the King has a secret chagrin."

"Bah!"

"He's in love."

"With whom?"

"A young girl that neither Monsieur de Richelieu nor Monsieur Sartine, nor anyone else, has been able to locate for him."

"What are you telling me?"

"Now," Porion continued, "I'll wager that if you tell the King that Monsieur Van Roëk, one of your friends from Holland, had come to Versailles expressly to give him news of that girl..."

"What!" exclaimed the Maréchale. "You know where she is?"

"Perhaps." And Porion added: "Remember, my lovely friend, that it's a matter of a hundred thousand écus."

The last words electrified the Maréchale. "I'll do it," she said. "Wait for me here. I'll come back to fetch you in a quarter of an hour."

"Poor Maréchale," Porion murmured, when she had gone. "She'll pull a terrible face tomorrow when she takes my diamond to Monsieur Bossange tomorrow to have it valued."

And the fellow waited for the Maréchale to come to fetch him, in order to take him to the King.

IX

In fact, the King could not sleep.

He was in his underwear and a dressing-down, his feet in slippers, beside the fire, and was in a mood that would have caused a courtier with the most flexible spine to shiver.

A page was in a corner, mute and inflexible, telling himself silently that the honor of approaching His Majesty and serving him was not worth as much as the happiness of sleeping peacefully on a good pillow of goose- and duck-down.

At first the King had gone to bed, and had even closed his eyes. Then he had woken up abruptly, complaining of indigestion. Someone had gone in search of the physician, Monsieur Fagon, the son of the doctor who had cared for Louis XIV for more than twenty years.

Monsieur Fagon had taken the pulse of his august client, had made him put out his tongue, had ausculated him carefully, and had ended up replying that the digestion was excellent, and that if the King could not sleep, it must be because of something other than a state of malady.

With that, the King had started to yawn, saying: "I'm suffering from ennui!"

He had sent for the Marquise. The Marquise had a migraine. He had asked for Monsieur de Richelieu. Richelieu was in Paris, at the Pavillon de Hanovre, in pleasant intimate company. Then the King had asked for the Maréchale. He had been told that she was at the Opéra, but that she would be returning to Versailles that evening. And the King had waited, yawning as if to strain his jaw.

Finally, the Maréchale arrived.

"Oh, my beauty!" cried Louis XV. "Take pity on me; I'm dying of ennui."

The Maréchale had taken advantage of the confidence of the pretended financier Van Roëk. "Sire," she said. "Your Majesty believes himself to be much more ill than he really is."

"Oh, my darling, I'm suffering greatly."

"That's because Your Majesty has a great preoccupation," said the Maréchale.

The King shuddered.

"An acute mental preoccupation," she continued.

"What do you mean by that?" said the King.

"Oh, Sire," said Madame d'H***, "I don't mean that Your Majesty has political anxieties. Affairs of State are going very well, thank God!"

"That's not what my Ministers say, my beauty."

"Your Majesty's Ministers are zealous."

"That might be true, but they claim that everything is going very badly." And the King sighed again.

"Your Majesty," the Maréchale continued, "has what they call a bee in his bonnet."

"About what, my darling?"

"A certain young woman."

The King made an abrupt movement in his armchair. "You know that?"

"Yes, Sire."

"That chatterbox Sartine!"

"Monsieur de Sartine hasn't told me anything, Sire."

"Then it's the Marquise..."

"Nor the Marquise."

"Then how do you know?"

The Maréchale was a woman of imagination, as you shall see. "Sire," she said, "I have an extraordinary friend, a Dutchman, a rich banker, Monsieur Van Roëk, who has been at Versailles for a few hours."

"Good."

"That banker devotes himself a little to the practice of sorcery. He knows that sorcerers are no longer burned, and that tolerance encourages him. He is the one who told me that Your Majesty is sighing deeply after a young woman, undiscoverable, it seems, although Monsieur de Sartine has the pretention of being infallible..."

"But how does your Dutchman know that, Maréchale?"

"Because he is something of a sorcerer, Sire."

"That's true. Well, it's necessary for me to find her..."

"That's what he proposes to Your Majesty, on condition that Your Majesty will receive him tonight..."

"Where?"

"Here."

"But where is he?"

"In my apartment, Sire."

The King extended his hand toward a bell-cord. The Maréchale stopped him. "No need," she said. "If Your Majesty wishes, I'll go fetch him."

"What!" exclaimed the King, almost joyful. "I wish it!"

The Maréchale stood up, as nimble as a sylphide, in spite of her forty-eight springs. And she headed for the door, murmuring: "that's my hundred thousand écus earned."

Ten minutes later she came back with the pretended financier Van Roëk.

Porion bowed to the King, like a man who is no stranger to fine manners.

"Is it true, Monsieur," the King said to him, "that you are something of a sorcerer?"

"A little, Sire," Porion replied, having been brought up to date briefly by the Maréchale.

"How do you proceed?" asked the King, curiously.

"Sire," said Porion, "if Your Majesty will give me ten minutes, I shall demonstrate my methods to him. And he made a small sign to the Maréchale with the corner of his eye.

"Very well," said the latter. "I'll withdraw."

The King saluted her with his hand and allowed her to leave.

Then Porion, left alone with the King, unbuttoned his coat and removed from beneath his waistcoat the folder of the poor painter Mardochée de Mardoche.

"What's that?" asked Louis XV.

Porion opened the folder, took out one of the two pastels, and showed it to the King."

The King uttered an exclamation. "That's her!"

"Really?"

"Her! It's definitely her!" repeated the King, in ecstasy before the portrait.

Porion started to smile. "Poor Maréchale," he said.

"What?" said the King.

"Sire," the police again said, "the Maréchale is an intelligent woman, but she has a weakness: she believes in sorcerers."

"And she's right," said the King, smiling.

"She's wrong," Potion countered, "given that there's not the slightest sorcery in all this."

"What?"

"Will Your Majesty deign to listen to me for ten minutes?"

"Yes, if you'll reply to my questions first."

Porion waited.

"Where is this young woman?"

"In Paris. Your Majesty has only to order it, and she'll be in Versailles in a matter of hours."

"That's good. Speak now."

Then Porion related to the King, very frankly and very wittily, how Monsieur de Sartine had sent for him, and how in a matter of hours he had uncovered all the threads of the tangle, stolen the painter's folder after getting him drunk, changed his costume and how, thus clad, he had turned the Maréchale's head.

The King laughed until he shed tears—which certainly had not happened to him for a long time.

"So," said the King, when Porion had finished his story. "You're not Dutch?"

"No, Sire."

"Not a financier?"

"Alas."

"And you're a policeman?"

"At Your Majesty's service, and who would certainly," said Porion, proudly, "make a better Lieutenant General that Monsieur de Sartine."

"Oh, yes!" said the King.

"If Your Majesty would deign to make the trial…," the impudent fellow suggested.

"Well," replied Louis XV, "Bring me the girl, and we'll see!" Then he started laughing again. "But the poor Maréchale—where will she get the hundred thousand écus on which she's counting?"

"Your Majesty will be so content tomorrow that it's not impossible that…"

"*Ventre-saint-gris!* as the Béarnais my ancestor used to say," exclaimed the King. "A hundred thousand écus. If I had them in my money-box, Madame de Pompadour would have spent them a long time ago!"

She summoned one of the pages and gave the order that Porion should be let out of the palace by means of a hidden stairway and a secret door.

When Porion had gone, the King started laughing again, writhing in his armchair. Suddenly, however, he heard cries—genuine cries of distress, and the bewildered Maréchale entered the King's apartment, holding the famous button that the pretended financier had dropped in her boudoir.

"Oh, my God!" she said. "The wretch! The swine! It's paste!"

"Maréchale," replied Louis XV, his good humor increasing further, "You're a woman of experience, and you ought to know that *all that glitters is not gold!*"

X

Let us abandon for the moment Porion, King Louis XV, the Maréchale and even Monsieur de Sartine, and return to an individual that we met at the beginning of this story.

You will remember that the unfortunate young man, after having seen death at such close range, guided by the duenna, had reached the terrace of the mysterious house where so much human blood had already been shed; that from the terrace he had climbed on to the roof of the next house and had run from roof to roof until, his strength running out, he had fallen, dying, into a mansard occupied by a young woman.

Now, it was two months after that episode that the King had commanded his Lieutenant de Police to find him a young woman with whom he was in love.

It was two months since Hector de Pierrefeu had left the inn in the Rue des Enfants Rouges, two months during which he had heard no mention of his younger brother.

What, then had happened?

That is what we are about to summarize briefly.

It is difficult to describe the amazement and fear that initially took hold of the young woman when she saw the young man covered with blood fall into her mansard, who said to her, in a faint voice: "Help me…in the name of heaven!"

They were, however, the only words that the young man pronounced, for, his strength abandoning him, he closed his eyes and lost consciousness.

The young woman did not lose her head. She laid Hector on her bed, made him respire vinegar, and, as she did not succeed in bringing him round and the blood was still flowing from the bullet-wound, she ran out of the mansard to seek help. She did not have far to go.

The house in which she lived, which was situated in the Rue Saint-André-des-Arts, was occupied by small households of workers, clerks and students. On the same floor, under the roofs, there was a young man who bowed respectfully to the young woman every time they met on the staircase. He was a poor student of surgery by the name of Firmin. Poor and studious, tormented by a thirst for knowledge, he spent part of his nights copying music in order to earn enough to pay for his lessons and follow the courses of the famous professors then practicing in the hospitals. Well before the young woman, who was exceedingly hardworking, Firmin was awake and at work.

She knocked on his door. He came to open it.

"Come quickly!" she said. "It's a matter of a man's life!"

Firmin picked up his medical bag and followed her. He saw Hector, sounded his wound, extracted the bullet, and answered for the life of the wounded man.

A few hours later, in fact, Hector recovered consciousness—but he only proffered incoherent words, full of delirium and fever.

Where had he been wounded?

Where had he come from?

Those were the two question that the two young people, the seamstress and the surgeon, asked, without being able to resolve them

Several days went by.

Firmin's mansard was a little larger than his neighbor's. Hector had been transported there. The young surgeon and the young woman lavished their cares upon the wounded man, but the latter did not recover his reason.

Firmin, who was already a skillful man, said to his neighbor: "That young man has experienced some terrible commotion. He will get better physically, but I fear that he might remain mad."

In fact, nearly two months went by, and Hector de Pierrefeu entered into convalescence, but his smile remained indecisive and almost idiotic, his eyes vague and his intelligence obscured. Sometimes, he attached a grateful gaze to his two saviors, but when he tried to speak, his voice expired in his throat, and he suddenly took his head in his hands and dissolved in tears.

Meanwhile, the young woman and the surgeon had exhausted their last resources caring for the unknown man. They had had to work for two hours more, vainly abridging their nights and lengthening their day. Distress was beginning to make itself felt in the two mansards that had so generously entered an association in order to save the young man, whose name they did not know, when a little money arrived in an unexpected fashion.

Who was that young woman?

In the house where she had lived alone for six years she was known as "the little Madonna," so beautiful and good was she. The clerks the students and the shop assistants who lodged on the lower floors saluted her deferentially. No one dared lack respect for her. She no longer had a mother. Her father was what was known as a "house man"—which is to say, a domestic servant. He came to see his daughter once a week, but, being poor himself, he could only give her very limited aid, and Cécile—that was the young woman's name—worked fifteen hours a day to earn eight sous.

She had nevertheless amassed some meager savings with a view to her establishment, if ever she encountered an honest man who wanted her for a wife, when Hector de Pierrefeu fell into her home.

As one can imagine, the seamstress' savings and the poor surgeon's resources, had soon been exhausted.

One morning, however, a sum of twenty écus reached them that they were not expecting.

Cécile's father, as we have said, usually came to see her once a week, but he had not put in an appearance for a month. As he was sometimes required to be absent from Paris, however, in accordance with the caprices of the masters he served, Cécile was not unduly worried by that.

Finally, one morning, a letter was brought for the young woman. It bore different postmarks, which announced that it came from abroad, and it enclosed what was then called a cashable bond, payable at the establishment of the Fermiers Généraux. It was for twenty écus—which is to say, sixty livres.

The letter was dated from Amsterdam.

Cécile recognized her father's handwriting, and read:

My dear child,

It's more than a month since I've seen you, and I don't know when I shall see you again. I've changed condition; I'm in the service of the Comte de A***, a disgraced courtier who was obliged to quit the realm precipitately and take refuge in Holland. If anyone asks about me, don't tell them where I am. I'll explain the reason for that recommendation later. In the meantime, I'm sending you all that I can assemble of my savings, and I shall always remain, your devoted father,

Robert Damiens.[16]

Cécile had just read that letter, sitting next to the window, when, raising her head, she perceived a gaze fixed upon her, in one of the mansards of the house next door. A man was standing at that window, contemplating the young woman with mute ecstasy.

It was Messire Mardochée de Mardoche, painter and gentleman, who, newly installed, was perceiving his neighbor for the first time.

---

[16] This name would have been instantly recognizable to Ponson's contemporary readers, and would have provided them not only with a context in which to construe subsequent scenes involving the character in question but also some inkling as to where the convoluted story-line might eventually end up—a benefit that the author presumably appreciated himself, although it relocates the setting of this part of the story to 1756, making Sartine's role as Lieutenant de Police anachronistic. Robert-François Damiens was charged with attempting to assassinate Louis XV, although the circumstances of the alleged attempt strongly imply that he had no such intention; at any rate, he was tortured and then subjected to a gruesomely cruel public execution that became legendary for its excess, and was recalled in many subsequent literary works. One description was provided by Giacomo Casanova's highly unreliable but widely read memoirs, in which he claimed to have witnessed the execution.

XII

Messire Mardochée de Mardoche was a bold companion when it was a matter of drinking, roughing up the sergeants of the watch or brawling in a tavern with anyone at all, but he lacked a certain audacity when it was a question of a woman.

The Rue Saint-André-des-Arts, which has been successively broadened in various epochs, was then very narrow, and its houses had overhanging roofs that protected passers-by from the rain. From his window, Mardochée could see Cécile Robert's. From his roof, by taking an appropriate run-up, he could have leapt to the neighboring roof and reached that window.

On the day when he had perceived the young woman, Mardochée had fallen in love. But Mardochée was timid, and he had been in love with Cécile Robert for more than a month without her even having noticed him. Sheltered behind the frame of his casement, the poor devil spent entire hours contemplating the young woman.

Then he took up his brushes and made her portrait.

Hunger, which was the only thing that chased him out of his mansard from time to time, tore him away from the contemplation of his idol. He had ended up becoming acquainted with all her habits. Cécile went out every evening between six and seven o'clock, traversed the Seine and went to the Rue Saint-Denis, to a lingerie establishment that gave her work. Then she came back, prepared herself a frugal meal, and returned to work until ten or eleven o'clock in the evening.

One morning, the poor artist had woken up with a bold idea. It was a matter of nothing less than lying in ambush for her by the water's edge, at the entrance to the bridge that the young woman crossed, approaching her boldly and declaring his love, while taking full advantage of his status as a gentleman.

But between the conception of an idea and putting it into execution, there is sometimes a world of difference, as you shall see.

Mardochée de Mardoche was indeed on the Pont au Change at six o'clock in the evening, but when Cécile Robert came to pass by, he was seized by such a fit of timidity that he did not even have the strength to salute her.

She went by without seeing him.

The following day, he came back, and the same thing happened.

The day after, he raised his hand to his hat, but Cécile did not see him.

Finally, the painter's distress made him decisive, to the point that he swore to himself that he would approach Cécile boldly that very evening. That was the day that he encountered Père Cinnamon and his suffering stomach imposed silence on his heart.

So, Mardochée de Mardoche was in love with Cécile Robert, and Cécile Robert had no suspicion of it. Nor did the poor young woman suspect that, on the day when she had gone, in all honor, to Marly, in the company of a few young women and several shop assistants who were friends of her cousin Agénor Chapuzot, that she had turned the head of the King. Nor, finally, at that moment, did she know about the tragic death of that poor devil, whose hand she had refused with a loud burst of laughter.

So, Mardochée de Mardoche had supped at the Pomme Verte tavern, had allowed Père Cinnamon to get him drunk, had fallen under the table, without any suspicion that the pretended bourgeois whose portrait he was to make was going to take singular advantage of his drunkenness.

Twelve hours had gone by and Mardochée was still asleep.

It is true that good care had been taken of him. The landlord of the Pomme Verte, handsomely paid by Père Cinnamon, aided by his waiters, had transported the stranger to a room. He had been undressed and put to bed without even opening his eyes.

The night had passed; the day had come, then the sun, and Mardochée was still asleep.

Finally, Porion arrived.

The brilliant financier Van Roëk had disappeared, to give way once again to the amiable Père Cinnamon.

It was then ten o'clock in the morning.

"What have you done with my drunkard?" he asked.

"He's upstairs," said the landlord.

"In bed?"

"Sleeping blissfully."

"Let's go wake him up," said Père Cinnamon.

And he went up to the bedroom, guided by sonorous snoring. It was necessary to shake him rudely to wake Messire Mardochée de Mardoche, but he finally opened his eyes, paraded an astonished gaze around him, and wondered where he was. Then he perceived the worthy Père Cinnamon.

"Have you slept well?" the latter asked.

"Oh, it's you, Papa."

"Yes, my boy."

"But where am I?"

"Still at the Pomme Verte."

"Really? I was drunk yesterday, wasn't I?"

"As a lord."

"What time is it?"

"Ten o'clock."

"I suspected as much. I'm dying of hunger."

"Damn," said Père Cinnamon, innocently. "I'd offer you lunch, but you'd get drunk again, and I wouldn't have my portrait."

"Oh, that's true," said Mardochée, whose memory was gradually returning. "It's you who paid the bill yesterday?"

"Of course."

"Three écus on account."

"Yes—but I need my portrait."

"It's just that I don't work well when I'm hungry…and thirsty." And he clicked his tongue.

"I'd be glad to give you lunch," said Père Cinnamon.

"Oh, you're a good man, Papa."

"But not here."

"Why not?"

Papa Cinnamon winked. "I'll tell you later. Get dressed, and come with me."

"Where are we going?"

"The Latin Quarter."

Mardochée got dressed. When he was ready he looked for his box of paints and his folder. They were both placed on a table; as you can imagine, before waking the painter, Porion had taken care to replace the pastel.

They quit the Pomme Verte together, therefore, descended the faubourg and then the Rue Saint-Martin, crossed the Place du Châtelet and went into the Latin Quarter.

Mardochée was beginning to show signs of anxiety.

"Where are we going to have lunch, then?" he asked.

"In your studio."

"What?"

"We're going to have a nearby tavern send up sausages and eggs, and two bottles of wine.

Mardochée pulled a face.

"It's because I want my portrait," said Père Cinnamon. "When it's done, we'll go back to have dinner at the Pomme Verte."

"But will my three écus stretch to that?"

"Not, it's me who'll pay."

"You're the king of bankers," said Mardochée. And he took Père Cinnamon up to the mansard that he referred to pompously as his studio. The latter went to the window and looked out.

Cécile Robert was working placidly beside her own.

"Aha, my lad!" said the amiable fellow, turning to Mardochée.

"How beautiful she is!" murmured the latter, who was no longer thinking about lunch.

Imbecile! thought Porion. *You don't suspect that you've just introduced the wolf to the sheepfold.*

XII

Two hours later, Porion, alias Père Cinnamon, had organized all his plans.

Mardochée and he had eaten a frugal lunch. The painter, condemned to meager salt-pork and a bottle of cheap wine, had accepted that fortune with mild philosophy, all the more so as Père Cinnamon had said to him:

"I don't have the honor of being an artist, nor a gentleman, but if a gentleman has the right to eat his fill, an artist must spare himself. I want to have a portrait with a good resemblance, with a view to sending it to one of my sisters who lives in the provinces, and if you'd drunk as much as you did yesterday, your hand would tremble.

"There's some truth in that," Mardochée replied, having set to work, sketching the debonair visage of Père Cinnamon with broad strokes of the pencil.

The latter was holding himself stiff and straight—which did not prevent him from chatting, however. "So you're in love?"

"You've just seen her, Papa Cinnamon," the painter replied, enthusiastically. "Tell me whether it's possible not to be seriously smitten."

"I certainly can't deny it." Then Père Cinnamon sighed: "Oh, it's good to be young!"

"Really?"

"And if I were your age..."

"Well?"

"We'd be cutting one another's throats for that *tender shoot*," Porion finished, who had read the novels of Mademoiselle de Scudéry.

Mardochée frowned.

"But don't worry," said the amiable fellow, "I'm sixty, and I no longer have any amour except for the juice of the vine. All for Bacchus, my friend, no longer anything for the goddess Cypris."

While working, Mardochée darted inflamed glances at the frame of the mansard under the window of which Cécile Robert was working relentlessly. But the young woman did not even raise her head, and was doubtless far from suspecting that she was the object of such sustained attention.

"Ah," said Père Cinnamon, "are you at least paid in return?"

Mardochée shivered.

"I don't know...I don't think so...," he stammered.

"What!"

"I'll even confess," the painter went on, who had a strong dose of naivety, "that I don't know whether she's ever noticed me."

"Get away!"

Mardochée sighed deeply; then he confessed, simply, that he had already gone to lie in ambush for her at the Pont au Change several times, with the firm intention of stopping the young woman and declaring his love, but that his courage had always failed him at the solemn moment.

"It's because you're still very young," murmured Père Cinnamon, with a hint of mockery.

"Really?"

"Of, if I were in your place..."

"Well, what would you do?"

"Instead of waiting for the young woman at the Pont au Change, I'd go to see her in her house."

"You'd dare to do that!" exclaimed Mardochée, who, despite his warrior appearance, was the mildest man in the world.

"Of course I'd dare," said Père Cinnamon.

"But...finally, how would you gain entry to her house?"

"Through the door, of course!"

"And what is anyone asks me where I'm going?"

"You'll reply that you're carrying out a small mission for Mademoiselle Cécile Robert."

"Oh, that's true," said Mardochée, whose face cleared. "We know her name now."

"So, nothing is simpler," Père Cinnamon continued. "You go right to the top of the staircase."

"Good!"

"You knock on the young woman's door, you fall at her feet..."

"And she throws me out," said Mardochée, ever naïve.

Père Cinnamon shook his head. "My God," he murmured, "the young men of today are entirely lacking in audacity. Look, my dear Monsieur Mardochée. I'll wager that if I took a hand in your affairs, I..."

"You, Père Cinnamon?"

"Me,"

"What would you do?"

"I'd go to find the young woman and I'd give her such an account of you that her mouth would be watering. You can imagine that an old fellow like me doesn't inspire any suspicion," Porion concluded, sighing deeply.

"You'd do that for me?" exclaimed Mardochée.

"I'm ready to do it."

The painter threw his arms around him and embraced him effusively.

"But you can imagine," Porion went on, "that it's not at present that it's necessary to try that step."

"Oh! Why not?"

"It's necessary for me to obtain some petty information, so that I can introduce myself into the house on some pretext."

Mardochée slapped his forehead. "The pretext isn't difficult to find," he said.

"Really?"

"On passing by the door, I saw a notice indicating lodgings for rent."

"Perfect!" said Porion. "I'll go this evening. In the meantime, work."

And the worthy fellow seemed to be setting the price of his future kindness at the completion of his portrait. So Mardochée worked for a part of the day with unparalleled ardor, and, as the frugal lunch he had had could not obscure his mind, he found himself the master of his full intelligence, and had recourse to the naïve flattery of painters who always embellish their model.

Under Mardochée's brush, Porion became an Adonis. And every time he abandoned the pose that the painter had made him take momentarily, in order to take a look at the work, he uttered cries of admiration and found a perfect resemblance therein.

Finally, as the afternoon wore on, Mardochée said to him: "I don't need you any longer now."

"Why is that?"

"I can finish the portrait without putting you to the trouble of posing any longer.

"Really?"

"And if you'd like to take a little stroll…"

Porion winked. "I see where you're going, my young friend. You think it's time to set out on campaign?"

"I agree."

"Well, I'll go…but wait for me here."

"I promise."

Porion took his coat and tricorn, and went out.

Mardochée continued working.

He no longer had any cause for distraction, in any case, for the young woman was no longer at her window. She was doubtless preparing her evening meal in a corner of the mansard.

An hour went by; the daylight faded away, and Mardochée would have been very embarrassed to work by lamplight, for he did not have so much as the stub of a candle in his attic. For more than a month the poor devil had been going to bed by moonlight or the light of the stars.

As he abandoned his work, however, footsteps sounded, initially on the staircase, and finally came to a halt outside the door of his mansard. Then Père Cinnamon appeared—but the amiable fellow was not alone.

Behind him, a tavern waiter was advancing, who was carrying an immense hamper on his head, from which penetrating perfumes were escaping that tickled Mardochée's sense of smell very agreeably.

Porion was radiant. "I have good news," he said.

"Really?" exclaimed Mardochée.

"And I'll give it to you glass and fork in hand, my young friend. It's me who'll pay again."

So saying, Père Cinnamon mad a sign to the waiter, who started unpacking the contents of the hamper, taking out successively a cold fowl, a ragout of pork, a few smaller dishes, and venerable bottles covered with cobwebs.

"By the turrets of the Château de Mardoche!" cried Mardochée. "You're more magnificent, Papa Cinnamon, than the greatest lord in the French Court. You put me in mind of Maecenas: *Maecenas atavis edite regibus!*[17] he concluded—for Messire Mardochée de Mardoche had a smattering of Latin.

---

[17] "Maecenas descendant of kings" (the beginning of one of Horace's *Odes*.)

XIII

The hour that had just gone by, in fact, had not been unfruitful for Porion, and had permitted him to complete the most tortuous of his plans.

The placard indicating vacant lodgings had served him quite naturally as a pretext for penetrating into the neighboring house. The two doors, moreover—Mardochée's and the young woman's, were opposite one another.

The house in which the latter lived had a tavern on the ground floor, and it was in that tavern that Père Cinnamon had, a little later, ordered dinner to be sent up to Mardochée's lodgings. To begin with, however, he had contented himself with going inside and seeking information about the vacant lodgings.

The tavern-keeper, who was also the principal tenant of the house, had hastened to take him upstairs, and as he was naturally loquacious, Porion had not had any difficulty making him talk.

While visiting the rooms, Père Cinnamon had learned a great many things. First of all, Mademoiselle Cécile was the daughter of a valet de chambre; she lived alone and was good, although a mild intimacy had been established between her and a young physician named Firmin.

Would they marry some day?

It was probable, but the tavern-keeper affirmed that the young woman was virtuous and that the student had the greatest respect for her. What the tavern-keeper was unable to reveal to Porion was the presence on the top floor of the house of a third person —which is to say, Hector de Pierrefeu, who, as we know, had entered via the roof and whom the young surgeon had hidden in his room. Neither he nor Cécile had told a living soul about the poor madman, and no one in the house suspected his existence.

Perhaps, if Porion had had knowledge of that, he would have modified his plans considerably, but what resulted for him from the conversation with the tavern-keeper was that the young woman had a defender, and that it was indispensable, if the young woman were to be abducted, that the latter be made to disappear, or at least drawn out of the house—which would be easy, a surgeon being unable to refuse the aid of his ministry to anyone who had need of it.

When he left, Porion had given the tavern-keeper a pistole. That was the usual deposit for the rent of a room on the second floor, which he had retained for his nephew, he said, Messire Mardochée de Mardoche, who thought himself too poorly lodged in the house opposite.

"Mardochée!" the tavern-keeper has said. "But I know him, Monsieur!"

"Oh, you know him?"

"He's a painter, always drunk, who never has any money. I've refused him credit of late."

"Fortunately, I'm here, and as I'm his uncle, I shall pay his debts," Porion had replied. And he had given him another two or three pistoles and ordered in addition the fine supper that the poor artist had see arriving shortly thereafter in his mansard.

On leaving the tavern, however, Porion had not gone back up immediately to Mardochée's lodgings. He had gone as far as the Carrefour Buci and gone into the shop of a merchant of comestibles. The latter was doubtless known to the policeman, for he gave him a mysterious little sign and passed immediately into the back room of the shop.

There, Porion said to him: "I have need of you."

"Just me?" asked the greengrocer, who was a big man, with a heightened complexion, who appeared to possess Herculean strength.

"No, bring one of your lads with you."

"Very well. Where to?"

"First of all," said Porion, "I'll tell you that there's twenty pistoles to be earned."

"Oho!" said the greengrocer. "Is it the boss who's paying?"

"Monsieur de Sartine?"

"Yes."

"No, it's better than that."

"Monsieur de Clermont?"

"Better still…it's the King."

The greengrocer opened his eyes wide. "And what is it necessary to do?"

"Abduct a young woman who has had the honor of pleasing the King."

"She shall be abducted," said the greengrocer. "Where is she?"

"Ta ta ta!" said Porion. "Don't go so quickly. I'll lead the expedition."

"Then command, Master," said the big man, who was not, as you can imagine, under arms on Porion's behalf for the first time.

"You'll procure a hired carriage with two horses."

"Right."

"Whose driver is one of ours."

"As good as done. Half the coachmen hereabouts belong to us body and soul."

"The carriage will be waiting at the corner of the Rue Saint-André-des-Arts at nine o'clock."

"What else?"

"Then you'll procure a plank strong enough to support the weight of two men, long enough to be placed like a bridge between one roof and another, and broad enough for someone to be able to pass over it without risk of falling."

"All that will be ready," replied the greengrocer and police agent.

"Do you know a painter named Mardochée?"

"Certainly. He's a drunkard."

"Do you know where he lives?"

"Of course. I've often climbed his six floors to go and collect what he owed me."

"And has he ever paid you?"

"Never."

"You'll get that as well as your twenty pistoles."

"But why are you talking to me about Mardochée, Papa Cinnamon?"

"Because it's to his attic that you'll bring the plank."

"When?"

"In an hour."

"Ah! Very well."

Having given his instructions, Porion had returned to the Rue Saint-André-des-Arts, had made a sign to the waiter to go up with him, and half an hour later, Mardochée and Père Cinnamon were supping with a hearty appetite.

"You have good news to give me, then?" said Mardochée, who had already emptied his glass three times.

"Excellent, my boy."

"What is it?"

"I've seen the girl."

"Ah!"

"And you're foolish to think that she's never noticed you."

"What are you saying?"

"Not only has she noticed you, but you please her a great deal. However," Porion added, "she's under surveillance."

"By whom?"

"By a young man, a surgeon, who is very much in love with her, who pleases her father, who has got it into his head to marry them."

Mardochée clenched his fists, angrily.

"The girl," Porion continued, "finds the surgeon execrable."

"Really?"

"She would even be very glad if a charitable soul would get rid of him for her."

"I'll kill him," said Mardochée, darting a glance at the sword hanging on the wall.

"I've got a better idea," said Porion. "Killing a man is stupid, as well as dangerous, for Monsieur de Sartine, the Lieutenant General of the Police always gets mixed up in those affairs."

"What's your idea, Papa Cinnamon?"

"You'll see," said Porion, emptying a large glass of wine in his turn.

XIV

Mardochée put both his elbows on the table.

Porion went on: "I have a good idea, as you'll see."

"I'm listening," said Mardochée, exasperated by the thought of a rival.

But Porion did not have time to explain his project, because someone knocked on the door.

Mardochée went to open it, and stepped back abruptly. He found himself in the presence of the greengrocer who had tormented him so much regarding his bill. The fellow was carrying the famous plank ordered by Porion on his shoulder. At the sight of Mardochée looking crestfallen, he started to laugh.

"Don't be afraid," he said to him. "I haven't come to make demands today."

"Ah!" said Mardochée, breathing out. "What do you want, then?"

"He's come to lend us a hand," said Porion.

"What?"

"I'm a friend of Père Cinnamon's," said the greengrocer, smiling broadly.

"You have fine acquaintances," stammered Mardochée, who had always had a holy terror of his creditor.

"Do you owe him a lot of money, then?" said Porion, who had begun to address the gentleman painter as *tu* without the latter's nobility suffering in consequence.

"Hmm—I don't know..."

"Twenty pistoles and one écu," said the greengrocer.

"I'll pay then," said Porion, majestically.

Mardochée almost fell over. "But you're not a man, you're a god!" he cried.

"Let's admit it, for the moment," Porion replied, modestly, "and occupy ourselves without delay with our little affairs—I mean yours."

"What do you mean?"

"Do you know what this plank is for?"

"No."

"To make a bridge between the roof of your house and the one where the girl is."

"Famous!" murmured Mardochée. "Except..."

"Except what?"

"As it's not very broad and when I've been drinking..."

"You walk in zigzags."

"Precisely."

"You'd best make use of it as soon as possible, then, for you're beginning to get drunk."

"Your words are golden, Père Cinnamon." And the amorous Mardochée stated to get up from the table.

"Ta ta ta!" murmured Porion. "Don't go so quickly, my lad."

"Eh?"

"Have you forgotten the surgeon?"

"Oh, that's true!" And Mardochée clenched his fists.

"Before going to see the girl, who will receive you with open arms, it's necessary for us to get rid of the surgeon."

"How?"

"You'll see. We're all three of us at table..."

"Good!" said Mardochée, who observed that, indeed, the greengrocer had sat down casually at the table and was eating and drinking."

"I'm your uncle..."

"Yes!" said the painter. "I'd like that."

"Aha! And why is that?"

"Because you appear to me to have straw in your boots and that I'd be your heir. But let's go on. You're my uncle..."

"Yes."

"Well, what has that to do with the surgeon?"

"I'm eating and drinking; I have a rush of blood."

"You're joking, uncle."

"The greengrocer here, who is one of our friends, will run to fetch the surgeon to in order to care for me."

"I'm beginning to understand."

"He arrives without any suspicion, and while he's preparing his medical bag, you throw yourself on him and knock him down."

"And I kill him!" said Mardochée. At the same time, overcome by drunkenness, he seized a knife and brandished it.

"No," said Porion. "One only kills people when one can't do otherwise."

"What are we going to do with him, then?"

"We're going to bind his hands and feet."

"Good!"

"And we're going to put this gag in his mouth, to prevent him from crying out." And Père Cinnamon took out of his pocket a gag with a metal mouthpiece, which Mardochée examined curiously.

If the painter had not been drunk, he might certainly have wondered how a peaceful bourgeois like Père Cinnamon came to have a police agent's or watchman's instrument in his pocket, but Mardochée was beginning to see double and Père Cinnamon never ceased pouring him more to drink.

"Let's go, Comrade," said the later, when he judged that Mardochée would be under the table within half a hour. "The time has come. It's necessary to go and fetch me the surgeon."

The greengrocer stood up. Porion and he exchanged a glance, while Mardochée put his nose in his glass again, and then the greengrocer left. He was known throughout the quarter. He went downstairs, went in to see the tavern-keeper in the house opposite and asked him whether the surgeon was at home.

"Oh, definitely," was the reply. "He came back at dusk and we haven't seen him come down again."

"What floor?"

"At the very top, the door on the left."

The greengrocer went along the damp and black alleyway and up the spiral staircase for which a greasy rope served as a rail. As you can imagine, the stairway was not illuminated, but thanks to the rope that greengrocer went up without difficulty.

When he reached the top, he groped momentarily, saw a thread of light passing under a door, and knocked.

A young woman came to open it. It was Cécile Robert. The greengrocer had mistaken the door.

"Excuse me," he said. "Doesn't the surgeon Firmin lodge here?"

"Pardon me," replied a voice—and Firmin came out of the neighboring room.

The greengrocer, solely occupied in looking at the young woman, did not think of darting a glance into the surgeon's room. Otherwise, he would have perceived Hector de Pierrefeu sitting in a large armchair and smiling, with the bewildered grimace that almost never abandons the lips of a madman. Perhaps he would even have been so struck by the young man's presence that he would have reported it to Porion, and the latter would have modified his plans. But the greengrocer did not see anything.

In any case, Firmin closed the door swiftly and said: "I'm the surgeon Firmin. What do you want with me?"

"I've come to ask for the help of your art."

"For whom?"

"For an old drunkard, a friend, who has an indigestion and needs bleeding."

"I'll follow you," said Firmin, who always had his lancet on him and had no need to go back into his room. "Is it far?"

"No, in the house opposite."

The two young people exchanged a smile, and then Cécile closed the door, and Firmin followed the greengrocer.

In the meantime, Père Cinnamon had finished getting Mardochée drunk. But in order to avoid any misfortune, for the painter was a bad drunkard, he had briskly taken away his knife.

"Pay attention!" he said, suddenly.

"To what?"

"Someone's coming up the stairs."

"Good."

"It's them."

"The surgeon! Aha! You don't want me to kill him?"

"No, imbecile."

And Père Cinnamon slumped back in the chair and assumed the attitude of an unconscious man.

At the same moment, the door opened and the greengrocer reappeared, followed by the surgeon.

XV

Firmin knew Mardochée by sight, like all the inhabitants of the quarter, for the painter was even more celebrated for his drunkenness and his wayward habits that his two- or three-écu portraits. He had also seen Père Cinnamon before, and recognized him immediately.

Porion was playing the unconscious man so well that the young surgeon was taken in.

"What's the matter, then?" he asked Mardochée.

"It's my uncle," the painter replied, darting a flamboyant gaze at the painter.

"Pay no attention to him," the greengrocer said. "The young man is drunk. Our poor friend has been taken ill."

The surgeon picked up Porion's limp arm and took his pulse.

"No," he said, "The pulse is calm. Perhaps it's a rush of blood."

"You're not going to bleed him, then?"

"Wait—we'll see..." And he leaned over Porion, applying his ear to his breast in order to listen to his heartbeat.

But at that moment, Porion opened his eyes abruptly; his sagging arms moved, and knotted around the surgeon's neck. At the same time, the greengrocer tripped the young man, who fell to the floor, seized by the throat by the iron hands of the pretended old man.

The greengrocer was robust; he held Firmin down and put a knee on his chest while Porion said to him: "If you move, or cry out, I'll kill you!"

That happened in the blink of an eye.

Firmin did not have time to recover from his surprise, or to struggle, before he was tied up solidly with a rope brought by the greengrocer, and the gag had been introduced into his mouth.

Mardochée had tried to get up in order to lend a hand to his two acolytes, but drunkenness nailed him to his chair. He drank one last glass of wine and slid under the table.

"There's one who won't get in our way," murmured Porion, pushing him with his foot. Mardochée uttered a dull groan, but the groan soon degenerated into a sonorous snore, and Père Cinnamon laughed, saying: "I know that imbecile's drunken fits. He's good for fifteen hours."

Firmin was making vain efforts to break his bonds.

"As for you, my lad," said Porion, who had straightened his stooped stature and whose eyes were shining with virility, "if you want to live at liberty and not go to rot in the Bastille, I advise you to keep quiet." Then he addressed the greengrocer: "Is the carriage ready?"

"I saw it at the street corner as I came up just now."

"Good. To work!"

And Porion opened the window of Mardochée's studio wide, while, at a sign from him, the greengrocer extinguished the lamp.

The night was black. No sound was coming up from the street, and the curfew had rung.

"The devil's with us," murmured Porion, "And no one will disturb us in our work. Bring the tool."

The greengrocer brought the plank. It required a man of Herculean strength like his to be able to push that plank from one roof to the other, holding it in his outstretched arms. The operation succeeded marvelously.

Then Porion said: "Hold it well."

"I'm holding it, don't worry."

"Is it solidly supported?"

"Like the arch of a bridge."

"Let's go, then," murmured Porion, recovering the audacity of a police agent. And he ventured on to the plank, having nothing to guide his march in a straight line but the young woman's lighted window.

Cécile Robert was sitting behind the window, next to a table, and working, awaiting the young surgeon's return. Calm, her expression candid, the young woman had no suspicion that her doom had been decided.

Suddenly, a noise made her tremble. She raised her head, at the same moment as a window cut with a diamond fell to the floor and a hand passed through the pane tripped the window-catch and the casement opened.

A man leapt into Cécile's room.

She uttered a cry, and tried to flee.

The man had a knife in his hand and he said to her: "If you scream, you're doomed."

More dead than alive, Cécile ran to the door of the mansard, but Porion got there before her and placed himself across it. Then Cécile, panicked, threw herself to her knees. "Mercy!" she begged, putting her hands together.

"I'll grant you mercy if you're good," Porion replied.

She looked at him fearfully, saying: "Mercy! What have I done to you? What do you want with me?"

"I want you to be good and follow me without resistance," said Porion. And he wrapped his arms around her.

"Help Me! Firmin! Help!" Cécile cried, struggling.

Porion tried to put his hand over her mouth, but she bit him.

"Ah! Little viper!" he said, angrily. "If you weren't the King's morsel, I'd strangle you!"

She did not understand those sinister words, and continued to struggle.

Then Porion made a supreme effort, loaded her on to his shoulders, and lifted her up like a feather.

But at that moment, unexpected help arrived for the young woman.

The door opened abruptly, and a half-dressed man precipitated into the room.

"Help me, Monsieur Hector! Help!"

It was, in fact, the poor insensate Hector who, hearing the noise and cries, had come running instinctively.

He threw himself on to Porion, who was obliged to let the young woman go momentarily.

"Wretch!" he said. "Wretch!" He was young and robust; in spite of his madness, he had the instinct of danger, which had caused him to run to the woman who had saved him from death, and that instinct redoubled his strength.

He succeeded in knocking Porion down, but as he was about to put a knee on his chest he uttered a terrible cry and his clenched hands relaxed. Then he collapsed heavily, while Porion got up. The wretch had picked up the knife that was lying on the floor, for he had dropped it in order to take possession of the young woman, and with that knife he had struck Hector de Pierrefeu in the side.

At the sight of the blood suddenly reddening the floor of the mansard, Cécile Robert uttered one last scream and fainted.

"I like that better," murmured Porion. And he loaded the young woman on to his shoulder for a second time.

This time, the young woman was no longer struggling. She was unconscious, and one might have thought that Porion as carrying a cadaver.

The man who was known as Père Cinnamon, and had such an amiable face, and ordinarily walked with a stoop, leaning on a cane, had recovered the energy and audacity of youth. He did not tremble on the threshold of the aerial bridge two feet wide, on to which he was about to venture with his burden, and might bend under his weight.

When coming, he had had Cécile's light to guide him, but in order to reach Mardochée's basement, he no longer had anything but his instinct, for the night was still black and the greengrocer, who was waiting, anxious and motionless, in the painter's studio, had not thought of lighting a lamp again.

But Porion ventured boldly on to the plank, at the risk of making a false step and falling from a height of fifty feet into the street.

That false step he might perhaps have made if Cécile, reanimated by the cold nocturnal air, had started struggling again. But as he had said to the greengrocer, the devil was definitely with him, and the young woman did not recover her senses.

The wretch reached the sill of Mardochée's window safe and sound, without a hitch.

The greengrocer saw the young woman's white dress outlined against the darkness

"Have you killed her then?"

"No, she's fainted. Silence!"

Firmin, lying on the ground, who finally understood why he had been lured into the trap, made a supreme effort, and a few inarticulate sounds passed through the gag.

"Shut up, you!" said Porion, suppressing him with a furious kick.

Under the table, Mardochée was still snoring like a church organ.

"Wait while I light the lamp," said the greengrocer.

"No," replied Porion. "It was necessary to do it just now, because I nearly broke my neck, but now, there's no need. Open the door and don't make any noise.

And Porion went down the tortuous stairway of the house first.

I'm beginning to think, he said to himself, *that I'll be Lieutenant de Police one day*.

Mardochée's house, like Cécile's, was inhabited by humble folk, scrupulous observers of the edicts, for whom the curfew was not a dead letter. Mardochée was the only one who returned at all hours of the night, and if any tenant heard footsteps on the stairway at an undue hour, he never failed to say: "It's that drunkard of a painter." After which he turned over on his pillow and went to sleep.

The door to the street opened by means of a latch.

The greengrocer turned it.

"Go fetch the carriage," said Porion. "We don't want to encounter the watch. That white dress would give us away, and it would be necessary to give them a host of explanations."

The greengrocer launched himself into the street, and Porion, still with the young woman on his shoulders, remained in the damp black alleyway.

Two minutes later, the numbered carriage, of which Maître Boileaux-Despréaux had spoken sixty years earlier, stopped at the door, driven by a man of whom Porion was sure.

The police agent placed the young woman on the cushions at the rear and sat down beside her.

"Where are we going?" asked the coachman.

"Versailles, at top speed," Porion replied. At the same time, he put a handful of gold in the greengrocer's hand. "Here's your twenty pistoles," he said. "It's the King who's paying."

"A good King," murmured the greengrocer, with a hint of irony, while the carriage drew away at a rapid trot.

Cécile was still unconscious.

XVI

The carriage got half way to Versailles without Cécile Robert recovering her senses.

At the hill rising to Bellevue, however, the horses slowed down, and Porion opened the window to see where they were. The fresh nocturnal air came into the carriage and ended up bringing the young woman round.

She uttered a sigh, stirred on the banquette, opened her eyes and murmured: "Where am I?"

Porion had taken advantage of the silent part of the voyage and made up a little story that ought to work wonders.

"Mademoiselle Cécile?" he said.

The young woman shivered, opened her eyes wide and looked around.

She saw that she was in a carriage, understood by the shaking that the carriage was moving, and, looking at Porion more attentively, recognized him as the man who had engaged in a struggle with her and stabbed Hector de Pierrefeu with a knife.

"Ah!" she said. "That man again!"

"Mademoiselle Cécile," said Porion, in a tone full of mildness, "don't be mistakenly alarmed. You're safe here. I'm a friend of your father."

He had calculated the effect that that name would produce."

"My father?" the young woman exclaimed. "My father? You're talking to me about him?"

"I'm his best friend," Porion replied.

"You're a friend of my father?"

"Yes, and it's on his orders that I'm acting."

But she shook her head dubiously. "My father," she said, "is a gentle and good man, and it can't be him who ordered you to treat me like this."

"If I'm acting like this, Mademoiselle, it's to save you."

"To save me?"

"Yes."

"Oh," she said. "I was living happily and calmly, and not running any danger."

"You're mistaken, my child, and I'll prove to you that I know your father."

"Oh!"

"His name is Robert."

"That's true."

"You had a cousin named Agénor Chapuzot."

"I still have."

"No," said Porion, "for he's dead."

"Dead!" exclaimed Cécile, with a tone mingling astonishment and fear.

"He killed himself," said Porion, "for love of you."

"Oh my God!"

"And in dying, he calumniated you."

"Me?"

"He said that you were the mistress of a surgeon who lives in your house."

"Horror!"

"Who tried to prevent me from abducting you, and whom I stabbed," said Porion, naively.

The wretch had calculated the range of his lie.

But Cécile cried: "You're mistaken—it wasn't him!"

"It wasn't him!" exclaimed Porion, feigning the most profound surprise.

"No."

"Who was it, then?"

"A poor madman that he and I took in."

"It doesn't matter," said Porion, "it was necessary to save you."

"But save me from what?" she asked.

"From the calumny."

Cécile rebelled. "But if it's on behalf of my father you're acting," she said. "Tell me..." And she stopped, trembling.

"Yes," said Porion. "I know what you're going to ask me. You find it strange that your father hasn't come to see you himself."

"Alas, yes," she said.

"And to tell you that, in order defeat the calumnies of the infamous Agénor Chapuzot, it was necessary for him to quit the house, where you lived ...or put the surgeon in a position to marry you?"

"Certainly," she said, struck by the logic of the argument.

"That's because your father is not in France," said Porion. "And then..." He stopped, deliberately.

"And then?" she said.

"You can't marry Firmin."

He expected an explosion of dolor, but she remained almost calm.

"I love Firmin like a brother," she said, "but I don't know why, if Firmin loved me amorously and I loved him, I wouldn't be able to marry him."

"Why?" said Porion. "Because he's married."

"Married—him!"

"Yes, two years ago...to a great lady who, after becoming smitten with him, threw him back on to the streets of Paris from which she had taken him."

Cécile Robert passed from fear to astonishment, and Porion perceived that.

"What you're saying astonishes me strangely," she said.

"Then you don't love Firmin?" Porion said.

"I love him like a brother."

"Good. But what about him?"

"He's never said an amorous word to me."

Porion sighed. "Then I regret having taken you away from your home so brutally, but it's an evil for a good end."

"What do you mean?"

"Did you ever know your mother?"

"She died giving birth to me."

"And your father never told you about your birth?"

"What could he tell me?" asked Cécile, ingenuously.

"Your mother was the nurse of a Prince of the Blood."

"Oh."

"The King is your godfather."

The young woman passed from astonishment to astonishment.

"Now," said Porion, "the King is anxious about his goddaughter, and wants to see her."

Cécile had begun to tremble again. "What interest can the King have in a poor girl like me?" she said.

"It's quite simple, since you're his goddaughter."

"Is that possible?"

"And you'll be well content in an hour, and you'll only regret having been so afraid of me."

"But…the King…?"

"The King wants to endow you."

"Oh my God," she murmured, with a sudden fear.

"While leaving you free to take the husband appropriate to you," Porion finished.

The last words were consummately perfidious, and they put to sleep the young woman's last suspicions. From that moment on she believed everything that Porion told her.

The carriage had arrived at the top of the hill; it had traversed the woods and gone past the ponds at the hermitage of Saint Cucuphas. Soon, the sonorous pavement of the streets of Versailles resounded under the horses' hooves, and Cécile asked again: "But where are we?"

"We're entering Versailles," Porion replied.

Indeed, shortly thereafter, the gates of the palace opened before the hired carriage. Porion only had to say one word for them to rotate on their hinges: "Service of the King!"

And the carriage rolled all the way to the perron.

As it was the middle of the night, there was no one in the courtyard but the guards and the officers on duty. Porion had changed his clothes in the carriage while Cécile was unconscious, putting on a fine coat with crystal buttons, and he said to the valet who came to open the carriage door: "I desire to speak to Monsieur Lebel immediately."

Cécile heard that name, but it did not make her shiver. Innocent and naïve as she was, having always lived in that placid street in the Latin Quarter where the distant rumors of the Court did not penetrate, how could she know the name of the abject man who was the obliging valet of the King's pleasures?

Porion left her in the carriage, exceedingly emotional, and stepped down to the ground.

Five minutes later, Lebel arrived.

He knew Porion, because he was the one who, the previous night, had enabled the pretended fancier Van Roëk, the trickster of the poor Maréchale d'H***, to leave the palace furtively. He knew that Porion had promised to bring the young woman the memory of whom was troubling the King's sleep.

"Well?" he said, anxiously.

"Well, she's here."

"In the carriage?"

"Yes."

And Porion, briefly and in a whisper, brought Lebel up to date with the fable he had made up.

"That's very good," said Lebel, "but..."

"But what?" said Porion, anxious in his turn.

"The King is asleep."

"It's necessary to wake him up."

"Oh, no! If he wakes up in a bad mood, he's capable of sending us all to the devil."

"Even the girl?"

"Yes."

"Well, what are we going to do?"

"Something quite simple, as you'll see." Lebel went to the carriage door, opened it, and said: "Mademoiselle Cécile, the King, your august godfather, has given orders for you to be taken to the chamber destined for you. He'll visit you tomorrow morning."

"What!" said the young woman. "The King has deigned to occupy himself with me?"

"He has designated me to be at your service," added Lebel.

Cécile thought she was dreaming.

Lebel had the white hair and respectable face of an old man. That was vice imprinting a paternal mask.

Cécile descended from the carriage without suspicion, and took the hand that the old procurer of the king's alcove extended to her.

"Well, Monsieur Lebel," whispered Porion in the valet's ear, "do you think I'll be Lieutenant de Police?"

"I'm beginning to think so," replied Lebel, "for you're a bold rogue, and Monsieur de Sartine is only a simpleton devoid of intelligence by comparison with you."

XVII

Then, even though the palace of Versailles was plunged in slumber, as a poet of those days put it, there were still a considerable number of people awake there.

In addition to the doormen on duty, the guardsmen and musketeers encumbering the waiting rooms and the servants coming and going through the corridors and stairways, there was, here and there, a page in a merry mood, a gentleman beating the retreat from a maid of honor and a soubrette who had given a rendezvous to some light-horseman.

The arrival of that hired carriage before which the gate had opened as if it were a question of a Maréchal or a Duc and peer, had caused a certain sensation.

The doormen had gathered. A few guardsmen, seeing Lebel come running, had looked at one another, smiling.

There were twenty people around the carriage when poor Cécile, ignorant of the fate that awaited her, set foot on the ground and leaned, innocently, on Lebel's soiled hand.

Among those twenty people there was a page. That page was a living legend. His name was Noël. He was fifteen years old. He was as pretty as a woman, brazen, mocking, full of wit. Where did he come from? No one knew, exactly. One morning, the Duc de Choiseul[18] had introduced him to the King as the son of a poor gentleman. The King had found him polite and intelligent, and had taken him on without any further ado.

Noël was adored by all the Marquises, Duchesses and Comtesses who lived in the palace. The Maréchale d'H*** had been his first instructress, the Marquise d'O*** his second, and after those two ladies, all the ladies, all the maids of honor, and all the women presented, with or without a footstool.

Noël had a demonic wit; he said what he thought to everyone, and no one got annoyed. He betrayed the women he had loved, and the discarded beauties hastened to make peace with him. The most serious individuals—Abbé Terray,[19] for example, who was the Minister of Finance—could not keep their faces straight when listening to his sallies.

---

[18] Étienne-François, Duc de Choiseul (1719-1785) became France's Minister of Foreign Affairs in 1758 and had an important influence on the nation's foreign policy thereafter, but prior to that his had been a diplomat in Rome and Vienna, so his role in the present story is anachronistic.

[19] Joseph-Marie Terray (1715-1778) was still a counselor in the Parlement de Paris in the 1750s and did not become Controller-General of Finance until 1769, so his role in the present story is also anachronistic.

One day, he had said something extremely improper about Madame de Pompadour. Everyone had trembled for Noël, who did not tremble. The Marquise had sent for him, had scolded him, rebuked him and reprimanded him, behind closed doors, and had sent him away absolved, to the great astonishment of the entire Court.

And among the people who saw the young woman emerge from the carriage was Monsieur Noël.

The page had seen a lot of pretty faces, sown with murdered flies,[20] but he could not help uttering a cry of admiration at the sight of Cécile.

"How beautiful she is," he murmured.

A guardsman tapped him on the shoulder.

"You have good taste, Monsieur Noël," he said.

"You think so?" said the page.

"But that game isn't for your table, my young friend," the guard continued.

"In truth!"

"That's royal flesh, as you can imagine."

There was a small group around the guardsman and the page, and everyone was listening The guardsman was young and well turned-out, whom one of the Maréchale d'H***'s chambermaids honored with a few favors. The soubrette had learned first-hand the story of the fake diamond, and hence that of the young woman of whom the King dreamed.

The guardsman had known everything right away, for the simple reason that he was with the soubrette when the Maréchale came back from the Opéra, and the soubrette had only just had time to hide him in a cupboard, from which he had heard, if not everything, almost everything. In consequence, the guardsman took a malign pleasure in telling the audience the story of the young woman, who could not be any other than the one over whom the King had lost his head, since he had recognized Porion as the man accompanying her, for he had heard the previous evening, through a crack in the cupboard door, the fake financier Van Roëk.

Noël listened to that story. Then, with his usual boldness, he said: "The King is truly luckier than one might think."

"You think so, my darling?" said a maid of honor, who had mingled with the group in the main courtyard.

"Oh, certainly."

"She's a pretty girl, it's true, but..."

"Oh, it's not for that reason that the King is lucky," said Noël.

"What is it, then?"

"He's lucky that the affair doesn't concern me."

---

[20] Artificial "beauty spots" applied to the cheek, very much in fashion at the time, were known in French as *mouches* [literally, flies].

There was a general burst of laughter around Noël, but the page was not disconcerted.

"What are you laughing at?" he said.

"You!" said those around him.

"Nothing is more serious, though."

"How's that, my darling?" asked the maid of honor, who found the page to her taste and was devouring him with her gaze.

"Suppose that young woman were my sister."

"All right."

"Or simply my cousin."

"So?"

"Or even a young woman who pleased me and for whom I was amorous."

"What would you do?"

"The King would be obliged to don his mourning."

"That child is mad," said a musketeer.

"He spends his life," said one of the guardsmen, "making pirouettes at the gates of the Bastille."

"You'll all go before me, Messeigneurs."

"That's possible, but..."

"But if I took it into my head to save that young woman..."

"You'd save her, eh?" said the maid of honor.

"I give you my word," replied the page, placing his hand on his hip in a challenging attitude.

"Fortunately," said the musketeer, "she's neither your sister, nor your cousin, nor..."

"Nor the woman you love, is she?" the maid of honor interjected.

"You know that full well, naughty girl," said the page, and kissed her, briskly.

The maid of honor uttered a little scream to acquit her conscience, and fled. Noël ran after her, and the group broke up.

Instead of pursuing the maid of honor, though, Noël, when he reached the first step of the staircase, turned nimbly to the left and went o the pages' hall,

There, nothing was known about Cécile Robert's arrival, and the pages on duty were playing chess. Noël went to sit down next to the players, appeared to take an interest in their game, and, in spite of himself, began to dream about the young woman.

Oh, he thought, *if I were sure that she didn't have a handsome lover in some quarter of Paris whose affair I'd settle, how I'd take it into my head to save her! But what's the point of causing the King chagrin with nothing to gain?*

While he was addressing this little monologue to himself, a woman came into the pages' hall on tiptoe, drew closer without anyone raising his head, and placed a gloved hand on Noël's shoulder.

The page turned round and recognized Mademoiselle Bellamy, one of Madame de Pompadour's chambermaids.

As he bowed to her, she whispered in his ear: "Come into a corner over there; I have something to tell you."

The game of chess was so animated that no one paid any more attention to Noël's retreat than to Mademoiselle Bellamy's entrance.

Noël followed her, and the demoiselle said to him: "You know, my darling, that insomnia is the malady of the Palace of Versailles. Everyone is in bed, but no one is asleep there."

"What you're saying has some truth in it, Mademoiselle," said the page, who did not know what Mademoiselle Bellamy was getting at.

She went on: "When the Marquise sleeps, it's the King who can't sleep. If, perchance, the King closes his eyes, the Marquise has a migraine."

"I know that," said Noël.

"It's a singular illness, is migraine, my darling," Mademoiselle Bellamy went on. "One can neither move, nor remain in place, and it's necessary to try all kinds of distractions to master it."

"And the Marquise has a migraine?"

"Yes."

"What is she doing to distract herself?"

"She's was doing absolutely nothing when she was told of the arrival of the little girl abducted for the King's pleasure."

"And did the Marquise's migraine improve at that news?"

"At first."

"That's good."

"But when she was told that the girl was very pretty..."

"She's dazzling," said Noël.

"The migraine got worse."

"Imagine that!"

"Then, the Marquise was told what you had said down there in the courtyard."

"Ah! Damn!"

"And the Marquise laughed, and her migraine dissipated slightly."

"Really!"

"And the Marquise sent me to find you."

"To do what?"

"To take you to her. She wants to see you."

The page put his hat under his left arm, offered his arm to Mademoiselle Bellamy, and said: "Well then, let's go see the Marquise!"

The game of chess continued, and when the lady in waiting and the page left the hall, no one looked up.

It was not far from the pages' hall to Madame de Pompadour's apartments. It was sufficient to traverse a gallery, two small reception rooms and a secret corridor that the King was accustomed to follow.

Madame de Pompadour did, indeed, have a migraine. She had gone to bed at first, but had not been able to remain there; then she had got up, and Noël found her sprawling in a wing-chair, her head supported by a pyramid of pillows.

"Oh, my darling," she said, extending her pink hand to the page, who brushed it with his lips, "if you haven't come to tell me one of those stories that you tell so well, I believe I'll end up throwing myself out of the window."

"Madame," said Noël, "command; I will obey."

The Marquise made a sign, and Mademoiselle Bellamy left.

Then Madame de Pompadour looked at Noël, and smiled. "So you saw the girl that the King has had abducted, my darling?"

"Yes, Madame."

"What is she like?"

"Almost as beautiful as you," replied Noël, who knew his métier as a courtier.

"Brunette or blonde?"

"Blonde."

"How old?"

"Seventeen or eighteen."

"Has she been taken to the King?"

"No; Monsieur Lebel has said that the King is asleep."

"Very good."

"And he has taken her to the lilac chamber, the chamber from which one never emerges as one went in," said the page, with a malicious smile.

"However," said Madame de Pompadour, "it appears that that isn't what you said a little while ago, my darling."

"Madame..."

"Didn't you regret that the young woman wasn't your sister?"

"Heu!" said Noël.

"Or your cousin?"

"Heu! Heu!"

"Or even your mistress?"

Noël feigned great terror. "Oh, Madame," he said, putting his hands together, "I swear to you..."

"Don't swear, my darling. In any case, you have too much intelligence to think that I would hold much of what you said against you."

The smile returned to the young page's lips.

The Marquise went on: "Come and sit here, at the foot of my wing-chair...and let's chat."

Noël sat down on the edge of the chaise-longue, and dared to plant a kiss on the arched foot clad in a silk stocking, at the end of which the Marquise was making a little red slipper dance. The Marquise was not irritated by that liberty, and continued: "Would you to like us to make suppositions?"

"I'm listening," said the page.

"That girl is your cousin."

"All right,"

"Better than that—your sister."

"And?" said Noël.

"Better still. You find her to your taste, and you think that it's offending God to throw her into the arms, of the King, who is past fifty."

"Well, Madame...?"

"Suppose, in addition that...I'm jealous..."

"Of that girl?"

"Yes."

"I'm waiting," said Noël, calmly

"Then I say to you: Noël, my darling, if you have a means of making that girl disappear from the lilac chamber, you can do it."

"Truly, Madame?"

"You'll incur neither my displeasure nor my anger."

"Oh, if I knew that..."

"I assure you of it."

"However..."

"Well," said Madame de Pompadour, "if the King finds out about it, I can't promise you that you'll conserve your employment as a page."

"Damn!"

"That you won't be thrown in the Bastille."

"Oh, my God!"

"And that if you appeal to me. I won't reply that you're a brazen liar."

"Then, Madame," said Noël, coldly, "as the girl is neither my sister, nor my cousin, nor my fiancée, and that I have everything to lose and nothing to gain in the adventure..."

"You're renouncing it?"

"Well..."

The Marquise had a demonic smile. "I thought you bolder," she said.

"That depends on the circumstances."

"And if you'd listened to me until the end..."

Noël planted a second kiss on Madame de Pompadour's dainty foot, and waited.

"Let's suppose, then," the Marquise went on, "that you make the girl disappear, and everything is discovered."

"The King will expel me."

"Naturally."

"And I'll be sent to the Bastille, as you sent Monsieur de Latude,[21] who is still there, for a poor quatrain..."

"Shh!" said Madame de Pompadour. "That doesn't concern you."

"So be it."

"But the governor of the Bastille is a friend of mine."

"Ah!"

"On the very day of your incarceration he lets you out."

"Marvelous!"

"You're no longer a page, but I send you to one of my châteaux to wait for the King's anger to calm down—and you know very well that within a fortnight, the King will no longer be thinking about you or the girl."

"That," said Noël, "is quite different."

"Well, my darling, think about it."

"Yes, Madame."

"Do you have debts?"

"Oh, trivia, a few hundred louis."

"I'll pay them. Is there anything you desire?"

"Perhaps..." And the page looked at the Marquise brazenly.

"Effrontery!" she said. "Go away."

When Noël the page had gone, Madame de Pompadour murmured: "It's singular, but it seems to me that I no longer have a migraine."

---

[21] Jean-Henri Latude (1725-1805) was thrown into the Bastille on Madame de Pompadour's orders in 1749 after he tried to trick her by warning her about a non-existent plot. Transferred to Vincennes a year later he escaped, but was re-captured and sent back to the Bastille, from which he famously escaped in 1756, but only briefly. He subsequently cemented his fame by escaping yet again from Vincennes after being transferred there for a second time. After the Revolution Madame de Pompadour's heirs were obliged to pay him compensation for her harassment of him.

XVIII

In the meantime, Monsieur Lebel had taken the naïve and credulous Cécile Robert to what was known as the lilac chamber.

An infernal genius had presided over the decoration of that apartment. One might have thought it the innocent and perfumed bedroom of a young woman who does not yet have a fiancé. Bright lilac fabric covered the walls. The bed, the chairs and the furniture were yellow sandalwood with ivory and ebony marquetry. A carpet with a large flower pattern covered the floor. Each toilette item was marked with an enlaced C and R.

"As you see," said Lebel, smiling, "the King has been awaiting his goddaughter for a long time, and he has taken care to have everything marked with your initials."

"That's true," said the young woman, naïvely, "who had never seen or dreamed of so many marvels."

"The King," Lebel went on, "has instructed me to tell you that you have no reason to be anxious wither about your father or the people that you love. He is watching over them."

"Truly?"

"When the King protects people," Lebel added, "they have nothing to fear."

"But Monsieur," said Cécile, "what have I done, for the King to be so god to me?"

"You're his goddaughter."

"And that's sufficient?"

"No, but the King knows how beautiful, good and hard-working you have been."

"Oh! He knows that?"

"The King knows everything, my child."

"Monsieur," said Cécile, "since the King knows everything, will he tell me why my father has left France without even coming to embrace me?"

"I can tell you that myself."

"You, Monsieur?"

"Yes, my child."

And Lebel made the child sit down, and stood in front of her. "The King," he said, "has sent your father outside France."

"Where to?"

"To Holland," said Lebel, at random.

Now, it was from Holland from which Robert Damiens' letter, received a few days earlier, had been sent. Cécile could no longer doubt Lebel's good faith. In any case, for the people, royalty is always surrounded by such prestige that it sufficed for Cécile to be at Versailles, in the palace of King Louis XV, to believe herself to be safe.

The lilac chamber was not alone; a small boudoir preceded it and it was followed by a dressing-room to which Madame de Pompadour had given her approval. Lebel acquainted the young woman with all the features of the pretty redoubt, to which so many poor creatures had come before finding dishonor. He asked her whether she was hungry and whether she desired supper.

Cécile refused. But the emotions of the evening and the tedium of the journey had made her thirsty. She asked for something to drink.

Lebel went out and returned a few minutes later, carrying a tray on which there was a glass of redcurrant syrup. Cécile drank it in a single draught and found the beverage delicious.

"Now, my child," said Lebel, "you can go to bed and sleep until morning."

"I shan't see the King this evening, then?" she asked, ingenuously.

"No, tomorrow morning. The King is in bed, but when he wakes up, he will hasten to come and visit you."

And Lebel, the man with white hair, the scoundrel rotten with vice who had the appearance of a respectable old man, kissed Cécile Robert's hand respectfully, and left her alone.

For her, there was then a phase of respite and reflection.

Until then, in a few hours, passing from anguish to terror and from terror to astonishment, she had not had a minute to herself to envisage her situation calmly, to analyze events and to remember—but finally, now she was alone: alone with herself; alone in the Palace of Versailles, where the name of the King curbed all foreheads.

Then she remembered...

She remembered that the man who had brutally abducted her had struck Hector de Pierrefeu with a dagger.

Now, Hector, whose full name she did not know—for the poor madman, since he had entered convalescence, had only been able to stammer a few incoherent words, and had had difficulty in saying that his name was Hector—was young, handsome and he was suffering; he had nearly died...

And is not the road of dolor sometimes the road to amour?

Firmin, too, was young, he was handsome, he loved Cécile tenderly, and Cécile reciprocated, but, as she had told Porion two hours before, that affection was purely fraternal on both sides.

For a month, almost always sitting with their poor invalid or leaning over him during his nights of fever and delirium, Cécile had sensed her heart beating as it had never beaten before. Sometimes, in the midst of his folly, Hector looked at her...he looked at her with a kind of ecstasy and intoxication...

And Cécile, bewildered, lowered her eyes and fled.

Since she had been snatched from her mansard, Cécile had hardly thought about Hector. But when she found herself alone, a remorse bit her heart. And then she remembered...

She remembered that Porion had struck the unfortunate young man with a dagger-thrust. Perhaps he had even killed him. And at that memory, Cécile uttered an exclamation: "My God! My God!" she said. "And I was no longer thinking about him!"

Then she was gripped by a serious fear. She ran to the door and tried to open it.

The door resisted.

She rushed to the window. But the window had a system of fastening that was unknown to her, and all her efforts to operate it were futile.

She rapped on the walls, but the walls were dull, for beneath the silky fabric there was a thick padding designed to muffle the cries of victims.

Finally, she perceived a cord of blue silk on the edge of the alcove; it was a bell-cord. She seized it and pulled it violently.

Almost at the same moment, footsteps resounded outside; then the door opened and the benevolent old man with the kindly face, the infamous Lebel, reappeared.

"Do you need something, my dear child?" he said, in a honeyed voice.

"Oh, Monsieur, Monsieur," she said, in a frantic voice.

"What's wrong?"

"Oh, I'm a wretch!"

"You, my child?"

"I've forgotten Hector."

"Who is Hector?" And Lebel frowned slightly.

"He's the poor young man that the man who brought me here stabbed, mistaking him for the surgeon Firmin."

Fortunately, Lebel remembered perfectly everything that Master Porion had told him on getting down from the carriage. "Don't worry," he said, smiling. "Your father's friend made more noise than effect, and that's very fortunate."

"My God!" she said, in anguish, "What do you mean, Monsieur?"

"Your father's friend wounded Monsieur Hector in an insignificant fashion. His knife slid over a rib."

"Oh, is that true, Monsieur?"

"It's not me who says so, it's the surgeon who was charged with dressing his wound, and who has arrived from Paris just now," Lebel replied, rapidly. "Would you like to see the man? Say the word and I'll have him here in five minutes."

How could she not believe the word of that white-haired man who had the appearance of a patriarch? Cécile fell to her knees and thanked God.

Lebel went away, seeing that she was reassured.

Then Cécile thought about going to bed. Her head was heavy; she had a certain unusual warmth in her stomach, and an invincible need for sleep was beginning to take possession of her. She did not think, poor child, that the glass of redcurrant syrup she had drunk with so much pleasure might have been mixed with a narcotic. Did she even know, in any case, what a narcotic was? Surely not.

Scarcely had she undressed and slid into the large soft bed, which bore no resemblance to her poor hard camp-bed, and scarcely had the light of the candles that she had blown out been replaced by the voluptuous muted glow of the night-light burning in the alcove, than her heavy eyelids closed abruptly and she fell into a profound slumber.

When Cécile opened her eyes again, a ray of sunlight was playing on the white curtains of the bed and the lacy pillow over which the young woman's blonde hair had spilled while she slept.

Her head was still rather heavy, and there was an inexplicable malaise throughout her body, but she had no great difficulty in reassembling her scattered memories and telling herself that she really was the King's goddaughter, that she was at the Palace of Versailles in a chamber that her august godfather had fitted out expressly for her, and that the moment was doubtless imminent when she would receive his visit.

Then she thought about Hector, remembered Lebel's reassuring words, and uttered a sigh of satisfaction. After that she got up, enveloped herself in a peignoir that she found open on an armchair next to be bed, and ran to the window again.

Once again, though, the fastening was a mystery to her, and she could not open the casement. She looked through the panes, however; she had before her the beautiful park of Versailles designed by Le Nôtre, which was the pride of the late King Louis XIV.

Sunbeams were streaming over the lawns, caressing the white statues, and reverberating in myriads of sparks from the blue water of fountains. Birds were fluttering from branch to branch through the trees, which were beginning to lose their foliage, and although Cécile could not hear them, she divined that they were singing.

She had been contemplating those marvels for a few minutes when she heard a slight noise behind her.

She turned round abruptly.

A man came in. It was not Lebel.

It was a man who appeared to be still young, and whose fresh and rosy face was heightened by beautiful, carefully-powdered hair. He was clad in a gray coat, over which passed, diagonally, the blue sash of the Ordre du Saint-Esprit.

The buttons of the coat were diamond, the collar and cuffs magnificent lace. He was wearing a small sheathed épée with a nacre hilt enriched with gems, and the silver buckles on his shoes were garnished with pearls.

"*Bonjour*, my child," he said, coming in and closing the door.

Cécile could not suppress an exclamation of surprise. In the gallant seigneur whose was smiling at her, the young woman had recognized the worthy gentleman who had looked at her so keenly one Sunday in the tavern at Marly-le-Roi.

"*Bonjour*, my child," he repeated.

"Oh my God!" she said, ingenuously. "It's the King!"

"Yes, my child," he replied. And the King—for it was indeed him—took the young woman by the hand and led her to a wing-chair, sat down on it first, and tried to sit her down on his knees.

"Oh, not that!" she said, blushing.

The King did not insist, but he started kissing her hands with enthusiasm.

Retained by respect and fear, Cécile, utterly confused, dared not withdraw her hands.

"But she's truly charming!" exclaimed the King, enthusiastically. And he planted a kiss on her neck.

Cécile uttered another cry.

"How timid we are!" said Louis XV, for whom that confusion made her a morsel truly fit for a king.

"Sire...my godfather...," she stammered.

"Oh, yes, that's true," said the King, laughing. "I wasn't thinking about that any longer. I'm your godfather, my beauty...Lebel reminded me of it..."

And he stole another kiss.

Cécile uttered another cry.

"How wild we are!" said the King. And, increasingly enterprising, he took the young woman in his arms.

But she pulled away with an abrupt movement. "Oh!" she said. "You've tricked me."

"Me, my beauty?"

"You're not the King."

"What a joke!"

"If you were the King..."

"I am, and I find you adorable...and I'll prove it to you, my beautiful angel."

And the King set about pursuing Cécile around the room; she fled in bewilderment, calling for help.

"Wonderful!" murmured Louis XV, delighted by that resistance, which irritated his amorous fantasy. "Wonderful! That's virtue, or I don't know it...oh, it's not the women of my Court who behave like that."

But just as he was about to reach the exhausted young woman, whose cries of terror were muffled by the padded walls, there was a loud noise, and the King stopped, mute with horror.

A black ball, which seemed to have fallen from the sky into the middle of the room, dancing of its own accord, vomited fire, and ended up exploding with a noise like that of thunder. It was a grenade loaded with powder.

And the King, with sweat on his brow, no longer thinking about pursuing the young woman, seemed to be wondering whether the wrath of Heaven was thus manifest.

At the same time, there was another sound. It was that of a human voice. That voice, which seemed to emerge from the alcove where the young woman had spent the night, said:

"Divine wrath attains kings as well as peoples."

Superstition was not a weakness of the victor of Fontenoy. He had not believed in divine wrath for a long time, but he thought that a man might be hidden behind the bed, and, drawing his sword, he hurled himself toward the alcove. But he searched in vain: the alcove was empty.

The voice, however, could still he heard—except that it was no longer coming from the depths of the alcove but seemed, on the contrary, to be coming from the friezes of the ceiling. And the voice said: "King, if you do not want to attract frightful misfortunes on yourself and your people, you will respect this young woman and you will send her back to her father!"

"Help!" cried the King. "Help me! Lebel...!"

But no one came.

King Louis XV had had the lilac chamber established in the most remote part of the palace, and when he was there, no one dared go near it.

XIX

"Help! To me!" repeated the King.

This time, he ran to the door and opened it. But there was no one in the corridor, and no one in the neighboring rooms.

The King was tempted to run away, but he made the reflection that the girl might also take advantage of the opportunity to flee. He therefore stayed, and swiftly closed the door again.

Cécile was no longer thinking about escaping. Mad with terror, her eyes wild, she had taken refuge at the other extremity of the lilac chamber, and was huddled in a corner.

The voice had fallen silent.

Louis XV stamped his foot. "Death of my life!" he said. "Never have I encountered such trickery. I don't believe in celestial wrath any more than Monsieur Voltaire, but I believe that some audacious rogue is making mock of me."

And, having comforted himself with those words, addressed to himself, the King advanced toward Cécile Robert again. The poor child was on her knees. She extended imploring arms toward the monarch and seemed to be appealing for justice. But that comedy had been renewed so often, he had seen so many poor girls imploring him, with the sole objective of putting a higher price on their defeat, that he did not believe in Cécile's tears or her supplications. He took her in his arms again and gave her a kiss on the lips.

But the voice immediately thundered—except that it was no longer coming from the depths of the alcove or descending from the friezes of the ceiling; on the contrary, it was resonating like a drum beneath the king's feet.

"Beware!" it said. "A great misfortune threatens you, King devoid of modesty! Beware!"

The King released Cécile once again, and his anger knew no bounds. This time, instead of running toward the door he ran to the alcove and agitated the bell-cord furiously.

Two minutes went by-two centuries for Cécile, two years for the King, whose anger was increasing; then footsteps resounded in the corridor, and Lebel finally appeared. On seeing the King in distress, with sweat on his forehead, as red as a poppy, the valet de chambre stopped on the threshold, nonplused.

"Lebel!" said the King. "Lebel! Lebel!" He repeated the word in three different tones.

"Sire..."

"Ah! Lebel...! And the King was gripped by a kind of suffocation.

"But what is it, Sire? What's wrong?"

And Lebel looked, alternately, at Cécile, who had ended up weeping copiously, and the King, who was threatened with falling ill.

"Look!" said Louis XV, finally. And he kicked the grenade that had exploded, and was now no more than a deformed fragment of blackened sheet metal.

"A grenade!" Lebel exclaimed.

"Yes—which exploded here, at my feet..."

Lebel thought that the firework had been thrown by Cécile. "Oh, you little wretch!" he said, running toward her with his fists raised.

But Louis XV stopped him. "No," he said, "it wasn't her."

"Who, then, Sire?"

"I don't know...it fell from heaven...!"

"Oh!" said Lebel, who no more believed in heaven than the King himself.

"The voice...the voice...," murmured Louis XV, whose face passed from crimson to a livid hue.

"What voice?" said Lebel.

"A voice that threatened me with the wrath of Heaven."

"Bah!" said the valet de chambre.

"And which sometimes comes from there, sometimes from there and sometimes from there!" And the King indicated the three places from which the voice had successively made itself heard.

"Sire," said Lebel, "it's impossible that anyone could have dared to disrespect Your Majesty thus. I'll call the guards, the château will be searched...and the temeritous individual will certainly be found..."

Louis XV stopped Lebel once again. "No, I don't want that."

"But Sire..."

"There's no need to have everyone laughing at my expense before the arrant rogue is caught..." At the same time, the King looked at Cécile. "I'm too upset now," he said, "to occupy myself with gallantries, but keep watch on this child—she's charming...and I hope that she'll be humanized before long..."

"Oh, Your Majesty can be tranquil," said Lebel. "The bird is in the cage, and the cage is solid. It won't fly away."

The King took a step toward the door, and then came back to Lebel. "Not a word of all this," he said.

"Yes, Sire."

"And send me the governor of the château." At the same time, the King picked up the carcass of the grenade and put it in his pocket.

Then he went up to his apartments, leaving Cécile in Lebel's hands.

The latter said, severely, to the young woman: "Someone has attempted to assassinate the King before your eyes, that's certain—beware of being an accomplice!"

And he left her prey to a new fear, that of the scaffold, succeeding the fear of dishonor.

Cécile heard him close and lock the door, and draw away. "Oh, my God! My God!" she said, bursting into sobs. "My God, have pity on me!"

While she fell to her knees, and as if God, whom she invoked, deigned to respond, the voice that had frightened the King made itself heard yet again, so close to the young woman that one might have thought that an invisible being was whispering in her ear.

The voice was no longer threatening. It was as tender and gentle as a consolation, and it said: "Have patience and courage; someone is watching over you, and protecting you...and you shall be saved!"

In the meantime, the King, whose emotion was beginning to calm down, had summoned the governor of the château to his study.

The man who fulfilled those functions was neither a great aristocrat nor a courtier. He was an old soldier, a former cavalry captain, to whom Louis XV had given that post in recompense for the fact that the brave man's left arm had been carried away at Fontenay by a cannonball that might well, but or that interruption, have gone on to kill the King. His name was Monsieur de Beautreillis.

The King showed him the grenade, told him what he had seen and heard, and said to him: "If you value your post, Monsieur, you'll have given me the explanation of this mystery tomorrow."

"Yes, Sire."

The poor captain was a devoted man who had performed marvels on the battlefield, but he was a paltry policeman, and, for all his efforts, dusk fell without him having discovered anything. The château was, however, searched conscientiously. Lebel having locked Cécile in another room, the lilac chamber was investigated carefully, the padded walls were sounded, and a search was made for trap-doors that did not exist.

Even though the King had demanded that the secret be kept, and had said nothing to Madame de Pompadour, and even though the searches had been made in great secrecy, the story leaked out. By eight o'clock in the evening a dozen courtiers were recounting it in whispers; by ten, the pages knew it; by eleven, it had made the journey to Paris, for Monsieur de Sartine arrived in all haste.

All day long, Master Porion had remained at the Château de Versailles, waiting for the King to deign to grant him an audience. Perhaps, if Porion had been employed, he would have fund the key to the enigma at the first attempt—but no one, not even Lebel, thought of him. And, as we shall see, that was a great misfortune for him.

Monsieur de Sartine, to whom the King recounted everything that had happened, and how Porion had brought the girl to him, exclaimed: "Search no further, Sire!"

"What?" said the King.

"The trickster is found."

"What are you saying, Sartine?"

"It's the fellow who, after having thought it good to by-pass me and deal directly with the King, has become His Majesty's trickster."

"Is that possible, Sartine?"

"I'm certain of it, Sire," replied the Lieutenant de Police.

"Oh! The arrant rogue!"

"I'll have him arrested, Sire, with Your Majesty's permission."

"I should think so!" said the King. "Arrest him, Sartine, and send him to rot in the Bastille."

"After which he'll be put to torture, Sire, and he'll confess what means he employed."

And Monsieur de Sartine, quitting the King, went to give the order to arrest Porion, while the latter was waiting quite tranquilly for his audience in the hall of the junior officers of the château, and who screeched like a peacock on finding himself seized by the collar. He tried to disculpate himself, to speak, to protest his innocence, even to offer his collaboration in finding the real trickster. But the police sent to arrest him closed his mouth, threw him into a carriage and shouted to the coachman:

"To the Châtelet, by order of the King!"

XX

At almost the same time as Père Cinnamon was being taken to the Châtelet, a small conference was held in great secrecy in Madame de Pompadour's boudoir.

The Marquise had two people with her; her chief lady-in-waiting, Mademoiselle Bellamy and the page Noël. The Marquise was writhing with laughter.

"Now, my darling," she said, looking at Noël, "now that you've shown your prowess, tell us how you did it."

"It's quite simple," said Noël.

"What! Quite simple!"

"I'm a ventriloquist."

"What?" said the Marquise.

"A ventriloquist," repeated Mademoiselle Bellamy. "What's that?"

"I speak with my belly."

"What are you telling us, my darling?" said the Marquise de Pompadour.

"Would you like proof of it?"

"Let's see."

"A ventriloquist has the gift of making his voice resonate wherever he wishes," said Noël. "Listen."

Suddenly, Madame de Pompadour and Mademoiselle Bellamy uttered exclamations of surprise, almost of fear. A voice, which seemed to be coming from the depths of the parquet, said, dully: "In my family, we are all ventriloquists."

The Marquise looked at Noël. His lips were moving, but the sound, instead of escaping from them, seemed to be emerging from beneath Mademoiselle Bellamy's chair. There was no doubt, however, that it was him who was speaking.

"That's marvelous!" exclaimed the lady-in-waiting.

"Miraculous!" said the Marquise.

"And that permitted me," said the page, laughing, "to speak in the name of Providence."

"But it was still necessary for you to be hidden in the lilac chamber?" said Madame de Pompadour.

"No, certainly not," said Noël.

"Where were you, then?"

A new smile brushed Noël's red lips. "I was in my room, tranquilly," he said.

"Your room?"

"Yes—it's directly above the lilac chamber. Pages are lodged in the attics."

"And you were able to traverse the thickness of the ceiling with your singular voice?"

"Not exactly."

"However..."

"The ceiling is hollow, like all ceilings," Noël went on. "Which is to say that there's a gap between the beams of the room below and the parquet of the room above."

"Good."

"At Versailles, in the time of the Great King," Noël continued, who knew his history, "everything was done royally. Instead of simply lodging mice, the ceiling could lodge men, and that good-for-nothing Monsieur de Beautreillis should have thought of that and had the ceilings sounded instead of searching the cupboards."

"Go on, my darling," said the Marquise, more and more interested by Noël's story.

"I unsealed one of the leaves of my parquet and slid into the ceiling."

"Very good. And then?"

"Then, with a drill, I made a little hole in a corner of the alcove. The lilac chamber is entirely padded, and the extended cloth covered the hole completely. It was through that hole that my voice passed, and which I could direct as I liked."

"I understand that now," said the Marquise. "But the grenade?"

"It passed through the hole."

"It was very small, you said."

"I enlarged it."

"And Monsieur de Beautreillis' men didn't find it?"

"No, the padding covered it. I only had to part a little of it momentarily in order to throw my projectile; then, with my fingertips, I put the cloth back in place."

"All that is marvelous," said Madame de Pompadour, "but afterwards?"

"The poor devil that Monsieur de Sartine has designated as the trickster has been arrested."

"Good. And if you continue the same comedy tomorrow, the King..."

"There will be no tomorrow, Madame."

"What's that, my darling?"

"I count on taking the child away this evening, while the King is at supper."

"Taking her away?"

"Yes."

"In spite of Lebel?"

"Of course."

"But what will you do?"

"I'll make use of a silken ladder that was a great help to me two months ago, for getting out of my room through the window."

"Why did you go out through the window instead of the door?"

"Noël smiled. "I don't want to compromise anyone," he said, "and I beg you not to interrogate me about that."

"So be it. Go on."

"So, I attach my ladder to a window."

"Good."

"And I descend as far as the lilac chamber."

"All right. But it's closed."

"Undoubtedly. Except—look..." And Noël set before the Marquise's eyes a superb diamond that he was wearing on his finger, which she had given to him. "With that," he said, "I cut a pane without the slightest noise, and I penetrate into the lilac chamber."

"The child, frightened, starts to cry out," said Mademoiselle Bellamy, "And Lebel comes running."

"No," said Noël. "I've anticipated that, and the mysterious voice has warned the girl that someone is watching over her and working to save her."

"You have an answer for everything," said the Marquise.

Smiling, Noël continued: "I take the girl in my arms, I climb back up the ladder to my room, and I wait for first light."

"And then?"

"At first light, I dress her as a man in one of my costumes. She's tall and slim, she'll look exactly like a page. We go out together. No one takes any notice of two pages going through the corridors and going downstairs. The guards, half asleep, hear me cry: "Service of the King!" and open the gates for me. Now we're in the streets of Versailles; we climb into a carriage, and 'Whip, Coachman!' I take the child back to Paris."

"To her father?"

"Well, that depends," Noël replied. "I find her charming."

"Rogue!" On that word, Madame de Pompadour seemed to reflect. Eventually, she said: "Listen, my darling, I believe that, beautiful as the girl is, she's no longer dangerous to me."

"Why is that, Madame?"

"Because, in three days' time, the King, still remembering his misadventure, will take a dislike to her."

"That's quite possible."

"But after all," Madame de Pompadour continued, "if she pleases you, and if you can carry the adventure to the end, I don't oppose it."

Noël kissed the Marquise's hand. "You're good," he said.

"Only," the Marquise added, "beware of letting yourself get caught."

"Oh," said Noël, laughing, "there's no danger of that." And he stood up.

"Where are you going?" asked Mademoiselle Bellamy.

"Well, it's the King's supper time."

"Oh, that's right."

"I'm going to save the girl. *Au revoir!*"

And Noël slipped away on tiptoe, leaving the Marquise laughing uproariously.

XXI

Cécile Robert had been locked up all day. She had not seen anyone except Lebel.

The old man horrified her now, and she knew what a wretch she was dealing with. Lebel brought her something to eat, but she had refused to touch any nourishment, first of all because she was too desperate to be hungry or thirsty, and secondly because the voice had made itself heard again, saying: "Don't eat anything but bread or drink anything but water, if you eat and drink. The wine is mixed with a narcotic, the aliments are doctored."

What was that voice, then, who spoke to her almost in her ear?

The young woman was no more tempted than the King to believe in anything supernatural; but she believed what the voice had said—which is to say that there were people at the Château de Versailles who were working to save her.

She had spent the day sometimes praying and sometimes weeping, sometimes abandoning hope and sometimes preventing herself from dissolving in tears.

Night had fallen.

Lebel, who had cast aside the mask, arrived at eight o'clock carrying a candle. He darted a glance at the table, which was still laden with the young woman's untouched meal.

"Ah!" he said. "It appears that we're not hungry?"

Cécile did not reply.

Lebel lit the candles that were on the mantelpiece. Then, looking at Cécile, he said: "My dear child, the wretch who has dared to play a trick on the King has been arrested, and the King is convinced that you were not his accomplice. The King still loves you and he will come to visit you. I therefore engage you, my dear child, to receive him well this time, and not to play the prude. Your future depends on it. If you're docile to the generosity of our august master, you'll be suitably endowed, and it will be permissible thereafter for you to marry your fiancé, if you have one."

With those ignoble words, Lebel went out.

Cécile only understood one thing, which was that the one who had already saved her had been arrested. From then on, she lost all hope, and dissolved in tears again.

Suddenly, however, the two candles went out, as if under a powerful breath.

Cécile, who was on her knees, got up, frightened, and uttered a cry. But the voice immediately made itself heard close by, as if in her ear. It said: "Lebel lied; the man who wants to save you has not been arrested, since it is me. Soon, I shall be with you...don't be afraid...don't cry out...your salvation depends on your silence."

Cécile's heart was beating as if to burst. She went to the window and leaned her burning forehead against the pane. The night was not luminous like the previous one; it was, on the contrary, black and rainy, and silence had fallen in the château, troubled only, from time to time, by the sonorous and regular tread of the sentinels, who sometimes, simply to acquit their conscience, deigned to emerge momentarily from their sentry-boxes and receive a few raindrops.

Suddenly, Cécile threw herself backwards sharply. Between the black sky and the window, something even blacker had just slid. That something, which appeared to be a human body, seemed to be swinging in mid-air on the end of a rope.

Cécile was tempted to cry out, but she remembered the recommendations of the mysterious voice, and did not budge. A small sound became audible; it was the diamond cutting the pane.

When the pane was detached, a hand passed through the casement and opened the catch, which Cécile had tried to do in vain several times. Noël—for it was him—knew the secret of the mysterious fastenings in the lilac chamber.

"It's me," he whispered.

Cécile was trembling in all her limbs, but hope swelled her breast. She could not make out the features of her liberator, but he had such a youthful and gentle voice! And he continued; "Trust me. I've come to save you."

"Who are you?" Cécile asked.

"I'll tell you later. Now, we don't have a minute to waste. If you stay here one more hour, you'll be completely lost, and I'll no longer be able to do anything for you. Do you have confidence in me?"

"Yes," said Cécile, into whose heart that suave and sympathetic voice descended like a hope.

"Then let me take you in my arms, and don't be afraid."

And as the page was robust, in spite of his elegant and dainty figure, he put his left arm round Cécile's waist, climbed back up on to the window-sill, seized the silken ladder that was hanging along the wall, and climbed back up boldly, paying no heed to the drop of forty or fifty feet beneath him.

"If you're scared," he said to Cécile, "close your eyes."

It was an affair of a few minutes. Noël soon reached the sill of his own window, and deposited the palpitating Cécile in his page's bedroom. Then he detached his ladder, which he hastened to hide under his bed, closed the window again and said to the young woman: "You're safe now."

He struck a briquette and lit a candle, for he had accomplished all those prodigies in pitch darkness.

Then Cécile was able to see her liberator.

Noël was pretty enough to eat, and had she not had the memory of Hector...but Cécile thought about Hector, and thought about him so well that, after having pressed his hand effusively, she said: "Oh, thank you...for me, and for him..."

Those words had the effect on Noël of a cold shower. "Who's *him*?" he said.

"Hector."

Good! thought Noël. *I was sure of it. These things only happen to me. Now I've just settled the affair of another.* Aloud, he said: "Ah! His name is Hector?"

"Yes," said Cécile, blushing.

"Why didn't he defend you when you were abducted?"

That question made Cécile shiver. "My God!" she said.

"What?"

"Oh! That man was lying to me!"

"What man?"

"The old man...the king's man."

"Oh, yes...that scoundrel Lebel."

"Yes," she said, nodding her head. Then Cécile told Noël, naively, everything that there was to tell, everything that she knew, from the fable that Porion had told her to the reassuring news that Lebel had given her regarding Hector."

Noël listened to it attentively. Then, when she had finished, he said: "Well, we'll know in a few hours what has happened to him."

"We'll know?"

"Of course, since I'm taking you back to Paris."

"Oh, you're noble and good," the young woman murmured, squeezing the page's hands again.

"Except that," said Noël, "it's necessary not to lose our heads, and to be prudent. You're not in the lilac chamber, but you're not far away as you'll soon see—and it's a matter of not going back there."

He approached Cécile and put his shoulder next to hers. "That's good," he said, "you're my height."

She looked at him in astonishment.

"You can't imagine, my dear demoiselle, "that you can get out of here dressed as you are."

"Ah!"

"The first guard or doorman you encounter would arrest you." The young woman's face expressed fear again. "Whereas, with the disguise I've prepared for you, we'll be able to leave the château freely."

At the same time, Noël opened a cupboard and brought out, piece by piece, a blue and red page's uniform—that of the King's pages.

"I have to put that on?" asked Cécile, ingenuously.

"Yes."

And Noël, who knew how to preserve the modesty of women, approached the window and turned his back on the young woman in order not to embarrass her during that metamorphosis. The instinct of danger, which had only been

140

partly dispelled, gave Cécile promptitude and activity. In less than a quarter of an hour, she had exchanged her feminine garments for a masculine costume.

Then Noël turned round again and put the finishing touches to her attire. He rolled up her hair in such a way as to make it seem short, plumped up the chemisette between the trousers and the jacket, placed a little braided tricorn boldly on Cécile's head, then fitted a fine épée around her waist, and said: "Now, there's only Lebel and the King who might be able to recognize you if they encountered you, and they won't encounter you. Come."

And he took the young woman by the hand. As he was about to go out, though, he changed his mind.

"Oh," he said. "It's necessary to anticipate everything. Monsieur de Beautreillis will doubtless mount a new search. Wait a minute."

He knelt down. Armed with a little knife that he took from his pocket, he swiftly detached one of the leaves of the parquet. Then Cécile, increasingly astonished, saw a gaping hole appear. It was the hollow ceiling about which Noël had spoken to Madame de Pompadour. The pages pushed the clothes that the young woman had just taken off into the hole. Then he replaced the section of parquet so adroitly that it was impossible to perceive that it had been displaced.

"Now, let's go!" he said.

But it was written that Noël and Cécile would not get out of the palace that night. As they arrived at the extremity of the corridor, which ended at one of the service staircases, a great racket suddenly became audible. Pages, guards and officers in service were coming and going in great haste.

Lebel's voice resounded, tearfully and nasally, saying: "What a misfortune! What a misfortune!"

And suddenly, the imperious voice of the King drowned out Lebel's, saying: "Close all the doors and all the gates! Don't let anyone out!"

Damn! thought Noël. *The King has finished supper earlier than usual today, and we've lost a quarter of an hour.* He turned to the trembling Cécile. "Your disappearance has already been perceived, but have no fear—they won't find you."

And he took the young woman back to his room, lifted up the leaf of the parquet again and said: "Here's a hiding place where no one will come to look for you. Stay there, don't budge, and count on me."

Then he replaced the piece of wood and launched himself out of the room, murmuring: "Let's go see what the King and Master Lebel think about the fashion in which young women fly away, exactly as if they were birds."

XXIII

Meanwhile in spite of his protests and denials, Porion was taken to the Châtelet, and Monsieur de Sartine, climbing into his own carriage, had given the order that the carriage carrying the poor devil should go at top speed.

It is easy to explain the sudden rigor of the Lieutenant de Police against the agent in whom, until then, he had had the most confidence. Potion had wanted to go over his chief's head, to do everything himself, to deal directly with the King and claim all the honors of the enterprise. That was enough for Monsieur de Sartine, whom subaltern agents had informed of Porion's arrival in Versailles, to take umbrage and ill-humor. So he had not hesitated to accuse Porion of the mysterious events of which the lilac chamber had been the theater.

The King had believed Monsieur de Sartine all the more easily because a man who had done what that one had just done, who had succeeded in finding the girl and making a fool of the Maréchale d'H***, appeared to him to be capable of anything. So the King had wanted whatever Monsieur de Sartine had wanted.

The two carriages headed for Paris with a vertiginous rapidity.

Darkness was just falling when the two entered beneath the somber vaults of the Châtelet.

Porion solicited an interview with his chief in vain. Sartine refused. Poor Père Cinnamon was thrown into a dungeon, and told that he would appear before the members of the criminal court. That meant, as clear as day, that he would be put to the torture. However, the preparations for the standard torture, which was to be abolished a few years later, under the following reign, required a certain time. It was necessary to summon the judges. It was necessary, by order of the King, to provide a clerk. Finally, it was necessary that Monsieur de Paris and his aides by alerted.

Two or three hours went by. Finally, the fatal moment arrived, and Porion was taken out of his dungeon. The unfortunate fellow was more dead than alive.

He was taken to the torture chamber, and he almost fainted at the sight of the rack, the ardent furnaces and the funnels. The rack was the instrument on which he was going to be extended. In the furnaces, the irons destined to roast the soles of his feet and to pinch the fat of his arms and legs were being raised to white heat. The funnels would serve to force him to ingurgitate bucketfuls of water into his stomach until he decided to talk.

He went pale at the sight of all those instruments of torture, and he was tottering as he advanced as far as the table at which the magistrate in a red robe charged with interrogating him was seated.

"Accused," the latter said to him, "you are charged with having made an attempt on the life of the King."

"Me!" cried Porion, putting his hands together.

"With the aid of a machine of war known as a grenade," the magistrate went on.

Porion raised his eyes to the heavens. "I don't know what you mean," he said.

The magistrate continued: "You arrested a young woman?"

"Yes, to obey the King."

"But that young woman, locked in the Palace of Versailles, you wanted to save?"

"Me!" Porion's tone was even more astonished than fearful.

"Believe me," said the magistrate, in a softer tone, "don't abuse the bounty of the King. Confess your crime."

"But I haven't committed any," said Porion.

"So you persist in your denials?"

"I can't say what I don't know."

"That's what we're going to see."

The magistrate made a sign, and the executioner's aide took hold of Porion. Porion started to yell. But he was dealing with two vigorous fellows, who reduced him to impotence and lay him down on the rack, to which he was solidly bound.

"With what shall we begin?"

"With the pincers," said the magistrate.

Monsieur de Paris picked up the red-hot pincers from one of the furnaces, and when his aides had laid Porion's arm bare, he approached the fuming iron to his flesh.

Porion uttered a terrible scream.

The magistrate made a sign, and the executioner stopped.

"So you confess?" repeated the man in the red robe.

"I don't know anything," said Porion.

"Continue, then," said the magistrate.

But as the executioner was about to obey, the door of the torture chamber opened and a voice cried from the threshold: "Stop!" At the same time, Monsieur Lebel, the King's valet de chambre, appeared.

"Who is that man?" asked the man in the red robe, who had never been to Versailles in his life and did not know the important personage before whom the entire Court inclined.

"Order of the King!" replied Lebel.

"What does the King want?"

"That this unfortunate fellow be taken away from here," said Lebel.

And he placed a parchment before the eyes of the nonplussed magistrate.

The King had written, with his own hand:

Monsieur de Sartine, do not put your agent Porion to the question and bring him to me in all haste

Louis.

Monsieur de Sartine was not at the Châtelet when Lebel arrived. Only half-believing in his agent's culpability, but glad enough to punish him for his insolence, Monsieur de Sartine, on arriving at the Châtelet, had given orders for the torture; then he had put on a gala costume and gone to spend the night with Mariette, a celebrated woman who had succeeded La Bravanne in the Rue des Blancs-Manteaux.

But there was no one at the Châtelet who would have dared to doubt the King's seal and signature. All doors were opened before Lebel, and even the magistrate inclined.

Porion, who was hastily detached, was howling as if he had been broken on the wheel.

"Calm down, my worthy friend," Lebel said to him, into his ear. "The King holds you in great esteem, and you're closer than you think to being Lieutenant de Police.

"Oh, if that ever happens," Porion cried, "I'll have Sartine put to torture."

A surgeon was summoned hastily. The surgeon placed a dressing on Porion's horribly burned arm designed to prevent inflammation, and Lebel said to him: "Now come with me."

"But where are you taking me?" asked Porion, who was suffering horribly.

"To Versailles."

"Why?"

"The King has need of you."

"Ah!"

"The girl has been abducted."

"Really?"

"And you're the only one who can find her."

And Lebel, to the great amazement of the magistrate and the torturers, took Porion by the arm, had all the doors opened, and led the police agent to his carriage, which was waiting on the quay.

XXIV

Why that abrupt reversal?

We shall explain it briefly.

The King, as the page Noël had remarked, driven by his amorous fantasy, and further excited by a few glasses of Tokay and Aï wine, had cut short his supper and headed in all haste for the lilac chamber. Lebel, candle in hand, had preceded him. When they arrived at the door the valet turned to the King and said: "I believe that Your Majesty will have no difficulty with the child."

"Why is that?"

"She's very frightened, and I've told her that if she resists Your Majesty any longer, she might be accused of complicity with the man who threw the grenade."

"Really! You told her that?" said the King, who started to laugh indecently.

"Yes, Sire."

"You're a clever rogue, Lebel."

Lebel bowed, blushing with pleasure beneath his white hair. Then he turned the key in the lock and opened the door. Suddenly, however, he uttered an exclamation

"What is it?" said the King, coming in behind him.

Lebel had stopped, sweat on his brow, breathless and voiceless, before the open window.

The cut pane lay on the floor. Evidently, someone had come to the girl's aid and had taken her away.

Lebel raced into the dressing-room and the boudoir. No one! Then he started uttering loud cries, and a few seconds later, the whole palace was in uproar.

It was at that moment that the King, drunk with anger and rage, had shouted in a resounding voice: "Close all the doors and all the gates! Don't let anyone out!"

It was also at that moment that the page Noël had thought it prudent to beat a retreat and hide Cécile within the thickness of the hollow ceiling.

All the valid men in the palace were immediately mobilized. Monsieur de Beautreillis, trembling for his position, redoubled his zeal. They set about searching the château from top to bottom, but it was a waste of time.

In the meantime, Noël smiled maliciously within the nascent down that served him as a moustache and said: "Search! Search! You won't find anything, good people!"

The sentries, interrogated, affirmed that no one had left the château. Lebel swore to the great gods that he had seen the girl not an hour before. From all that, it was necessary to conclude that neither the girl nor her abductors had yet left the château.

Suddenly, the King's anger subsided. "Lebel," he said, "come with me."

More dead than alive, the valet de chambre followed his master, who shut himself up in his study with him.

Then the King said: "Sartine is an imbecile."

Lebel looked at the King.

"And doubtless," continued Louis XV, "he has arrested an innocent man and is about to put the poor devil to torture."

"That's quite possible," said Lebel, who had a weakness for Porion, deep down.

"It's certain," said the King. "Would you like proof?"

Lebel waited for the King to explain.

"When that man was taken away, the girl was still in the lilac chamber, wasn't she?"

"Certainly, Sire."

"So it isn't him who's abducted her?"

"Evidently not."

"If it isn't him who abducted the girl, it isn't him who threw the grenade."

"I agree with Your Majesty."

"So Sartine is an imbecile."

"I don't deny it, Sire."

"And Monsieur de Beautreillis is another, since he hasn't found anything."

Lebel made a gesture, which signified: *The stupidity of Monsieur de Beautreillis is indubitable.*

The King went on: "Well, you see, Lebel, I've got an idea."

"What, Sire?"

"It's that if neither Sartine or Beautreillis can do anything, the man who has already give us such great proofs of ability is the man we need."

"I believe so," said Lebel,

"Climb into a carriage and take my best horses, Lebel."

"Yes, Sire."

"Run to Paris and bring me back that man; he'll find the girl."

"I'm certain of it," said Lebel.

And less than a quarter of an hour later, Monsieur Lebel was on the road to Paris.

In the meantime, Monsieur de Beautreillis was summoned by the King.

"Monsieur," Louis XV said to him, "Give your guards the order to shoot anyone trying to leave the palace."

Monsieur de Beautreillis inclined.

Then the King ordered that everyone should retire to their rooms in an orderly manner, that the ladies and the pages should go to bed and that everyone not on duty should stay in their apartments.

An hour later, the most profound silence reigned in the Palais de Versailles and the King, who seemed to be in a god mood, went to play tric-trac with Madame de Pompadour.

The Marquise did not know that the King had sent Lebel to Paris, so she said, smiling: "I see that Your Majesty is being reasonable."

"Why is that, my beauty?" asked Louis XV, kissing her hand.

"Because he doesn't bang his head against a wall more than is reasonable."

"Oh, you think so, my love?"

"Of course!"

"Well, you're mistaken," said the King.

"How so, Sire?"

"I've sent Lebel to Paris."

"To do what?"

"To bring back the man who found the girl."

"The same one who dared to make a fool of Your Majesty?"

"No, it wasn't him, my love."

"Who was it, then, Sire?"

"I don't know, but I'll find out."

"In truth!"

"And he'll find the girl."

"I hope so, Sire."

"And finally," the King concluded, with a glint of anger in his eyes, "justice will be done, and it will be terrible."

Madame de Pompadour and Mademoiselle Bellamy, who were standing behind the King, exchanged a rapid glance. That glance meant: *Look out for Noël—he might pay dearly for his escapade!*

A few minutes later, someone came to inform the King that Lebel had returned and that he had brought back Porion, alias Père Cinnamon.

XXV

The King left the Marquise and returned to his study.

Lebel was there, in company with Porion.

Porion was suffering like a damned soul, and putting his hand to the arm burned by the executioner's red-hot iron.

"Sire," said Lebel, who definitely held Porion in high esteem, "I arrived too late. Monsieur de Sartine had started on the poor devil."

"Aye!" said the King, "When it's a matter of doing bad work, Sartine is always in a hurry."

Lebel continued: "It will be necessary for your Majesty to compensate this poor man."

Porion thought it appropriate to utter a few groans.

"He'll be given a thousand livres," added the King.

"And if I find the girl?" said Porion, in a tone of great conviction.

The King turned to him. "Anything you wish," he said.

Porion looked at the King. "Your Majesty will allow me to choose?"

"Speak, fellow."

"I would like to put Monsieur de Sartine to torture," said Porion, modestly.

"Oh, my friend," said the King, "what you ask is impossible."

"Why is that, Sire?"

"Because one doesn't pinch the flesh of a gentleman, like that. Ask for something else, and we'll see."

"Well," said Porion, mingling his requests with very effective groans, "I'd rather like to be Lieutenant de Police."

"Really?"

"After, of course," the fellow finished, "I've proved to Your Majesty that I'm worthy of it."

"Well, prove it, and we'll see..."

Porion stopped groaning. "I'm ready to go to work," he said, "and I await Your Majesty's orders."

"The girl has disappeared," said the King.

"Right!"

"And some wretch has permitted himself on play tricks on me."

"Both will be found, Sire, except that..."

"Except what?"

"I shall be obliged to address a host of questions to Your Majesty."

"Speak."

"First I should like to know exactly what happened to Your Majesty."

"When?"

"When he was with the girl."

"I saw a grenade fall at my feet, which nearly put my eye out."

"And then?"

"And then, damn it, I heard a voice…"

"Coming from where?"

"Almost everywhere—sometimes from above, sometimes below."

"Right!" said Porion. "I know that trick."

"What?"

"Your Majesty was dealing with a ventriloquist."

"Get away!" said the King, who knew the meaning of the term that Porion had employed.

"Yes, Sire."

"Now," Porion continued, "How did the girl, fleeing on her own or abducted—it doesn't matter which—get out of the room?"

"Through the window."

"Sire, said Porion, "every time I am charged with carrying out a search of a house, instead of going in, I begin by making a tour of it, thinking that the best means of knowing the interior is to know the exterior by heart."

"So?" said the King.

"I would like, instead of going into the lilac chamber, to go down into the courtyard and look at the window from outside."

"That's easy," said Lebel. "I'll guide you."

"I'll come too," said he King, who, although being furious, observed that he was no longer suffering from ennui.

On the king's orders, Monsieur de Beautreillis had given such strict instructions that the Palace of Versailles resembled a veritable necropolis, in spite of a mild night and beautiful moonlight. The pages were not trailing back and forth on the staircases; the musketeers were not harassing the maids of honor; no more amorous rendezvous in little corners and dark corridors. Who, in truth, would have permitted themselves to make love when His very Christian Majesty the King deigned to have heartache, like a simple mortal?

So the three individuals, Lebel, Porion and Louis XV, descended the grand stairway of Versailles in the midst of a profound silence and almost complete isolation. But the news had spread very rapidly that Lebel had been sent to Paris to fetch the clever man who had put his hand on the girl once already, and that the man had returned to Versailles. The King and Porion were scarcely in the courtyard before the rumor had run throughout the palace.

When they had entered the courtyard, they were alone. By the time they were under the window of the lilac chamber, there were nearly fifty people keeping respectfully at a distance.

"Sire," said Porion, in a low voice. "I can only answer for success on one condition."

"What?"

"That I have *carte blanche*."

"What do you mean?"

"And that if I put my hand on someone's collar, Your Majesty will have him arrested..."

"But..."

"Until I have demonstrated that he is the guilty party."

"So be it," said the King.

Porion examined the window.

Almost vertically beneath it, there was a sentry-box.

"Sire," said Porion, "it isn't the route of the street that the girl followed."

"What?" said the King.

"As she's an angel," continued Père Cinnamon, in a mocking tone, "the thing is quite natural: she took the skyward route."

"How's that?"

"What is the window that is vertically above?" Porion went on.

"That's the window of a page's bedroom," said Lebel.

"And that page...where is he?"

Lebel darted a glance around the group of courtiers, soubrettes and pages who appeared to be taking a great interest in Porion's operations from a distance. He perceived Noël, who had wanted to judge Porion's skill for himself, but who was too far away to be able to hear what Porion and Lebel were saying to one another.

"Over there."

"Which one?"

"The young brown-haired lad with a blue toque."

"That's good," said Porion. And he began walking backwards as if he wanted to see the open window from a greater distance, but in reality to get closer to the group of curiosity-seekers.

Then suddenly bounding like a tiger, and as rapid as lightning, he turned round, fell upon the page, seized his collar and shouted: "I have him!"

Noël uttered a cry.

"Who is it?" said the King, immediately turning round himself.

Noël was struggling in Porion's iron grip.

"What!" exclaimed the King. "Little Noël!"

"Yes, Sire."

"One of my pages?"

"Yes, Sire," Porion repeated, with conviction

"But that's impossible!" said the King.

"The man's lying," said Noël, who was still struggling.

"Sire," replied Porion, in a tone of conviction, "If I'm mistaken, Your Majesty can hang me from the gallows."

"I'm a gentleman," said Noël.

"But if Your Majesty," Porion went on, "will have confidence in me for a quarter of an hour..."

"Well?" said the King.

"Let me go, vile rogue!" said Noël, whom Porion was still holding by the collar.

"My young friend," said Porion. "I'll let you go when the King has confided you to two of his men, who will watch over you and prevent you from leaving the courtyard."

"Sire, sire," stammered Noël, "this man is mad..."

"I believe as you do my child," said the king, "but it's my fault; I had the weakness to grant him *carte blanche*." And he made a sign to two guards, who made sure of Noël's person.

"Now," said Porion, "let's go make a tour of the lilac chamber."

The King and Lebel followed him, and, curiosity prevailing over respect, the crowd of courtiers went with them.

Porion paraded his fist over the walls, went into the alcove, climbed up on the bed, hesitated momentarily, and then detached the fabric and the padding that covered the ceiling.

In a corner, a hole as big as a fist then became visible.

"It's from there that the grenade was thrown," said Porion.

The King uttered a cry of admiration.

"But we have nothing more to do here," Porion went on.

"Where are we going?" asked Lebel.

"To the page's room."

And Porion went upstairs.

A few minutes later, he had inspected the alcove and the walls. Tapping with his foot, he said to the bewildered King: "Sire, the bird isn't far away."

The King shivered.

"It's beneath our feet," added Porion.

And he bent down in order to detach the section of parquet that covered the hollow ceiling.

XXVI

Let us return to Paris now and penetrate into the mansard that Messire Mardochée de Mardoche, painter and gentleman, pompously called his studio.

Fifteen hours after the abduction of Cécile Robert, things were in the same state as when Porion and the greengrocer had left—which is to say that Firmin, still tied up and gagged, had exhausted himself in vain efforts to break his bonds and call for help; the plank was still extended as a bridge between the two roofs; and finally, Mardochée had not interrupted his sonorous snoring for an instant.

In the house where he lived, the painter's vagabond habits and interminable drunkenness were well known. No one, therefore, was anxious to know whether he had spent the night outside or whether he was at home sleeping off his wine.

In addition, as he lodged at the very top and had no neighbors, no one had heard Firmin's dull groans as he tried to cry out through his gag.

But everything comes to an end in this world, even drunkenness. Professional drunkards have the rare quality of entering instantaneously into their presence of mind when the wine has worn off and linking the moment when they went to sleep with the present moment.

The reawakening of the mind operates within them before that of the body.

Mardochée suddenly stopped snoring.

His eyes were still closed, but his mind awakened, clear and precise, and he said to himself: *I got drunk, and fell asleep like a veritable brute at the very moment when poor Père Cinnamon abducted my pretty neighbor, not on his own account, for he's too old, but on mine. Ah! Is he drunk and asleep too? And the girl...or, did his foot slip as he passed over the plank?*

As you can see, Mardochée remembered everything.

He made a desperate effort and opened his eyes.

Dazzled by the light that was entering the mansard in floods, he started looking around, but saw nothing at first.

"No one!" he said. "Where have they gone, then?"

Firmin uttered a new groan.

"What?" said Mardochée. And he shook himself, stretched his arms and turned his head. Then he saw Firmin, bound and gagged, and as his memory was still faithful, he started laughing and exclaimed: "It's the medical student! Poor Père Cinnamon! There's a friend!"

Then he stood up, still tottering, marched toward Firmin, sniggering and, his jealousy gripping him again, he picked up a knife. "Since Papa Cinnamon isn't here," he said, "I'll take advantage of that to kill my rival."

And, brandishing his knife, he advanced on Firmin, who was still lying in a corner of the mansard. But there are certain hatreds in which the gaze of a man has more power than his arm, in which his eyes are charged with an electric fluid whose influence is insurmountable. Half way, Mardochée stopped. He stopped because Firmin's soft and supplicant gaze was fixed upon him. And, fascinated, he dropped his knife and started staring at his rival in his turn.

Firmin's gaze was animated at that moment by an expression of profound pity. That gaze seemed to say: *You're a victim, like me, and furthermore, you're a dupe. Oh, if you would get rid of my gag and my bonds, I could tell you everything, and after you'd heard it, we'd be friends and not enemies!*

Mardochée understood everything that that gaze was trying to say. He bent down and picked up the knife, but it was not to strike Firmin; it was to cut his bonds and his gag.

And Firmin, once free, got up, exclaiming: "Oh Monsieur, what wretches!"

"Who are you talking about?" asked Mardochée, stupefied.

"Those two men who have abducted Cécile."

"That was for me," said Mardochée.

"For you?" said the surgeon, shrugging his shoulders. "Get away!"

Mardochée's jealousy returned, and he began to snigger. "They tied you up, all the same, you, her fiancé!"

"Me, her fiancé?"

"Yes, you."

"Never!"

"What do you mean, never?"

"I loved Cécile like a sister," said Firmin, in a voice full of sobs, "but as a sister only."

"Really?" said Mardochée.

"I swear it."

"Then," said the joyful painter, "give me her hand. I'll marry her, and we'll be brothers."

But Firmin responded to those hopeful words with a groan. "Oh, Monsieur," he said, "what you say will never happen."

"Why?"

"Because neither you nor I will ever see her again."

"Ah!"

"Those wretches have kidnapped her…they took her away unconscious."

"But since I tell you it's for me," said the naïve Mardochée.

"For you, alas!"

"Of course. I know Père Cinnamon well, damn it! He's my friend."

"I don't know whether he's your friend," said the painter, sadly, "but what I can affirm to you is that I heard that man, as he was leaving, say to his accomplice: 'The King will be content.'"

"The King!"

"Yes," said Firmin, in a tone of conviction. "Cécile, whom I love, whom you love, is perhaps at this moment an inmate of the Parc-aux-Cerfs."

Mardochée uttered a cry of rage. Firmin might well be right. The painter commenced by exhaling his fury in blasphemies, then he beat his head against the walls, and then his nerves relaxed and he wept.

Firmin's dolor was calmer, and more concentrated, but no less violent.

Finally, the two men extended their hands to one another. Then they both experienced the same desire: one to see again, the other to see for the first time, the room from which the unfortunate Cécile had been seized. They exchanged glances, but understood one another without saying a word.

The plank was still there. Mardochée was no longer drunk. He stepped over the sill and boldly ventured on to that new kind of bridge. Firmin followed him. As Mardochée penetrated into Cécile's room, however, he uttered a cry of horror.

A man lay extended on the floor, in the middle of a pool of semi-coagulated blood.

"Hector!" cried Firmin.

It was, in fact, Hector, who appeared to be dead, but was only unconscious. Firmin placed a hand over his heart. The heart was beating feebly, but it was beating.

"He's alive!" he exclaimed. Then the man in despair was effaced, to give way to the surgeon—and the surgeon summoned up all his sang-froid and all the resources of his art. Aided by Mardochée, he transported Hector to Cécile's bed. Then he began to sound and examine the wound.

Lebel had told the truth without knowing it. The wound received by Hector was a veritable scratch; the knife had indeed slid along a rib, Except that, as the hemorrhage had been abundant, Hector, still weak, had lost consciousness

"Another hour," said Firmin, "and he'd have been dead."

"So he isn't grievously wounded?" asked Mardochée.

"No, I'll answer for him," said Firmin.

Then the two young man, seeking to numb their dolor—a dolor without remedy, alas, for who would dare to take on the King?—undressed Hector and put him to bed, and while Firmin put an initial dressing on the wound, Mardochée rubbed his hands and arms in order to restore warmth to them. While they were occupied in that task, someone rapped softly on the door.

Firmin went to open it.

A man was standing on the threshold: a man whose garments were covered in dust and whose shoes were caked in mud, declaring that he had made a long journey on foot; a pale, emaciated man, exhausted by cold and hunger.

Firmin murmured: "Cécile's father!"

It was, in fact, Robert Damiens, who had been traveling all night and all of the previous day in order to come and embrace the daughter he adored.

XXVII

Robert Damiens appeared so changed to Firmin, who had not seen him for several months, that the young man, on seeing him pale, distressed, with his eye flamboyant, wondered whether he might not already know the extent of his unhappiness.

Nothing of the sort, however, for scarcely had he crossed the threshold than, instead of asking: "Who are these men?" he asked: "Where is my daughter?"

He asked that question is a strange and seemingly fearful tone.

Mardochée exchanged a rapid glance, and understood one another. A pious lie was immediately agreed between them.

"Monsieur Robert," said Firmin, "you know that your daughter works for a shop in the Rue Saint-Denis. She's gone to take back her work."

"Oh," said Damiens, still in his strange and seemingly unhinged voice. "I'll wait for her."

And he sat down. Then he looked at Mardochée. "Who is this man?" he asked Firmin.

"He's one of my friends," said the surgeon.

"And the other?" Damiens pointed at the man who was lying down, without appearing to take full account of the fact that he was lying in his daughter's bed.

"That one," said Firmin, "is an unfortunate madman who fell to us, not from the sky, but from the roof."

Damiens, who had sat down near the entrance to the room, got up and approached the bed. He slipped in the blood that was covering the floor, in the same place from which Hector had been picked up, and which he had not noticed. The man was scarcely clinging to the earth, to judge by his gaze, shining with fever.

Hector was beginning to come round. At the moment when Damiens leaned over him, he opened his eyes.

Suddenly, Cécile's father uttered a cry: "Him!" he exclaimed. "Him!"

Firmin looked at him.

"Him!" repeated Damiens, with a fearful expression.

"You know him, then?" said Firmin.

"Do I know him?" cried Robert Damiens. "You're asking me whether I know him?"

"Yes."

"He's the young man from the inn in the Rue des Enfants-Rouges."

"What?"

"It's for having protected and defended him, Firmin, that you see me in this state." His troubled brain then appeared to recover a complete lucidity. And, seizing Firmin's arm forcefully, he said to him, pointing at Mardochée: "Can that man be trusted?"

"As I can," said Firmin.

"I've come here," Damiens went on, "in order for my daughter and you to hide me."

"You're being pursued, then?"

"Yes."

"By whom?"

"By the blood-drinkers. See what a state they've put me in!"

Then the man, who appeared to have recovered all of his sang-froid and all of his reason, told the young men a frightful story. He told them about the monstrous fantasies of the Tartar and the sanguinary treatment to which he subjected himself for his skin disease: the baths in human blood that he took at the Blue Dragon inn in the Rue des Enfants-Rouges, and the mysterious suctions that he operated upon young men put to sleep by means of a narcotic.

The two young men listened, shivering, momentarily forgetting the unfortunate Cécile, and wondering whether the man might not be completely mad. But he gave details so precise, so explicit, that it was difficult not to believe him. In addition, he was talking about Hector.

Hector, on hearing his name pronounced, had propped himself up on his elbow, and he was looking at Robert Damiens and listening with a somber avidity. And Damiens related how, one night, he had obeyed the voice of remorse; how, suddenly converted by the words of the duenna Lénore, he had resolved to save the unfortunate young man from a certain death.

He did not forget a single detail, neither the fashion in which the cataleptic Hector had been recalled to life, nor the combat on the stairway, nor the flight across the rooftops. There, Damiens' story was completed by Firmin's memories.

He divined what must have happened. Running away from roof to roof, Hector had come to fall into Cécile's mansard, not suspecting that the young woman who was going to collect him and care for him was the daughter of his savior. But what Firmin did not know, and could not divine, was what had become of Robert Damiens after that moment.

The men devoted to the Tartar had captured him. The Tartar having come running, had judged him personally, and had condemned him to a slow death. For a week, a pint of blood had been extracted from him every morning. Then, at the end of that time, he had been put in a carriage and taken on the journey for forty-eight hours. The Tartar, who was returning to Russia, had taken him as far as Holland; there he had granted him mercy. He had abandoned him, devoid of strength and near to dying.

And Robert had come back...

156

He had come back on foot, frightened, racked by remorse...and when he had concluded that frightful story, he cried: "Oh, divine wrath will end up striking the depraved Prince under whose reign such crimes are accomplished in peace!"

Hector, mute until then, uttered a cry. "Oh!" he said. "I remember..."

And he slapped his forehead, looked at Robert Damiens again, and said to him: "Yes, it's you who saved me!"

"It was, in fact, me," replied Damiens.

"And you have cared for me?" he said to Firmin.

The surgeon nodded his head.

Then Hector de Pierrefeu took his head in his hands, as if he wanted to re-assembled his scattered memories. And suddenly, a new cry sprang from his breast, and a name brushed his lips: "André!" As all three of them looked at him, he added: "My brother! What have you done with my brother?"

"Your brother?"

"Yes," said Hector, "my young brother André, a child who, on that fateful night, I left asleep in the Blue Dragon inn."

Firmin and Mardochée looked at one another. Robert Damiens lowered his head and did not reply.

Then Hector de Pierrefeu, whose strength was returning with his reason, leapt out of bed, came to Damiens, seized him by the arm and repeated: "My brother! Where is my brother?"

Damiens made a desperate effort, and, looking at Hector in his turn, said: "You're asking me what became of our brother?"

"Yes."

"He was a child of fourteen or fifteen?"

"Yes."

"And you left him at the accursed inn?"

"In order to go to the amorous rendezvous that had been given to me." And Hector, shivering, with sweat on his brow, bowed his head in his turn. "I had confided him," he said, "to the hotelier himself, who was a former servant of my family."

"The hotelier was a wretch!" said Robert Damiens.

"What do you mean?" cried Hector.

"I mean," replied Cécile's father, with a savage energy, "that the hotelier was the Tartar's accomplice."

"My God!"

"And during the same night when you went to sleep under the influence of a narcotic, your brother's throat was cut, and the monster took a bath in his blood."

Hector uttered a terrible cry. "Oh, vengeance, vengeance!" he cried.

"Vengeance!" repeated Mardochée and Firmin.

"The King will do justice!" added Hector, in an excited voice.

At the name of the King, Mardochée and Firmin looked at one another with a sort of fear, and it was in a solemn one that the surgeon said, in his turn: "Don't count on the King's justice."

"My daughter—where's my daughter?" repeated Robert Damiens, at that moment.

"Your daughter!" exclaimed Firmin. "You want to know where your daughter is?" And he started laughing in a frightening fashion. He too felt himself gained by the current of madness and fear that seemed to be flowing through the room.

"Your daughter," said Mardochée, "has been abducted."

"Abducted, my daughter! By whom, Seigneur?"

And as the unfortunate father asked that question, a voice answered him: a broken, bewildered, dying voice that came from the threshold.

"Your daughter," said that voice, "has been abducted by the King's men."

They turned round, and uttered a single cry; "Cécile!"

Cécile was, indeed, standing on the threshold. Pale, her eyes feverish, her garments in disorder, the poor child came to kneel before Robert Damiens, and said to him "Father, I'm dishonored!"

And Robert Damiens leapt upon a knife that was within arm's reach, and, brandishing it, he said in a crazed and savage voice: "this is the arm that will accomplish God's justice…!"

PART TWO: THE KING IS DISTRACTED

I

Winter had come, somber and cold, and November, the black month, had caused the last leaves to fall from the trees. Paris and Versailles had resumed their customary pleasures, and everyone was having a good time.

When we say "everyone" we do not mean the bourgeoisie, who were subject to the curfew, nor the peasants, who were dying of hunger, nor the people of the cities, who were dying of cold. "Everyone," in those days, consisted of the nobility, the clergy, the great lords and the great ladies.

There was dancing in Paris, in, in the houses of the aldermen and the magistrates, at Versailles in the homes of the Maréchale d'O*** and the Duchesse de Pli, and at the château. Comedies were even being staged in the King's residence, and Madame de Pompadour, who got younger every year, found an extreme pleasure in that diversion.

Except that the King, as usual, was suffering from ennui, and that ennui was the Marquise's sole chagrin.

How to distract the King?

Monsieur d'Argenson himself had lost his science.[22] His lewdest reports on the gallantries of the court and the city and his spiciest anecdotes had ended up making the King yawn. The King no longer even opened his mouth regarding the lovely Cécile, whom we have seen returned home half-dead with shame and mad with dolor.

One evening, however—the evening when this story recommences—something bizarre happened to the King, which brought a little color back to his cheeks and a gleam of youth to his extinct eyes.

That bizarre thing was, however, as we shall see, something quite simple.

As he was going to bed with the vague hope of sleeping—for he did not always sleep—the King perceived that his golden snuffbox was empty of Spanish tobacco. The King took no other, and his brother in Madrid—which is to say, his uncle, the King of Spain—had the custom of sending him an enormous packet every year, via his ambassador. That tobacco was contained in a vase of

---

[22] Marc-Antoine de Voyer de Paulmy, Marquis d'Argenson (1722-1787), not to be confused with his more famous father and grandfather, the previous holders of the title. His main claim to enduring fame was as a book collector; his collection eventually became the Bibliothèque de l'Arsenal, where Charles Nodier hosted his famous cénacle.

Saxe porcelain, which was itself in a pretty sandalwood escritoire placed in a corner of the royal bedroom.

Instead of handing his snuff-box to a page or one of his gentlemen of the bedchamber, His Majesty, like a mere mortal, opened the escritoire himself.

Underneath the shelf that supported the tobacco jar, there was a drawer. Mechanically, the King opened that drawer, which was full of old papers, mostly love letters, unique relics of his vanished passions. Louis XV leafed through them with a distracted finger. By the color of the paper he recognized the vanished hand that had written the letter, and there were papers in the drawer of all colors, from sky-blue to straw-yellow.

Suddenly, the King shivered A small rectangle of yellow paper had caught his eye. That piece of paper was neither folded not in an envelope. A name had been written in the middle of it: *Maître Dumas*. And beneath it, in smaller and more delicate handwriting, but evident the same were the words: *Discover the truth about that when the Monsieur le Régent is dead.*

The sight of that piece of paper, that name and the words written beneath it plunged the King into such a reverie that the lords assisting at his retirement to bed, seeing him still standing in front of that open drawer, looked at him in astonishment.

Suddenly, the King turned round.

His eyes were shining. A slight redness colored his face, and it was in an almost joyful voice that he said: "Messieurs, I've just been rejuvenated by thirty years in one minute."

The Maréchal d'H***, the husband of the poor indebted Maréchale who, six months earlier, had mistaken the police agent Porion for a Dutch financier, was the seigneur standing closest to the King at that moment. The King handed him the piece of yellow paper, saying: "You see this, Maréchal?"

"Yes, Sire."

"Well, I'm the one who wrote that name and that line."

"Ah!" said the Maréchal. And he waited.

"That name," the King went on, reminds me of one of the most mysterious stories that occupied all Paris in the times of Monsieur le Régent, and the end of which was never known."

"In truth!" said the Maréchal.

"I was fifteen years old then, and it had excited my vivid imagination keenly. I was the King, but it was Monsieur le Régent who ruled; when I mentioned it to him he shrugged his shoulders and replied that nothing of what I was saying was true and that someone was making fun of me. That did not prevent me from searing an oath that when Monsieur le Régent was dead, I would discover the truth about that story."

"Monsieur le Régent has been dead for a long time, Sire," observed the Maréchal.

"And I still only know the first half of the story," said the King sighing.

At the same time, he pushed back the drawer, closed the escritoire and sat down in the large armchair in which he was accustomed to being undressed.

Then a smile came to his lips.

A smile on the King's lips was something as rare as a ray of sunlight shining among the thick fogs of winter.

"Your Majesty appears to be in a good humor this evening," said the Maréchal.

"Such a good humor, Maréchal, that I no longer have any desire to go to bed."

All the courtiers took the view that it was necessary to smile, and all lips then expanded.

"Messieurs," the King continued. "For a long time, people have sought to distract me by telling me stories; I believe that the time has come to pay my debt."

The courtiers looked at one another.

"I'm going to tell you a story," said the King. And he crossed his legs and leaned back in his armchair.

"Sire," said the Maréchal, "we are listening to Your Majesty with joy and avidity."

"Don't laugh, Messieurs," said the King. "My story is more amusing than you might suppose."

"So amusing that Your Majesty would like to know the end of it," said the Maréchal.

"Exactly."

The King took a pinch of tobacco and commenced thus: "There is a little street in Paris called the Rue de l'Hirondelle."[23]

"We all know it very well, Sire."

"In that street," the King went on, "there was a tall, black, smoky, narrow house with a little door that gave access to a damp and dark alleyway."

"That's promising," murmured the Maréchal, wanting to encourage the royal narrator.

"In that house lodged an old procurator, his son, his daughter and a maid-servant.

---

[23] The story the King tells his courtiers is not original to Ponson. A slightly different version of it, including an account of the King's dual involvement with it, can be found in the multi-volume *Mémoires tirés des Archives de la Police de Paris* (1838), by-lined "J. Peuchet, archiviste de la police," which is available on *gallica*. Jacques Peuchet was a writer of miscellaneous non-fiction, who was not, in fact, a police archivist, and who co-authored the work in question with Étienne de Lamothe-Langon, a prolific forger of supposed historical documents; the anecdote bears all the hallmarks of the latter's ingenious imagination.

"The son was old, the daughter was old and ugly, which gives you the age of the procurator, who was said to be nearly a hundred years old. It had certainly been fifty years since he had sold his sacks, his papers and his clientele to a colleague, and forty since the people of the quarter had seen him set foot in the street.

"Sometimes, when night fell, he was seen to appear at a window at the top of the house. Was he simple taking the air, like a good bourgeois, or was he interrogating the stars, like an astronomer? The latter version was the most accredited.

"The old women of the Rue de l'Hirondelle and the neighboring streets had no hesitation in saying that the procurator, whose name was Maître Dumas—I forgot to tell you that—entertained a clandestine commerce with Hell. That belief was based on strange events.

"The son of the procurator—who was, it was said, fabulously rich, so relentlessly had he pressured, racked and ravaged unfortunate litigants—had a whim to get married. He was already old, rather ugly, even a trifle hunchbacked, and walked with a limp. In spite of his meager advantages, he thought it ought not to be difficult. His father gave him a large bag full of gold and he set forth in search of a woman. He found one: a widow, quite passable, very devout and without a sou or property.

"The marriage took place at the Église Saint-Germain-l'Auxerrois. Maître Dumas did not appear—prevented by gout, it was said.

"The widow had lodgings in the Rue des Lions-Saint-Sauveur, and it had been agreed that, when the wedding feast was concluded, the husband would go to live in the wife's house.

"Thus far, as you see, nothing extraordinary.

"But scarcely had the crowd that escorted the newlyweds to the prosecutor's house, where the party was being held, begun to dissipate when the bride was heard to utter horrible screams, and she was seen to run out, terrified, saying that she had seen the Devil.

"Her husband tried in vain to retain her; she fled in fear to her lodgings, shut herself in and refused to come out again. The next day, the neighbors, not seeing her appear, had the idea of breaking down the door, and they found her hanged.

"Two years later," the King continued, who was getting a taste for his own story, "the same fantasy took possession of the daughter of the procurator, in spite of the tragic example of her brother, who had not dared to show himself in the streets since then.

"She was past fifty, and her face resembled a skimmer, so pock-marked was it, but amour comes at any age, as they say, and the old spinster had encountered an avid old soldier attracted by Maître Dumas' écus, and the marriage was decided.

162

"The mercenary went for eight nights in succession to the procurator's house to pay his court to the old spinster, and saw nothing very extraordinary. On the ninth night, however, the eve of the marriage, when he had just gone in, a noise was heard at the door. It was the clatter of iron horseshoes on the pavement of the street.

"At that sound, which died away at the door—proof that the mount was stopping—the procurator went pale, the son started to tremble, and the daughter hid her face in both hands.

"'It's the man with the mule,' said the procurator.

"The raised door-knocker fell back violently on to the striking-plate.

"'It's necessary to open up,' said the procurator

"'I'm not going to,' said the son.

"'Nor me,' said the daughter.

"The procurator did not budge from his seat, and the knocker resounded for the second time, but with even more violence.

"Seeing and hearing that, the old soldier, who had seen many others, got up, saying: 'I'll go open up, and even if it's the Devil, I'll confront him.'

"At those words, the daughter and the son made the sign of the cross, and the procurator started laughing like a damned soul."

Having arrived at that point in his story, the King looked at his audience with a cheerful expression.

"Well, Messieurs," he said, "what do you think of that beginning?"

"Sire," replied the Maréchal d'H***, "we could believe that we were hearing the reading of a veritable romance."

"It is one, in fact," said the King. "You'll see."

And he continued: "So, the mercenary opened the door. The night was black and there was not a single light in the Rue de l'Hirondelle. Nevertheless, the mercenary saw a man of tall stature, holding by the bridle an almost gigantic mount.

"In a hoarse voice, which made the mercenary shudder, the man said: 'Is Maître Dumas at home?'

"'Yes,' replied the mercenary.

The unknown man hitched his mount to an iron ring fixed in the wall next to the door, and then he came in.

"As he was enveloped in a large cloak and his hat was pulled down over his eyes, the soldier saw nothing at first, and stood aside to let him enter. Then the man opened his cloak and took off his hat. Suddenly, the mercenary was struck in the face by two jets of flame that emerged from the eyes of the stranger, at the same time as they illuminated his visage.

"That visage was hideous. A gaping wound extended across the whole breadth of the forehead, from ear to ear, and the nose appeared to be eaten away by a cancer.

"The mercenary was brave, and had proved it in many a battle; nevertheless, he was afraid—so frightened, in fact, that his legs buckled under him, his heart beat faster, his eyes closed and he collapsed heavily against the wall of the narrow corridor. He had just fainted, like a woman.

"What happened then? How long did that faint last? The mercenary never knew.

"When he came round, reanimated by the cold night air coming into the corridor through the door, which was still open, he got to his feet unsteadily and headed, with the tread of a drunken man, for the low room in which he had left Maître Dumas and his children when he had got up to go and answer the door.

"Maître Dumas was no longer there. The son was lying full length on the floor, giving no sign of life. As for the daughter, the mercenary's fiancée, she was on her knees, praying.

"The mercenary tried to talk to her, put she pushed him away and gave him a sign to kneel down like her.

"Then our man tried to reanimate Maître Dumas' son, but could not succeed. A coarse oath escaped him, and he fled like a devil that someone has tried to steep in a font.

"When he got out of the door, curiosity triumphed over his fear. He approached the unknown man's mount. It was a mule: a superb mule, plumed and harnessed like that of a Spanish canon, with little bells around the neck-strap of the bridle.

"Suddenly, the mercenary shivered.

"It seemed to him that a blue flame ran over the mule's rump. That flame illuminated a large and gaping, bloody wound that extended along the left flank, descended as far as the teats and allowed a glimpse of the intestines, which looked ready to slide out. A few drops of blood were falling, one by one, on to the pavement of the street.

"The mercenary recoiled at first, then made an effort to collect himself, drew nearer, and put his hand on that strange wound. But suddenly, he uttered a terrible scream and withdrew it sharply, reddened and reeking of burning. The blood appeared to be molten lead, and the pain that the mercenary felt was so intense that he fainted again and fell down in the middle of the street.

"He was extracted from that second faint by the sound of the door closing again, and that of the mule's hooves, striking sparks from the pavement.

"The man with the gaping wound had just emerged from the house, had climbed back into the saddle, and was tranquilly drawing away.

"The mercenary got to his feet. 'Mordioux!' he cried—for he was a Gascon—'I'll have the key to this enigma.' And, drawing his sword, he set off after the mule. The mule was trotting and the mercenary was running. He was a good runner, but the mule was already thirty paces ahead of him.

"It went out of the Rue de l'Hirondelle into the Rue Saint-André-des-Arts, reached the river's edge, passed over the Petit-Pont, traversed the Cité, then the Pont-au-Change, and arrived in the Place du Châtelet.

"The mercenary was running out of breath, but the mule, which was traveling at its ordinary pace, was still thirty or forty paces ahead of him. In the Place du Châtelet, the rider stopped ad turned round in the saddle, and the mercenary received full in the face the two jets of flame that had already dazzled him in Maître Dumas' corridor—which caused him to stop in a similar fashion and stagger again, as if he had been hit by two bullets.

"Then the mule set off again.

"The mercenary summoned up all his energy and started running again.

"The mule plunged into a labyrinth of narrow and black side-streets, which radiated all around the cemetery of the Innocents. The mercenary ran after it.

"When it reached the gate of the cemetery, the mule stopped again. 'Ah, bandit!' shouted the mercenary, brandishing his sword, 'I'll catch you in the end.'

165

"For a second time the rider with the gaping wound turned round, and the flames of his eyes burned the mercenary's face again. The latter was obliged to sit down on a boundary-marker, for his strength was exhausted.

"Then the mule went tranquilly into the cemetery, and the mount and its rider suddenly disappeared. One might have thought that the earth had opened up and closed over them.

"The mercenary was so weak that he had neither the will not the force to get up. He stayed there until the first glimmers of dawn, prey to fever and frissons. When daylight appeared, he saw a tavern whose doors were open, a short distance away. Recovering his strength, he went in and asked for something to drink.

"The tavern-keeper, astonished by his pallor, questioned him, but to no avail. The mercenary did not want to say anything. When he had been restored by two or three glasses of wine, however, he left the tavern and headed resolutely toward the cemetery.

"The mule's hoofprints were visible in the soil. The mercenary followed the tracks through the middle of the tombs, and he noticed the singular fact that they always kept a respectful distance from the crosses that stood on mounds here and there.

"Suddenly, the tracks stopped. At the place where the mercenary found the last imprint, the earth seemed to have been freshly moved. It was doubtless there that the mule and its rider had been abruptly swallowed up.

"Frightened, the old soldier left the cemetery—but he did not return to Maître Dumas' house; he went to spend the rest of the day in the tavern where he had had a drink in the morning, recounted his nocturnal adventure, and left that same evening to rejoin his company, which was about to go to campaign.

"He was not seen again thereafter."

The king stopped momentarily to draw breath. You could have heard a fly buzzing in the royal bedchamber, so much had the story impressed the listeners.

"Sire," said the Maréchal, "that's a story that would render Monsieur de Voltaire himself credulous."

"Wait a while," replied Louis XV. "I haven't finished."

And the King continued:

"Those two stories would have been sufficient to establish the belief that Maître Dumas entertained relations with the Devil, but the mercenary was not the only one to have seen the mule with the bloody flank and the rider with the gaping wound.

"Four or five times a year, the people of the Rue de l'Hirondelle were witnesses to that spectacle. The man arrived, hitched his mule, went into the house, and spent several hours there—after which he went away again, and no one knew where he went.

"A shopkeeper, a druggist, bolder than the others—for all doors were closed when the mule's hoof-beats were heard—had the audacity one day to approach the strange animal.

"The mule launched a kick at him that cracked his skull.

"The druggist's death put the quarter in uproar. A complaint was made to the chevalier of the watch. The latter established a sergeants' post in the street. The sergeant remained in watch for forty-five nights in succession. The man with the mule did not come.

"On the forty-sixth night, as it was summer and the heat was stifling, then sent for wine and started drinking. An hour later, they were all asleep. That night, the man with the mule came back. A panic terror took possession of the entre quarter.

"The alarmed people were talking about nothing less than setting fire to the old procurator's house, and the chevalier of the watch had been obliged to send two sergeants to protect him, when a new event, even more bizarre than the others, occurred.

"Until then, the rider with the gaping wound had not come by night.

"One day, in broad daylight, he was seen to turn into the street, advance at his tranquil pace to the procurator's house, dismount and lift the door-knocker. As he did not take off his hat, the frightened inhabitants of the street could not see whether he still had the wound on his forehead—but the mule appeared to have healed, and in the place of the wound, white hair had grown, which contrasted with the rest of its coat, which was bay brown.

"However, while the rider was in the house, no one dared approach the mule. The latter was stamping its foot impatiently, and scratching the ground, seemingly in a hurry to leave.

"Several hours went by.

"Finally, the rider reappeared. He was carrying a sort of valise under his arm, which he threw over his saddle-bow, and which rendered a metallic sound. After which, he leapt into the saddle and departed, not at a trot but at a gallop, in such a fashion that no one could follow him.

"Some said that he had taken away all the procurator's money; other claimed that it was his soul that the valise contained, and that if the valise was so heavy, it was because the soul was laden with sins and crimes."

III

The King stopped again. A visible satisfaction was painted on his face, so glad was he of the success of his narration.

"Well, Maréchal," he said, "what do you think happened next?"

"In truth, Sire," replied the Maréchal, "I'm incapable of guessing."

"Then I'll tell you."

And the King went on: "Several hours went by. At the end of that time, the procurator's son was seen to emerge from the house and knock on a neighboring door. He seemed very emotional, and his legs were buckling beneath him, while a nervous tremor appeared to have taken possession of his entire body.

"The door at which he had just knocked was that of a neighbor, a woman, who was perhaps the only person in the quarter who was on good terms with the procurator and his family. A former market-trader, she was tall and still robust, in spite of her seventy years.

"She was proud of being string-minded, and had always shrugged her shoulders when anyone had said to her that the procurator had relations with the Devil, who was none other than the man with the mule.

"'Lord God!' she exclaimed, on seeing the procurators son enter in that state. 'What's the matter?'

"'Come...come...,' the fellow replied. The market-trader followed him.

"When she was in the house she saw the daughter on her knees, praying devoutly, with her eyes full of tears.

"'But what's happened, then?' she asked, again.

"'I believe that my father is dead,' said the son.

"'Your father?'

"'Yes.'

"'Where is he, then?'

"'Upstairs.'

"And he went upstairs. Now, it's necessary to tell you that there was indeed, at the very top of the house, a redoubt into which the procurator's children had never penetrated, where the procurator had the custom of shutting himself away for hours on end.

"'Oh! Your father is up there?' said the market-trader.

"'Yes.'

"'And he hasn't come down?'

"The son shook his head.

"'Well, it's necessary to call him.' And, making a loudhailer with her hands, she shouted: 'Hey! Maître Dumas!'

"Maître Dumas did not reply. Her son said, then: 'The man with the mule has just come.'

"'Ah!'

"'My father wasn't expecting him. When he realized, he cried: '*I'm doomed!*'

"The procurator's son went on: 'The man came in, and my father, making a violent effort, went up to the top of the house with him. They shut themselves in, and several hours went by.'

"'And then?' said the market-trader.

"'The man came back down. He laughed as he went past me. "Don't disturb your father," he said, "he's very busy up there." And he left, taking I know not what with him under his arm. Then my sister and I were frightened, and we went to knock on the door.'

"'And your father didn't reply?'

"'No.'

"'Perhaps it's because he's ill,' said the market trader. 'Let's go see.'

"And she went upstairs at a deliberate pace. When she reached the door of the redoubt, she knocked, as the procurator's son had knocked, but obtained no more response than he had.

"She had the idea of looking through the keyhole. Then she saw Maître Dumas, as white as snow, his eyes extinct, but alive, sitting in a large armchair at a table laden with alembics, retorts and books of alchemy.

"The market-trader was vigorous, as I told you. With a thrust of her shoulder she broke down the door.

"Then Maître Dumas breathed in noisily, as if the air that had suddenly reached him had rendered him a life that was ebbing away. The neighbor picked him up in her arms and carried him downstairs. She took him back down to the room on the ground floor that I have already mentioned, installed him in front of a good fire and started massaging his entire body.

"The procurator recovered the use of his tongue and shook his head. 'You're cares are futile, my children,' he said. 'I'm a dead man.'

"From that day on, in fact, the procurator, who was already very thin, began to diminish in a frightful fashion. One might have thought that he was melting away. Meanwhile, he ate and drank as usual, but he no longer spoke, and his children, desolate, tried in vain to get a word out of him.

"Finally, one day, he asked by means of signs to be taken back to the mysterious room where he had received the man with the mule for the last time. His children obeyed him and took him up, supporting him bodily. When he was there, he recovered a little strength. He closed the door, locked it, and remained there alone.

"The evening passed, and then the night. The children, frightened, had recourse to the neighbor again.

"The latter went back up with them and, like the first time, she looked through the keyhole again. She could see the armchair, but not the procurator. The armchair was empty. She called out to Maître Dumas. There was no reply.

"Then, having consulted the children with her gaze, the good woman broke the door down again. Surprise! The procurator was no longer in the redoubt. There was only the table laden with books and the instruments of alchemy in the middle of the room.

"This time, the market-trader was afraid, and began crying out. Other neighbors arrived, and then the police, who were alerted in all haste. The house was searched from top to bottom, but the procurator was not found.

"Finally," the King concluded, "that mysterious event made so much noise that it reached all the way to the ears of the Regent. The Regent ordered a further investigation, which produced no result."

"What!" said the Maréchal. "They were never able to discover the truth."

"Never."

"And Your Majesty..."

"My Majesty," said the King, laughing, "was no further forward than anyone else. I was fifteen years-old then, and I was only King in name. I promised myself, as you have seen just now, that when I was the master, I would discover the truth."

"Your Majesty has been the master for a long time," said the Maréchal d'H***."

"Yes," said the King, "but I've had other concerns, and that entire story slipped my memory—and it required, to bring it back, my finding that piece of paper."

"But it was thirty years ago," said the Maréchal.

"At least."

"And it will be very difficult..."

"Perhaps the house has been demolished," said another courtier.

"That's possible."

"And perhaps all the witnesses to the adventure are dead."

"That's probable."

"Your Majesty would therefore be wise," said the Maréchal, to put that piece of paper back in the drawer, or throw it in the fire."

"Certainly not," said the King. The King had pronounced those two words in a tone that denoted a firm determination. "Since I've remembered all that," he said, "I want to go on to the end." And, as they looked at him, he said: "Which of you, Messieurs, remembers a fellow who made some noise at Versailles and found me a girl whom a certain page had abducted on his own account?"

"Your Majesty," said one of the courtiers, "might be referring to a certain Porion?"

"Exactly."

"I know him," said the Maréchal.

"Aha!"

"Porion has lost the good graces of Monsieur de Sartine, Sire."

"That might well be the case."

"The Lieutenant de Police has even persecuted him somewhat."

"Really?"

"The fellow has left the police, but, as one does not renounce that métier easily, he continues to follow it as an amateur."

"How?"

"Madame de Pompadour has taken him into her service."

"And what service can he render *her*?" asked the King, emphasizing the word.

"He keeps her informed of a host of things."

"Really!" And the King started laughing. Then, after a pause, he said: "The man is at Versailles, then?"

"I believe so, Sire."

"Have him brought to me."

"He will be present at Your Majesty's *petit lever* tomorrow," said the Maréchal, hastily.

"It's not tomorrow, but tonight that I want to see him." And the King, seeing that the astonishment of his entourage was increasing, added: "Tomorrow, I'm capable of no longer giving it a thought. What time is it, Messieurs?"

"Midnight, Sire."

"Well, Maréchal, go to the Marquise's apartments. If she's in bed, wake her up."

"Yes, Sire."

"And tell her I have need of Porion."

The Maréchal departed at a run.

Half an hour later, he returned, and Porion, whom he had found drinking in a tavern a short distance from the château, was with him.

The King then started to tell him the story of the procurator Dumas.

Porion started to smile. "I know it, Sire," he said.

"Ah! Do you know what became of the procurator?"

"No."

"It's necessary to find out."

"I shall find out, Sire."

"When?"

"I'll go to Paris tonight, but..."

"But what?"

"I'll need an order from Your Majesty."

"For whom?"

"For Monsieur le Lieutenant de Police."

"You'll have it," said the King. And he dictated a letter to the Maréchal for Monsieur de Sartine, and placed his seal upon it.

"Now, Messieurs," said Louis XV, "I'll go to bed, and I believe I'll sleep well. I've told you—I'm thirty years younger. Bonsoir!"

IV

An hour later, Porion, alias Père Cinnamon, was on the road to Paris. He had taken an old hired carriage and promised the coachman a good tip if he went at top speed. So the vehicle was flying along the road, which was rather poorly maintained, shaking Porion's entrails and sometimes drawing a cry of pain from him.

In an hour and a half, he reached Paris. A quarter of an hour later he arrived at the door of Monsieur de Sartine, who was even more firmly ensconced as Lieutenant de Police.

The young magistrate had nocturnal work habits that were in harmony with his redoubtable functions. It is good that the police are alert while Paris sleeps.

The Lieutenant de Police had spent the evening at a ball, at the home of a pretty magistrate's wife, who did her best to console herself for not being at Court, and he had got home shortly after midnight. As was his custom, Monsieur de Sartine had taken off his formal attire, but in a dressing gown and gone into his study, where a large fire was lit every night, and had started work.

It was the hour when certain of his agents, who were waiting patiently in a nearby room for their chief to return, came to make their reports, one after another. The Lieutenant allowed his door to open and close, continuing to work, only raising his eyes when the agent reached his desk, in the circle of light described by his work-lamp.

That night, there was no one in the Lieutenant's antechamber when Porion arrived. The old fellow knew all the personnel of the household so well that he had come in without anyone paying attention to him. Finding himself alone, he knocked twice, discreetly, on the study door.

"Come in!" said Sartine's voice.

Porion went in without the Lieutenant raising his head.

The former agent, who was a physiognomist, could see that Sartine's expression was troubled, and said to himself: *Perhaps I won't be as poorly received as I thought.*

On hearing Porion coming forward, Sartine removed his gaze from the papers in front of him in order to direct it at the newcomer.

"Porion!" he exclaimed.

"In person, Monsieur."

"Scoundrel!" said the Lieutenant, frowning. "Do you dare to appear before me?"

"In truth, Monseigneur," said Porion resolutely, "I am sufficiently aware that my presence is disagreeable to you not to be here of my own choice, believe me."

"What do you want, then, wretch?"

"The King has sent me."

"The King?" said Sartine, and made a gesture of impatience.

"What do you expect, Monseigneur?" continued Porion, in a mocking tone. "The King has a different opinion of my person, my feeble talents and my merits, than Your Lordship."

"The King in, in truth, very benevolent," sniggered the Lieutenant de Police.

"I don't deny it, but that is the way it is, Monseigneur, and it's necessary to play your part."

"Well, what does the King want?"

"The King summoned me tonight."

"So?"

"And he confided a mission to me to which he attaches a great importance."

"Oh, really?"

"The King is even convinced," Porion continued, "that Monsieur le Lieutenant de Police could not carry it out as well as me."

"Insolent!" said Sartine. And he reached for his cane in order to lift it against Père Cinnamon.

"Monseigneur," said the latter, coldly. "Will Your Lordship please deign to take cognizance of his order."

And he placed before Monsieur de Sartine's eyes the following script, to which the King had put his signature and his seal:

Order to Monsieur le Lieutenant de Police to furnish Monsieur Porion with the money and men he might need in order to complete the mission I have given him.

Louis.

Monsieur de Sartine inclined, and then looked at Porion. "What is your mission?" he asked.

"That's the King's secret."

"But, scoundrel," said Sartine, with a movement of anger, "you're permitting yourself, I believe, to poach on my preserves."

"Monseigneur," said Porion, coldly, "you have sacked me; I'm earning my living as I can."

"And what if I took you back into my service?"

Porion smiled thinly. "It's a little late, Monseigneur," he said.

Sartine shrugged his shoulder. "My dear Porion," he said, suddenly softening, "you ought to know the King better."

"If you please?"

"The King will give you a hundred louis when you've satisfied his caprice, and won't give you another thought the day after."

"Perhaps."

"But if I take you on again myself..."

Porion looked at the Lieutenant de Police mistrustfully, and did not reply.

Monsieur de Sartine divined the meaning of that gaze. "If I extend my hand to you," he said, "would you believe me?"

"Perhaps...but..."

"But what?"

"I want to make conditions."

"All right. Speak."

"You see, Monseigneur," Père Cinnamon continued, "I'll tell you what you think, and what I'm worth, which is absolutely the same thing. Of all your agents, there isn't one who's worthy to tie my shoelaces, and that's your opinion."

"I agree," said Sartine, frankly.

"In the six months since you've dismissed me, the police, who ought to know everything, no longer know anything."

Monsieur de Sartine did not protest.

"Personally," Porion went on, "I'm living tranquilly in Versailles on the small pension that Madame de Pompadour gives me, but I know everything that's happening in Paris."

"Oh, really?" said Sartine dubiously.

"With your permission, I can bring you up to date," said Porion.

"Go on—I'm listening."

"Your Lordship doesn't always know which way to look," Père Cinnamon continued.

"And?"

"First of all, the disappearances of children are continuing..."

"Ah!"

"Baths in blood are more fashionable than ever."

Sartine shrugged his shoulders. "You're mad," he said. "It's true that the Tartar had a few children abducted from the Rue des Enfants-Rouges..."

"That's ancient history."

"But the Tartar has gone and we have no news of him."

Porion winked. "If Your Lordship won't put his cards on the table, we'll never reach an understanding."

"Speak, then."

"Your Lordship knows full well," Porion continued, "that there's another seigneur in Paris, far more powerful than the Tartar, who is treating himself by means of the same system."

Sartine paled slightly. "Shut up," he said.

"If I shut up, Monseigneur, we'll never reach an understanding."

The Lieutenant de Police curbed his head.

Porion went on: "Monsieur le Comte d'Auvergne, the king's cousin, a Prince of the Blood, takes a bath in human blood every morning.[24] The people are murmuring increasingly, but the precautions that have been well taken thus far...and nothing has reached the King..." Porion bowed. "In that regard, I must agree that Your Lordship has deployed great skill."

"Let pass on," said Sartine.

"A young provincial gentleman," Porion continued, "named Hector de Pierrefeu, arrived in Paris six or even months ago..."

"Oh, you know that too?"

"I know everything, Monseigneur."

"Continue."

"A young gentleman," I said, "has seen his brother abducted, who perished by order of the Tartar, and he only escaped an identical fate himself by fleeing. He has come to request justice of the King, but thus far, he has been unable to reach Versailles. Sooner or later, however, he will succeed."

"You think so?"

"Yes, for he has a protector."

Sartine shuddered, and demanded, sharply: "Who is it?"

"That's what I'll tell you tomorrow, because today, I don't know."

"Ah!" said Sartine.

"As that is no longer my concern, I'm not unduly occupied with it," said Porion, negligently.

"But you'll occupy yourself with it now?"

"If we succeed in reaching an understanding."

"I've told you: state your conditions."

"Not yet."

"Why?"

"Because it's necessary to tell you what I can do first."

"Go on."

"When the King suffers from ennui, he's capable of doing anything to distract himself," said Porion.

"That's true."

"If someone proposed to him to make Monsieur le Comte d'Auvergne appear before Parliament, he might accept."

Sartine jumped in his seat.

"The trial," said Porion, "might amuse him."

"Shut up."

---

[24] This reference is curious; the title of Comte d'Auvergne had lapsed during the previous century and no Prince of the Blood was awarded it. The Comte de Clermont had, however, notoriously been the lover of the wife of a member of a cadet branch of the family, who employed the surname de La Tour d'Auvergne, several of whom were at Louis XV's court.

"It's necessary, however, to amuse the King."

"That's difficult."

"I've found the means—or rather, the King has found it himself."

"Ah!"

And Porion told Monsieur de Sartine, in detail, the old story of the procurator Dumas and the whim the King had to know what had become of the old sorcerer.

"But all that's absurd!" said Sartine.

"Agreed."

"The house might have been demolished?"

"No."

"Al the people are dead..."

"We'll resuscitate them."

"What?"

"I have a little plan, Monseigneur."

"Let's have it!"

Porion, weary of standing up, sat down casually, and Sartine did not get annoyed by that lack of propriety, so pressed was he to have the old man's secret.

"Monseigneur," Porion went on, "there was a man at court two years ago who amused the King greatly."

"Who's that?"

"An adventurer who called himself the Comte de Saint-Germain and claimed to be several centuries old."[25]

"So what?"

"I desire to find a new Comte de Saint-Germain."

"To do what?"

"To amuse the King and deflect the storm that is gathering over the head of the Comte d'Auvergne."

"But..."

"If Your Lordship promises me a thousand écus a month and a pension of ten thousand livres for my old age. I'll explain."

"Granted," said Monsieur de Sartine.

---

[25] The adventurer who called himself the Comte de Saint-Germain first appeared in the French Court in 1748 and was entrusted with a diplomatic mission by Louis XV in 1749. He surfaced again in 1760, apparently operating as an agent of the Duc de Belle-Isle, a jealous rival of the foreign minister, the Duc de Choiseul, and a notorious schemer. Giacomo Casanova, who similarly posed as a sorcerer and also claimed to have functioned as a dubious diplomat, claimed to have met "Saint-Germain" several times, initially in 1757, although he naturally dismissed him as a charlatan; much of what is "known" about him comes from Casanova's mostly-fictitious memoirs.

Sartine and Porion remained in conference all night, and no one knew what passed between them—except that, at daybreak, Père Cinnamon, older, more broken-down and more amiable than ever, went away murmuring:

"I've waited a long time for fortune, but I believe it's finally knocking on my door."

V

The next day, the King had scarcely opened his eyes, and Monsieur de Chamillac had the honor of putting on his chemise, when a page came in and said that Monsieur Porion, whom His Majesty had charged the previous evening with an important mission, was soliciting the favor of being received in order to render an account of that mission.

"Send him in!" said the King, swiftly.

Porion was introduced. He had the proudly modest air of a man who has succeeded.

"Well?" said the King.

"Sire," Porion replied, "I have things so mysterious and so confidential to tell Your Majesty that I beg him to send away the people surrounding him."

"But all these Messieurs were assisting at my bedtime yesterday," said the King.

Porion bowed.

"They all know the beginning of the story."

"Agreed, Sire."

"And it would be agreeable or us to inform them of the end."

"It's just," said Porion, "that it isn't the end of the story that I'm bringing Your Majesty."

"Ah!"

"It's one chapter more, that's all."

"But the denouement?"

"I can only guarantee that to Your Majesty if I have the honor of telling him in the utmost privacy."

"You heard him, Messieurs," said the King, smiling. And with a gesture, he sent all those surrounding him away.

Then Porion, left alone with the King, said: "I've discovered the procurator, Sire."

"You mean his house?"

"No, Sire."

"Or his son?"

"His son and daughter have been dead for a long time."

"All the more reason why he must be dead himself, given that he'd be at least a hundred and twenty years old."

"A hundred and twenty-five, Sire."

"Are you making fun of me, scoundrel?"

"No, Sire. What I'm saying is the exact truth, and I beg Your Majesty, who cannot accompany me, to give me one of the men in whom he has the greatest confidence."

"To do what?"

"To come with come to Paris and see the procurator Dumas with his own eyes."

"A man a hundred and twenty-five years old?"

"Who appears to be scarcely thirty, Sire."

The King shrugged his shoulders, but Porion was undeterred and continued: "But Dumas was an alchemist."

"All right!"

"He has found the elixir of long life."

"What a joke!"

"Your Majesty cannot, however, have forgotten the Comte de Saint-Germain."

"No, certainly not—he was a fine charlatan."

"He boasted of having lived a dozen lifetimes already," Porion continued, "and he was telling the truth."

"Oh!"

"I'm convinced of that, Sire, since I've seen the procurator Dumas."

The King started to laugh. "What connection can there be," he said, "between the Comte de Saint-Germain and the procurator Dumas?"

"The knowledge of the same secret."

"What?" And the King looked at Porion with more astonishment than skepticism.

"Sire," the police agent said, "the Comte de Saint-Germain has found the means of living several existences."

"He said so, at least."

"The procurator Dumas has found the same means."

"Ta ta ta!" said the King. "Let's understand one another, fellow!"

Porion waited.

"You say that the procurator isn't dead?"

"Yes, Sire."

"But that if people old enough to have known him could be found, they wouldn't recognize him?"

"That's true."

"Then," said Louis XV, "either you're a rogue or you're making fun of me."

Porion raised his eyes and hands to the heavens.

"Or you're an imbecile, the victim of a schemer."

"That's what I thought at first, Sire, but..."

"But?" said the King.

"The man told me that there was a certain mark by which to assure his identity."

And that mark?"

"He can only show it to the King or to a man in whom the King has invested all his confidence."

"Word of honor," murmured Louis XV, "I no longer know whether I should laugh or get annoyed."

Porion did not blink.

"Where is this man?" the King demanded.

"In Paris."

"That's not an indication. Paris is so big!"

"Sire," said Porion, with imperturbable calm, "if Your Majesty will deign to listen to me..."

"Speak."

"Last night, furnished with the letter that Your Majesty had given me for Monsieur de Sartine, I went to Paris."

"So?"

"Instead of going to see Monsieur de Sartine, I went to the Rue de l'Hirondelle. I wanted to make sure first that the procurator's house was still standing."

"And it exists?"

"It was renovated after the death of the son, who was buried twelve years ago."

"And sold?"

"Yes, Sire, sold and bought."

"By whom?"

"By a merchant draper who calls himself Ulysse Carnot, who is none other than the procurator Dumas."

"This is too much," said the King.

"Sire," said Potion, "I'm a paltry individual whom Your Majesty can break by making a sign, and if Your Majesty doesn't believe me, I'm doomed."

The King said nothing.

"Your Majesty can throw me out, or, worse than that, have me whipped, or worse still, have me hanged."

"Continue."

"It is therefore, with that perspective that I have come here, determined in advance to tell the King everything, at the risk of being hanged high and low, as people used to say. So, if I dare to speak, it is because I'm convinced."

"As all that amuses me greatly," said the King, "you can continue."

Porion bowed. "So, as I told Your Majesty, I went to the Rue de l'Hirondelle."

"Yes. Well?"

"It was then after midnight, and the quarter was as silent as the tomb. No one in the street, no light at the windows...no, I'm mistaken; there was one...only one..."

"Ah!"

"Toward the middle of the street, behind the shutters of a ground-floor window. As I drew nearer, that window opened and a man who seemed young leaned toward me. 'Why, Monsieur Porion,' he said. 'You're out late.'

"You can imagine, Sire, that I was quite astonished to see a man that I didn't know, whom I had never even seen, addressing me by my name. I approached him, and my astonishment was redoubled when he said to me: 'Are you looking for the house of the procurator Dumas?'

"How could he have known that? I stammered a few words at hazard and he went on: 'The house for which you're looking is this one. The King, who sent you, will be convinced, like you, when you tell him that this house is said to be that of François I, for he knows full well that that's the one inhabited by the procurator.'"

"That's true!" the King interrupted. "I'd forgotten that detail."[26]

"The man went on: 'Even before you, for it's not two hours since the King summoned you, I knew that you were coming.'

"'Monsieur,' I said to him, 'I can see that you're making fun of me.'

"He started laughing. 'No, by God,' he replied. 'I knew that because I know everything: the past, the present and the future. I knew that the King would open a drawer, that he would find an old piece of paper that would remind him of events long forgotten, and that, finally, he would charge you with finding the key to the enigma regarding the mysterious disappearance of Maître Dumas, the old procurator.'

"I was amazed on listening to the man. 'And so,' he continued, 'I didn't want to go to bed, and I waited or you, for there's no one but me who can give you the information for which you're searching.'

"'Oh!' I exclaimed, completely bowled over by the man's audacity. 'You've been waiting for me?'

"'Yes.'

"'For a long time?'

"'Since I discovered that you were coming.'

"So saying, he closed the window and shouted through it: 'Wait there; I'm going to open the door for you.'

"And he did, in fact, open it for me two minutes later.

"I'm neither a coward nor superstitious, Sire, but I admit to Your Majesty that I hesitated before entering that house, so extraordinary did what I had heard seem to me. Then the unknown man said to me: 'If you don't trust me, go away and come back tomorrow after having obtained information. My name is Ulysse Carnot; I'm a merchant draper; I have a wife and three children and I count among the notable businessmen of the quarter.'

---

[26] The detail in question can be found in the Peuchet/Lamothe-Langon forgery.

"He had an honest and attractive face, seemed to be aged between thirty-five and forty, and his voice had a frank tone that testified in his favor. I was ashamed of my hesitation and I went in.

"He introduced me into a small room on the ground floor and said: 'This is where Maître Dumas usually sat.' And he offered me a chair.

"The lamp that he had placed on the mantelpiece illuminated the room, the simple and elegant furniture of which had nothing diabolical about it. 'When I moved in here," he said, 'I had the whole house renovated.'

"'I should think so,' I said.

"'Except for my observatory, which I left in its original state.'

"'Your…observatory?'

"'Yes.'

"'That's what you call it?'

"'The room situated at the top of the house, in which I received the man with the mule when he came to visit.'

"'Who?' I said, stupefied.

"'Ah!' he said to me, smiling, 'for a man of my age, I'm truly a little confused. I've forgotten to tell you that the procurator Dumas is me.'

"As you can imagine, Sire," said Porion, in a humble and naïve tone, "at first I took the man for a lunatic."

"Such is my opinion," said the King.

"But Your Majesty will think otherwise soon."

"Bah!"

"When I have told him what the man confided to me."

"Go on," said the King, increasingly amused by the absurd story.

And Porion continued.

VI

"The man's physiognomy had modified considerably since I had entered his house. His amiable manner had given way to a cold and arrogant expression, and there was a dark glint in his gaze.

"'My dear Monsieur Porion,' he said, 'the man with the mule, about whom you will think it good if I maintain a prudent silence, had given me the secret of not dying.'

"'It's as well that you possessed that secret,' I replied, in a mocking tone, 'if you really are Maître Dumas.'

"'I am.'

"'How old are you now?'

"'About a hundred and fifty years.'

"'Damn!'

"He was not annoyed by my incredulity, and went on: 'That secret consisted of an elixir contained in a little bottle. When I sensed death approaching, I had to rub myself all over my body with that liquid.'

"'And that's what you have done?'

"'Wait. The elixir was to procure me a sleep of ten or fifteen years, after which I would wake up at the age I wanted to be. I immediately chose the finest age of life, in my opinion, twenty years.'

"'You were right.'

"'So I shut myself up in my laboratory and I rubbed myself with the elixir of long life; but I was in such a hurry to be twenty years old that I forgot one of the parts of my body, the left leg.'

"'Ah!'

"'I therefore went to sleep, and when I woke up, people had been talking for fifteen years about the mysterious disappearance of procurator Dumas. I was twenty; I was young and rosy—except that my left leg, which had been deprived of the regenerative elixir, had remained that of an old man.'

"'Get away!'

"'You shall see,' he said.

"And he took off his shoes, unbuckled his garters, and first laid bare his right leg. That one was strong, vigorous and well-muscled, and young blood was circuiting in its veins.

"Then he lowered his left stocking, and I saw a false calf fall on to the floor. At the same time, I saw a frightful thin, fleshless tibia covered with yellow, wrinkled parchment. It really was the leg of an old man."

"Oh, scoundrel!" cried the King, finally interrupting Porion. "You're definitely making fun of me."

"Sire," replied Père Cinnamon, "Ulysse Carnot—which is to say, the man I firmly believe to be procurator Dumas, can show his leg either to Your Majesty or to any person the King designates, and then…"

"Continue," said the King. "It's a fanciful tale you're telling me, but it's amusing."

Porion went on: "When he had readjusted his stocking, the draper said to me: 'If that proof isn't sufficient for you, I can give another to the King.'

"'Ah! What's that?'

"'The King might have forgotten one important detail, which signaled my disappearance.'

"'What is it?'

"'When I was a procurator, I was charged with a very important case, on which the entire fortune of the Bois-Rosé family, which is a noble family of Saintonge, depended. I lost that case. I lost it because I had mislaid an important piece of evidence. After my death—which is to say, after my disappearance—the heirs of the Baron Bois-Rosé obtained permission to mount a search of my papers, but they did not find anything.'"

"Indeed," said the King, interrupting Porion for a second time, "I remember that perfectly. I also believe that ten years ago, the case was brought again, and the Bois-Rosés won."

"Thanks to the mislaid piece of evidence being found, Sire."

"How do you know that?"

"Because the man who says that he is procurator Dumas claims that the young Baron Bois-Rosé, who is no longer young today, and who must be over fifty, will prove to Your Majesty that the late procurator Dumas and Ulysse Carnot are one and the same."

"Oh! What!"

"'Monsieur Porion,' the man said to me, in conclusion, 'I have said all that I can tell you.'

"'Oh, pardon me,' I said, 'but you're forgetting one thing.'

"'What?'

"'That procurator Dumas, having gone up to his laboratory, disappeared.'

"'Certainly.'

"'And he would have been found rubbed with the elixir and sleep if what you say weren't pure invention.'

"My objection is not disconcert him. 'My dear Monsieur Porion,' he said, 'you can imagine that the man with the mule did not make me a gift of his secret.'

"'He sold it to you?'

"'And very dear, since the last time he came, he took away a large bag full of gold. But in addition, he imposed a certain condition on me…'

"'Ah! What?'

"'I swore him an oath, under pain of losing my life immediately, never to reveal during my new existence the place where my metamorphosis would be accomplished.'

"'You have an answer for everything,' I said, laughing. For I was intent on proving to him that I was not his dupe.

"He did not blink, and continued: 'It's unfortunate that Monsieur de Saint-Germain has left Paris.'

"'Why?'

"'Because he would have been able to tell you or the King what you desire to know.'

"'What do you mean?'

"'He would have been able to indicate to you in such a precise manner the place where I slept and awaited my second youth that it would have been impossible for you not to find it.'

"'That's possible,' I replied, 'but after all, Monsieur de Saint-Germain is no longer in Paris.'

"'Yes, but there's a man who is as knowledgeable as him regarding the mysteries of life indefinitely prolonged.'

"'Oh?'

"'That man can tell you everything that Monsieur Saint-Germain could have told you.'

"'And who is that man?' I asked.

"'He's a Tartar Prince.'

"'His name?'

"'Trespatky.'"

At that name, the King shivered. "The man with the skin disease?"

"Exactly. It's him that the supposed rejuvenated procurator meant. 'There's only one thing wrong with that,' I told him. 'The Tartar is no longer in Paris.'

"'That's true; he left Paris six months ago; but he'll return tomorrow morning.'

"'How do you know that?'

"'Haven't I told you that I know everything?'

"And, careless of my incredulous attitude, Ulysse Carnot added: 'Be at the Porte Saint-Antoine at seven o'clock in the morning. You'll see a carriage arrive, and in that carriage the prince, who is returning from Germany. That, my dear Monsieur Porion, is all that I can tell you; the Prince can explain the rest.'

"And with those words, he got up from his chair, like a great seigneur giving an audience, making it understood that the audience is concluded. I wanted to question him further, but an invincible and mysterious force pushed me toward the door.

"I found myself in the street without knowing how I had arrived there, and the door of the man who had been procurator Dumas had closed before I had recovered from my surprise."

The King looked at Porion again. "Do you know, fellow, that if ever I have proof that you're making a fool of me, I'll have you perish under the whip."

"Sire," said Porion, "I haven't finished."

"In truth?"

"It's necessary now that I talk to Your Majesty about the Tartar Prince."

"You've seen him, then?"

"Of course."

"Where and when?"

"I followed the draper's indications, and I went to the Porte Saint-Antoine."

"Good."

"At seven o'clock precisely, as day had barely broken, a cloud of dust rose up in the faubourg, and I saw a traveling coach appear drawn by four horses covered with little bells, which was making a deafening racket. Four lackeys on horseback preceded the carriage. For others followed it. That did not present Messieurs the tax-collectors stopping the carriage in order to see what was inside. Then a man emerged, speaking very loudly and in a tone that was somewhat harsh. It was the Prince."

"Really?" said the King. "And you weren't afraid?"

"Why would I have been afraid, Sire?"

"Because he's horrible to behold," said the King.

Porion smiled.

"Covered with a vile leprosy..."

"He is, on the contrary, a very handsome man, Sire, a very handsome youth, even, who has a very white skin."

"No skin disease?"

"No more than my hand."

"He's cured then?"

"Radically, Sire."

The King frowned. "So," he said, "all the reports I've been given are true."

"About the Prince?"

"I've been told that he was treating himself by taking baths in human blood."

Porion stated to laugh again. "Sire," he said, "in the epoch when that rumor ran around Paris, Monsieur de Sartine still employed me, and I was better informed than anyone with regard to the truth."

"Well?"

"Well, there isn't a word of truth in all that. The Prince has been cured thanks to the care of his physician, a Tartar like him."

"But children were disappearing?" said the King.

"That's true."

"What became of them?"

"That I don't know. All that I can tell Your Majesty is that disappearances of that sort were observed long after the prince's departure."

"But after all," said the King, "how can that man know what Monsieur Saint-Germain knew?"

"Ah, that, sire..." And Porion adopted a mysterious air. Then he darted a furtive glance at the clock. "I fear," he said, "that it's time for Your Majesty to confer with his Ministers..."

"My Ministers will wait," said the King.

Good, thought Porion. I'm becoming a person of importance. *For me, the Ministers will have to wait!*

And he waited for the King to ask him another question.

VIII

Louis XV remained pensive momentarily.

Then, looking at Porion, he said: "So you really believe," he said, "that the draper Ulysse Carnot is nothing but a new incarnation of the procurator Dumas?"

"I believe it firmly, Sire, after all that I've seen."

"And you've seen the Tartar cured?"

"Yes, Sire."

"I can't amuse myself," the King went on, "by bringing the draper here, until we've clarified this whole story. But I can summon the Tartar."

"That's impossible, Sire."

"Impossible!"

"The Tartar wouldn't come."

"Why?"

"Because he's a Russian subject."

"So?"

"And the French court is at odds with Czar Ivan."[27]

"Oh, that's true," said the King. "The Tartar has functions with regard to the Czar, then?"

"He's an Aide-de-Camp."

"Very well," said the King. "I'll send him Richelieu, then."

The King had scarcely pronounced hat name than someone knocked softly on the door and a page showing his alert face there, said: "Monseigneur le Maréchal de Richelieu is waiting to pay his court to the King."

"Talk of the Devil and he shows his tail," said the King, laughing. "Send the Maréchal in."

Richelieu appeared. On seeing Porion, he made a slight grimace. Porion reminded him of one of his misadventures. In fact, the police agent had done what he, Richelieu, had not been able to do; he had found the girl with whom the King had been infatuated a few months before. But as the King appeared to be in a good mood, which was rare, Richelieu thought he ought to be cheerful, and he returned Porion's bow.

"Maréchal," said the King, "do you remember the Tartar?"

"Certainly, yes, Sire. He returned to his own country to die of that horrible skin disease that covered his entire body."

"You're mistaken, Maréchal."

---

[27] Although Ivan VI (1740-1764), who had been nominally tsar of Russia as an infant in 1740-41, was still alive when the story is set, the actual ruler at the time was Empress Elizabeth Petrovna, who reigned from 1741-1762.

"He isn't dead?"

"He's marvelously well."

"With a skin disease?"

"With no skin disease, given that he's completely cured."

"If that's the case, Sire," said Richelieu, "I beg Your Majesty to make peace with the Czar and appoint me as ambassador to him, because until I can go to Saint Petersburg or Moscow to see the Tartar, it will be impossible for me to believe in his cure."

"My dear Maréchal," replied the King, "you won't need to go so far."

"Oh!" said Richelieu, astonished.

"The Tartar is in Paris."

"Since when?"

"Since this morning, and I'm going to give you a mission to visit him."

Amazed, Richelieu considered the King and Porion by turns, appearing to search for the key to an enigma.

"Master Porion," said the King, "tell the Maréchal the singular story that you've just told me."

And the King rang to request his chocolate, which was brought to him immediately on a small table that was placed before the fireplace.

While the King took his chocolate, Porion told Richelieu succinctly about his adventure with the draper in the Rue de l'Hirondelle, and what had followed it.

During the narrative, the Duc shrugged his shoulders more than once, but Porion was able to give his face such an expression of naivety and amiability than the most skeptical man in France and Navarre felt himself invaded by a sort of mysterious terror mingled with curiosity.

When Porion had finished, Richelieu turned to the King. "I await His Majesty's orders," he said.

"Where is the Tartar staying?" the King asked Porion.

"The Rue du Pas-du-Mule, Sire, in the vicinity of the Place Royale, in a house that belongs to Monsieur le Comte d'Auvergne."

"Well, Maréchal," said the King, "you're going to take Porion with you."

"Yes, Sire."

"You'll go to the draper's house."

"And I'll have him show me his leg?"

"Precisely. Afterwards, you'll go to see the Tartar on my behalf, and you'll tell him that if he really possesses the marvelous divinatory qualities of Monsieur de Saint-Germain, he will give me great personal pleasure by casting some light on this strange affair of the procurator Dumas."

Richelieu bowed.

"Go," said the King. "Hurry up, and come back as soon as possible."

Porion and the Maréchal went out.

After their departure, the King said to himself: *All this is very amusing. It's already noon and I haven't yawned once all morning. Richelieu has a grudge against Porion. If Porion's lying, Richelieu will unmask him. I couldn't find a better pairing.*

And with that reflection, the King swallowed his last gulp of chocolate.

The page reappeared. "Sire," he said, "Monsieur le Duc de Choiseul, Your Majesty's Prime Minister, solicits the favor of coming to work for an hour with the King.

This time, the King yawned, but he accepted his part in the work bravely. "Send Monsieur de Choiseul in," he said.

And Monsieur de Choiseul having come in, the King set to work conscientiously and courageously for two full hours. From time to time, however, Louis XV glanced at the clock, thinking: *It seems to me that Richelieu can't be much longer.*

Monsieur de Choiseul was not only a great minister, but also a courtier, full of wit. He knew that with the King, it was necessary not to abuse labor. At a given moment, he put all his papers back into his portfolio and said: "Sire, I have the honor of taking leave of Your Majesty." He did not, however, take single step backwards.

"Have you something to ask me, Duc?" said the King.

"Yes, Sire."

"A favor?"

"No, an act of justice."

"Speak," said the King.

"Sire," said Monsieur de Choiseul, "Your Majesty will remember that at the battle of Fontenay, he owed his life to a poor captain named..."

"The Comte de Pierrefeu, of course" said the King. "I believe so. A worthy gentleman, that poor Pierrefeu, who wasn't rich. I gave him a pension of a hundred louis. Has it not been paid precisely, by chance?"

"It is no longer being paid, Sire."

"And why is that, Monsieur?"

"Because Monsieur de Pierrefeu died several years ago, Sire, on his modest estate in Bourgogne."

"Oh, the poor man!" said the King. "He certainly saved my life at Fontenoy."

"The Comte is dead," Monsieur de Choiseul went on, "but he left two sons."

"It's necessary to send them to me, Duc, and I'll occupy myself with them."

"Sire," said Monsieur de Choiseul, "will Your Majesty permit me to abuse his leisure momentarily? What I have to say is rather complicated."

"Go on," said the King.

"Six months ago, Monsieur de Pierrefeu's two sons set out for Paris; the elder was twenty-five years old, the younger fourteen or fifteen, I believe. The elder was carrying a letter written by the old Comte on his deathbed addressed to Your Majesty. In that letter, he solicited an employment in the guard for his elder son, and a page's jacket for the younger. The two young men arrived in Paris toward evening and stayed in the Rue des Enfants-Rouges, at the Blue Dragon inn."

"And that was six months ago?"

"Yes, Sire. In the evening the younger went to bed; the elder was drawn into an amorous trap. From that moment on, the two brothers have not been seen."

"How is that, Duc?"

"Lured to a mysterious house, the elder was attacked by armed men who tried to kill him."

"A jealous husband, no doubt?"

"No, Sire."

"Thieves?"

"Not that either."

"Why, then did they want to kill him?"

"In order to bathe in his blood."

The King shivered.

"At the same hour," the Duc de Choiseul went on, "while young Hector de Pierrefeu was defending himself valiantly, and, pierced by sword-thrusts, succeeded in escaping his assassins..."

"Ah!" said the King, with a sigh of relief. "He's not dead, then?"

"No, Sire, he survived, but he was mad for several months. Will Your Majesty deign to let me finish?"

"Speak."

"At that moment," the Duc went on, "in the inn in the Rue des Enfants-Rouges, the younger brother's throat was cut, and a highly-placed person voluptuously took a bath in his blood."

"God!" cried the King. "What are you telling me? But it's true, then? In France, under my reign, baths have been taken in human blood?"

"Yes, Sire, and they still are..."

"But Monsieur de Sartine has sworn to me..."

"I don't know," said Monsieur de Choiseul, coldly, "what the Lieutenant de Police might have said to Your Majesty, but I beg the King to grant an audience this very day to Monsieur le Comte Hector de Pierrefeu, who can tell you better than I can frightful things, which cannot go unpunished."

"Duc," said the King, "justice will be done. Where is Monsieur de Pierrefeu?"

"In Paris."

"Send him to me; I'll receive him."

"He will be here at four o'clock, Sire."

"That's good," said the King. And he dismissed Monsieur de Choiseul,

Scarcely had the Prime Minister gone than Monsieur de Richelieu arrived.

"Sire," he said, "I have brought Your Majesty good news."

"Know, Maréchal," replied the King, "that after what Monsieur de Choiseul has just been telling me, I'm in dire need of distraction."

VIII

The King's last words intrigued Monsieur de Richelieu somewhat. He looked at Louis XV and appeared to be waiting for his gracious sovereign to explain.

But the King said, abruptly: "Come on, what's this good news?"

"I've seen the Tartar Prince."

"And?"

"He consents to be presented to Your Majesty."

"Ah! Truly!"

"But on condition that the interview will be secret, so fearful is he of displeasing his sovereign, the grim Czar."

"That's quite simple," said the King. "I'll receive him in the Marquise's apartments."

"I thought of that," said Richelieu.

"Ah!"

"So I've brought the Prince in my carriage."

"Where is he?"

"Downstairs in the courtyard. The blinds are lowered and no one can see him."

"'Well," said the King, "there's no reason why I shouldn't see the individual right away. I'll go warn the Marquise."

"There's no need, Sire."

"Why not?"

"Porion is with her. Your Majesty has only to go to Madame de Pompadour's apartment by way of the corridor to which he alone has the key. In five minutes, the Tartar Prince will be there."

And Richelieu took a step toward the door.

"One moment!" said the King.

The Maréchal stopped and waited.

"Have you seen the draper?"

"Yes, Sire."

"And his leg?"

"A genuine old man's leg," said the Maréchal.

"So you believe what he says?"

"Hmm!" said Richelieu. "I have that temptation, Sire, in spite of my skepticism."

"In truth?"

"And the Tartar Prince believes it completely."

"This Tartar Prince is definitely an adept of Monsieur de Saint-Germain, then?" said the King.

"Yes, Sire."

"He claims to have lived before?"

"Naturally."

"And his skin disease?"

"The skin disease has disappeared in the wreckage of his last existence."

"What! He has died and been resuscitated, then?"

"He says so, at least, Sire. In any case he's a very curious individual. Your Majesty will be delighted to have seen him."

"Very well," said the King. "I'll come."

Richelieu went out.

The King called for his pages, had a sprinkle of powder put on and a little carmine on his lips, adjusted the pleats of his ruff and opened a door at the back of the royal alcove.

That door, which was masked by a curtain, and to which the king alone had a key, led to a narrow and obscure corridor that ended in Madame de Pompadour's apartments. The King had followed the route so often that he went into the corridor without a light, reached a second door, and, having opened it, found himself on the threshold of is favorite's boudoir.

Four people were already there: Madame de Pompadour, the Tartar Prince, Richelieu and Porion. The last-named was standing respectfully by the door.

The eyes of the King alighted on the Tartar with an avid curiosity.

He was, in truth, an exceedingly handsome man, very tall, almost a colossus, but admirably proportioned, with beautiful hands on which rings of fabulous price were sparkling, and relatively small feet. His face displayed the typical features of the Caucasian race rather than the Tartar race. He had large blue eyes, admirable teeth, affine white skin, a broad forehead and magnificent dark chestnut hair, while his beard was almost red.

He was dressed with the elegance of a great Muscovite lord, and his blue fox pelisse with diamond clasps suited him marvelously. By the fashion in which he saluted the King and bowed before him, kissing his hand, one divined a man brought up in familiarity with sovereigns.

"Monsieur," the King said to him, "I'm very grateful to you for having come."

The Tartar Prince bowed again.

"Sit down, Monsieur."

The Prince sat down without saying a word.

"Monsieur," the King continued, "I've been told truly extraordinary things about you."

The Prince smiled. "And yet very easy to explain," he said.

"How is that, Monsieur?"

"Sire," said Prince Trespatky, "only living a hundred years is very little. If I'd limited myself to that modest figure, I'd have died a long time ago."

The King performed a veritable somersault on his chair. "What age do you claim to have, Monsieur?" he asked.

"Sire," the Tartar replied, "I made the first expedition to Sweden with Czar Ivan the Terrible."

"You're joking, Monsieur."

"It was in the year of grace 1545, and I was then twenty years-old. Let Your Majesty deign to count. I'm no less than two hundred and forty years-old."

"Bah!" said the King, "you look scarcely thirty."

"That," said the Tartar, without being disconcerted, "is because I have died and resuscitated seven times since then."

This time, the King, astounded, stood up.

"In truth," he said, "I believe I'm hearing Monsieur de Saint-Germain."

"He's one of my good friends," said the Tartar, coolly.

"Really?"

"We both came to France at the beginning of the reign of King Henri IV, Your Majesty's glorious ancestor."

And as the King looked by turns at the Marquise, Richelieu and Porion, who were mute, and seemed confounded, the Tartar went on:

"If Your Majesty would care to listen to what I shall have the honor of telling him, all of that which seems extraordinary now will seem to him as limped as the water of a rock-pool."

"To be sure, Monsieur," replied the King, "I haven't brought you here for any other reason than to listen to you. In consequence, speak."

The Tartar went on: "It was precisely during that expedition to Sweden undertaken by Czar Ivan the Terrible, which I mentioned just now to Your Majesty. On the eve of a bloody battle, seven of us found that we had gone astray in the mountains separating Sweden from Norway. Only three of the seven were Russian, including me. One of the other four was Portuguese, one German, the third French and the fourth Italian. The Czar had gathered under s flags adventurers of all nations, having said that his subjects needed to learn the art of war from foreigners.

"We were fatigued and dying of hunger, seeking a meal and shelter. Suddenly, a light shone through the gigantic pines of a centuries-old forest. It was a woodcutter's cabin. We approached. The door was closed. We knocked, but a cracked voice replied, telling us to be on our way. As Your Majesty, can imagine, the door was broken down by the thrust of a shoulder.

"Then we found ourselves in the presence of a little old man, so old that he had become diaphanous. We asked him for something to eat and drink. He replied that he had no bread, or eau-de-vie, or any beverage of any sort.

"We searched the house, but it was a waste of time. Then, furious, we resolved to hang the old man. But he threw himself on his knees and said to us: 'If you grant me mercy, I'll give you a secret that is worth more than all the treasures on earth.'

"'And what is this secret?' we demanded.

"'That of never dying,'" he replied.

"We started to laugh, as Your Majesty laughed just now, and one of us said: 'But since you possess that secret, you ought not to be afraid of us.'

"'Oh no,' he replied. 'If you give me a quarter of a hour's respite and give me time to rub myself with a certain oil that I've buried here at the foot of an old tree, you can hang me afterwards in all liberty. I'll no sooner be dead than I'll be resuscitated.'

"The curiosity that gripped us triumphed over our anger of starvelings. We consented to the old man's request and we went with him a hundred paces into the forest. He was armed with a spade, and stated digging a hole with it at the foot of a tree.

"After a short while, he disinterred an enormous earthenware jar that could have contained as much as a dozen bottles. It was so heavy that he couldn't carry it, and I took charge of it.

"We returned to the cabin

"Then the old man undressed and laid himself as naked as a rat. Then, having take the stopper out of the demijohn, he poured into a wooden saucer the equivalent of half a glass of a brown liquid, in which he then dipped a piece of wool. After which, with the wool steeped in the mysterious liquid, he rubbed himself over his entire body.

"When that was done, he looked at us, smiling, and said: 'Now you can hang me if you wish.'

"The most virtuous of us being unable to resist the temptation, we put a rope around the old man's neck and hanged him from the branch of a fir-tree a short distance from the cabin. Ten minutes later he was dead. Then we took him down and went to lie down next to a big fire we had lit, having decided to spend the night in the cabin and sleep with empty stomachs.

"For three or four hours the cadaver went cold. When day broke, it was frozen rigid. 'We ought to bury him,' said one of us.

"'Bah!' said another, 'perhaps the wolves are hungry; he'll make a good meal.' But suddenly, the cadaver agitated, uttered a sigh, extended his arms and then his legs, and came to his feet. At the same time his eyes opened and looked at us in an amiable manner.

"'You're very kind, my children,' the resuscitated dead man said to us. At the same time his white hair turned black, his emaciated limbs filled out visibly with flesh and his empty mouth was furnished with magnificent teeth. Suddenly, we had before us a man as young as us.

"'My good friends,' he said to us, again, 'you've kept your word, I'll keep mine, and give you each a little bottle of the elixir of long life.'"

"Monsieur!" exclaimed the King, interrupting the Tartar, "if I died, could you resuscitate me?"

"Of course," said Prince Trespatky, coolly.

"Go on," said the King.

IX

Prince Trespatky went on:

"I have had the honor of telling Your Majesty that we were seven, three Russians, a Frenchman, a German, an Italian and a Portuguese. The old man who had become young again gave us each a small phial containing the equivalent of approximately three glasses of his elixir. After which he said to us: 'Now you're going to drink and eat.'

"He took us to the foot of another fir-tree and started to dig with his spade, no longer with difficulty, as he had the previous day, but with all the strength and ardor of youth. Soon, he had uncovered a kind of hiding-place constructed of wood, which served him as a larder of provisions.

"When winter comes, Norwegian peasants bury their food stores, in order that they do not fall prey to the wild beasts that populate the forest, and against which they are defenseless. That hiding-place contained his bread, his salted meat and Holland's gin in abundance. We drank and ate avidly.

"Then the old man who had become young said to us: 'You're men, and I owe you some good advice.'

"'Speak,' we said.

"'I've made you a gift that no human power could have given you. I've given you the means to live for thousands of years, but if you aren't careful, that gift will be fatal for you.'

"'Why is that?' asked the Frenchman.

"'We live in a time of superstitions,' our host went on, 'in which the Devil plays a large role. That elixir, whose power you have just been able to appreciate, is not, however, his work. I am a scholar, an alchemist, and I have not made any pact with Hell. But if I boasted of having the secret of resuscitation, you can be sure that the priests and the doctors would not fail to cry sacrilege, to affirm that I am possessed by a demon and then burn me alive. Now, as they would not give me the leisure to rub myself with my elixir, I would be dead for good and all.'

"'That's probable,' I observed.

"'To want to do good to others is sometimes to do harm to oneself,' the resuscitated man went on. 'I therefore engage you to keep your secret to yourself and when, having grown old, you feel the need to rejuvenate, do not fail to change your country and your name; that is the way to avoid persecution and the pyre.'

"The advice of the former old man appeared wise to us, and when we quit him we made an oath to keep our secret religiously. That evening, we had rejoined the Muscovite army.

"The next day there was a murderous battle. The two Russians and I were killed..."

"Ah!" said the King.

"But only I was resuscitated."

"And the other two?"

"The other two had neglected to rub themselves with the precious liquid before the battle. Of the seven of us, only five remained. The German returned to his homeland and became a physician. He was a philanthropist; he made such benevolent use of his elixir to resuscitate others that he exhausted it to the last drop."

"Which meant that he died and was not resuscitated."

"As Your Majesty says. The other four, including me, were wiser, and kept the oath that we had sworn."

"And the other three are alive?"

"Yes, Sire. The Italian retired to Naples two hundred years ago and is in good health."

"What became of the Portuguese?"

"Your Majesty has admitted him to your intimacy; he is the Comte de Saint-Germain."

"And the Frenchman?"

"It is a good fifty years since I lost sight of him, but everything leads me to believe that he is Maître Dumas, the procurator."

"And in consequence, now the draper Ulysse Carnot?"

"Yes, Sire."

The King became pensive again, and neither the Tartar, nor Richelieu, nor Madame de Pompadour breathed a word.

As for Porion, he was still standing by the door, not budging any more than a statue.

Finally, the King raised his head. "Monsieur," he said, "your story is certainly clear, and I'm very tempted to believe it—but permit me to ask you a few questions."

"I am ready to reply to Your Majesty."

"The old man from whom you obtained the elixir resuscitated ten or twelve hours after his death?"

"Yes, Sire."

"And you?"

"Similarly."

"And your companions also?"

"Undoubtedly."

"Then explain to me why Maître Dumas took so long—fifteen years, I believe."

The Tartar smiled. "It was doubtless because he waited too long."

"What do you mean?"

"After eighty years, life is much more difficult to recall. Then again, it depends on the dose of the elixir. Finally..."

That Tartar stopped and adopted a mysterious expression.

"Finally?" said the King.

"Finally," replied the Tartar, "as it depends absolutely on us to prolong our deathly sleep..."

"Ah! That depends on you?"

"Yes, Sire. Perhaps Maître Dumas had his reasons for not reappearing immediately."

The Tartar awaited a further question from the King.

"What about the man with the mule?" said Louis XV, finally.

"Sire," the Tartar replied, "must I tell Your Majesty everything?"

"Yes, certainly."

"I believe that the man with the mule was an accomplice."

"What!"

"Maître Dumas had awakened the suspicions of the Jesuits, who were accusing him loudly of sorcery."

"All right."

"And he will doubtless have paid some poor devil who played that role, and amused the superstitious minds of good people, with the sole purpose of dying and resuscitating in peace."

"Ah! That's what you think, Monsieur?"

"Yes, Sire. I myself, last year, allowed an absurd rumor concerning me to be accredited in Paris."

The King shuddered. "What is that rumor, then?" he asked.

"I had a skin disease, as Your Majesty might have been told, which was mortal and gave me a horrible aspect. Hermann, my physician, had not hidden it from me that I was going to die."

"Ah!"

"He even determined the day and hour of my death."

"That's a skillful physician," the King observed.

"But Hermann did not know that I had the power to resuscitate, and when I said that I would cure myself, he shrugged his shoulders. As it entered into my plans for people to believe that I might be cured, I let the good Parisians talk."

"And what did the good Parisians say?" said the King.

"That I was having children abducted, Sire, and that I was bathing in their blood."

"In fact, Monsieur, that claim was made," said the King, fixing the Tartar with a severe gaze.

"It was made wrongly," said the Prince, coldly. "When, according to Hermann's advice, I had no more than a fortnight to live, I left for my lands in the Caucasus, where I arrived dying. On the last day, I had myself rubbed with my elixir. A few hours later, my skin disease having killed me, I resuscitated, full of life and health.

"That is my story, Sire, and, as you see," The Tartar concluded shamelessly, "it's quite simple."

"So be it," said the King, "but it does not cast any light on that of the procurator Dumas."

"What does Your Majesty desire to know?"

"The truth."

"If Your Majesty can have someone give me a pitcher full of water, I will be able to answer with regard to things of which I am ignorant for the moment, but which I can discover in a matter of seconds."

Madame de Pompadour stood up and passed into a dressing-room adjacent to the boudoir. She came back with a silver-plated ewer filled to the brim with water.

Then the Tartar took the vessel, placed it on a table and plunged both his hands into it.

For a few moments, he had his eyes fixed on the water, which gradually lost its natural color and became a tender pink, then a dark violet, and finally arrived at indigo blue.

The King was stupefied. The Tartar definitely enjoyed a supernatural power.

"Sire," the Prince said then, "the procurator Dumas is definitely the Frenchman that I mentioned to Your Majesty."

"Ah!"

"He did not want to resuscitate immediately, because he wanted to wait for his children to die."

"Very well—but where was his body for fifteen years?"

"In a subterrain beneath his house, where his procurator's smock and the phial, which only contains a few more drops of the elixir, can still be found."

"But how can that subterrain be reached?"

"By taking up a section of the parquet in what he calls his laboratory, in the center of the window and against the wall, a secret stairway can be found."

"Bah!"

"That stairway, hollowed out in the thickness of the wall, descends all the way to the subterrain."

The King turned to Richelieu. "Maréchal," he said, "you will go see that."

"Yes, Sire."

At that moment, someone knocked softly on the door and a page appeared. "Sire," he said, "a young gentleman, the bearer of a letter from Monsieur le Duc de Choiseul, is waiting in Your Majesty's antechamber."

The King frowned. "Oh, that's true," he said. It's four o'clock. Ask the young man to return tomorrow at my *petit lever*. Introduce him before anyone else."

"Yes, Sire."

"Who is the young man?" asked the Marquise.

"Comte Hector de Pierrefeu," replied the page.

At that name, Porion and the Tartar shuddered, and they exchanged a furtive glance, while the page left to carry out the King's orders.

"I believe we've had a narrow escape," murmured Porion, who was still standing in the shadows.

X

Let us now abandon the Château de Versailles, King Louis XV and the Tartar and take a step backwards, with the sole purpose of explaining how our poor friend Hector de Pierrefeu had found a protector in the most powerful man in France after the King.

We left our hero, six months before the events that we have just narrated, in the mansard where Cécile Robert had lodged, in which she had lived poorly and honestly on the fruit of her labor, with Firmin the surgeon for a neighbor, adored without knowing it by Messire Mardochée de Mardoche, the painter, who lived in the house opposite, on the other side of the street.

You will also remember that on seeing Robert Damiens again, Hector de Pierrefeu, whom Cécile and Firmin had cared for, but who had nor recovered his reason, had suddenly had a flash of lucidity. Memory had come back to him, one recognizing the man who had aided the duenna to snatch him away from his executioners.

The return of Cécile, dying and dishonored, had completed that scene of bleak despair.

What had happened since?

You can guess.

The news of the death of his young brother André, whose blood had served for the Tartar's bath, had plunged Hector de Pierrefeu back into grim madness. For three further months, the unfortunate had hovered between life and death once again.

Cécile, who had wanted to die at first, had become reattached to life on seeing Hector so close to the tomb. The poor dishonored child had forgotten her own despair in order to think of nothing other than the limitless despair of the man she loved.

Firmin, the devoted friend, had lavished his cares on Hector.

Robert, Cécile's father, had installed himself with them. Somber and taciturn, the man did not pronounce ten words a day. He read the Bible from morn till evening, and appeared to be living in an imaginary world himself. Sometimes, sinister words escaped him. "The justice of God is slow," he said, "but it arrives inexorably, sooner or later."

Alongside the poor madman, the dishonored girl and the poor physician whose dogged labor sustained all those miseries; alongside that somber and fatal man what had appealed to divine justice, another face had been grouped: that of Messire Mardochée de Mardoche.

At first, the unhappy painter had been inconsolable. "It's me," he often said, "who was the innocent cause of Cécile's abduction; it's me who served as that wretch Père Cinnamon's instrument." And twenty times a day, Mardochée raise his fist toward the heavens, saying: "Oh, if I ever find him again, he won't die by any other hand than mine!"

But Mardochée had run around searching Paris in all directions for several days. Père Cinnamon—he did not know him by any other name—had disappeared.

After a few weeks, Hector de Pierrefeu's fever had calmed, and when the fever was gone, reason returned.

One evening, the three young men and Cécile's father were talking in low voices. Cécile, who had resumed work, had gone to deliver her needlework. Robert Damiens talked about vengeance.

Firmin shook his head. "One doesn't take vengeance on the King," he said.

A wild gleam passed through the eyes of the former lackey. "Who knows?" he said.

Hector had been told about Cécile's misfortune, but Hector did not want to believe it. "No, no," he said. "The King has been served and deceived by wretches, but the King will do justice, as he will do justice to me."

"Oh!" sniggered Robert Damiens, "you believe in the King's justice?"

"Yes," said Hector who remembered at that moment that he was a gentleman. Addressing Firmin, he said: "When can I go out?"

"In a week."

"That's good," said Hector, in a resolute tone.

"Why, what are you going to do?" asked Mardochée.

"I'm going to find the King."

"Good."

"And reveal the truth to him."

"And?"

"And the King will repair the wrong he has done you, and will punish my brother's murderers."

Robert Damiens shrugged his shoulders and made no reply. But Mardochée shook his head. "One doesn't reach the King like that," he said.

"I shall reach him." Then a memory came to mind; he asked for his coat: the coast of coarse cloth that he was wearing on his arrival in Paris, and in which he had gone to the mysterious rendezvous in which he had nearly found death. The letter that his father, the old Comte de Pierrefeu, had addressed to the king on his deathbed was still in the pocket of that coat. "There," he said, showing it to those who were listening to him, "that will open all doors to me."

"I doubt it," murmured Mardochée.

The weeks went by, and Firmin declared that Hector, who had no longer been confined to bed for some time, could go out.

The day before, Mardochée had made two portraits in the Pomme Verte tavern and brought back two pistoles. He insisted that Hector take one of them.

Hector climbed into a hired carriage and went to Versailles. He presented himself successively at all the gates. Everywhere he found sentinels who sent him away, saying that the King did not grant audiences to just anyone. Finally, an officer appeared, took an interest in him and said to him: "My gentleman, you're from the provinces, I can see, and you don't know the usages of the court. Will you allow me to give you some advice?"

"Speak," said Hector.

"Do you want your letter to reach the King?"

"I haven't come here for any other reason," said Hector.

"Then listen to me. I'll take you across this courtyard."

"Good!"

"You see that door on the left?"

"Yes."

"It's the petition office."

"Ah!" said Hector.

"Go in; you'll find a very amiable old gentleman there, Monsieur de Pompionne, who is responsible for receiving everything addressed to the King."

"And I hand my letter to him?"

"Yes—and if he likes you, for his humor is very bizarre, I have no doubt that you'll obtain what you ask..."

"Thank you," said Hector.

Thanks to the service officer, he was able to come through the first gate. He therefore traversed the courtyard and arrived without hindrance at the petition office.

A lackey in the King's colors introduced him to the presence of Monsieur de Pompionne, one of the ordinary gentlemen of the bedchamber.

Monsieur de Pompionne was smiling, and in a good mood. There was a simple reason for that; an hour before, he had traversed the Orangery and had crossed the path of Madame de Pompadour, who had deigned to smile at him. He therefore received Hector very graciously, took charge of the letter, and promised him that he would have a response within three days.

Hector went away delighted, and returned to Paris.

But the hope he had in his heart was not shared by his friends. In vain the young man said that his father had saved the King's life at the battle of Fontenoy. Robert, Mardochée and Firmin shook their heads, saying: "The King won't receive the letter."

The three days went by, and then three more. No message reached Hector. Then the young man returned to Versailles. This time, there was no money in the poor domicile in the Rue de Saint-André-des-Arts, and he was obliged to go on foot.

By dint of negotiating with the sentinels at the first gate, he ended up entering into the courtyard. The petition office was still there, and Monsieur de Pompionne was there, as usual; but the gentleman of the bedchamber was no longer in the same humor.

That morning, Monsieur de Pompionne had had a misadventure. Monsieur de Richelieu had come up to him rather abruptly and had said: "You're permitting a host of petitions to reach the King, requests for money or help, which are annoying him greatly. I engage you to mend your ways." And the Maréchal had left without even listening to Monsieur de Pompionne's excuses. The latter, furious, ordered his lackeys to throw out anyone who presented himself.

Hector was therefore treated very rudely and expelled unceremoniously.

When he returned to Paris, in despair and exhausted by fatigue, he only found Cécile and Firmin. Robert had gone out in the morning. As for Mardochée, no one had seen him for three or four days. The painter had gradually resumed his nomadic habits and was drowning his despair in the somewhat acidic wine of the Pomme Verte.

While Hector was relating his fruitless steps to his friends, however, Mardochée arrived. The artist was radiant; he was also slightly inebriated.

"Well," he said to Hector, "have you seen the King?"

"Alas, no."

"And Monsieur de Pompionne?"

"He had me thrown out."

"I was sure of it."

"It is, however, necessary that I reach the King," said Hector, in a wrathful tone.

"You'll get there," said Mardochée, "with a protector."

"How is that?"

"Because I've involved myself up in the affair."

"Oh?"

"My dear friend," said the painter, "I've found you a protector."

"You?"

"Me."

"And that protector is…?"

"Ah!" said Mardochée, "that's a long story. Let me get my breath back first, and then you'll see."

And Mardochée sat down, to get his breath back.

XI

Mardochée then assumed a self-satisfied expression and said: "I've become the friend of a friend of the valet de chambre of Monsieur le Duc de Choiseul."

"The Duc de Choiseul?" said Hector.

"Yes—the Prime Minister."

Firmin and Cécile looked at one another dubiously. Mardochée was slightly tipsy, and at such moments, he tended to be boastful.

"All right," said Hector. "You have a friend..."

"Who has a friend who knows his valet de chambre," said Mardochée.

"Where will that get us?"

"I'll introduce you this very evening."

"This evening?"

"Yes, to the Pomme Verte tavern."

"All right."

"I'll introduce you to my friend."

"Very good."

"Who will introduce you to his friend."

"At the same tavern?"

"No, elsewhere."

"Oh."

"The latter can introduce you to the Prime Minister's valet de chambre, the valet de chambre can introduce you to the Minister, and he can introduce you to the King."

"But the valet de chambre isn't the Minister," said Hector, with a sad smile.

"He's the only man who has any influence over him."

"Why is that?"

"Eh? How do I know. Because he has to be, because it can't be otherwise; that in the same way that no man is a hero to his valet de chambre, he can't be a Prime Minister to that same valet. One can see that you're from the provinces, my dear friend; you don't know anything about the world of the Court and the city."

And as Hector did not seem to be convinced, Mardochée went on: "I can assure you that you'll reach the King within a week, unless you don't want to go with me to the Pomme Verte."

Mardochée was speaking with such a tone of conviction that Hector consented to go with him. He was very weary, though, and dying of hunger—but Mardochée whispered in his ear: "I have credit out there; we'll sup marvelously.

They left the Rue Saint-André-des-Arts together, therefore, before Robert Damiens had returned, and went over the bridges, crossed the Place du Châtelet and started walking along the Rue Saint-Martin. Mardochée described a few arabesques here and there, but he was speaking with so much fire, and was so convinced of success that our poor friend Hector allowed himself to share his hopes.

They arrived at the Pomme Verte tavern.

It was crowded that evening. All of the regulars were there. "Here's Monsieur Mardochée!" they cried. "Long live Monsieur Mardochée!"

"De Mardoche," added the painter, who was clinging more tenaciously than ever to his title of gentleman.

And he cleaved through the crowd, whose members looked at Hector curiously, distributing a few handshakes right and left. At the back of the tavern, there was a man drinking alone at a table.

"There's our man," said Mardochée, nudging Hector with his elbow; and they both approached the individual in question.

The latter was a short, obese man, completely bald, clad in a gray coat and having the appearance in his person and his attire of a petty rentier who has made his fortune in retail commerce.

"My friend," said Mardochée, "may I introduce my friend Monsieur Samuel." Intending his introduction to follow all the rules of etiquette he added: "My friend the Comte de Pierrefeu."

Hector bowed in his turn.

"Monsieur le Comte," said Monsieur Samuel, "Monsieur Mardochée has deigned to give me the hope that you will overlook the disparity in our conditions and that, even though I am a man of humble status, you will do me the honor of accepting supper."

Hector smiled sadly and sat down. He was neither hungry nor thirsty. He was thinking about his unfortunate brother, whose phantom was standing up before him and demanding vengeance.

At a sign from Monsieur Samuel, the waiter set three places, and brought wine and cold meats. Then the bourgeois said: "I made my petty fortune in the grocery trade. That has permitted me to buy a house. Among my tenants there is a worthy man, a former lackey of the Duchesse de P***, who is an intimate friend of Monsieur Vénault."

"Who is Monsieur de Vénault?" asked Hector.

"He's the valet de chambre of the important personage that Monsieur de Mardochée has mentioned to you."

"Oh—very good," said Hector.

"My tenant," Monsieur Samuel went on, "has a daughter of seventeen, to whom Monsieur Vénault is paying court, for good motives. The latter will do anything that the father, whose name is Jean Mordu, wishes."

Hector was beginning to understand that the thread indicated by Mardochée as not so bad.

"When we have supped," Samuel continued, "I beg you to accompany me to my house. We shall go up to see Jean Mordu, and I'll wager that we'll find Monsieur Vénault there."

And, indeed, things went like clockwork, and Mardochée proved to have been right. An hour later, Mardochée, Hector and the latter's singular protector quit the Pomme Verte and went to the Rue des Marais-Saint-Martin. It was in that street that Monsieur Samuel was a landlord.

Jean Mordu, the former valet, was at home. He and his daughter were awaiting the daily visit of Monsieur Vénault—for, since he had become the young woman's fiancé, he came every evening.

Hector recounted his horrible adventure and his brother's tragic death. He interested Jean Mordu's daughter, and when Monsieur Vénault arrived, he was converted in a matter of seconds to Hector's cause. He said to him: "Monseigneur is departing tomorrow for Chanteloup. He'll spend the day there and won't be back in Paris until nightfall. But I'll find an opportunity within two days to speak to him about you, and I promise you that he'll consent to receive you."

That evening, Hector returned to the poor lodgings in the Rue Saint-André-des-Arts full of hope. Whether or not he saw the King was of little importance now. Would not the Prime Minister avenge the death of young André?

Two days went by. On the evening of the second, Mardochée returned. He had come up at a run, and was completely out of breath.

"Come," he said to Hector. "Come quickly."

"Where are you taking me?"

"There's a carriage down below."

"Ah!"

"In that carriage is Monsieur Vénault." Hector shivered. "And Monsieur Vénault will take you to see the Minister."

O my brother! Thought Hector, whose heart was beating terribly—and he followed Mardochée.

There was, indeed, a carriage at the door of the poor house, which bore no coat of arms, but in the form of which the carriage of a man of quality was visible. The populace had formed a crowd around it. In the carriage was the Duc's valet de chambre. He made a sign to Hector to get in.

"We're going to Versailles," he said.

"Good luck!" shouted Mardochée.

And the carriage pulled away.

In fact, the valet de chambre had kept his word, and Monsieur de Choiseul, who was sometimes glad to listen, thinking that the truth comes more often from below than above, had lent an attentive ear to the unfortunate young man's story. When his valet de chambre had finished, he exclaimed: "Finally, I have in my hand the living proof of these mysterious crimes that have been committed in Paris for more than a year, and in which the King doesn't want to believe!"

The Duc had therefore consented to receive Hector. He was in such haste to see him, in fact, that he had sent his valet de chambre to Paris with orders to bring Hector back.

The young man, with his dignified and concentrated sadness, pleased Monsieur de Choiseul. He received him kindly, listened to him attentively, and had recounted to him in all is details the horrible drama of the Rue des Enfants-Rouges and the Tartar's house.

When Hector had finished, he said to him: "I'm due to work with the King tomorrow, and I promise you that he will know everything. Better than that, the King will receive you, and you can tell him everything that you have just told me. Come back and see me tomorrow at three o'clock."

At the same time, the Minister opened a drawer, took out a roll of gold coins, and handed them to Hector "This is on account of the pension that the King owes you and will give you."

Hector smiled.

"Take it," said Monsieur de Choiseul. "It's for your equipment. You can't appear before the King in those ragged clothes."

As you can imagine, Hector left Versailles full of hope. Then again, was not the gold that he was carrying worth months of wellbeing to his friends in the Rue Saint-André des Arts?

As he left Versailles in the Duc's carriage in company with Monsieur Vénault, an old man stood aside to let the carriage pass, but as he did so, he darted a glance inside, and shivered. That old man, who had recognized Hector, was none other than Porion, alias Père Cinnamon.

XII

Now, the day when Hector had presented himself to the Duc de Choiseul was the same day when Louis XV, discovering at the back of a drawer, on a piece of yellow paper, the name of Maître Dumas, had recounted to the people assisting at his retirement the singular story of the old procurator and sent some-one to fetch Porion, whom we have seen invested with his confidence.

Porion had not had time to examine the carriage that was taking Hector away, but on seeing him in that carriage, he had concluded that the young man had found a protector and that he would end up reaching the King. For, it is nec-essary to say, although Père Cinnamon was no longer attached to the police and had become Monsieur de Sartine's bête noire, and although he was only charged by Madame de Pompadour with maintaining surveillance on the intrigues of the favorite's enemies, he was nevertheless obedient to the need that policemen have to know everything that is happening.

Thus, he had known about Hector's fruitless steps and attempts to reach the King. That evening—and hour or two before the King sent for him—after perceiving Hector in a carriage that evidently belonged to some important per-sonage. Porion had addressed the following petty monologue to himself:

It doesn't concern me, but I believe that Monsieur de Sartine will have to repent not having that young man watched. If he reaches the King, he'll tell him everything. The Tartar is no longer here, but Monsieur de Clermont hasn't quit the court, and things might turn out badly for him.[28]

Rubbing his hands at the thought that Monsieur de Sartine, in spite of the protection of Madame de Pompadour, might well be disgraced soon, Porion had added: *But that's not my concern.*

Porion had thought thus at six o'clock in the evening. At midnight, as we have seen, his opinions had been singularly modified, and at two o'clock in the morning, having made peace with Monsieur de Sartine, he had every interest in preventing Hector de Pierrefeu, by any means possible, from reaching the King.

The next day, however, Hector, whom Mardochée had taken to a second-hand clothes dealer of his acquaintance, arrived at Versailles, newly clad, and was introduced to the Duc de Choiseul's residence.

The Prime Minister was leaving for Chanteloup.[29]

---

[28] The author has now abandoned that substitution of a fictitious "Comte d'Auvergne" for the Comte de Clermont, but in so doing he seems to have abandoned the allegation that the character in question is taking daily baths in human blood, perhaps in response to an editorial instruction.

[29] In fact, the Château de Chanteloup did not become the Duc de Choiseul's country residence until 1760.

"My friend," he said to his protégé, the King will receive you today at four o'clock. At the same time, he took a pen and wrote on a piece of paper: *On behalf of Monsieur the Duc de Choiseul*. Then, handing the piece of paper to Hector, he said: "You only have an hour to wait; my valet de chambre will take you to the grand apartments.

And Monsieur de Choiseul had departed for Chanteloup with the conviction that Hector would see the King that same day.

In fact, Monsieur Vénault, who was an important person by virtue of his functions, had taken Hector to the royal antechamber. All doors opened before Monsieur Vénault. A page had taken the piece of paper and had gone into the King's apartments. But the King, at that moment, was in Madame de Pompadour's apartments, where he was listening to the singular story of the Tartar Prince, and when the page, arriving through the secret passage, had come to tell him that Monsieur de Choiseul's protégé was there, the King, who was amusing himself greatly and did not want to be saddened, had postponed the audience until the following day.

Then Monsieur Vénault had said to Hector: "It's almost nightfall. Don't go back to Paris; sleep in Versailles. I'll take you to a hostelry where you can spend the night, and I'll come to collect you tomorrow at the time of the King's *petit lever*."

Hector had followed Monsieur Vénault's advice. He had allowed himself to be taken to the hostelry of the Singe Vert, very near to the château, where gentlemen stayed who came to solicit at Versailles.

Monsieur Vénault had quit him saying: "Until tomorrow."

But Monsieur Vénault was unaware that it was at the Singe Vert that, for reasons known only to him, Porion, alias Père Cinnamon, lodged in a mansard under the roofs.

While Hector de Pierrefeu reconciled himself to that hitch, with the conviction that he would have his audience the following day, for the page had reported the king's words faithfully, the Tartar Prince took his leave of his Majesty and left Madame de Pompadour's apartments.

As he arrived at the stairway, in company with Porion, a page ran after him.

"Monseigneur," he said "Madame la Marquise begs you to return."

A smile came to the Tartar's lips. "I know why," he said. And he followed the page.

The King and Monsieur de Richelieu had gone. The Marquise was alone.

"Monsieur," she said to the Prince, "you dipped your hands in that jug?"

"Yes, Madame." The ewer was still on a side table, but the water, which had changed color several times on contact with the Prince's hands, had become clear again."

"Did you drop this ring into the water?" asked Madame de Pompadour. And she took out of the ewer a magnificent diamond as big as a hazelnut.

"Indeed!" said the Prince, feigning astonishment.

"Take it," said the Marquise.

"Madame, said the Prince, "you see me in great embarrassment."

"Bah! Why is that?"

"A prophecy is attached to that ring. A Bohemian woman predicted to me one day that it would only quit my hand for the hand of a Queen."

"I'm not a Queen," said the Marquise.

"Permit me to believe the contrary," replied the Prince. And, taking Madame de Pompadour's hand, he kissed it respectfully and slipped the diamond on to her finger.

The Marquise smiled. "You're worthy of being French," she said.

The Prince bowed and left.

"I believe," the Tartar murmured in Porion's ear, "that the Marquise will be with us from now on."

"I should think so," said Porion. "A diamond worth thirty thousand écus."

"Very nearly," said the Prince.

"But we've had a narrow escape, Monseigneur."

"Indeed?"

"If the young man whose name you heard pronounced just now had seen the King..."

"The King won't believe him."

"All the same," said Porion, "it's better that the King doesn't see him."

"How can that be done?"

"I don't know, but I'll find a means between now and tomorrow."

The Tartar and Porion separated in the courtyard. The former climbed into his coach in order to return to Paris.

Porion went through the streets of Versailles, thinking: *I have a blank* lettre de cachet *in my pocket, which Sartine gave me just in case, but it's a poor means. I know the name of his protector now, and Monsieur de Choiseul is bound to wonder what has become of his protégé.*

As he went further, Porion continued: *It's improbable that my man has returned to Paris. His audience has been postponed until tomorrow morning, so he'll stay in Versailles. Let's find him.*

And he headed for the hostelry of the Singe Vert.

Night had fallen. It was November, the month of fog and frost.

Instead of going into the hostelry, Porion remained in the street and approached the windows of the main room. Through the widows, he perceived Hector, who was sitting at a table, having supper served to him.

Good, he said to himself. *I'm not mistaken.* He slapped his forehead. "I've got a famous idea," he murmured. And instead of going into the hostelry, he turned round and retraced his steps toward the château.

There was a kind of tavern directly outside, frequented by guardsmen and soldiers of fortune in quest of employment. Porion went into it. No one paid any attention to him, except for a young man who wore a blue uniform, and belonged to the lansquenet corps.

The young man in question had a long nose and thin lips, something angular about his person, and an evil gaze. He was a gentleman, but a poor gentleman of the Alsatian nobility. Incorporated in the lansquenets, he had had all the difficulty in the world becoming a sergeant. Nevertheless, he was treated with a certain consideration, and even the officers were very polite to him. Why? It was because Monsieur d'Erishem, that being his name, had a reputation as a formidable swashbuckler. He had fought ten duels and had killed his man ten times.

Porion approached him and said in a whisper: "How are the finances?"

"Agonizing. My purse is empty."

"What would you say to a hundred pistoles?"

The swashbuckler shivered, and looked at Porion attentively.

"If you wish" he latter said, amiably, "we can have a little chat."

XIII

Porion sat down beside Monsieur d'Erishem and summoned the waiter.

"What can I offer you?" he asked the Alsatian.

"A glass of Cyprus wine," the latter relied. "I'm dying of thirst."

"Two large glasses of Cyprus wine," Porion ordered.

Since the police agent had been in Versailles he had resumed the inoffensive mask of Père Cinnamon. He was encountered in taverns, inns and promenades, aged, debilitated and amiable, dressed like a well-to-do petty bourgeois. No one, except perhaps Monsieur d'Erishem, had suspected his veritable profession.

Among the soldiers who were in the tavern when he entered, there was no one of a high enough rank to be involved with the intimate life of the château. In consequence, no one knew what had happened the day before in the King's apartments and it would have astonished those brave men greatly if anyone had told them that the worthy man with the appearance of a simpleton had just come out of Madame de Pompadour's apartment, where he had been chatting familiarly with the King and the Maréchal de Richelieu for more than an hour.

Porion, therefore, did not attract anyone's attention. Only Monsieur d'Erishem had shivered on seeing him come in. That was because Porion had already employed him once for a tenebrous task, a month before.

A month before, a drunken soldier had permitted himself to say something improper about Madame de Pompadour. The soldier was a bad lot, belonging to a great family related to the Choiseuls and the Praslins.

The Marquise had summoned Porion and said to him: "My dear Porion, Monsieur de B*** is nothing but a ruffian. I don't want to importune the King by asking him for a *lettre de cachet*, nor do I want to involve Monsieur de Sartine in the affair, who runs with the hare and hunts with the hounds, and wouldn't fail to raise the objection that he's the Prime Minister's cousin. Finally, I wouldn't want to be personally disagreeable to Monsieur de Choiseul. However, I'd like the insolent fellow punished. Can you find me a means of doing so without a fuss and without any finger of suspicion being pointed at me?"

Porion had asked for a credit of fifty pistoles. Then he had entered into communication with Monsieur d'Erishem.

The following day, as Monsieur de B***, half-drunk, was holding forth in a tavern, the Alsatian gentleman had come in and jogged his elbow in passing. A quarrel had ensued. As it was dark, the two gentlemen had left the tavern and had fought under the first street lamp. At the third pass, Monsieur de B*** had fallen, mortally wounded.

On learning of his death, Monsieur de Choiseul had simply said: "That gets rid of an embarrassment for his family and me." And no one had suspected that Madame de Pompadour and Porion had had anything to do with it.

That is why Monsieur d'Erishem, having not a sou in his purse, had quivered with hope on seeing Porion come into the tavern.

When the Cyprus wine had been brought, Père Cinnamon lowered his voice. "So, you're short of money?"

"I've spent my last écu, and it's a long time until pay day."

"In consequence, a hundred pistoles wouldn't displease you?"

"Certainly not."

"I'll make you the observation," said Porion, winking, "that's it's exactly double the sum that I offered you for the first affair."

"That's probably," said Monsieur d'Erishem coldly, "because the individual is more important."

"You're mistaken."

"Bah!"

"It's a petty provincial gentleman, unknown in Versailles, whose death wouldn't preoccupy anyone."

"Why are you offering me a hundred pistoles, then?"

"Bah!" said Porion. "With the sole aim of encouraging you."

"You're joking, Père Cinnamon."

"Not at all."

"And if the gentleman is so unknown, what interest do you have in him disappearing?"

"Oh, that's another story."

"Well?"

"The Marquise has nothing to do with it."

"Really!"

"It's Monsieur de Richelieu who sees him with an unkind eye."

"Why?"

"Because the young man is tormenting him for an audience with the King. The King is in a good mood. The young man would sadden him."

"How?"

"By telling him some stupid story—and rays of sunlight are too rare in Versailles to allow the skies to be covered like that. For three days the King hasn't yawned once."

"That's superb!"

"But if the young man in question succeeds in reaching him tomorrow morning..."

"Ah! It's tomorrow morning."

"Yes."

"So it's necessary for him to disappear before then?"

"Well, it's for that reason that I'm offering you a hundred pistoles instead of fifty. It's the Maréchal who's paying, anyway."

The Alsatian scratched his ear. "Damn!" he said.

"What?"

"The Maréchal is deeply indebted."

"Agreed."

"Will I be paid?"

"Immediately," said Porion. "I have the money." And after darting a glance around to make sure that no one was paying any attention to him, Porion took a greasy portfolio from his pocket and showed a wad of cashable bills at the bottom. "It will even be paid in advance," he said.

"Then I'm ready."

"Another glass of Cyprus wine?" asked Porion.

"Gladly, for it's cold."

And Monsieur d'Erishem drank to the Maréchal's health.

"Now," said Porion, "let's go."

"Where is my man to be found?"

"At the Singe Vert."

"Good, that's only a few steps away."

The Alsatian and Porion left the tavern without attracting any attention. It was very cold and the fog was thick.

"Brrr!" said Monsieur d'Erishem. "The Maréchal's chosen a nasty moment for the young man. To die in weather like this is to die twice over."

They lengthened their stride, and a few minutes later, they arrived at the door of the Singe Vert. Porion took the Alsatian by the arm and drew him to one of the windows of the main room. Inside, through the frosty windows, they could see twenty provincial gentlemen, mostly eating at different tables in groups of two, four or six.

Hector de Pierrefeu was alone.

"That's him," said Porion.

"The black doublet?"

"Yes."

"Is he already wearing mourning for his death?" the Alsatian sniggered. For in buying his clothes, Hector had put on mourning for his brother.

"You can see the effect he'll produce on the king's presently-rosy spirits tomorrow, with that funereal costume."

"You're right," said the Alsatian.

Porion opened his portfolio. "You're a man of honor," he said, "and one can trust you."

The Alsatian bowed. At the same time, Porion slipped the cashable bills into his hand.

"Are you going away?" asked Monsieur d'Erishem, pocketing the bills.

"No, but I'll stay outside."

"To see the provocation?"

"Of course."

"Oh, it won't take long—you'll see."

And the Alsatian went into the hostelry.

On seeing him, the master of the Singe Vert could not suppress a grimace. Monsieur d'Erishem paid badly, or even did not pay at all, but no one dared refuse him credit, so redoubtable was his reputation. The hotelier's grimace did not escape him, and he understood its meaning. So, as he had money, instead of going directly into the main room, he went to the kitchen and showed one of his bills. "Change it for cash," he said.

The sight of the cashable bill brought the most gracious of smiles to the hotelier's lips.

"And serve me supper," added Monsieur d'Erishem. With those words he went into the main room and headed for the back. It was there that Hector was eating. There was a vacant table next to him, and the Alsatian sat down at it. Then he looked around insolently.

The gentlemen who were there looked at the individual with the appearance of a brawler, and a few exchanged uncomplimentary remarks in low voices. Monsieur d'Erishem even glimpsed smiles and overheard fragments of remarks that displeased him, but it was not to pick a quarrel with others that he had come to the Singe Vert, and he said nothing.

Only Hector paid no attention to him. The poor young man was eating slowly and seemed to be absorbed in dolorous thoughts.

Monsieur d'Erishem began to eat.

At first he limited himself to staring at Hector, but Hector did not see him. Then he coughed.

Hector did not raise his head.

Then, impatiently, the ruffian got up and approached him.

"Hey, Monsieur," he said.

This time, Hector shivered, looked at his interlocutor and said: "What do you desire, Monsieur?"

"You're dressed in black."

"I'm in mourning, Monsieur."

"I can see that, and it's for that reason that I beg you to go and eat elsewhere. The sight of black garments causes me a very disagreeable melancholy."

Hector looked at him in amazement.

"Go on," said the Alsatian. "Hurry up and get out!"

This time, Hector de Pierrefeu's face went red, and he instinctively put his hand on the hilt of his sword.

XIV

The Alsatian had spoken in a low voice. Nevertheless, some of the gentlemen who were in the room had heard. Others scented a quarrel.

It was unanimous. All conversations stopped, all gazes were concentrated on the table that the Alsatian had just approached.

Hector, clad in black, with his handsome face imprinted with sadness and distinction, had something that immediately attracted favor. Monsieur d'Erishem, with his insolent manner, his negligent attire, his dubious linen and the knot of faded ribbons borne on his sword, was displeasing a first sight. That instinctive aversion had been manifest as soon as he came into the room.

When he saw that he was the focus of general attention, the Alsatian felt obliged to raise his voice and become even more insolent.

"Go, on, quickly," he said. "Get out."

But Hector was a gentleman. Furthermore, he had drunk, instead of milk, the generous wine that streams beneath the blessed sun of Bourgogne and makes men brave and strong. All his blood flowed to his heart; all the pride of his face suddenly burst forth in the visage.

"Monsieur," he said, "you're a madman, a fool or a scoundrel."

"Be careful!" said Monsieur d'Erishem, pale with anger. And he wrenched a glove from his hand, ready to strike Hector in the face.

But Hector was young and strong. He rushed upon the Alsatian, who was thin, short and paltry, snatched the glove from him and said. "If it's a quarrel you want, I'm your man!"

"Ah!" said Monsieur d'Erishem. "Good! He can talk!"

"Did you think I would run away?" said Hector, ironically.

"No…but…"

The Alsatian had felt the vigor of Hector's wrist. He was sure that he could kill him with a sword in hand, but he was not sure that he would not be knocked out by a punch, so he prudently kept his distance.

"Monsieur," said Hector, coldly. "God is my witness that I am seeing you for the first time. I don't know what motive you have for seeking a quarrel with me."

"I'm seeking a quarrel because you're dressed in black."

"What does it matter to you?"

"It displeases me."

"Oh," said Hector, "really?"

"And you'll fight me," said the Alsatian, who was honest in transactions and intended to earn his hundred pistoles.

"Oh, wholeheartedly."

"Then let's go."

And Monsieur d'Erishem took a step backwards,

"Excuse me, Monsieur," said Hector calmly, "but I've arrived from the provinces and..."

"That's obvious," sniggered the Alsatian.

"I know nothing of the usages of the Court."

"In truth!"

"I didn't know that one fought at night."

"That's the custom at Versailles, Monsieur."

"What! In the dark?"

"No, under a street-light."

"You have a response for everything, Monsieur, but..."

"But what?"

"In spite of the pleasure I'd have in crossing swords with you, that appears to me to be impossible."

"Any why is that, my little Monsieur?" said Monsieur d'Erishem, ironically.

"First of all, because I haven't finished my supper," replied Hector, calmly.

"Very well, I'll wait."

"And secondly, because tomorrow, between nine and ten in the morning, I shall have the honor of seeing the King."

"I'll offer him your apologies."

"No," said Hector. "At noon, I'll be your man, but between now and then I have a sacred duty to fulfill, in which I shall not fail."

"Even if I slap you with my glove?" said Monsieur d'Erishem, furiously. And he took of his left glove, Hector having taken possession of the right.

But his raised arm did not fall, for a vigorous arm seized it, while a Stentorian voice said to him: "The two of us, Monsieur Assassin!"

The Alsatian turned round, stupefied, and even uttered a cry of pain, for his arm was caught in a vice. He then found himself in the presence of one of the provincial gentlemen supping at the nearby tables. He was a sort of colossus, nearly six feet tall and proportionately broad: a big man with an expansive and ruddy face, with blond hair and blue eyes. One might have thought him some warrior divinity of ancient paganism.

"Monsieur," he said to the Alsatian, "as true as my name in Vicomte Gontran de Mauroy and I was born in Saint-Omer, that I've been appointed captain of the arquebusiers of my native town, and as true as I could fell you with a blow of my fist, I'm going to break your back and tear you into little pieces if you don't make your apologies to this young man."

"Monsieur!" said the Alsatian, going pale,

"Tomorrow, at noon," said Hector, "I shall be at Monsieur's orders." And he looked at Monsieur d'Erishem.

"No," said the latter. "Not tomorrow. Today."

"Oh, you want to fight by night?" said the colossus.

"Yes," said the Alsatian.

"Well, then," said Gontran de Mauroy," be satisfied." And he applied a resounding slap to the swashbuckler's pale face.

Monsieur d'Erishem uttered a screech. "To me!" He cried. "I need blood!"

"You can fight me if you wish," said the Fleming, with the phlegm typical of his race. "Come on, then, there's a street-light a few steps away."

And as Monsieur d'Erishem did not get out quickly enough, and concentrated his hateful gaze on Hector, astounded by the sudden intervention, the Fleming took him by the shoulders and shoved him rudely ahead of him.

"I've been told who you are," he said. "You're a fine blade, it appears, and you kill your man with a sure thrust; we shall see."

So saying, he applied a second shove, and threw him out of the room, bruised, to the applause of all those gathered there.

There was, indeed, a street-light by the door, at the corner of the hostelry.

Everyone emerged in a tumult on the heels of the Fleming, who was still pushing his enemy in front of him.

In the cold night air, the Alsatian recovered all his composure.

After all, it was only an annoying hitch of short duration. He was sure of himself. He knew full well that at the point of a sword, brute force is worthless against skill. *I'll kill this one*, he thought, *and then I'll be able to force the other to draw his blade.*

Having arrived under the street-light, the two adversaries looked at one another, blades drawn.

"Be careful," a charitable soul had whispered in the Fleming's ear. "He's a dangerous fighter."

"We shall see," Vicomte Gontran de Mauroy had replied.

Then commenced a singular, bizarre and perhaps unprecedented combat.

The Fleming stood directly in front of his adversary, sword in hand and arm extended. The Alsatian began with a few sketchy feints, then his play acquired finesse, and then his épée fluttered like a serpent around the heavy rapier of the colossus. But the arm did not bend, and the sword it held resembled an iron bar planted in a wall. As it was longer by at least a foot than the Alsatian's, and the Vicomte was still directing it at the body, the swashbuckler consumed himself in vain efforts. If the Vicomte had bent his arm, or if his word had deviated, the Alsatians would have easily found a route to his breast, but it was like dealing with a statue, which did not budge any more than the bronze colossus beneath which triremes passed with all sails flying.

Then losing patience, the Alsatian cried: "Ah, Monsieur, are we going to be here until tomorrow? I'm in a hurry to finish."

"As you wish," said the Fleming." Then, with his arm still extended, his sword still menacing his adversary's body, he took a step forward.

The Alsatian dropped back.

The Fleming took another step forward, and then another.

The Alsatian fell back again. The Fleming continued marching. The Alsatian continued to fall back before that blade, which seemed to be coming after him as immutable and rigid as destiny. They covered fifty or sixty paces like that, one advancing and the other recoiling.

The street was narrow, and the people who had emerged from the Singe Vert had invaded it. For a long time, the two combatants had emerged from the circle of light descried by the street-lamp.

Now, the Alsatian, gripped by a secret fear, was retreating into the darkness.

There was a bend in the street, almost a right-angle. The Alsatian, who was still moving backwards, did not see that bend, and suddenly bumped into an obstacle. It was a house in the pivot of the bend. Then the Fleming extended his arm, and his adversary uttered a cry, while the épée escaped from his hand. The terrible rapier, piercing him all the way through, had just nailed him to the wall.

The Fleming then withdrew his sword, and, no longer having anything to sustain him, Monsieur d'Erishem fell to the ground like an inert mass.

"Brrr!" said the Fleming, with his customary phlegm, "it's damnably cold. Is it permissible to disturb honest men thus, who are warmly installed around a well-served table?"

He wiped his sword on his knee and put it back in its scabbard.

Then veritable applause burst forth among the gentlemen who had followed him. But to that applause, a dull cry of rage and despair responded from the other end of the street. That was Porion, who had just seen the scaffolding of his Machiavellian plan crumble, and who could no longer contain his fury.

XV

The Fleming was a simple man.

When he had wiped his sword and replaced it in its scabbard he started walking back to the hostelry, tranquilly. But in his passage he found Hector, grave and sad, who extended his hand to him and said, simply: "Thank you."

The Vicomte took his hand, and said: "Don't thank me, Monsieur; I did what anyone else, including you, would have done in my place. It's sufficient to look at you to have no doubt of your courage, and I immediately understood the motives that obliged you to adjourn an encounter with that wretch, who had insulted you, until tomorrow. It's me who has done you wrong in killing him, for he belonged to you somewhat."

And the colossus shook Hector's hand cordially.

Then, drawing him into the hostelry, he went on: "That fellow interrupted us in our supper, which is always bad for the stomach. Let's return to table. Will you permit me to sit with you?"

"Gladly," said Hector.

And they both resumed their supper.

Flemings are cold, but wine easily releases their tongues. Then they become expansive. When he had emptied a third bottle of Burgundy wine, Vicomte Gontran de Mauroy put his elbows on the table and felt the need to talk about his affairs a little.

"It's fifteen years since I was last in Versailles," he said, "and I see that nothing has changed. Fifteen years ago, the King was suffering from ennui, as he is today; the gentlemen of the antechamber were as insolent as they are today, the great seigneurs were indebted, and as everyone is on their knees before Madame de Pompadour today, they were then at the feet of Madame de Châteauroux.[30] Only the people have changed, but things are the same."

"Really?" said Hector, naively.

"I'm not a solicitor by métier," the Fleming relied "I even have a certain horror of the condition of courtier, and I much prefer the coarse doublet and leather boots that I wear in my château to a court costume and tight silk stockings, but I don't like people making mock of me either."

Who dares to mock you, then?" asked Hector, timidly.

"The Minister of Finance, Abbé Terray."

"Ah!"

---

[30] Marie-Anne de Mailly, one of four sisters who all became Louis XV's mistresses; she became his official "first mistress" in 1742, but died not long afterwards in 1744, a month or so before Madame de Pompadour inherited that position.

"First of all, I ask you, is it common sense to mistake an abbé for a financier? But that's not my concern; that's the King's business, not mine. What does concern me is that, in the last war with Holland, an entire army corps passed over my land, installed themselves there, beasts and man, and lived there for nearly a month. My fodder and my crops, all passed that way. Naturally, I addressed myself to the governor of the province He sent his officers to assess the damage. Between swordsmen, one always reaches an understanding, and we fell into accord regarding the figure of the indemnity. Six thousand livres!"

"A fine figure," murmured Hector.

"The King approved the sum, and I was sent to the Minister of Finance."

"Who paid?"

"No, who has put my steward off at three month intervals for three years. As my steward was on his tenth voyage to Paris, I made the decision to come myself. I arrived this evening, and I hadn't been in Versailles for an hour when I had the pleasure of rendering you the small service that you know."

Hector inclined.

"By the way," said the Fleming, "what insect had stung that poor devil—let's be indulgent, since he's dead—and pushed him to seek a quarrel with you?"

"I don't know."

"However..."

"I've never even seen him before."

"Really?"

"I swear to you."

The Fleming frowned. "This," he said "seems shady to me."

He summoned the hotelier.

The worthy man who presided over the destinies of the Singe Vert came running all the more urgently because he had just experienced a great consideration for the Fleming, who had just rid him forever of a man who not only did not pay but was always causing trouble in his establishment.

"Ah, Master," said Vicomte Gontran de Mauroy, "it would be very kind of you to give us some information about the man I've just killed."

"He's a low-ranking officer in the lansquenets, as Your Lordship could see," the host replied.

"Yes. His name?"

"Monsieur d'Erishem."

"German?"

"No, Alsatian."

"Perhaps he was drunk?"

"Oh, no," said the hotelier. "He hadn't eaten yet, and he was perfectly composed."

"Monsieur," said the Fleming, indicating Hector, "was seeing him for the first time."

"There's nothing astonishing about that."

"What!" said the Fleming, naively. "There's nothing astonishing about seeing a man with an empty stomach, who has all his reason in consequence, seeking a quarrel with a man he doesn't know and who has never seen him before?"

"Astonishing to the part of anyone else," said the hotelier, "but not the Alsatian."

"Ah!"

"He's killed more than ten men in five years."

"But why?"

The hotelier hesitated to speak, but then lowered his voice. "Because it brings him fine pistoles and bills."

"What?"

"As he had remarkable skill with the épée and was almost sure of killing his man, it was to him that people addressed themselves."

"But who?"

"People who had an interest in getting rid of someone," the host continued, looking directly at Hector. "Believe me, Monsieur, he was hired to kill you."

"Ah!"

"And he's even collected the price of your blood in advance."

"Oh!" said the Fleming.

"This morning," the host went on, "he didn't have an écu."

"And this evening."

"He showed me, when he came in, a wad of cashable bills."

"But I don't know anyone in Versailles!" exclaimed Hector, stupefied.

"Truly?" said the Fleming. At the same time, the Vicomte dismissed the host with a gesture. Then, lowering his voice and leaning toward Hector's ear, he said: "My young friend, I've only known you for an hour, and yet you inspire a veritable sympathy in me."

"You're too kind," said Hector.

"You're young; your mourning dress tells me that you've experienced a great misfortune."

"Very great," murmured Hector, his eyes filling with tears.

"I'm therefore interested in you," the Fleming went on, "And if you'll permit, I'll take you under my protection."

"Monsieur," said Hector, effusively, "what have I done to merit such generosity?"

"That's how I am," the good Fleming replied. "When people please me, I'd throw myself in the fire for them." And he shook Hector's hand for a second time Then, as they had finished their supper, he said: "Come and get some air for a moment. We can talk better outside, for the excellent reason that there are no walls, and walls often have ears." With those words, he stood up.

Then Hector, slightly astonished, saw him take a pipe from his pocket, load it methodically, and light it with the candle, scandalizing the gentlemen who were in the room. Very few people smoked in those days, and hardly anyone except a mercenary or a Fleming would have permitted himself such an incongruity.

Vicomte Gontran de Mauroy did not appear to perceive the mild scandal he had occasioned, and, taking Hector by the arm, he went out, leaving behind him a magnificent corkscrew of blue smoke.

"Now, my friend," he said, when they were in the street, "let's talk seriously."

"I'm listening, Monsieur."

"The man who was supposed to kill you is dead, and we won't occupy ourselves any further with him," the Fleming went on, "but if the arm is no longer to be feared, the head that directed it still exists."

"That's where my reason is lost," said Hector.

"Ah."

"I don't know of any enemies in Versailles."

"But you might have some in Paris."

"I don't know."

"Come on, confide in me, my poor friend, and tell me what you've come to ask the King."

"Justice and vengeance!"

This time, the Fleming looked at Hector with a kind of amazement.

"Justice and vengeance for an unfortunate murdered brother," completed the young man.

"Speak," said the Fleming, shaking his arm. "Perhaps it's Providence that put me in your path."

And he waited for Hector to explain.

XVI

Vicomte Gontran de Mauroy was one of those gigantic blue-eyed Flemings to whom God seems to have granted physical strength with the sole aim of given men a lesson in sagacity and moderation. A man less young and less confident than Hector de Pierrefeu would have felt drawn to him by a mysterious sympathy. After scarcely an hour, Hector felt at ease with him, as with an old friend.

Thus, he did not hide anything of his life or his misfortunes. He told him about his simple and naïve childhood in the shadow of the gray turrets of the old paternal manor; then his departure for Paris with his younger brother, whose mentor he had sworn to be, and his meeting in the forest with the Tartar; and finally, his arrival at the Blue Dragon inn.

He did not omit any detail. His memory, at that moment, served him with perfect lucidity. He recalled the slightest details of the fatal evening in which he had almost fallen under the danger of assassins, perhaps at the same moment when his brother's throat was being cut. He even recalled certain circumstances that had marked the time of his madness, and which he had forgotten. Thus, he remembered having quit his bed and vainly opposed the abduction of Cécile Robert.

At that point in his story, the Fleming stopped Hector, whom he had only interrupted thus far with gesture of horror and indignant exclamations.

"Have you ever seen that man again?" he said, alluding to Porion.

"Never. Oh, but his face is engraved here…!" And he placed his hand on his forehead.

"So you'd recognize him?"

"In a thousand, even if he were lost in a crowd or passed at a precipitate gallop on horseback."

"That's good," said the Fleming. "Continue."

When Hector had finished his story, the gentleman said to him: "Now, my friend, you're astonished that someone wanted to have you murdered?"

"But…"

"You can be sure that too many people have an interest in your not reaching the King."

"That's true, what you say. However…"

"However what?"

"The Tartar has left Paris."

"How do you know?"

"Have I not told you that the father of the unfortunate Cécile was in his service?"

"So?"

"And he separated from him in Holland. The Tartar was returning to Russia, he said, where he was going to complete his cure," Hector added.

A smile came to the Vicomte's lips. "Dear child," he said, "you know as well as I do the truth of that."

"You don't believe that the Tartar has gone?"

"It's not a matter of the Tartar, but of those who served him. They have certainly not left Paris; and they, even more certainly, know that you've escaped the fate that awaited you..."

"Oh! You think so?"

"I'm convinced of it, and they're perhaps watching over you relentlessly."

Hector was walking beside his companion, his forehead pensive, and he thought that the latter was right.

"Your audience is for tomorrow morning?"

"Yes."

"It's quite natural, then, that someone wanted you dead this evening."

"Oh!" said Hector, his hand clenching the hilt of his sword. "When I've seen the King, they can assassinate me then; I'd die sure of my vengeance."

"Do you no longer have anyone left in this world?"

At that question, Hector shivered; a name rose from his heart to his lips: "Cécile."

The Fleming went on: "My friend, you have faith in the King, as that is our duty—the duty of all of us, as gentlemen. Oh, if the King were named Henri IV, or even Louis XIV, I would say to you: you're right."

"The King is always the King," said Hector.

"Undoubtedly, but this one reigns and does not govern... at least, not always."

"What do you mean?"

"King Louis the Beloved, as he is known, perhaps a little derisively, is less occupied with is subjects than his mistresses, and more with his pleasures than the well-being of the kingdom. He will listen to you, my friend, he will believe you, he will be moved, he will promise you prompt and severe justice, and he will certainly be sincere in is promises."

"Well?"

"But when you have gone, someone will talk to him about something else, and then..."

"Then he will forget me?"

"I fear so."

"It is, however, necessary that my brother be avenged."

"On whom, since the Tartar has gone?"

"On the wretches who aided in his death."

"You mean the two hoteliers?"

"Of course."

"And do you not think that the Tartar might have had other accomplices?"

227

"I don't know."

"Let's see, have you not told me that on the day when the man was in the forest of Sénart, he was hunting with a great seigneur?"

"Yes, the Comte de Clermont."

"A Prince of the Blood, my friend, and Prince about whom strange rumors are going around."

"Ah!" said Hector,

"Did the Comte not offer you his protection?"

"Of course."

"Well, instead of going to address yourself to Monsieur de Choiseul, why did you not go and knock on Clermont's door?"

"Oh, I don't know... but that name alone, at present, inspires a certain aversion in me."

"You see," said the Fleming, his reasoning triumphant, "that albeit reluctantly, you are holding the Comte de Clermont responsible for the death of your brother."

"Oh, be quiet, Monsieur, please!" said Hector, trembling.

"And it is against such adversaries that you are struggling, my poor friend."

"I want to avenge my brother." The young man pronounced those words in a tone of grim resolution.

"And Cécile Robert," the Fleming went on, "the young woman you love, perhaps without admitting it to yourself, but whom you surely love, I have understood by the tone of enthusiasm with which you talked about her just now, Cécile, who the King has dishonored—will you avenge her?"

A cry of dolor escaped Hector. "Oh my God!" he said.

"Look," the Vicomte went on, "would you like me to give you some good advice?"

"Speak."

"Have you what you need to live on? Perhaps not. Then it's necessary for you to carve out a small place in the sun, and for that task, a gentleman only has his sword. Come with me to my domain. I'll keep you for a month in my château, and I'll ask you permission to lend you a hundred pistoles. With that money you can go to Holland, and you can take service in the army of the Netherlands."

"And Cécile?"

"You'll take her with you and make her your wife."

"But it's necessary that I avenge my brother!"

"Well," said the Fleming, "try to find yourself one evening, in the corner of a deserted street in Paris, face to face with the Comte de Clermont. That's easy enough, because, bad lot that he is, he courts women of low society, grisettes and bourgeoises."

"And then?" said Hector, his voice suddenly trembling with anger.

"Then, put the point of your sword in his face, and if he refuses to cross blades with you, kill him like a dog."

"And afterwards?"

"After you've killed the Comte de Clermont, you start searching for the Tartar. The world isn't so large that one can't find a man when one has hate for a torch and duty for a guide."

"What you're advising me to do," said Hector, "I'll do; but before then, I want to see the King. It shall not be said that a gentleman, before doing justice himself, did not address himself to the man who is placed above all."

"And who will do justice to the King, for the honor of the woman you love?"

"God," said Hector, gravely. "God, who is above kings, and punishes them if necessary." And he raised his hands toward the heavens.

"As you wish," said he Fleming, with a sigh, "but in the meantime, permit me to be your companion until tomorrow."

"Oh, with all my heart."

"The nights are long in winter, and there's nothing to say that you won't be in further danger between now and tomorrow. If you wish, we'll sleep in the same room, and place our swords under our bolster."

"I will do as you wish," said Hector.

That conversation, as we have said, took place in the open air, in the street that ran alongside the Singe Vert. The sky was black and there was fog. The cold and the obscurity contributed not a little, as you can imagine, to rendering the street deserted. However, a man had followed the Fleming at a respectful distance.

Had he heard what they had said?

It was not probable, for they were talking in low voices, and, in any case, he would only have been able to seize a few fragments of their conversation. Assuredly, however, he was spying on them, for when the Fleming suddenly turned round, the man stopped.

Vicomte Gontran de Mauroy as a great hunter, like the majority of provincial gentlemen, and hunters have piercing sight. He perceived a black form in the fog, stopped abruptly and seized Hector's arm.

"Did you see?" he whispered.

"Yes...a man..."

"The fellow might have been listening to us..."

"That's possible..."

"In fact, we'll soon know." And the Fleming retraced his steps and marched straight up to the man, who appeared to want to dissimulate himself in the fog.

As the Vicomte and Hector advanced, the man began to retreat. Seeing that, the Vicomte lengthened his stride. The man did the same.

"Hey, friend!" called the Fleming. "Wait a moment!"

But the unknown man paid no heed to the injunction, and started running. As he took flight, he passed under the street-lamp under which Monsieur de Mauroy and the Alsatian had drawn their swords. Suddenly, his face, which he was not, in fact, trying to hide, was fully illuminated.

Hector and the Fleming were no more than ten or fifteen paces away from him. It was only for the duration of a lightning-flash, but it was enough.

Hector uttered a cry. "It's *him!*" he said.

"Who?" said the Vicomte, amazed.

"The man who abducted Cécile!" cried Hector.

And he launched himself in pursuit of the man, who was still fleeing in the fog.

XVII

Him, was Porion.

Hector was not mistaken.

Père Cinnamon, who had witnessed the duel of the Fleming and the Alsatian from a distance, the duel so unfortunately concluded for the latter, had divined in the colossus who had made himself Hector de Pierrefeu's protector a dangerous enemy. So he had promised himself not to lose sight of him for an instant, and when the Fleming had come out with Hector, he had started to follow them.

But Porion was a prudent man, and he had kept at a respectable distance, as you can imagine—which meant that, when the Fleming summoned him to stop, he took to his heels and ran away.

Hector had then launched himself in pursuit. Perhaps, in Paris in a labyrinth of obscure side-streets, Porion would have been able to escape him, but in Versailles, in the midst of those broad streets arranged in a grid, the outcome of that race was not in doubt. Porion was old, Hector was young and alert.

In a matter of minutes, Hector had caught up with Porion and had grabbed his collar, saying; "Ah, wretch, I've got you at last!"

"What do you want with me?" replied Porion, trying to free himself. "I don't know you... I'm a poor old man...Père Cinnamon...everyone in Versailles knows me. Ask anyone. I swear to you that you're mistaking me for someone else."

In speaking thus, he had assumed a paltry and debilitated aspect, rendered his voice quavering, curbing his back and giving his visage an expression of piteous fear.

But Hector did not let go of him, and said. "I recognize you... oh, I'd recognize you in a thousand, rogue!"

In the meantime, the Fleming, who was not running as fast as Hector, arrived. "Well, what is it?" he asked.

"It's *him*," said Hector, still gripping Porion by the throat.

"The man who was spying on you?"

"Yes, for one thing. He's also the man who abducted Cécile and stabbed me with a knife."

"The young man is mad," said Porion, in a lamentable tone. And, joining in his hands and addressing the Fleming, he added in a lamentable tone: "My good Monsieur, I beg you, come to my aid!"

But Hector had spoken with a tone of conviction that had impressed Vicomte Gontran de Mauroy.

"My good man," he said to Porion, "it's possible that my young friend Monsieur de Pierrefeu is mistaken, but there's no great harm in that, given that neither he nor I want to murder you, at least for the moment."

Porion breathed out. But Hector was still holding him by the collar.

"The street is a poor place for explanations," said the Vicomte. "For one thing, we can't see, and for another, it's cold."

Porion had the courtesy to shiver.

"Come to our hostelry, then, over there, the Singe Vert. We'll see whether our friend is mistaken or not.

And the Fleming took Porion's arm and placed it under his own. Then Porion felt as if he was caught in a vice.

"The hostelry of the Singe Vert," he said. "But that's mine, Monsieur."

"Ah! That's where you lodge?"

"Of course."

"Then you're known there?"

"Most certainly."

"Very good. But can you explain to me why you were following us just now?"

"I wasn't following you. I was taking the air."

"Bad reasons, my good man."

"But I swear to you..."

"If you weren't following us, why did you run away when we called to you?"

Porion recovered his quavering and broken voice. "My good Messieurs," he said, "I know that appearances are against me, but when I've told you that there's not a day goes by when someone doesn't molest me and do me some bad turn, you'll understand...I'm timid...and that..."

"Let's walk," said the Vicomte. "We'll see if all that's true. Come on Hector, and trust me; I have a solid fist, and the fellow won't escape."

Hector and the Fleming therefore took Porion, who seemed resigned, back to the hostelry of the Singe Vert. Having pushed him into the kitchen the Fleming summoned the hotelier. "Do you know this man?" he asked.

"Of course he knows me," said Porion.

"Eh?" said the hotelier. "That's Père Cinnamon."

"Who is Père Cinnamon?"

"A worthy man who lodges here," said the hotelier, astonished to see Porion a prisoner of the two gentlemen.

"You see," said Porion.

But Hector said, in a tone of conviction: "I swear that it's him."

"So," said the Fleming, "this man lodges here?"

"Yes."

"On what floor?"

"At the very top."

"Very good. Give me my candle."

Porion thought he was free and wanted to pay in audacity. "You can see that I'm neither a thief not a deliverer of knife-thrusts," he said. "In consequence, *bonsoir*, Messieurs, and no hard feelings." And he tried to disengage himself from the Vicomte de Mauroy's grip—but the Fleming did not let him go.

"I believe all that you tell me, but I want to have a little chat with you."

"Ah!"

"And we're going to go up to your room."

"Why can't we chat here?"

"We'll be more comfortable in your room."

"As you wish," said Porion, increasingly anxious.

"Go on ahead," the Fleming said, when they were at the foot of the staircase, "and don't try to run away, as you did just now, or I'll plant my sword in your back."

Porion started climbing the stairs of the hostelry with a tottering tread.

At that moment, the Fleming looked round and saw the hotelier making him a mysterious sign.

"Hector," said the Vicomte, "don't lose sight of this man for an instant, and wait for me at the top of the stairs."

Hector went up behind Père Cinnamon, while the Fleming went back down.

The host winked in a significant fashion. When he saw that the Fleming was coming down again he retreated to a corner of his kitchen. The Vicomte followed him.

The hotelier said, in a whisper: "Be careful."

"Of what?" asked the Fleming.

"You don't know that man?"

"Certainly not, since I've just asked you who he is."

"If you wish, I'll give you some good advice," said the host.

"Speak."

"That old man who seems paltry and amiable is a most dangerous man."

"Ah! Really?"

"I'd rather have all the seigneurs of the Court for enemies than that man, my gentleman."

"Does he possess some magic power, then?"

"No, but he's Madame de Pompadour's secret agent."

"Ah! Very good."

"If it pleases him to make a head fall..."

"Bah!"

"No one knows that at Versailles," the hotelier continued, lowering his voice even further, "but I know it. He had the Alsatian kill a gentleman who spoke ill of the Marquise."

"The Alsatian that I nailed to a wall a little while ago?"

"Yes, my gentleman, and it's because you rendered me a real service in ridding us of him that I wish you well and am permitting myself to give you this advice."

"Thank you," said the Vicomte.

"If you believe me," the hotelier finished, "you'll make your apologies to the fellow instead of molesting him and you won't stay in Versailles for long. You can imagine that, in saying that, it's not in my interests to send away my customers, but I repeat, the fellow has a long arm and he's full of rancor."

The Fleming extended his hand to the hotelier.

"You're a worthy man," he said, "and I thank you, so I'll profit from your advice."

And he went back to the staircase, which he went up four at a time.

Porion and Hector had preceded him. Having arrived at the top floor, Hector had taken Porion in hand again, saying: "Let's wait here." Porion had tried to protest again, but Hector had replied: "It's you, definitely you, who abducted Cécile Robert."

The Fleming rejoined them.

"My dear Papa Cinnamon," he said. "Show us your lodgings."

"It's this way," said Porion, taking a corridor feebly lit by a lantern. Then he stopped in front of a door, took a key out of his pocket, and opened it.

Then the Fleming and Hector found themselves on the threshold of a rather large room, but completely contained under the mansard roof, with very meager furniture.

"My dear Monsieur Cinnamon," said the Fleming, "it would be too uncomfortable to chat here; we'll have chairs for everyone. Come to my room; it's much better."

"But in sum, what have you to say to me?" said Porion, increasingly frightened.

"This, first: if you raise your voice, if you utter a cry, if you refuse to walk, I'll kill you!" And, joining pantomime with threat, the Fleming drew his sword.

Porion resigned himself. He closed his door again and, still followed by the Fleming and Hector, went back down to the first floor. It was there that Vicomte Gontran de Mauroy, who was rich, was luxuriously installed. He had a veritably complete apartment.

Once inside, the Vicomte locked his door.

"My dear friend," he said to Hector, "You see this man? Well, not only is he the one who abducted Cécile Robert, he's also the man who paid the Alsatian to kill you."

Porion stepped back, stupefied.

The Fleming went on: "The hotelier, who fears him greatly, has given me the advice to beware of him and make him my apologies, so I'm going to follow that advice." At the same time, he tripped Porion, throwing him to the floor, put his hand over his mouth to prevent him from crying out, and said to Hector: "We're going to tie him up, and I swear to you that it isn't him who'll prevent you from presenting yourself at the King's *petit lever*."

I've been rolled over like a schoolboy, Porion thought, despairingly. But the fellow was too prudent to risk his life, and as the Vicomte was a man who might kill him, he allowed himself to be tied up without the slightest resistance.

When that was done, the Fleming picked him up and carried him to his own bed. Then he said to Hector:

"It's necessary not to look ghastly tomorrow, my friend. Place yourself in that armchair and sleep. I'll watch this fellow."

XVIII

The night advanced.

Hector de Pierrefeu had followed the advice of his new friend, Vicomte Gontran de Mauroy. He had sat down in a large armchair, had crossed his legs, and had not taken long to close his eyes.

The Fleming had stuffed his pipe, thrown an armful of wood on the fire and had said to himself: *A bad night is soon passed.*

As for Porion, trussed up as he was, it was impossible for him to move. For a moment, the fellow was gripped by a sort of concentrated despair. *I'm caught,* he thought, *caught and reduced to impotence. In consequence, the best thing to do is resign myself to it. Evidently, these two men will kill me.*

But Porion was not a man to despair and lament for long. He was a man of energy, in whom audacity had soon regained the upper hand. He was tied up. Had he been free, the Fleming could have knocked him unconscious with a punch. Nevertheless, Porion was thinking about escape.

After ruminating for a quarter of a hour, he said to himself: *If I can get out of here, I could do one of two things: either I could go to warn the Tartar, or I could make an arrangement with Madame de Pompadour to prevent our young man from having his audience tomorrow morning.*

But it was necessary to get out of that room, where he was a prisoner with his hands and feet bound, and of which the Fleming, having locked the door, had put the key in his pocket.

For anyone other than Porion, the thing would have seemed implausible and impossible.

The Fleming had taken a newspaper from his pocket that did not get into France easily, the *Gazette de Hollande*.[31] That paper, which was an insulting diatribe against France, the King and the Court, which attached Madame de Pompadour and the royal institution of the Parc-aux-Cerfs vehemently, was strictly prohibited. It was sufficient to be found in possession of such a sheet to be gravely compromised, and there were poor devils and gentlemen in the Bastille whose only crime was to have traded that pamphlet, which almost always included an epigram or a couplet about the omnipotent Marquise

But Vicomte Gontran de Mauroy, a rich and independent man, raised in the provinces in the scorn of courtiers and the Court, and whose lands, moreover,

---

[31] The *Gazette d'Amsterdam*, popularly known as the *Gazette de Hollande*, had been founded by Huguenots forced to flee France when Louis XIV revoked the Edict of Nantes, and it continued publication almost to the end of the 18th century, maintaining a relentless propaganda war against the Bourbons. Its contents were almost entirely written by French emigrants bearing grudges.

were in the frontier, had no scruples about being a subscriber to the *Gazette de Hollande*. The administration, moreover, took responsibility for getting it to him, at its risk and peril, and it arrived very regularly. The latest issue had reached him just as he was mounting his horse to set off for Versailles, so he had stuck it in his pocket without reading it and had climbed into the saddle.

During the four days that his journey had lasted, Gontran de Mauroy had always gone to bed too late to read, and that explains how he had arrived in Paris without having opened his paper. The obligation he had that night to keep his eyes open and watch Porion thus gave him the leisure. So the Vicomte had gone to a side-table near the fireplace, placed a candle on the mantelpiece and rolled up an armchair next to it. Then, with his pipe in his mouth, he had started reading tranquilly, sometimes interrupting his reading in order to ascertain that Porion was not moving.

Porion was pretending to be asleep, but when the Vicomte returned his eyes to his paper, Porion opened one of his own. And that eye, which was piercing, had succeeded after a quarter of an hour in deciphering the title of the newspaper.

Then Porion said to himself: *Let's suppose that, instead of being tied up, I'm free, and that instead of being a prisoner, I can get out of here, and, for an hour or two, neither of my guardians perceive my escape... I run to the château... it's midnight, but what does it matter? I have the means of reaching the Marquise at any hour. Oh, then, I believe that Monsieur de Pierrefeu would not have his audience, and that Monsieur Gontran de Mauroy's indemnity would not soon be regulated.*

Poor heads, narrow minds that bump into an obstacle, cannot see beyond it. Strong minds suppress the obstacle in thought and meditate on what they will do when that obstacle has disappeared in reality.

While the Fleming read, Porion gradually drew up his battle plan. When he had settled that battle plan, he thought about an escape plan. The choice, as we have said and we shall see, was not, so to speak, practicable. A Hercules could not have broken the bonds securing Porion's arms and legs, and Porion was only an old man devoid of strength. Nevertheless, Porion thought seriously about escaping.

For a while he hoped that the Fleming might end up falling asleep. When sleep takes possession of such Herculean individuals, it grips them long and hard; it would require a cannon-shot or the sound of a bell to wake them. But the Fleming did not appear to have any desire to go to sleep. The bowl of his pipe was still burning, and enormous spirals of blue smoke were rising slowly toward the ceiling, tinted pink as they passed in front of the candle.

Oh, said Porion to himself, *if, instead of smoking, he took snuff, and he asked me for a pinch, how things would go like clockwork thereafter!*

In order to make such a reflection, it was necessary for Porion to have had an idea.

The Fleming continued reading, and Porion suddenly heard him laugh out loud.

"Damn!" he murmured. "Those are pretty verses and elegantly turned. Monsieur de Maurepas is truly a man of great wit."[32]

The *Gazette de Hollande* reprinted a famous quatrain that had earned it author exile a few months earlier.

On hearing the Fleming laugh, Porion pretended to wake up.

"Brrr!" he said. "It's damnably cold."

The Fleming raised his head. "Oh, are you cold, fellow?" he said.

"My gentleman," said Porion, humbly. "Since you persist in your error and remain convinced that I'm a spy, when I'm only a poor inoffensive bourgeois, don't show yourself to be inhumane."

"What do you want me to do for you, rogue?"

"Throw your cloak over my shoulders."

"Thanks you very much," said the Fleming, "my mantle is over my shoulders and fulfilling its employment very well. I'm a good fellow, though, and although you're scarcely worth the trouble, I'll do something for you."

With those words, the Fleming put his paper down next to the candle and, without abandoning his pipe, he got up, approached the bed, lifted Porion up bodily, like a feather, and carried him close to the fire, where he laid him out full length.

"Now," he said, "be careful not to get too hot, because I don't like being disturbed."

Porion tried to thank him, but his thanks were cut short by a formidable sneeze. "Since you don't like to be disturbed," he said, finally, when the sneezing fit had passed, "take generosity all the way to the end, Monseigneur."

"What do you want now?" said the Fleming.

"I'd like to take a pinch of tobacco."

"Indeed!"

"After which, I'll be quite tranquil...very tranquil...I promise you."

"For that, it would be necessary to untie your hands."

"You can tie them again afterwards."

"True. But I don't have any snuff; I rarely take it."

"I have some."

"Because I'm a smoker," said the Fleming, "I know how I'd suffer if someone took away my pipe. I'll take pity on you, rogue."

And as he would have been able to fell Porion with a blow of his fist if he tried to take advantage of the moment of liberty he was about to give him, the

---

[32] Jean-Frédéric Phélypeaux, Comte de Maurepas, was Chamberlain of the Royal Household and director of the secret police from 1742-49, but was removed as a result of a plot engineered by the Duc de Richelieu, and subsequently banished, ostensibly for writing an insulting epigram about Madame de Pompadour.

Fleming untied his hands and then helped him to sit up. Porion uttered a sigh of relief, put his hand in his pocket and drew out a beautiful tortoiseshell snuff-box, which he opened, and into which he plunged the thumb and index finger of his right hand with an ineffable voluptuousness.

The tobacco was Spanish. It was a veritable luxury then, and only people at Court made use of it. The tobacco was perfumed, and the aroma that escaped from his snuff-box tickled the olfactory nerves of the worthy Fleming very agreeably.

"Damn!" he said. "You have good tobacco, it seems to me, fellow."

Porion had closed his snuff-box, and with a movement so rapid that the Fleming had been unable to perceive it, he had turned it upside down. "Monseigneur," he said humbly, "it's not customary for a poor man to offer a pinch to a man of quality; otherwise..."

"Yes," said the Fleming, "but a man of quality can sometimes ask an inferior for a pinch. In consequence, give me one. Your tobacco is scented like balm."

"Oh, gladly," said Porion. And he opened his snuff-box again. The Fleming did not perceive that it had a double bottom, and opened on both sides.

"Excellent tobacco," repeated the Fleming, smearing his nose complaisantly.

Porion replaced the snuff-box in his pocket. After which the Fleming picked up the rope and said: "Give me your hands."

"Oh, whatever you wish, now," said Porion. "My nose is garnished, I'm warm and I'm resigned to being your prisoner until the time when you recognize your error."

And he allowed his hands to be rebound with a good grace and lay down in front of the fire.

Then the Fleming reloaded his pipe, lit it with a firebrand, picked up his newspaper and resumed reading.

After a few minutes, however, the Vicomte's eyelids began to flutter. He shook himself and continued reading, but he stopped smoking, and his pipe went out. Finally, the newspaper escaped from his hands. Then he tried to struggle against sleep and gripped his armchair, but an invincible force nailed him there.

At the same time, his eyes closed, and as if an immense weight had suddenly been placed on top of it, his head slumped on to his robust breast.

The Fleming was asleep.

Then Porion murmured: "Now, it's a matter of breaking my bonds. If I can do that, it's not him who'll stop me getting out of here.

Hector, also vanquished by fatigue, was sleeping the good and heavy slumber that is the prerogative of youth.

XIX

Porion had, however, been tied up by expert hands, and the rope that bound his feet and hands was as thick as his little finger. In order to succeed in escaping, three things were required, even assuming that the narcotic mixed with the tobacco contained in the double-sided snuff-box was powerful enough to prevent the Fleming from waking up henceforth.

First it was necessary for him to untie himself. It was then necessary for him to be able to retrieve the key to the room from Vicomte Gontran de Mauroy's pocket. Finally, he had to be able to go to the door and open it without Hector, who was sleeping quite naturally, waking up.

Those three difficulties, which seemed insurmountable, did not deter Porion.

His hands were tied behind his back, and any effort to break the rope would have been fruitless. But the fire was ardent, and Porion was only two feet from the grate. A brand that rolled toward him suggested an idea to him. Instead of rolling over—the only movement permitted to him—and drawing away from the brand, he drew nearer to it, executing the movement in the inverse direction, and, succeeding in turning his head in such a fashion as to be able to see behind him, he put his two hands to the brand and brought the rope into contact with it..

Then, with a heroic courage, without uttering a cry of pain—for the fire was so close to his hands that his skin was gradually roasting—the man waited for the rope to catch fire.

The hemp was dry. When he saw that the rope was burning, Porion drew away from the brand with little somersaults. That was the affair of a few minutes, during which Porion supported the bite of the fire stoically. Then, when the rope was partly consumed, he made a violent effort, and it broke. Porion's hands were horribly burned, but they were free.

"Oof!" he said. "That's a fine line to add to His Highness Prince Trespatky's bill. I've burned a thousand écus' worth of flesh."

Once his hands were free, he had soon untied his legs and he was on his feet. The first difficulty had been overcome. The other two remained.

He made an eye-shade of his hand and looked at Hector. The young man was asleep, and there was a smile on his lips. Perhaps he was dreaming that the King was listening to him kindly, and ordering the punishment of André's murderers.

Having tied Porion up, the Fleming had only taken incomplete precautions. He had placed on the table beside the candles not only his sword but also two fine pistols with shiny butts, carefully loaded and primed.

That's what will protect my retreat, Porion said to himself. And he took one of the pistols, put his finger on the hammer and cocked it silently. *If the oth-*

er wakes up, he thought, *I'll have blown his brains out before he's had time to get up*.

Holding the pistol in his right hand, he employed the left to search the Fleming's pockets. The later was snoring like a cathedral organ. While searching for the key, Porion encountered papers. He was curious, and drew out the papers as well as the key. Still holding the pistol and watching the sleeping Hector from the corner of his eye, he started riffling through them and scanning them.

They were letters concerning the famous indemnity that the Vicomte was claiming. Among them there was one from the Ministry of War. Porion scanned it rather lightly at first, but at the third line he shuddered, slipped to the signature and read: *Normand*.

Now, as we have said, Porion knew everything, or almost everything. As much by inclination as his métier, he liked to have informants everywhere. He had one in the Ministry of War, the portfolio of which was then confided to a man who was to leave behind a renown for parsimony and avarice, Abbé Terray.

Now, by virtue of that secret intelligence, Porion knew that the abbé was not liked by his subordinates, who resented him, and that among them there was a bureau chief named Normand, who had often tried to send reports concerning his minister to the King. Porion therefore took cognizance of Monsieur Normand's recently-dated letter, which had doubtless determined the Fleming's voyage.

The bureau chief wrote:

My dear Vicomte.

This is completely confidential. Your indemnity will not be paid. The minister has had the report sent to him, has examined the evidence supporting your claim, and had recognized that it is just. But, having conceded that, he said that the treasury is heavily burdened with debt, and that he is very sorry, but as long as he is minister, he will elude the issue so well that you will never have a sou.

I believe that it is not only futile but imprudent for your steward to return, for that damnable abbé, for whom all means are good, is capable of employing against him one of the numerous lettres de cachet *that he always has in his portfolio. Follow my advice, therefore, come to Versailles and try to obtain an audience with the King. It is the sole means by which your claim will not fall by the wayside.*

I have the honor to be, etc.,

Normand.

Porion folded up the letter and put it in his pocket. Then he cast a glance at the *Gazette de Hollande*. The famous quatrain soon attracted his attention.

There we go! he said to himself, with a smile of satisfaction. *I think that things will go even better than I thought at first.* And he replaced the *Gazette de Hollande* in the Fleming's pocket.

Afterwards, still with the pistol in his hand, ready to fire if Hector woke up, he marched toward the door. The thickness of the carpet permitted Porion to muffle the sound of his footsteps so well that he reached the door without Hector stirring. To introduce the key into the lock and turn it was child's play for Porion.

The door swung on its hinges without creaking. Then Porion removed the key with the same precaution, and from the inside, replaced it in the lock outside. Once in the corridor, he closed the door slowly, and locked it with the same silent dexterity.

"Now," he murmured, "it's them who are my prisoners. Let's go see if there's a place for them in the Bastille."

Hector was still sleeping peacefully in his armchair, as Porion was able to assure himself by putting his eye to the keyhole.

As we have said, it was then after midnight. Everyone in the Singe Vert was asleep, with the exception of the hotelier, who was in a corner of the kitchen, sitting at a little table, counting the day's receipts. Porion, who was familiar with the layout of the hostelry, went down quietly to the kitchen.

Then the host raised his head and made a gesture of astonishment. "You, Papa Cinnamon!" he said.

Porion put a finger to his lips. "Shh!" he said. And he approached the host in great mystery, took a chair, said down beside him, and said: "It's necessary that I talk to you, Monsieur Aubert." That was the name of the landlord of the Singe Vert.

"Oh," said Master Aubert, as he was known in his inn, "What happened to you this evening with those two gentlemen, Papa Cinnamon?"

Porion assumed an even more mysterious expression. "My friend," he said, "you know who I am..."

"Certainly" said the hotelier, suppressing a slight shiver.

"It's better to do me good than harm..."

"Oh, certainly."

"Since I've been lodging with you, no unfortunate adventure has befallen you, has it?"

"None."

"And your establishment continues to prosper, does it not?"

"One makes ends meet, Papa Cinnamon.

"You have a grown-up daughter that you're thinking of establishing, haven't you?"

"Well, she'll soon be eighteen."

"You love your wife?"

"She's good-natured and a hard worker, my dear Monsieur. Why wouldn't I love her?"

"In sum," said Porion, "everything is going as you wish, is it not?"

"Very nearly, at least."

"Well, my poor friend," said Porion "all that could fall apart in no time at all."

"What do you mean?" said the hotelier, starting in his chair, his face suddenly taking on a slight pallor.

"Have you heard mention of the master of the hostelry of the Lion d'Or in the Rue Saint-Martin?"

"Yes?"

"Do you know what happened to him?"

"No."

"His inn was closed and he was put in prison."

"Why?"

"Because he had lodged conspirators."

"Poor man! But..."

"Well," said Porion, "you're in exactly the same situation, my poor friend."

"Me!" exclaimed the host, fearfully.

"You—and but for me, you might go to the Bastille." Master Aubert joined his hands fearfully. "For you know who those two men are who were maltreating me a little while ago?"

"But...they're..."

"They're wretches who introduce into France pamphlets against Madame de Pompadour."

"Lord God!'" exclaimed Master Aubert. "I'll throw them out now!"

"Refrain from doing that."

"What shall I do, then?" asked the host, whose fear was increasing.

"If you want your inn to be closed and to be imprisoned along with your wife and daughter, you have only to go upstairs and warn them."

"My God!"

"If you want nothing to happen to you, it's necessary, on the contrary, to take your hunting rifle..."

"All right!"

"And go lie in ambush in the corridor...."

"And then?"

"I've locked them in and they're asleep, but it's possible that they'll wake up and scent danger. If they break down the door to get out, shoot them."

"But what about you, Monsieur Cinnamon? Where are you going?"

"To fetch soldiers to arrest them," said Porion.

And he went out, firmly convinced that the landlord belonged to him body and soul henceforth, by virtue of the power of fear.

XX

Porion only had a short step to take from the small street where the Singe Vert was to the château. However, before approaching one of the posterns by which one entered when the gates were closed, he paused momentarily and paraded an investigative gaze over the façade of the palace, which was speckled here and there with the light of a few belated lamps.

Abbé Terray lodged at Versailles. For one thing, the King liked to have his Ministers around him, in order not to be put to any inconvenience, and secondly, the abbé, who was very miserly, preferred having free accommodation to renting a house or having one built. He was, moreover, a valiant minister, the little churchman who had restored the two departments of War and Finance.

He went to bed at eight o'clock in the evening, but, winter or summer, he got up at three o'clock in the morning to set to work, most of the time without a fire, enveloped in an old smock that his valet de chambre would not have wanted.

What Porion was looking for was the indefatigable minister's lamp.

It was not yet three o'clock in the morning, but it was after two. After a certain hour, the doors of the château no longer opened except for a few great seigneurs who had special permits. Those permits consisted of a round card, brown in color, in the middle of which was a golden fleur-de-lys. Madame de Pompadour had given one of those cards to Porion, but Porion so rarely made use of it that the sentinel guarding the postern was astonished to see him equipped with it. Porion's paltry appearance and worn apparel clashed with that favor in high places.

Nevertheless, the gate was opened to him—but the sentinel felt the need to take him to the chief of the guard-post at the main door. The officer looked Porion up and down at first and asked him how it was that a peasant like him was furnished with such a card.

"Monsieur," Porion said to him, "I'm going to see the Marquise de Pompadour, and if you'd like to accompany me, perhaps you'll be surprised to see that the Marquise will grant me an audience in the middle of the night."

The officer was a prudent man, who was determined to remain at court; he therefore allowed Porion to pass.

Porion set forth, and as he was traversing the courtyard he raised his eyes to the façade again. The window of Abbé Terray's study, previously dark, had just been illuminated. The minister had got up half an hour earlier than usual.

Marvelous! thought Porion. *I won't have any need to wake the Marquise.* And he went into the château.

The servants on duty, distributed here and there in the corridors and on the staircases, were more familiar with the brown card with the fleur-de-lys. Porion

244

passed everywhere. He arrived in the minister's antechamber, where he found an old domestic lying on a bench.

The domestic initially raised a few difficulties about introducing the matinal visitor, but Porion said to him: "It's matter of a sum of ten thousand écus that you'll cause your master to lose."

The lackey did not need any more than that. He opened a door, and Porion found himself on the threshold of Abbé Terray's study. The Abbé was in his underwear and slippers, and seemed to be paying no heed to the rigor of the temperature, as he had no fire. Sitting at a table laden with papers, he had just started work when Porion came in.

He raised his head, perceived the man, whom he was seeing for the first time, and said, abruptly: "Who are you?"

"My name is Porion," the latter replied, humbly.

"What do you want of me?"

"I desire Your Excellency to listen to me for a moment."

"If you're a solicitor," said the abbé, brutally, "you can go away; neither the State, nor the King, nor I have any money."

"Instead of coming to ask Your Excellency for money," said Porion, "I've brought you some."

Those words caused the Minister to make a veritable bound. He looked at the poorly-dressed man and wondered whether he might be in the presence of a madman. But Porion put his card before the Minister's eyes.

"That," he said, "will explain to Your Excellency how I was able to get this far."

"Who gave you that card?"

"Madame de Pompadour."

"Ah!" And the Minister looked at Porion with disdainful curiosity.

"Monseigneur," said Porion, "I'll tell you immediately who I am. I'm a police agent in the service of Madame de Pompadour."

"So?" said the abbé, whose lips accentuated the disdain.

"In the course of my service, I've found an opportunity to be agreeable and useful to Your Excellency."

"Really?" said the abbé, with a hint of irony.

"And if Your Excellency will deign to listen to me..."

"Speak."

"Your Excellency, it appears, has been fatigued and tormented by the claims of a certain Flemish gentleman, Vicomte Gontran de Mauroy."

The abbé shuddered. "How do you know that?" he said.

"Am I not a policeman?"

"That's true. Continue."

Porion went on: "That gentleman is claiming an indemnity of ten thousand écus."

"It isn't me who'll pay them," said the Minister.

"Perhaps…"

"Oh, indeed!"

"The gentleman has the intention of addressing himself to the King."

"To the King!" said the abbé.

"He has come to Versailles."

"When?"

"He's already here, Monseigneur."

Abbé as he was, the Minister could not suppress a forceful oath.

"And he has a letter of audience for this morning."

"Oh, that's too much!" said the abbé, striking the table with his fist.

"I thought that news might cause Your Excellency chagrin," Porion continued, "and it's for that reason that I've come."

"Well," said the Minister, curtly. "What can you do about it?"

"If Your Excellency will lend himself to it, I can prevent that audience."

"How."

"By getting rid of the Vicomte."

"What?" said the abbé, misunderstanding Porion's meaning.

"Don't worry, Monseigneur," said the latter. "It's only a matter of a simple *lettre de cachet*."

The Minister shrugged his shoulders. "One can't put people in the Bastille without a reason," he said.

"Permit me to explain, Your Excellency," said Porion, "and hear me out."

"Go on."

"If Vicomte Gontran de Mauroy were guilty of no other crime than claiming his ten thousand écus, it would, indeed, be absurd to ask for a *lettre de cachet* for him, but…"

"But what?"

"If I take a carriage," said Porion, "go to Paris and give Monsieur de Sartine a certain item of information, he will give me the *lettre de cachet*."

"What will you tell him, then?"

"That the Vicomte is in Versailles in the company of one of his friends, and that the two gentlemen have introduced into the kingdom an abominable pamphlet, the *Gazette de Hollande*, which contains frightful verses against Madame la Marquise de Pompadour."

"In truth!" said the Minister.

"Yes, Monseigneur."

"Ah!" said the Abbé Terray, who started rubbing his hands. "I know that people go to the Bastille for less than that."

"Undoubtedly."

"In consequence, my dear Monsieur, I engage you to hasten to Paris and ask Monsieur de Sartine for a *lettre de cachet* to send the two gentlemen to the Bastille. And you're right: in acting thus, you've rendered me a true service, for that Fleming's demands were irritating me horribly. I'll even promise you a small gratification."

"But Your Excellency is forgetting..."

"What?"

"That before I've returned from Paris and Monsieur Sartine has given his orders, the gentleman in question will have had his audience."

"Damn!" And Abbé Terray became pensive momentarily. Then his face cleared. "That's true, what you say," he said, "but the harm isn't as great as you think, Monsieur Porion."

"Why is that, Monseigneur?"

"The King doesn't have ten thousand écus in his pocket."

"Oh, I should think not."

"If he had them, it would be Madame de Pompadour who would obtain them."

Porion started to smile.

"In consequence, the King will limit himself to giving me orders."

"Good!"

"Orders that he'll retract as soon as he knows why the Vicomte is in the Bastille."

"Yes," said Porion, "but between now and then, the *Gazette de Hollande* might disappear, and the Vicomte might throw it in the fire. Then, *bonsoir!*"

Abbé Terray shivered.

"While at present," Porion continued, "the Vicomte is asleep. He was drunk yesterday evening, and he's sleeping like a log. Let us suppose that I have a *lettre de cachet*, that I penetrate into his lodgings with soldiers, and I begin by putting my hands on the *Gazette*."

"Ah! That's a good idea," said the Minister. And he opened a drawer and took out a *lettre de cachet*. But as he was about to hand it to Porion, he hesitated. "But," he said, "what proof can you give me that the gentleman you're going to arrest really is Vicomte de Mauroy? For if it isn't him, I don't want to meddle in Madame de Pompadour's affairs."

Porion took out of his pocket the letter written by Monsieur Normand to Gontran de Mauroy and showed it to the Minister."

The latter paled with anger after having read it.

"That's a man I'll throw out this very day," he murmured. Then, looking at Porion, he said: "In truth, you have an answer for everything." And he let go of the *lettre de cachet*, which Porion seized, quivering with joy.

XXI

Hector de Pierrefeu would doubtless have slept for a long time yet had he not been awoken by a certain racket. He stirred in his armchair, stretched his limbs, opened his eyes and came to his feet.

The candle was still burning on the table. Vicomte Gontran de Mauroy, slumped in his armchair, was sleeping noisily.

Hector, still numbed by sleep, cocked an ear in order to determine where the noise that had woken him up had come from, and its nature.

The heavy and measured tread of a night patrol had stopped at the door of the hostelry. Then those footfalls had been audible in the corridors, and appeared to be heading for the door of the room that he occupied with the Vicomte. A secret presentiment assailed Hector.

"Hey, Monsieur!" he called, in order to wake the Fleming—but the Fleming did not budge.

The Hector turned his eyes toward the bed on which they had deposited Porion, bound, the previous evening. Porion was no longer there.

"Monsieur?" Hector repeated.

And he approached the armchair and started shaking the Vicomte, but the colossus continued snoring loudly. Hector ran to the door then, and tried to open it. The door was locked and the key was not in the lock.

The young man thought he remembered that after having locked the door, the Vicomte had put the key in his pocket. He therefore went back to him and shook him harder, but still with no result. Placed as he was he was facing the window, and could see the first light of dawn sliding through the shutters.

Why was Porion no longer there? Why was the Vicomte sleeping so profoundly that he could not succeed in waking him up? Finally, why, instead of two, was there only one pistol on the table?

Hector asked himself those three questions successively, but he did not have time to resolve them. The key turned in the lock, the door opened, and the room was invaded by soldiers. More astonished than afraid, Hector took a step backwards. He had unbuckled his sword when be extended himself in the armchair the previous evening and had placed it in a chair within arm's reach—but he did not think of picking up the sword and putting himself on the defensive.

Evidently, the soldiers could not have anything to do with him, and there was some misunderstanding. At their head was a police runner. The policeman leapt toward the sleeping Fleming. At the same time, one of the soldiers took a step toward Hector, put a hand on his shoulder and said: "I arrest you in the name of the King."

"You're arresting me!" Hector exclaimed. He tried to move back toward the armchair and pick up his sword, but two other soldiers threw themselves upon him, and he found himself reduced to impotence.

The police runner had approached the Vicomte, who was still asleep, and searched his pockets. He soon put his hands on the copy of the *Gazette de Hollande*. "Ah!" he said. "Here's the *corpus delicti!* Now we can act without scruple." Then he shook the Fleming in his turn. "But he won't wake up!"

"Oh, not yet," said a voice that made Hector de Pierrefeu shiver. And the young man saw Porion appear, who had prudently stood back until then.

Porion looked at Hector, smiling. "I believe," he said, "that I'm taking my revenge, my young seigneur. What do you say about that?"

"Wretch!" said Hector.

"Oh," said Porion, calmly, "you can hurl as many insults at me as you like. I've heard many others. Don't inconvenience yourself, my gentleman. They slide over me like rain from a roof."

The police runner went straight to Hector. "Monsieur," he said, "by virtue of this *lettre de cachet*, in the name of the King, I arrest you."

"You're arresting me?"

"Yes," said the policeman.

"What crime have I committed, then?"

"You're the accomplice of this man." And he designated the Fleming, who was still snoring, and doubtless dreaming that he would be paid his indemnity of ten thousand us.

"What is his crime?" asked Hector, again.

"You'll be informed at the Bastille."

At that terrible name, Hector's hair stood on end. "At the Bastille!" he echoed, in a strangled voice.

"You'll be very comfortable there," said Porion, in a mocking tone. Then the rogue addressed the policeman. "Go on, Monsieur," he said, "do your duty."

The runner said to Hector: "It would be repugnant to me, Monsieur, to have the hands of a gentleman bound and to resort to violence against him. Will you go with me of your own free will?"

Hector inclined his head. Two soldiers placed themselves to either side of him. Then, at a sign from the policeman, two others took possession of the sleeping Vicomte, lifted him up bodily, and loaded him on to their shoulders.

The noise that the soldiers had made had set the entire hostelry abuzz. Domestics and scullions had got up in haste. The gentlemen who were sleeping in the inn had leapt out of bed and opened their doors to see what was happening. But the hotelier, Master Aubert, was talking loudly in the corridor, and, still armed with his hunting rifle, he was saying: "It's a *lettre de cachet* being put into execution."

Those words were sufficient for no one to think of taking the side of the two unfortunate gentlemen. So Hector, between two soldiers, and the Vicomte, carried on the shoulders of two others, traversed the corridor and the staircase and arrived at the door of the hostelry without anyone thinking of liberating them.

Equipped with the famous *lettre de cachet*, Porion had acted in accordance with the regulations. He had requisitioned an agent, who had placed himself under his orders; the policeman had taken soldiers with him and had been accompanied by four men from the constabulary.

The latter were downstairs, on horseback, arranged two by two at the door of a carriage of the kind then known as "chamber-pots." On Porion's orders, the Vicomte was carried to one, and then Hector was made to sit down beside him, while the policeman placed himself facing them.

Porion climbed up on to the seat beside the coachman. "To the Bastille!" he said.

The chamber-pot moved off and departed, escorted by the four men from the constabulary.

The effect of the narcotic was not eternal, however. About six hours after having absorbed the pinch of tobacco that had proved so catastrophic, Vicomte Gontran de Mauroy opened his eyes. When they were open, though, he started rubbing them, thinking that he was still asleep. In fact, he could not believe his eyes.

He was in a small room with bare walls, illuminated by a single window fitted with thick iron bars, set so high that even a tall man could not reach it.

He was lying on a camp bed, with a chair and a table facing him: a wicker chair and a white-wood table supporting a pitcher full of water.

"Damnation!" exclaimed the Fleming. "Where am I, then?"

Turning his head to the right and left he perceived another bed similar to his own, and, lying on that bed, Hector de Pierrefeu, who was looking at him sadly.

The Vicomte stood up in a single movement and repeated, in a Stentorian voice: "Where are we, then?"

"In the Bastille, my friend," Hector replied.

"In the Bastille?"

"Yes."

The Fleming took two steps forward, like a wounded boar turning toward the rifle shot. Then, as there was a door between the two beds, he rushed upon it—but the door was lined with iron and fitted with three large bolts and an enormous lock.

"I don't know whether we're in the Bastille," howled the colossus, "but what I do know is that we're in prison."

He quit the door and ran to the window. With an agility that one would not have suspected in such a big man, he leapt up and seized the iron bars with both hands. Then, with his Herculean strength, he levered himself up with his arms, high enough for his face to reach the bars. He perceived the Porte Saint-Antoine in front of him, and the black houses surrounding it. Then, letting go of the bars, he fell back to the floor saying: "Yes, we're definitely in the Bastille. But why? How? I slept very soundly, then?"

During the journey, Porion had given himself the satisfaction of relating his ingenious escape to his prisoner, through the open window of the carriage.

"Did you untie your man's hands?" said Hector.

"Yes, for a minute, for him to take a pinch of tobacco."

"And you took another?"

"Oh, thunder!" exclaimed the Fleming. "I remember now. I went to sleep like a brute!"

"And our man took advantage of it."

"But..."

"He's obtained a *lettre de cachet* against us."

"A *lettre de cachet?*"

"Yes; otherwise we wouldn't be here."

"But how? Why?"

"Didn't you have in your possession an issue of the *Gazette de Hollande*?"

That question was a flash of enlightenment for the Fleming. "A thousand thousand thunders!" he cried. "These things only happen to me!"

"You won't have your audience with the King," said Hector, sadly, "and nor will I."

"Bah!" said the Fleming. "It's a bad turn by Abbé Terray. Oh, the scoundrel! But..."

"But what?" said Hector.

"But it isn't sufficient to put me in the Bastille," said the Fleming, who had suddenly recovered all his calm. "It's necessary to keep me here."

"Oh," said Hector, shaking his head, "When one is in the Bastille by virtue of a *lettre de cachet*, one stays there."

"Or one escapes," said the Fleming. And as Hector looked at him in amazement, he said: "Well, do you think we have the time to stay here?"

He spoke with so much phlegm and assurance that a ray of hope penetrated Hector de Pierrefeu's desolate heart.

XXII

Let us leave our friend Hector had his companion in misfortune in the Bastille now, and follow Porion.

After having consigned his two prisoners to the Bastille and receiving the felicitations of the governor, Monsieur de Launay,[33] who was always charmed to see people arriving who had been able to displease the omnipotent Marquise, the police agent went to the Rue du Pas-de-la-Mule. It was there that the Tartar Prince Trespatky was lodged in a house that belonged to his friend the Comte de Clermont. It was then about nine o'clock in the morning. Porion was received by a Kalmuk domestic who did not know a single word of French, and was obliged to go and fetch the little old German who was the Prince's physician and whose name was Hermann.

Hermann arrived, and as he knew Porion he said: "You want to see the Prince?"

"Yes."

"You've come too early in the morning."

"Oh?"

"The Prince spent last night at supper; he's drunk. He's still asleep."

"Well," said Porion coldly, "it's necessary to wake him up."

"Oh!"

"It's necessary."

"You have something very important and very urgent to tell him, then?"

"Would I be insisting otherwise?"

Nevertheless, Hermann still hesitated. "Well," he said, "Since it's necessary to tell you everything, the Prince is taking a bath."

"Yes, a bath in blood," said Porion.

The old man shivered. "You know that?" he said.

"I know everything."

"Come, then."

Hermann took Porion by the hand, led him through a vestibule, and opened a door that revealed a stairway apparently descending into the cellars of the house. A lantern suspended from the vault illuminated it.

Potion allowed the little old man, who was walking ahead of him, to guide him.

---

[33] In fact, the governor of the Bastille in 1756 was Pierre Baisle, who had replaced Duc René Jourdan de Launay in 1749. The latter's son was to make the surname far more famous because he was the governor in 1789 when the Bastille was stormed during the Revolution and he was murdered.

After thirty steps, the later opened a second door. Then Porion found himself on the threshold of a small vaulted room from which a strong odor of blood emerged. In the middle there was a bath, and in that bath the Tartar, who appeared to be prey to an unparalleled voluptuousness.

"Aha!" said the Prince, on seeing Porion enter. "Hermann did well to bring you. I have no secrets from you. Besides which, it's ox-blood. I no longer have any need of the other.

Porion, wretched and criminal as he was himself, could not help a slight frisson.

The Tartar went on: "Sit down. It appears that we need to talk?"

"Oh, intimately," said Porion. He took a stool and sat down. Then the Prince made a sign to the old man, who went out.

"Monseigneur," Porion said, when they were alone, "you and I had a narrow escape last night."

"What!" said the Tartar. "You haven't found a means of getting rid of the young man for me?"

"Yes, but not without difficulty." And Porion told him what had happened.

The Tartar shivered on thinking that Hector had almost reached the King. Then he laughed aloud when Porion told him how he had succeeded in putting Hector in the Bastille.

"Well," he said, "how much do I owe you for that fine escapade, rogue?"

"Monseigneur," said Porion, "with a seigneur of the Court of France, I would have made my conditions in advance, but with you..."

"You're relying on my generosity?"

"Yes," he said.

"You'll have two thousand éus," said the Tartar.

Porion bowed, and seemed satisfied. Then, after a brief silence, he said: "Monseigneur, it's necessary for us not to go to sleep, in spite of that."

"Speak."

"The Duc de Choiseul, who, as you know, in the Prime Minister, won't fail to make inquiries about his protégé."

"All right."

"Perhaps he'll be able to get him out of the Bastille, and we'll have to begin again."

"What is it necessary to do, then?"

"Continue to amuse the King with the story of the procurator Dumas."

"Ah! Very well."

"And for you to go to court today to pay your respects to Madame de Pompadour."

"I'd thought of that."

Porion remained for a long time in mysterious conference with the Tartar, and it was after midday when he emerged into the Rue du Pas-de-la-Mule. He went in the direction of the Palais Royal, sniffing the air like a man satisfied with himself. The Tartar had paid the two thousand écus and Porion had pockets full of money, partly in coins and partly in bills. A fortune is sometimes inconvenient, or at least engenders numerous cares. Knowing that he had that much money on him, the police agent was afraid of thieves.

I'd do well to return to Versailles promptly, and to arrive there before nightfall, he said to himself. But he had not had anything to eat, and he was beginning to experience hunger pangs.

In the Place Royale, which he had just entered, there was a rotisserie that he had once frequented. *After all,* he thought, *I'm not so richly dressed that anyone would suppose that I had pockets filled with gold. And then, there's nothing to fear from thieves in broad daylight.*

And he went into the rotisserie.

After the kitchen, into which one penetrated first and where the spit was turning from dawn till dusk, there was a room in which small tables were aligned. Twenty people were having a meal there. Porion went to sit down in a corner and summoned the waitress, from whom he ordered a modest lunch. The people who were in the room were chatting loudly. They were petty individuals for the most part, shop assistants, scriptorium employees and lackeys without a place. Porion started eating, and by force of habit, listened to what was being said around him.

A tall lackey rubbed his hands and said: "It serves Monsieur le Duc right; it will teach him not to sack his best servants."

"What's happened to him, then?"

"His horses bolted yesterday evening."

"Where was that?"

"On the road to Chanteloup."

That name caused Porion to shiver.

The lackey went on: "The horses carried him away, the coachman fell off his seat, the carriage turned over, and Monsieur le Duc was trampled and bruised all over."

"Oh! Really?"

"He's been transported to Chanteloup, and they doubt that he'll budge for a fortnight."

A shop assistant, who mingled in politics in his spare time, said, ironically: "Affairs of State won't go any worse."

From then on, Porion was certain. The carriage that had overturned was that of the Duc de Choiseul, and it was the Prime Minister who was being discussed. *Good!* the rogue thought. *That's more god news. In a fortnight, Monsieur de Choiseul will have time to forget his protégé. At any rate, we have a fortnight to spare. There's always that.*

At a table neighboring the one where the former lackey of the Duc de Choiseul was holding forth. Honest bourgeois were having a conversation in low voices were having a conversation which attracted Porion's attention even more. The words *enfants rouges* had been pronounced.

One worthy man was saying: "It's impossible that the King knows about all this."

"How can the King not know?" said someone else.

"People hide what's happening from him, for I don't believe, personally, that a King of France would gladly allow poor children to be murdered."

"But is that really true?" said a third interlocutor.

"You can't doubt it, living as you do at the corner of the Rue des Enfants Rouges."

"I know that the Blue Dragon inn has an evil reputation."

"It's a den of cut-throats."

"The police have searched it several times, though."

"I don't deny it."

"And they've never found anything."

"That's because the police searched badly."

"Bah!"

"I'm sure that there are cadavers of children buried in the cellars."

"Oh, of course!"

"You won't rid me of the idea," said the old fellow. Then, winking: "But it's not the innkeeper and his wife who are the most guilty."

"Oh, you think so?"

"It's on the account of very highly-placed people that they're working, believe me..."

"And those people...?"

"Those people are powerful enough for the truth not to reach the King."

"My friend," said another bourgeois, "would you like some good advice?"

"Speak."

"You're sixty years-old and I'm sixty-six. It isn't you or me who'll have our throats cut at the Blue Dragon inn. You're a bachelor and so am I, so we have nothing to fear for our children."

"So?"

"Let's keep quiet, then, and not get mixed up in all that."

"Perhaps you're right."

"Well, personally," said a younger man, brandishing his knife, "if the people want to go to the house of the Lieutenant of Police and set fire to it, I'm with them!" And that man succeeded in making the entire room share his indignation.

Damn! thought Porion. *If anyone knew who I am, they might well do me a bad turn. Let's hurry up and finish lunch.*

But as Porion said that to himself, a newcomer entered the room. At the sight of him, Porion's expression changed, and he had gooseflesh all over his body. He had recognized Messire Mardochée de Mardoche, painter and gentleman.

XXIII

How did our friend Mardochée happen to be so far from his quarter and in an establishment that certainly did not give credit?

His affairs were not very brilliant, and for some time, Mardochée had been more hard up than ever. The evening before, however, he had embarked Hector for Versailles in Monsieur de Choiseul's carriage, and the latter's valet de chambre had slipped two pistoles into his hand. When Mardochée had two pistoles, he thought he was richer than a financier. So he went forth, sword buckled and a feather in his hat, with his box of colors in his hand, looking for clients in Paris, not much caring where he stopped, going into a tavern when he was thirsty and emerging thirstier than when he went in.

He had not returned to the old Rue Saint-André-des-Arts. A pretty grisette that he had encountered on the Pont Neuf had been the innocent cause of that. The grisette in question lodged in the Rue des Lions-Saint-Paul, in a small room under the roof. She had shared that humble lodging with him, and Mardochée had forgotten himself there for twenty-four hours.

When the painter separated from his conquest, the two pistoles were reduced to a petty écu.

From the Rue des Lions to the Place Royale is only a step. Mardochée crossed it with the intention of going into the Rue Saint-Louis, then the Faubourg Saint-Martin and from there to his dear Pomme Verte tavern. But man proposes and the stomach disposes. On passing under the arcades, Mardochée was seized by the throat by the lush perfumes that were escaping from a rotisserie.

"Bah!" he said. "I'll still have time to go have supper on credit at the Pomme Verte. Let's have lunch here, and death to my last écu!"

Having taken that resolution, he went in.

The room was rather obscure. When someone came in from outside, it took a few minutes for them to be able to see clearly where they were. Mardochée, who was very hungry, went to sit down at a table next to Porion's, but did not see him. Porion took advantage of that to pull his hat over his eyes as far as possible. He would gladly have taken flight, but to that it would have required him to go past Mardochée, and that would have been dangerous.

Mardochée, who had started devouring a chicken thigh doused in mustard, was drinking in small sips and listening to the noisy conversation that had had for its point of departure the mysterious crimes committed in the Blue Dragon inn, and for its point of arrival a general tirade against the Lieutenant de Police.

The police! Mardochée had reason to like them less than anyone. So, with his characteristic lack of inhibition, he joined in with the general conversation.

"Hey, my friends," he said, turning his back to Porion, who did not budge any more than a stone saint in his niche, "perhaps you don't know who I am?"

Everyone looked at him curiously.

"My name is Mardochée de Mardoche," he went on. "I'm a painter and gentleman, and believe me, if I had the Lieutenant de Police by the collar, I'd strangle him."

"What has he done to you, then?" someone asked.

"He has an agent who'll only die by my hand, a certain Porion, alias Père Cinnamon. Oh, the brigand!"

Porion trembled in every limb.

Mardochée continued, while pouring himself a drink: "This Porion, you see, is a wretch of the worst species. He abducts young girls for the King's shameful pleasures."

These words were greeted by a murmur of indignation.

"Everywhere he goes," Mardochée continued, "he sows desolation and mourning."

"Père Cinnamon?" said a voice, "It seems to me that I know that name."

Mardochée turned round and perceived a thickset individual whose face evoked a vague memory in him. "Eh?" he said. "It seems to me that I've seen you somewhere before."

"Yes, at the Pomme Verte."

"That's right," said Mardochée. "So you know him too, Père Cinnamon?"

"Yes, a little old man, very stooped."

"That's him. Oh, the brigand! If I got my hands on him..."

And Mardochée, whom wine made communicative, started telling all those people he did not know the lamentable story of Cécile Robert, and how he, Mardochée, had been the unwitting instrument of the abduction. At that moment, Porion would have given the two thousand écus he had in his pocket to be outside. The poor fellow! Before Mardochée had arrived, he had ordered a slice of black pudding. That black pudding was to be his undoing.

The waitress crossed the room carrying the black pudding on a plate and headed for Père Cinnamon's table. As the waitress was pretty, Mardochée followed her with his gaze. And suddenly, he uttered a cry: "Ah! Wretch!" he said. He got up, and in two bounds, he was upon Porion, whom he grabbed by the collar, saying: "Here he is! Here he is!"

Porion tried to struggle, but the thickset individual had recognized him too. "That's Père Cinnamon!" he said.

"Ah! Brigand! Blackguard!" howled Mardochée. "Your last hour has come!" And he shook Porion so forcefully that his coat ripped and a handful of gold coins rolled noisily over the flagstones.

All the people who were in the room had joined in the tumult and were surrounding Porion and Mardochée.

Porion tried to free himself from the rude grip. "This man is mistaken," he said.

"I'm not mistaken," Mardochée replied. "It's really you, wretch!"

And the other, coming to Mardochée's aid, responded in parallel: "As for Père Cinnamon, that's definitely Père Cinnamon."

"My friends," said Mardochée, "this man has committed enough crimes. Let me do him justice, I beg you."

And Mardochée drew from its scabbard his long rusty cabbage-cleaver, which had never killed a chicken. That did not prevent Porion from believing that he had arrived at his last hour, and uttering a scream of supreme terror.

Some of the bourgeois had bent down and had picked up the gold coins fallen from his pocket. "It's gold," they said.

"It's the price of some new misdeed," replied Mardochée. "It's money for crime!"

"My friends, my good Messieurs," howled Porion, "save me from this madman, and that gold is yours."

The indignation that the story of Cécile Robert's misfortunes had excited was too great for Porion to hope to find liberators among that society.

However, the man who had been talking about the disappearance of children a little while before stopped Mardochée's arm, as it was about to sheathe the entire blade conscientiously in Porion's body.

"Just a moment!" he said.

"Do you want to prevent me from killing this wretch?" exclaimed Mardochée.

"No."

"Let go of my arm, then."

But instead of obeying, the bourgeois went on: "Listen to me for a minute."

"Speak."

"You're a gentleman?"

"I'm proud of it."

"The sword of a gentleman shouldn't be soiled with the blood of this wretch."

"Give me a knife, then," said Mardochée.

"No, not that," said the bourgeois. "The rope is preferable for such a man; it's necessary to hang him."

"Yes! yes!" repeated all the people in the room, in tumult. "That's it! It's necessary to hang him!"

"But where?" asked Mardochée.

"There's a lantern at the door of the establishment."

"Ah! Very well."

"Hang him! Hang him!" howled the crowd.

Porion had thrown himself on his knees. He was begging them to spare his life. "Take my money," he said, "but let me go..."

They replied to him with cries of fury. When the bourgeois of Paris commits himself wholeheartedly, he is ferocious, and nothing can soften him.

As a hanged man has no need of money, Porion was searched, and they took everything they had, including the bills. Then, to the great scandal of the poor rotisseur, who was trembling with fear lest sergeants arrive who would hold him responsible for the summary execution, they took off his coat and dragged him outside,

Then, as today, the Place Royale was almost deserted at any hour of the day or night. Since the Court was at Versailles, the great seigneurs who lodged there had deserted their town-houses. Under the arcades, there were only sparse shops. In the garden, a few children and schoolboys were playing.

When they saw that furious crowd emerging tumultuously from the restaurant, pushing before them an unfortunate old man who was uttering horrible screams, a few people in the vicinity approached, and the children, curious, stopped their games—but no one thought about intervening.

There was, as one of the bourgeois had affirmed, a lantern at the door. Everyone knows that the Place Royale has arcades, above which the houses overhang. The lantern was, therefore, planted in the wall, a foot above the casements of the first-floor windows, at a height of ten or twelve feet.

A ladder was brought, which was set up against one of the pillars; a rope was procured, and the most agile of the band went up to attach it to the lantern. At the same time, Mardochée made a noose and passed it around Porion's neck.

Porion did not even have the strength to scream any longer. He was already half dead. When he had the rope around his neck, a robust bourgeois took him in his arms and climbed up to the middle of the ladder.

"Mercy!" stammered Porion, one last time.

"Hurry up!" cried a voice. "Here come the sergeants!"

Indeed, at the other extremity of the square from the direction of the Rue Saint-Antoine, a dozen sergeants of the watch could be seen running at a precipitate pace. The bourgeois launched Porion into space, and Porion found himself suspended by the neck, his feet in mid-air. At the same time, the improvised executioner came back down the ladder and the crowd took flight, leaving Porion struggling in the supreme convulsions of agony.

The square was broad, and the sergeants had a long way to run before they could cut the rope. Porion would have been well-and-truly dead if, at that moment, Heaven—or, rather, Hell—had not worked a miracle.

A window opened above the lantern, a man leaned out, seized the rope in both hands, and the rope and the hanged man abruptly disappeared through the window, which immediately closed again.

Mardochée had been one of the first to take flight, and he had not seen that unexpected denouement brought to the petty tragedy of which he was the author.

XXIV

How had that unexpected aid, perhaps a trifle belated, come to Porion?

That is what we are about to tell you, by going back in time a few minutes.

On that first floor of the Place Royale lived an old man and a young woman. The old man—we can give him that title because of his white hair and beard—was still tall and robust. The young woman was frail, dainty, and pretty enough to eat. Both of them rarely went out. They were scarcely known by sight in the neighborhood.

One Sunday, the young woman was seen, simply dressed but nevertheless like a young woman of quality, going devoutly to mass at the nearby church. The old man accompanied her, but he wore neither a sheathed épée, nor silver buckles on his shoes, nor powder in his hair, and his costume was entirely black, like that of a lawyer. The neighbors had concluded from that difference in attire that they were not father and daughter, but manservant and mistress.

An old woman looked after the cares of the household.

The old man rarely went out, and if he did, it was in the morning, and anyone who had followed him would have seen him head for the Île Saint-Louis, the quarter of the legal fraternity, with a voluminous portfolio under his arm, stuffed with dossiers, and go up to the apartments of judges, advocates and procurators.

It would not have been difficult for people more curious than the placid inhabitants of the Place Royale to penetrate the petty mystery that seemed to envelop the young woman and the old man. The young woman was named Mademoiselle Espérance de Beaulieu. She was an orphan of the Blaisois region, who had come to Paris a little more than a year ago under the conduct of Maître Patureau—that was the old man's name—who was a steward of sorts.

Mademoiselle Espérance de Beaulieu had come to Paris to sustain a lawsuit on which her entire fortune depended, and that of her brother, a child of fourteen. The daughter of an officer killed in the last war in Flanders, she had lost her mother a few months after her brother's birth. Patureau was the only man who interested himself in the two orphans. A cadet branch of the Beaulieu family had contested the heritage of an aged aunt, and it was to fend that heritage that the young woman had come to Paris, conducted by her old servant. On arrival, she had placed her brother with the Jesuit fathers of the Rue de l'Oratoire, and had installed herself in a large and gloomy apartment in the Place Royale.

Mademoiselle Espérance was an energetic young woman in spite of her slender appearance. She was defending her rights and those of her brother, and she had sworn to succeed. But lawsuits went less rapidly then than they do today, and her adversaries had obtained one postponement after another. Mademoiselle Espérance, who had counted on returning to her dear Blaisois home-land much sooner, found herself delayed indefinitely in Paris.

Thus, the days seemed very long to her, and she passed them in part behind closed shutters, looking through them with the curiosity of any young woman who is not in love and is, in consequence, suffering from ennui.

That day, as usual, she was sitting by the window, with a book in her hand, sometimes interrupting her reading to follow the joyful frolics of the band of children who were playing in the square, when she suddenly heard vociferations. Then she had seen that tumultuous crowd emerge from the rotisserie, pushing Porion ahead of them.

She had shivered on seeing the old man beg for mercy and his executioners preparing the rope, bringing the ladder and setting it up against the wall. Invisible behind her shutters, she had watched all those sinister preparations, and she had called the old manservant.

"Can't we save him?" she said to him.

Patureau frowned. "It's not our concern," he said.

"But we can't let the unfortunate fellow die," she said, in anguish.

"How can we save him?"

"I don't know."

"First of all, it's impossible," said the old man.

"No, no," said Espérance, "I've just had an idea, my friend."

"What, Mademoiselle?"

"The lantern is only a foot from the window."

"Yes—so?"

"When they've suspended him, if you open the shutters abruptly..."

"And then?"

"If you lean out and pull the rope toward you..."

"First of all, it's probable that he'll already be dead."

"What does it matter? It's necessary to try."

"Secondly, those people will invade the house...they might do us a bad turn..."

"Again, what does it matter?" said the young woman, in an authoritarian tone.

Patureau shook his head. "Mademoiselle," he said, "I'd like to obey you, but something tells me that we'd be doing something that will bring us misfortune."

"I want it!" repeated Espérance.

Patureau gave in.

Scarcely was Porion's body swinging in mid-air, than the shutters of the window opened abruptly and, while the crowd took flight, the old man drew the rope and the hanged man toward him.

All that was done so rapidly that neither the bourgeois, who were running away as fast as they could, nor the sergeants who were arriving at a run, had time to take exact account of what had happened. The latter hesitated momentarily over going into the house, and then renounced doing so and set off in pursuit of the bourgeois. Which meant that Porion, who was no longer giving any sign of life, but whose heart was still beating feebly, was carried to a bed, and that the old man and the young woman, after hastening to cut the rope and rid him of the noose, started lavishing cares upon him.

The resurrection took a long time to obtain. It required more than two hours before Porion recovered his senses. His temples and nostrils had been rubbed with vinegar; his feet had been wrapped in hot napkins.

Finally, the hanged man uttered a sigh, then reopened his eyes, thought for a moment that he was waking up in the other world, and was only convinced that he was still in this one when he saw, leaning over him, the adorable and youthful visage of Mademoiselle Espérance de Beaulieu.

If I were in the other world, he thought, *I certainly wouldn't be in paradise, and I'd see demons and not angels.*

He was too weak as yet to speak, but he was able to address a smile of gratitude to his saviors—the amiable and slightly foolish smile with which Père Cinnamon had so long deceived his society and passed for being essentially inoffensive.

Finally, when he had recovered his strength, when he was able to talk, he took the young woman's hand and raised it to his lips. Then he murmured: "How did I get here? Has God sent one of his angels to snatch me from my executioners?"

"I'm not an angel," the young woman replied, smiling, "but I was able to save you, and I'm very glad of that."

And she told him, simply, how the rescue had been effected.

Patureau continued frowning, and muttered to himself privately: "Something tells me that we've done the wrong thing, and that we'll repent of it."

A few hours later, Porion was out of danger and his strength had returned in full. Thanks to his fecund imagination, he had found a very ingenious little fable to explain the violence of which he had been the object.

"Can you imagine, my good demoiselle, that I am a man very unfortunate to have a brother?"

"You have a brother?"

"Yes, Mademoiselle, a brother a few years younger than me, but who resembles me so perfectly that we're often mistaken or one another. That brother went to the bad. While I meekly became a grocer-cum-druggist in the Rue des Lombards, at the sign of the Golden Pestle, my brother foolishly dissipated a part of our modest heritage; then he became a gambler, and then a thief, and then a police agent; he played tricks on everyone, worthy of getting him hanged, and I'm not astonished that those people wanted to hang me, on mistaking me for him."

"Oh, they mistook you for him?"

"Yes, Mademoiselle."

And Porion completed the fable with a host of small details that ended up gaining Mademoiselle Espérance's sympathy.

Patureau, on the contrary, as still shaking his head and saying to himself: *Perhaps it's him who's the police agent, and I'm very much afraid that we've done dirty work.*

Porion remained hidden in the house where he had so miraculously come back to life for the rest of the day. It was only in the evening, at dusk, when he had the near-certainty of being able to quit the Place Royale without running the risk of encountering his enemies of that morning, that he took his leave of Mademoiselle Espérance de Beaulieu—but he asked to come back the following day in order to make a visit of gratitude, and that permission was gracefully granted to him.

He slipped out of the house then, with his hat pulled down over his eyes and the collar of his coat turned up in order to hide his face as much as possible. When he had reached the Rue Saint-Antoine, he saw a carriage for hire passing and made a sign to the coachman, who stopped. He climbed inside and had himself taken to Monsieur de Sartine's house.

Porion had recovered all his composure and his infernal presence of mind. "Come on!" he murmured, as he climbed the Lieutenant de Police's stairs. "If I hadn't lost my two thousand écus in the brawl, all would be for the best, for I've made the acquaintance of a very pretty girl. Who knows? One day the King might suffer from ennui again, and perhaps we can use her."

And the wretch went into Monsieur de Sartine's antechamber, and said to a lackey: "Urgent business. It's necessary that Monseigneur receives me immediately."

While the lackey went to announce him, Porion thought: *A man who will be very astonished to find himself locked in the Bastille and to receive my visit there will be Messire Mardochée de Mardoche, my good friend!*

The lackey returned.

"Monseigneur is yours in a few seconds," he said. "He's in conference with Monsieur le Maréchal de Richelieu."

At that name, Porion frowned.

Am I not yet at the end of my misadventures? he said to himself, suppressing a slight frisson.

XXV

Why was Monsieur de Richelieu in Monsieur de Sartine's house?

In order to discover that, it is necessary to return to Versailles and go back to the moment of the King's *petit lever*.

His Majesty had woken up sooner than usual.

The captain of his guards, Prince de Bénavent, who was on duty that morning, had gone into the King's bedroom at the first ring of the bell.

The King had slept badly.

The extraordinary stories of the Tartar Prince, which had amused him so much during the evening, had procured him nightmare after nightmare during the night. He had dreamed that he had used the marvelous elixir, and as we shall see, he had been able to appreciate its inconveniences.

The Prince de Bénavent was a young seigneur whom the King liked very much, and he liked him for qualities entirely contrary to those that ordinarily succeeded with the King.

The Prince had the courage to tell the King the truth, and when everyone at Versailles pretended that the kingdom had never been more prosperous and the people happier, the Prince, with a brutal frankness, affirmed that the King was being deceived, that the people were dying of hunger, that the army was disorganized and that the State coffers were empty.

Anyone else would have been disgraced immediately. However, for several years the Prince had been speaking thus, and the King was not annoyed. The captain of the guard was the first person who went into the King's apartment in the morning, after the pages. He took the orders and had the custom of making His Majesty a summary report on what had happened at the château during the previous night.

On seeing him enter, the King said: "I slept badly last night, my poor Bénavent; I had absurd dreams."

"Perhaps Your Majesty had his supper too late," said the Prince. "Nothing brings on nightmares like bad digestion."

But the King shook his head. "It was the Tartar's stories," he said.

"Ah!" said the Prince. And the King told the captain of his guards, briefly, about the singular pretension that Prince Trespatky had published, the previous evening, in Madame de Pompadour's apartments, of having enjoyed several existences thanks to the marvelous elixir.

The Prince de Bénavent listened to the King, smiling, and said: "Did Your Majesty not throw the impudent liar out?"

"No," said the King, and perhaps I've been punished for my moderation, for I dreamed last night that I made use of his elixir."

"Oh, really?"

The King sat up, supported by a pile of pillows, took a pinch of tobacco, and went on:

"In my dream, I was twenty years older, and my grandson, the Duc de Berry, who is only three years old, was twenty-three.[34] In twenty years, I shall certainly not be young, my dear Prince, but in my dream I was horribly old—so old, my poor Bénavent, that a heap of physicians I didn't know but who, it appears, were attached to my person predicted to me that I was going to die. Among them, there was one whose face struck me; I seemed to have seen him before somewhere."

"I'll wager," said Prince Bénavent, smiling, "that it was the Tartar."

"Exactly!" said the King.

"And he offered Your Majesty his elixir?"

"In great mystery, when we were alone. 'Sire,' he said to me, 'you're old, decrepit, and you'll be dead in a week Trust me, consent to die immediately, and I'll resuscitate you, young and strong.' He spoke so well that I consented to everything he wanted."

"Your Majesty died?"

"I died that same evening, an hour after my mysterious physician had put his miraculous balm all over my body. Although my eyes were closed, my heart extinct and my body immobile and cold, I heard everything that was happening around me. A few of my courtiers wept, others were already talking about saluting my successor. Only the sobs of the princesses, my daughters, seemed to me to be really sincere.

"For three days I was exposed on a bed in this very room where we are, and as I could hear, although dead, I learned that they were about to proclaim as king my grandson, the Duc de Berry, who would reign under the name of Louis, the sixteenth of that name. All that made my slightly anxious already, I must confess, my dear Prince. I could not see, but I could hear...and what I heard only pleased me in part."

"What did the Marquise say?" asked the Prince, smiling.

"In truth," said the King, "I believe that the Marquise was dead, for I did not hear any mention of her, and I did not think about her at all."

The Prince de Bénavent bowed.

The King went on: "The day of my funeral arrived; it was in great pomp that I was transported to Saint-Denis. The coffin of my grandfather Louis XIV was still at the top of the steps of the crypt, for, as you know, Prince, tradition dictates that the last King to die awaits his successor at the door of the crypt. So

---

[34] The future Louis XVI, who was given the title Duc de Berry at birth, was, in fact, only two years-old in November 1756, which would have to be the date of this scene if it were correctly adapted to Robert Damiens' alleged assassination attempt on 5 January 1757.

Louis XIV was taken down into the interior and I took his place at the top of the stairs.

"The ceremony was long, but it finally ended, and when the last prayers had been said and holy water thrown on my coffin, everyone went away. I even heard the sound that the door of the crypt made as it closed.

"The Tartar had inspired me with such confidence in his elixir that I was not frightened by that abandonment and I made the reflection that when I resuscitated I was going to disrupt a host of petty calculations. Several hours went by, and then a sound struck my ears. It was the key to the crypt turning in the lock. At the same time, it seemed to me that my heart stated beating.

"Footsteps resounded, and then a voice reached my ear. 'Sire,' it said, 'it's me.' I recognized the voice of the Tartar.

"The Tartar opened the various locks of my four coffins, as he had opened that of the crypt, and the external air struck my face. At the same time, the Tartar said: 'Sire, this is the moment of resurrection, open your eyes.'

"Suddenly, my eyes opened, and I was able to see the Tartar standing before me, with a lamp in his hand. 'Get up!' he said to me. And I got up without effort. I flexed all my limbs one after another, and I found all the elasticity of youth in them.

"Then the Tartar, lamp in hand, started walking in front of me. He walked at a rapid pace, but I had rediscovered the legs I had at twenty, and I had no difficulty following him. We traversed the old basilica of Saint-Denis and emerged through a small door. I perceived then that it was night. The stars were shining in the sky, and the vicinity of the square was deserted.

"I turned to the Tartar. 'Where are my servants?' I said to him.

"'At Versailles, Sire.'

"'What! You haven't warned anyone?'

"'No,' he told me. 'I thought Your Majesty would not be annoyed to surprise his people.'

"'But at least you've brought a carriage?'

"'No, Sire.'

"'Where do you expect us to go, then?'

"'To Versailles, Sire.'

"'On foot?'

"'Oh, it's an insignificant journey for Your Majesty, who is young now.'

"Perhaps he was right, for I tensed by hamstrings and found myself as fit as in the best days of my youth. 'Well,' I said, 'let's go.'

"'That's your road, Sire: it's the Route de la Révolte, which Your Majesty had constructed, which, avoiding Paris, leads directly to Versailles.'

"'What! You're not coming with me?'

"'No, Sire, that's impossible,'

"'Why?'

"'Because I'm going to resuscitate a poor devil of a German Jew who was my valet de chambre, and to whom I promised a new life.'

"'But will I at least see you again?'

"'Yes, Sire, in sixty years, at the end of your new reign.'

"And having spoken thus, the Tartar appeared to me to become suddenly diaphanous and gradually faded away in front of me like mist in the sun. But bah!—it was all the same to me; I was resuscitated, and, he had told me, I had sixty years of reign before me. I therefore set out at a brisk pace. Surprisingly, it seemed to me that I had never marched as rapidly.

"On the way, I started thinking about a host of things that had never occurred to me before. Thus, for example, I thought very little about my courtiers and a great deal about my people, whom I promised to render as happy as possible."

"Ah! Your Majesty thought about that?" said the Prince de Bénavent, with a smile.

"OF course—but let me continue."

"I'm listening, Sire."

"It's nearly six leagues from Saint-Denis to Versailles, but I made the journey in less than three hours, I had such good legs. When I arrived at Versailles it was not yet light, only a slight blue tint was shining on the horizon.

"I had kept a key to the park, of which I often made use at night in order to leave the château incognito and go to the Parc-aux-Cerfs. Thanks to that key, I went in with no sound or fuss. A window, which I recognized as that of my study, was illuminated. *Damn!* I thought. *It appears that people get up early since I died.*

"A gardener I encountered bowed to me. 'My friend,' I said, 'who is up there?' And I pointed at the lighted window.

"'It's the King, who is working,' he told me,

"'The King?'

"'Yes, Monsieur.' The worthy man did not recognize me.

"'And why is he working at night?'

"'The King has just got up, Monsieur,'

"'Oh, he gets up as early as thus?'

"'Yes, Monsieur, for the well-being of his people.'

"*That's what I shall do henceforth*, I said to myself. Aloud, I said: 'And with whom is he working?'

"'With Monsieur de Maurepas, the Prime Minister.'

"'Oh! Very good.'

"And I continued on my way, wondering how it has come about that I had exiled Monsieur de Maurepas and that my successor has made him his Prime Minister. I reached the Orangery, went up the steps of a little stairway and arrived at the door of my study without encountering a living soul.

"Although I was at home, I thought it polite to knock discreetly twice on the door of my own study. 'Come in,' said a voice that I recognized as that of the Duc de Berry, my grandson. I opened the door and went in.

"I expected to see the Duc de Berry utter an exclamation and rush toward me with open arms. There was nothing. The new King looked at me with astonishment, turned toward his Prime Minister, and said: 'Who is that man?'"

XXVI

At that point in his story the King took a further pinch of tobacco and, replacing the snuff-box under his pillow, he continued:

"Can you imagine my astonishment and my anger, my poor Bénavent? The Duc de Berry had wept over my corpse the day before as I was being put into the coffin; he had even manifested an extravagant grief, and now he was pretending not to recognize me! He didn't want to return my crown to me, then!

"'Oh! You ask who this man is?' I cried. 'This man is your ancestor and our King, dead yesterday and resuscitated today, thanks to a powerful elixir...'

"The Duc de Berry looked at Maurepas, smiling, and said to him: 'The man is mad!'

"I took a step backwards, and, the anger that dominated me increasing, I put a hand to the hilt of my sword. Alas, I had forgotten that I had no épée. When laying me down in my coffin they had put the great sash of the Saint-Esprit over me, put the crown on my head and laid my épée beside me. The épée and the crown were still in the coffin, and I had only brought my sash.

"'Monsieur,' the new King said to me, kindly, 'what do you want of me?'

"'I want you to recognize me,' I said.

"'Insolent!' said Monsieur de Maurepas, who stood up and tried to take me by the arm.

"I raised my hand. 'Wretch.' I said to him, 'do you dare to lift your hand against your King?'

"But at that moment—I don't know how it happened—my eyes fell on a mirror, which reflected me in my entirety. I then had the secret of my grandson's astonishment. I was no longer myself. Between the King Louis XV buried at Saint-Denis and the King Louis XV who had been resuscitated there was an abyss. The former had been old and decrepit; the latter was young and appeared to be no older than twenty.

"I understood that it was necessary to give the Duc de Berry certain proof of my identity for him to consent to return my crown to me. 'Listen to me, I beg you,' I said to him.

"'Speak,' he said, generously.

"Then I recounted my adventure in all its details; I even went as far as to speak to him about a certain State secret that I had confided to him a few days before my death, and that only he and I knew.

"He smiled at me and said: 'If my aunts the princesses recognize you as their father, I'm ready to return the throne to you, but for myself, I confess to you that my religion forbids me to believe in the infernal practices about which you have just spoken to me.'

"'Oh, my daughters will certainly recognize me!' I cried.

"And I ran to the princesses' apartments.

"Madame Adelaide, who is the most devout person in my realm, was getting up to go to the first mass, and she was getting up without a fire, in a spirit of contrition and humility. I went in abruptly. At the sight of me, the saintly young woman uttered a scream. She was scarcely dressed, and no one ever went into her apartment at such an hour.

"'My daughter!' I cried. 'Don't you recognize me?'

"And I tried to tell her the same story that I had told the Duc de Berry. But she made the sign of the cross, fearfully, shouted that the Devil was in her room, went to fetch a bottle of holy water, and sprinkled me with it.

"Then I screamed in my turn, and that cry woke me up.

"That was my dream, my dear Prince," said the King. "I still reign, but I only have twenty years, and I believe that if I died, the Tartar's elixir would not have the power to resuscitate me."

"I believe as you do, Sire," said Monsieur de Bénavent.

"My dream has caused me a host of odd reflections," the King continued.

"So much the better, Sire."

"So, this Tartar is a charlatan."

"Oh, without a doubt."

"And he will have sent Madame de Pompadour some jewel of great price, so that she will take him into her affection."

Monsieur de Bénavent began to smile.

"However," said the King, "there's one thing that astonished me singularly about that individual."

"Oh?" said the Prince.

"Is it true that last year he was covered with scabs and leprosy?"

"Yes, Sire."

"Which all the physicians claimed to be mortal?"

"Yes, Sire."

"And yet he is cured..."

"Sire," said the Prince, coldly, "is Your Majesty in a humor to hear the truth this morning?"

The King shivered. "How you say that to me, Bénavent!"

"Your Majesty has never reprimanded me for my frankness," the Prince went on, "and I'm accustomed to say all. If your Majesty is not in a humor to listen to me, I will simply take his orders and withdraw."

"No, no, stay."

"Your Majesty will listen to me?"

"Yes," said the King. "The dream I've had has modified a host of things in my mind. I want to know what is happening in my kingdom and occupy myself with my people. Speak, Bénavent."

"Sire," said the captain of the guards, "Monsieur le Duc de Choiseul had recommended a young gentleman to Your Majesty's benevolence."

"Yes, certainly; let him be admitted this morning. I've given orders that he be introduced..."

Monsieur de Bénavent shook his head. "He will not come, Sire."

"Why not?"

"Because he has been in the Bastille since five o'clock this morning."

"In the Bastille?"

"Yes, Sire."

"Why?"

"By virtue of a *lettre de cachet* signed by Your Majesty."

"You're mad, Bénavent."

"If Your Majesty will deign to listen to me, he will see that I have all my reason."

"Speak."

"Monsieur de Choiseul left yesterday for Chanteloup. Fortified by Your Majesty's promise, but mistrusting a crowd of schemers who have an interest in deceiving the King, he had recommended his protégé to me, knowing that I was in service today."

"Very well."

"Your Majesty, who was amused by the Tartar's tales, had postponed the promised audience until this morning."

"Yes, certainly."

"There were people in Versailles who feared that audience greatly, Sire."

"Why is that?"

"Because Monsieur le Comte Hector de Pierrefeu, whose brother's throat has been cut, would have had the courage to denounce the guilty party."

"Ah!" said the King, frowning.

"And those people put everything to work to make sure that he did not reach Your Majesty."

"But why is he in the Bastille?"

"Your Majesty will see..."

"I'm listening."

"There was a low-grade officer, a rather bad lot, called Monsieur d'Erishem."

"I've heard mention of him," said the King. "He's a very dangerous duelist, isn't he?"

"Yes, Sire. Monsieur d'Erishem received money to kill Monsieur de Pierrefeu. He went to the hostelry of the Singe Vert and picked a quarrel with him."

"I can guess," said the King. "It's him who has killed Monsieur d'Erishem, and he's been put in the Bastille."

"No, Sire. Monsieur d'Erishem is dead, however. He was killed by a fine sword-thrust that nailed him to a wall, but it was not Monsieur de Pierrefeu who delivered it."

"Who was it, then?"

"A provincial gentleman, a Fleming, who was there by chance and did not know Monsieur de Pierrefeu. That gentleman, who is a giant of sorts, slapped Monsieur d'Erishem, and killed him five minutes later."

"Good," said the King. "And then?"

"Naturally, the Fleming and Monsieur de Pierrefeu formed a bond, and came back to the inn the best of friends, to such an extent that they slept in the same room. What happened then? I don't know exactly. All that I could discover this morning, when I went to inquire about my protégé, is that at five o'clock in the morning, a police agent named Porion, a police runner and soldiers from the constabulary invaded the Singe Vert and arrested the Fleming and Monsieur de Pierrefeu."

"But under what pretext?" asked the King.

"Under the pretext that the Fleming had an issue of the *Gazette de Hollande* in his pocket."

"A vile pamphlet, Bénavent."

"I don't deny it, Sire."

"Which continually insults the poor Marquise, to the extent that she cries all the tears in her body, grinds her teeth and loses her head. If I listened to her, I'd declare war on Holland again with the sole aim of exterminating the editors of that accursed newspaper."

And the King sighed. "But after all," she said, after a silence, "that's no reason to imprison Monsieur de Pierrefeu."

"He has been deemed an accomplice."

"Oh, truly? And who delivered the *lettre de cachet*?"

"Thus far, I haven't been able to find out."

"It's necessary to know."

"If Your Majesty will give me two hours, I'll find out."

"But the police agent who proceeded with the arrest is named Porion?"

"Yes, Sire."

"The rogue!" said the King. "So he had a great interest in my not seeing Monsieur de Pierrefeu?"

The Prince de Bénavent was in a frank vein. "Sire," he said, "did Your Majesty not hear mention of the Tartar from him?"

"In fact, that's true!"

"Well, the Tartar has taken a bath in Monsieur de Pierrefeu's blood."

"You believe those things, Bénavent?"

"Yes, Sire."

"The man is a wretch, then?"

"Yes, Sire."

"What would you do in my place?"

"I'd have him arrested."

"Good."

"Judged by the Parliament and broken on the wheel in the Place de Grève."

"But he's a subject of the Czar."

"Undoubtedly. Except that he has committed crimes in France, and it is up to France to punish him."

"Hmm!" said the King. "All this is to some extent my fault."

"Why is that, Sire?"

"It's that stupid story of the procurator Dumas that came back to my memory. I sent for this Porion, and I believe he's making a fool of me. He brought me the Tartar. The Tartar is now on the best terms with Madame de Pompadour. If I have him judged, she'll protest loudly. What would you do in my place, Bénavent?"

The captain of the guards did not have time to reply. Someone knocked on the door, and a page announced Monsieur le Duc de Richelieu.

"Ah!" said the King. "Here's the Maréchal, who will remove the nasty thorn from our foot. Come in, Duc."

Monsieur de Bénavent bit his lips, but he did not breathe a word.

Monsieur de Richelieu came in.

XXVII

The Maréchal was smiling and sprightly, which did not happen to him every day, and was an indication to the King that he had something malevolent to recount. A model courtier, the Maréchal had studied the tastes and caprices of his master so carefully that he had arrived at divining in advance the sudden changes that occurred in the mind of Louis XV.

The previous evening, in Madame de Pompadour's apartment, the Maréchal had seen the King greatly smitten with the Tartar, who attributed his marvelous cure to an elixir of longevity, so he would not have wanted to contradict the Tartar or attack him, for all the gold in the world.

The following day, however, the Maréchal's mental disposition had changed, as we shall see. In the royal antechamber he had found the page who slept during the night in a cabinet open to the King's alcove. He had exchanged a few words with him, asking how the King had slept.

"Badly," was the reply he had received.

"Oh, really?"

"His Majesty had a nightmare," the page replied.

"All night?"

"Very nearly."

"Ah!"

"I even got up several times, for the King was talking aloud, and seemed very frightened," the page added.

Good! thought Monsieur de Richelieu. *That Tartar's fanciful tales have disturbed the King's mind, and it's probable that he'd be poorly received if he presented himself this morning.*

In consequence, Monsieur de Richelieu, who had arrived at the château resolved to ecstasize about Prince Trespatky's cure and to believe in his elixir, changed that resolution in the antechamber and went into see the King armored by the finest skepticism.

"Well, Maréchal," said Louis XV, on seeing him come in, "How did you sleep last night?"

"Very badly, Sire." Richelieu was not a man to make any other response; from the moment the King could not sleep, none of his subjects had the right to sleep.

"Really? You slept poorly, my dear Maréchal?"

"Yes, Sire."

"And why is that?"

"I had a nightmare."

"Did you dream about the Tartar?"

"All night long."

"And his elixir?"

"Naturally, Sire."

"Aha!" said the King, triumphantly. "Well, what do you think of his elixir?"

Richelieu smiled mutely. Doubtless he was waiting for the King to formulate his own opinion.

The King went on: "I believe, my poor Maréchal, that the rogue was mocking us yesterday."

"I believe so too, Sire."

"There is, however, one fact..."

"Which?"

"That of the cure."

"Hmm!" said the Maréchal. "That depends...it's necessary to know..." And he looked at the Prince de Bénavent, as if to beg him to throw him a line.

The captain of the guards seized the ball on the bounce. "Sire," he said, "I believe much more in the efficacy of the baths that the Tartar has taken than that of his elixir."

"Me too," said Richelieu, who, by adhesion, passed with arms and baggage over to the enemy camp.

"Oh, you believe that too, Maréchal?" said the King.

"Well, Sire, it's the public rumor."

"Well, what would you do in my place?"

For a second time, the Maréchal looked at Prince de Bénavent."

"I'd have the Tartar arrested and judged, Sire," said the Prince.

"That's my opinion," said Richelieu.

"Ah! That's your opinion, Maréchal?"

"Yes, Sire, except..." And the Maréchal stopped.

"Let's hear your restriction, Maréchal," said Louis XV.

"I would put a certain form and a certain discretion into it."

"Why?"

"Your Majesty sent someone to look for the Tartar?"

"That true."

"Because a rogue, a police agent, affirmed that the Tartar could provide certain information about the fate of the procurator Dumas, who disappeared more than thirty years ago?"

"Yes," said the King, "that's the point of departure of this whole story."

"Now," Richelieu continued, "if the King will follow my reasoning..."

"Speak, Maréchal."

"The Tartar no more knew procurator Dumas than he knew Monsieur de Saint-Germain, and he is an audacious impostor, but it's still necessary to prove that imposture to him, Sire."

"How can it be proven to him?"

"Did he not tell you that procurator Dumas had hollowed out a mysterious stairway in his house?"

"Yes."

"And that the stairway in question, by why the procurator descended into a cellar where he slept for fifteen years, can still be found?"

"That's true."

"Well, I'll take charge of having the house searched, Sire, and it will be seen that the stairway doesn't exist."

"Oh, very good!"

"Then the Tartar will find it quite natural that, having made mock of Your Majesty, Your Majesty will take his revenge and abandon him to the punishment he merits."

"Your words are golden, Maréchal."

"Thank you, Sire," said the Maréchal. "If I obtain that result, may I request a favor of Your Majesty?"

"What?"

"The punishment of a rogue whose impudence knows no limits."

"Porion?"

"Exactly."

"In fact," said the King, "if the Tartar has tricked us, it's Porion who has been the instigator of the hoax, and I share your opinion, Maréchal, that the rogue merits a severe correction."

"Your Majesty will give me his full powers, then?"

"Certainly."

The animosity of the Maréchal against the infimal individual named Porion is explained by the success that the latter had obtained in finding Cécile Robert, for whom Richelieu had searched in vain for several weeks. Vengeance is not only the pleasure of gods; it is also the joy of great seigneurs. Monsieur de Richelieu did not have any grudge against the Tartar, but he had such a great hatred of Porion that he gladly sacrificed the Tartar for the pleasure of immolating the police agent.

"So," he said, "Your Majesty gives me his full powers?"

"Yes," said the King.

"I shall certainly have need of Monsieur de Sartine."

"Monsieur de Sartine will obey you." And the King took a piece of paper and wrote on it: *Do what Monsieur de Richelieu orders you to do. Louis.*

"Sire," said the Prince de Bénavent, then, "since Monsieur de Richelieu is going to Paris, can he not take responsibility for a supplementary task…?"

"Eh?" said the King.

"And have the young man who has been sent to the Bastille released?"

"What young man?" asked Richelieu.

"The one that I was to receive this morning," said the King.

"Why is he in the Bastille, Sire?"

"It's Porion who put him there, on his own authority."

"Oh, the rogue! But under what pretext?"

"Under the pretext that he had a friend who read the *Gazette de Hollande*."

"Hmm," said Richelieu. "Then the Marquise is no stranger to that arrest."

"Perhaps..."

"Sire," said Richelieu, "Your Majesty could write to Monsieur de Launay and charge Monsieur de Bénavent with the letter."

"Why not you, Maréchal?"

"It's just that the Marquise is susceptible...she's already quarreled with me once because, she said, I was meddling in her affairs."

"So be it," said Monsieur de Bénavent. "If Your Majesty cares to give me the letter, I'll go to Paris this evening, when my service ends."

"So," said the King, "that's agreed, Maréchal."

"Yes, Sire."

"You'll go to Paris and you'll have a search carried out in the house in the Rue de l'Hirondelle."

"Yes, Sire, and given that the stairway doesn't exist, the Tartar will find himself convicted of imposture."

"That's it. Go, Maréchal." And the King gave him his hand to kiss.

Richelieu went out, murmuring: "I'll have that Porion rotting in a dungeon."

Scarcely had Richelieu left than someone knocked with a certain violence on the door that opened at the back of the royal alcove, giving access to the mysterious corridor that led to Madame de Pompadour's apartments.

The King opened it and found himself face to face with the Marquise.

The latter was in a morning robe, and seemed to be prey to a great agitation. She even had tears in her eyes.

"Oh, Sire, Sire," she said, "are you going to allow me to be outraged perpetually?" And she let herself fall, almost fainting, on to a chair.

"What's the matter, my love?" said the King, emotionally. "What's happened?"

By way of response, the Marquise set before his eyes the same issue of the *Gazette de Hollande* that had been seized by the police officer from the person of the Fleming.

The King frowned, but, resolved to withstand the storm of tears by which he was menaced, he said: "What do you expect me to do about it, my love? We can't be in a state of perpetual war with Holland."

"So be it," said the Marquise, "but the wretches that transport these infamies into the kingdom, won't Your Majesty punish them?"

"It's done," said the King. "They're in the Bastille."

"But they'll stay there, at least?"

"Certainly," said the King. At the same time, he made a small sign to Monsieur de Bénavent, which meant: *That won't prevent your protégé from being released.*

And as the Marquise appeared to be in a frightful state, the King thought that it was necessary to console her at any price.

"Prince," he said to the captain of his guards, "leave us for a moment. This evening, when you quit your service, remind me of what I promised you."

"Yes, Sire."

And Monsieur de Bénavent went out in his turn, leaving the King in the power of his terrible and dominant mistress.

XXVIII

Once outside the King's apartments, Monsieur de Richelieu said to himself: *I believe I've done well to abandon the Tartar. In any case, there are already enough people who have an inconvenient influence over the King, without letting any more creatures acquire authority over him. Only one thing worries me, and that's knowing how the Marquise will take it?*

Hazard took charge of responding to the Maréchal. On the staircase he encountered old Lebel, who was coming back from the Parc-aux-Cerfs. "Well, my dear Lebel," he said, "what's new?"

Lebel assumed a mysterious expression. "The Marquise is furious," he said.

"Ah!"

"She's talking about declaring war on Holland."

"Right!" said the Maréchal. "I have it—it's a matter of the *Gazette*."

"Exactly."

"What has the terrible *Gazette* said now, then?"

"It has published Monsieur de Maurepas' quatrain."

"Is that all?"

"It's quite enough."

"No," said Richelieu, "for it's nothing new, given that the whole world knows that quatrain."

"Yes, but the Marquise didn't know it."

"Poor Marquise," said Richelieu, with a comical smile of commiseration. And he shook Lebel's hand and went on his way, without having thought to ask how the *Gazette de Hollande* had fallen under the eyes of Madame la Marquise de Pompadour.

Good, he said to himself. *The Marquise is no longer thinking about anything except exciting the King against Holland, against Monsieur de Maurepas and against all the latter's friends. She won't be thinking about the Tartar any longer.*

And the Maréchal climbed into his carriage and said to the footman: "To Paris!"

There is nothing like traveling to stimulate meditation. On the way, the Maréchal said to himself: *Monsieur de Sartine is certainly an enemy of that rogue Porion, who dreamed of replacing him, but he might be a friend of the Tartar. What if, instead of addressing myself to Monsieur de Sartine, I take it upon myself to demonstrate to the King that the Tartar is an impostor?*

Richelieu knew the story of the procurator Dumas by heart, and Porion had recounted with a host of details his interview with the draper of the Rue de l'Hirondelle, who was said to be the procurator Dumas resuscitated. The

279

Maréchal then had the idea of going to the Rue de l'Hirondelle to interrogate the draper himself.

For that, he first had himself taken to his house in the Rue de Hanovre, stayed there for half an hour, and spent that half hour summoning his steward and a valet de chambre who never quit Paris and was responsible for receiving the Maréchal's mistresses.

The steward was still a young man, of tall stature and Herculean appearance. The valet de chambre was also a sturdy fellow. With such bodyguards, the Maréchal could go anywhere and do without Monsieur de Sartine's men. It was not the first time that the Maréchal had taken them with him. Often, smitten with some woman of the petty bourgeoisie, the Maréchal, in disguise, went to prowl around the beauty's windows in the company of the two men, both solid enough to protect their master from any unfortunate encounter.

The Maréchal therefore ordered them to take off his livery and dress in somber clothing. He dressed himself like a provincial gentleman passing through Paris, and when that triple metamorphosis was accomplished, the Maréchal sent the in search of a chamber-pot and climbed into it with them, instructing the coachman to take them to the Rue de l'Hirondelle.

From the Rue de Hanovre to that airless and lightless back street was a long journey. The Maréchal took advantage of the time to give his two bodyguards their instructions. At the corner of the Rue de l'Hirondelle, he got down and sent the chamber-pot away.

The house was not difficult to find; it was in the very middle of the street, and a shop open on the ground floor had a pair of scissors for a sign. It was the draper's shop. He had even written his name over the door: Ulysse Carnot.

At least there's some truth in Porion's story, thought the Maréchal. And, followed by the valet de chambre and the steward, he advanced toward the shop.

The draper was at the door. At first he took the Maréchal and his two companions for clients and hastened to usher them into his shop, asking them what they desired.

"My dear Monsieur Carnot," the Maréchal said to him, "I desire to talk to you."

The draper seemed slightly anxious, but the Herculean stature of the steward impressed him.

At a sign from Richelieu the valet closed the door of the shop. Then the Maréchal looked the draper in the eye and said: "I've come on behalf of the King."

The draper shuddered.

"To see your withered leg," added the Maréchal.[35]

---

[35] The author has apparently forgotten that the King has already sent Maréchal de Richelieu with Porion to investigate Carnot's withered leg, and that the Maréchal brought back a report confirming that the leg in question was genuine.

"My leg?"

"Yes."

"But Monsieur..."

"My dear Monsieur Carnot," said the Maréchal, coldly, "the King doesn't like to be tricked, and that's why I've been sent to you."

"But Monseigneur..."

"How long have you owned this house?"

"About twelve years, Monseigneur."

"Really?"

"Since I was resuscitated," added the draper.

This time, the Maréchal looked at the man more severely still. "So, you have the pretension of being the procurator Dumas?" he said.

"But...of course..."

"Then show me the leg that you forgot to rub with the elixir of longevity, which remains that of an old man when the rest of your body became young."

The draper was still hesitant, but the colossal stature of the steward, the determined attitude of the valet de chambre and the severe aspect of the Maréchal imposed upon him.

"Is it true," he said, "that you've come on behalf of the King?"

"Certainly. Would you like proof?"

"Yes," he stammered.

Suddenly, the Maréchal opened his brown cloak, and the draper recoiled, dazzled. He had perceived the blue sash of the Saint-Esprit on the Maréchal's chest.

At the same time, the door to the back room of the shop opened and a woman appeared. It was the draper's wife: a pretty brunette of perhaps thirty-five, plump and dainty, with lively eyes.

"Don't you recognize Monsieur de Maréchal de Richelieu, wretch?" she said.

The draper uttered a cry of astonishment and fright, and wanted to fall at the Maréchal's knees. The latter stopped him with a gesture.

"Ulysse," said the brunette then, "you're not forced the play the role that has been imposed on you. Throw yourself at Monsieur the Maréchal's knees and beg his pardon."

"But this woman is mad!" stammered the draper.

Richelieu started to laugh. "I can see that she is," he said. "You ought to have been warned that the day when the King sent someone to see your leg, it would not go well—which is because your leg would not have been subjected to the preliminary treatment of which the people of the Cour des Miracles know the secret so well."

"What you are saying, Monsieur le Maréchal," said the pretty brunette, "is the pure truth. My husband is an imbecile who has let himself be twisted by a certain Porion, who promised him two thousand livres if he consented to pretend to be the procurator Dumas."

"You're going to doom me, wretch!" cried the draper.

"No," continued Madame Carnot—who, as is evident, was an energetic woman—"Monsieur le Maréchal takes pity on imbeciles, on condition that they repent. Isn't that so, Monsieur le Maréchal?" And the pretty brunette looked at Richelieu seductively.

"Yes, certainly," said the Maréchal, "And I'm ready, Madame, to pardon your simpleton of a husband and intercede on his behalf with the King, who is furious."

"You see," said Madame Carnot. "The King is furious."

"It's even probable," said Richelieu, delighted to see things take such a promising aspect, "that if the King had sent another seigneur of the Court in my place, your husband might well be going to the Bastille."

"To the Bastille" exclaimed the draper, in a tone of unspeakable terror.

"Yes, my friend," said Richelieu.

Then the Maréchal turned to the pretty brunette again. "So," he said, "it's a certain Porion who persuaded your husband to lend himself to this comedy?"

"Yes, Monseigneur."

"By promising him two thousand livres?"

"My God, yes."

Richelieu frowned. "Was he alone?"

"Yes, but it appears that he's one of Monsieur le Lieutenant de Police's men."

"Really?"

"It was to him that my husband addressed himself when he went to talk to him about the secret stairway."

"That stairway exists, then?"

"Yes, Monseigneur."

"I'd like to see it," said Richelieu.

"I'm ready to take you there, Monseigneur," replied the pretty brunette.

Richelieu looked at the draper. "My friend," he said, "I'll leave my steward with you, with orders not to let you out of his sight. Fear is dominating you; you might take flight, which would aggravate your situation singularly."

"Monseigneur is right," said the pretty brunette. "He's so stupid!"

And after that singular apology for her husband, she opened the door that gave access from the shop to the corridor where the principal staircase of the house was located, which led to the mysterious laboratory where, thirty years before, old procurator Dumas had disappeared.

Richelieu left his steward in the shop and made a sign to his valet de chambre to follow him.

XXIX

Madame Ulysse Carnot was rather loquacious. While going up the stairs she started jabbering. "It's truly very fortunate," she said, "that I was in the house when you come, Monseigneur. My husband is a greedy fool, whose love of money makes him do the most stupid things."

"In truth," said the Maréchal.

"When we bought this house," the draper' wife went on, "we were naturally entertained with all the nonsense that was running around on its account. My husband is so stupid that he didn't want to conclude the bargain. But I, who saw a good deal, give that we got it for virtually nothing, insisted on the acquisition. Once we were in, however, terrors without number took possession of him. He couldn't sleep, or if he slept, he had nightmares. At the slightest sound, he leapt out of bed and started shouting like a man possessed, saying that, for sure, it was the soul of the procurator coming back. He never wanted to go into the room at the very top of the house, and in which it was said that the old fellow had dealings with the Devil."

"But you went in?" said the Maréchal, putting his hands around the pretty brunette's plump waist.

"Yes, certainly," she said, pulling away with a little cry that was not at all fearful.

"And you discovered the stairway?"

"Yes, Monseigneur."

So saying, the pretty brunette arrived at the top of the house and reached the door of the room about so much had been rumored. The key was in the lock.

Madame Carnot turned the key, the door opened, and the Maréchal found himself on the threshold of the redoubt. It was a small rectangular room, obtaining daylight from a single window. The pushed-back leather curtain, the old furniture, the antique dressers filled with retorts and phials, the alembic in which the procurator had doubtless distilled his elixir: it was all there. Nothing had been touched, and one might have believed it the evening on which Maître Dumas has seen the man with the mule for the last time.

"All this is rather bizarre," murmured the Maréchal, casting an investigative gaze over those old things. But where's the stairway?"

The Maréchal's question was quite natural, for there was no door to be seen and no opening by which it might be entered. At the same time, he sat down in a sort of large armchair with a sculpted back, which had certainly been Maître Dumas' preferred seat.

Seeing that, the pretty brunette planted herself directly in front of him and said to him: "Monsieur le Maréchal, I'll show you the stairway in a moment, but permit me to give you a few details beforehand."

"Speak, my beauty," replied the Maréchal, who put his hands around the waist of the draper's seductive wife for a second time.

"It's necessary to tell you, Monseigneur," she said, "that, for several years, I've been coming up here alone. My husband didn't want to accompany me, much less the two shop assistants. But I have no fear of the Devil, and I was bitten with curiosity by all the bizarre stories that were told, and wanted to know the last word about the disappearance of old Dumas."

"Aha!" said the Maréchal.

"By virtue of spending entire hours here, sounding the walls and opening the dressers, I ended up discovering the stairway."

"Where is it, then?"

"Wait, Monseigneur." And the draper's lovely wife continued: "Once the stairway was discovered I forced my husband to come up here. When he saw it, he said to me: 'I'll go tell the police.' And although I did what I could to stop him, he went. Monsieur de Sartine received him..."

"Ah! Very good!" said the Maréchal.

"And after having listened to him," Madame Ulysse Carnot went on, "he threw him out, saying: 'My friend, no one in Paris remembers procurator Dumas and the mysteries of the Rue de l'Hirondelle. If you'll take my advice, you'll go home tranquilly and you'll meditate on the inconveniences that there might be in disturbing the police unnecessarily.'"

"Really?" said the Maréchal. "Monsieur de Sartine said that?"

"Yes, and he severely reprimanded the man named Porion, who had introduced him."

"And how long ago was this?" asked Maréchal de Richelieu.

"Two years, Monseigneur."

"Ah! Very good."

"I was therefore very astonished," Madame Carnot went on, "to see Porion arriving yesterday."

"I can guess the rest," the Maréchal interrupted. "Now my dear lady, where's the staircase?"

The pretty brunette headed toward a corner of the room, moved away a table that was placed there, took a large pair of scissors from her belt and introduced the end between two sections of the parquet. The Maréchal heard a dry click. At the same time, the section of the parquet, obedient to a hidden spring, lifted up, and Richelieu, who had come forward, was able to see an opening some three feet broad, and the steps of a staircase.

"Where does it lead?" he asked,

"You'll see, Monseigneur."

The draper's wife then went to a dresser on which there was a stout candle of brown wax and a briquette. She lit it.

"Now," she said "if Your Lordship will follow me..."

"Gladly," said Richelieu.

The valet de chambre got ready to go down behind the Maréchal—but the latter, to whom a tête-à-tête with the draper's wife, even in a cellar, did not seem in the least displeasing, made him a sign to remain—which meant that he and the draper's wife were engulfed in the stairway alone.

The draper's wife went down first. The stairway, it was easy to see, had been hollowed out within the thickness of a principal wall, and it had been constructed spirally. The Maréchal was obliged to duck down in order not to bump his head on the vault.

The draper's wife went down at a brisk pace, and did not find it necessary to cry out again at a certain moment when the Maréchal's lips brushed her neck.

The staircase was long. The Maréchal counted more than a hundred steps, but he finally felt the last one under his foot, and suddenly found himself on the threshold of a little vaulted cellar cluttered, like the laboratory, with flasks and retorts.

It was there that the spiral stairway terminated.

In whichever direction the gaze went, by the light of the stout candle that Madame Carnot as carrying in her hand, it encountered the vault or the wall. There was no other exit—apparently, at least.

"Is this all that you discovered?" asked the Maréchal.

"Yes, Monseigneur."

"Then you haven't discovered anything at all, my dear."

"But Monseigneur..."

"Undoubtedly," said Richelieu. "For, listen carefully..."

"Speak, Monseigneur." And the draper's wife fixed her large sparkling eyes on Monsieur de Richelieu.

The latter continued: "What does the legend say? That old procurator Dumas locked himself in his laboratory?"

"Yes."

"That after several hours, his children, having decided to break down the door, no longer found him in there."

"That's right," said the draper's wife.

"Therefore, my beauty," the Maréchal went on, "When you told me that you had found a stairway, I thought that the stairway would put us on the procurator's track."

"Ah!"

"I don't believe any of the story invented by Porion, and if the procurator died here, it's necessary for us to find traces of his body." So saying, the Maréchal started making a tour of the cellar, striking the wall with his closed fist, at intervals.

Suddenly, it seemed to him that the wall, instead of rendering a dull sound, became sonorous. He rapped again, and thought he could hear a kind of metallic vibration. One might have thought that he had struck an iron plate.

"Oh-ho!" he said. "What's this? Give me some light, my darling."

The draper's wife approached with her candle. Then the Maréchal took the large scissors that were still hanging from her belt, and stated scratching the wall, which was covered with an old layer of mortar that time had blackened. As the plaster fell away, the scissors returned a clearer and increasingly sonorous sound.

Soon, the Maréchal had uncovered an iron plate. He continued scraping, and the mortar, coming away in large fragments, laid bare a door.

The draper's wife watched the operation, quivering.

The door had a lock, but it was one of those locks, common in the Middle Ages, that did not open with the aid of a key but by means of a spring.

That spring, whose secret varied infinitely, was generally imperceptible, lost in the host of designs and arabesques sculpted in relief. Anyone but Richelieu would have found himself impotent in confrontation with that door—but for the Maréchal, it was mere child's play.

In fact, in his youth, the Duc, who was as curious as a woman, having made a voyage to Italy, had amused himself for several days studying the art of Florentine and Milanese locksmiths. Guided by a celebrated armorer of Milan, he had visited all the mysterious doors, and opened all the coffers, of the fifteenth and sixteenth centuries. So, running the tip of the scissors over the lock, he had soon found the spring, which was immediately activated, and the door swung on its hinges.

Then the Maréchal and the draper's wife found themselves on the threshold of a new staircase, which plunged down profoundly beneath their feet.

"Give me your candle," said the Maréchal. "I'll go down first."

"No, no," she replied. "I want to have the honor of lighting the way for you, Monseigneur."

"You won't be afraid?"

She replied with a burst of laughter, and the Maréchal took advantage of it to steal a second kiss from her.

Candle in hand, the draper's wife ventured on to the new staircase. The Maréchal followed her. They descended some thirty steps in that fashion. But suddenly, the draper's wife stopped abruptly and uttered a cry of terror.

At the same time, the candle escaped from her hand, fell, and went out.

XXX

The most profound obscurity enveloped Monsieur de Richelieu and the pretty draper's wife.

The later had thrown herself sharply backwards, and the Maréchal had caught her in his arms. He felt her shiver, and her heart, which was pounding, was beating next to his own.

"But what did you see?" he said.

"Oh!" she stammered. "I saw...*him*!"

"Who?"

"The procurator."

"Alive?"

"No...dead..."

"Him!" said the Maréchal. "What are you thinking? Are you afraid, then, when I'm with you?" And he hugged her gently in his arms, and brushed her face with his lips.

"Ah!" she said. "The candle's gone out." But her voice was less tremulous.

"Yes," said the Maréchal.

"How are we going to get out of here?" Her voice was firmer, and the Maréchal understood that she was entirely reassured.

"Don't be afraid," he said. "I'm a man of precaution, and when you picked up the candle upstairs I put the briquette in my pocket. So saying, he produced a shower of sparks, which permitted him to see the candle on the first step of the staircase. He bent down, picked it up, struck the briquette again, and the candle was relighted.

Then, passing in front of the draper's wife, whose terror had returned with the light, he walked forward. The stairway ended in a second cellar almost identical to the first, except that it was empty of bottles, flasks and alembics. In the middle, however, a man was lying. The man was dressed in a black robe, and it could not be anyone else, if the legend could be trusted, but Maître Dumas, the old procurator.

"Come on, my child," said the Maréchal. "When one is protected by the living, one need have no fear of the dead." And he took the draper's wife in his arms, sat her down on the last step in the staircase, and deposited a further kiss on her neck.

Then he approached the cadaver and set about examining it attentively. To tell the truth, it was nothing but a mummy, as yellow and dry as parchment. The flesh had vanished, and the skin was stick to the bones. The Maréchal tried to lift it up, and perceived that it was as rigid as wood. The fingers of the right hand were clenched around an object that attracted Richelieu's attention. The object in question was a little phial, empty of any liquid.

"Good!" he said. "I understand everything now."

The draper's wife had ended up reconciling herself to the sight of the cadaver. Seeing the Maréchal laughing, she asked him why.

The Maréchal replied: "The worthy man believed in the elixir of long life."

"Really?" said the draper's wife.

"I'll wager that the man with the mule was nothing but a clever trickster who passed himself off as the Devil. Do you believe in the Devil, my darling?"

"Not much," said the pretty brunette.

"Follow me carefully, then. The man with the mule—I'll wager that this is what must have happened—sold master Dumas, in return for a large sack full of gold, the secret of living forever."

"Ah, you think so?"

"They came down here. Then the man with the mule, in possession of the money, gave him this phial."

"Good."

"Enjoining him to drink the contents."

"And then?"

"Instead of an elixir of longevity, the phial certainly contained a poison. The fellow fell down stone dead, to judge by his hand clenched around the phial."

"And the man with the mule?"

"Went away tranquilly, taking the bag full of gold."[36]

Gradually, Madame Carnot had become accustomed to the sight of the cadaver. She had quit the last step in the staircase and had ended up putting her small hand on the Maréchal's shoulder.

"But have you thought of one thing, Monseigneur?"

"What?"

"That the door masking the stairway that comes down here was covered with plaster."

"Yes."

"The man with the mule wasn't alone, then?"

"I confess that that's the last mysterious corner of the adventure. But perhaps we'll also have the explanation of that. Come with me, darling; we'll go back upstairs."

"Aren't we going to give a sepulcher to this cadaver?" asked the draper's wife.

"What's the point? The absence of air has mummified it. It's quite comfortable here. Besides which, I have an idea that I'll explain to you shortly." And the Maréchal, passing one of his arms around the waist of the draper's wife, and

---

[36] This inference is inconsistent with the version of the story of Maître Dumas told by the King, in which the death of the procurator occurred some time after the last visit by the man with the mule.

still holding the stout brown wax candle, stated to climb the spiral stairway again.

They arrived thus in the first cellar, and there, after having closed the iron door again, the Maréchal undertook a further inspection. He soon discover, in a corner, a mason's trough and a trowel. The trough was still full of dried mortar.

"That's the explanation I was looking for," he said. "The man with the mule walled up the door before he left."

"But although you can explain that, Monseigneur," said the draper's wife, who, having drawn away from Maître Dumas' cadaver, had become cheerful again, "how do you explain the bleeding wound that the mule had in its flank?"

"Oh," said the Maréchal, laughing, "I don't explain that at all, my darling."

"But..."

"For one thing, the neighbors who saw, or claimed to see the wound are dead."

"Oh, most certainly."

"Then again, it was thirty years ago..."

"At the least."

"In thirty years," added the Maréchal, still laughing, "either the mule has died or healed. In consequence, we won't occupy ourselves with it any longer."

And he kissed the draper's wife again.

Meanwhile the Maréchal's valet de chambre had remained at the very top of the house, in the laboratory of the late Maître Dumas, facing the gaping hole where the stairway began.

A full hour had gone by, and the Maréchal had not come back. The valet was beginning to be a little anxious.

Finally, footsteps became audible on the stairway, and Richelieu reappeared, giving his hand to the draper's pretty wife, who was a trifle red-faced and disheveled, and who was complaining that the stairway was never-ending.

She closed the section of parquet carefully, and the Maréchal said to her: "So, darling, it's agreed?"

"Yes, Monseigneur."

"Your husband is an imbecile."

"Oh!" she said.

"And it's always necessary to mistrust imbeciles."

"I should think so."

"In consequence, it's unnecessary for him to know anything."

"Absolutely nothing, Monseigneur."

"Come, then."

And they both went downstairs, followed by the lackey.

Master Ulysse Carnot was pacing back and forth in the shop, visibly anxious. The steward had taken a malign pleasure, during his wife's long absence, in telling him about the Maréchal's numerous good fortunes. The draper, who was jealous, was foaming at the mouth.

Richelieu, on reappearing and divining what was passing through the fellow's mind, assumed an exceedingly severe expression. "Master Carnot," he said, dryly, "thank God for having a wife less naïve, less stupid and less credulous than you. Thanks to her, I want to forgive you for the hoax to which you lent yourself with such good grace; but never try it again, for I shall then be obliged to have you arrested, and you might well end your days in the Bastille."

The draper made a gesture of fright, but his wife responded with a menacing glare. And Monsieur de Richelieu kissed the hand of the pretty wife very gallantly and went away laughing, leaving the husband terrified.

Poor man! he said to himself. *Why the Devil did he listen to Porion?*

At the end of the Rue de l'Hirondelle, the Maréchal found a fiacre, climbed into it and, sending his steward and his lackey away, he had himself taken to the home of Monsieur de Sartine.

The day had gone by, and it was almost nightfall. The young Lieutenant de Police was proceeding with a scrupulous toilette and getting ready to go to supper with the beautiful wife of a magistrate who was very much to his taste when Monsieur de Richelieu was announced.

The Maréchal came in. At the sight of him, Monsieur de Sartine recoiled in surprise. Richelieu was, in fact, dressed as a man of the third estate, and might have been taken for a peasant had the point of his épée not lifted a corner of his cloak, the color of a wall.

"I see something's amusing you," he said as he came forward.

"Indeed," stammered Monsieur de Sartine.

"It's because I, too, have just been doing a little police work."

"The amorous police, no doubt," said Sartine, who thought he understood.

"No, police work for the King."

"Ah!" said the Lieutenant, looking at Richelieu and shuddering.

"The King has been deceived," the Maréchal went on, "and I've just discovered the deceivers."

And Richelieu sat down, while Monsieur de Sartine felt a few drops of sweat pearling on his forehead.

XXXI

There was then a moment of silence between Monsieur de Sartine and the Maréchal.

The former was anxiously asking himself: *What the Devil does he want to talk about?* The latter was maliciously enjoying the anguish to which he had given birth.

Finally, Monsieur de Sartine said: "Will you deign, Maréchal, to explain yourself more clearly?"

"Gladly, Monsieur." And the Maréchal crossed his legs.

"Someone has deceived the King?"

"Yes, certainly."

"But how?"

"My dear Lieutenant," the Maréchal went on, "the King had a whim, two days ago, to exhume an old story, that of the procurator Dumas."

"Ah!" said Monsieur de Sartine, feigning the most profound astonishment. "Who's that?"

"A man who possessed the elixir of long life, it's said, some thirty years ago."

"Good."

"And who disappeared."

"Ah," said Monsieur de Sartine. "I believe I do remember, in fact."

"The King, who is always suffering a little from ennui," Richelieu went on, "and who demands distractions indifferently from Heaven or Hell, addressed himself, in order to know the sequel to that story, to a rogue that you scarcely love, I'm sure of it."

"Who?"

"A certain Porion."

"He is, in fact, a schemer."

And Monsieur de Sartine played the most perfect impassivity and ignorance so well that Richelieu, caught in the trap, told him everything that he already knew only too well—which is to say, what had happened at Versailles in the last two days, from Porion's first departure to the introduction of the Tartar."

"Everything that you're telling me, Monsieur le Maréchal," said the Lieutenant de Police, "makes me indignant and amazed."

"Wait," said Richelieu. And after having told Monsieur de Sartine what he knew, he told him what he did not know: the arrival in Versailles of Hector de Pierrefeu, the desire that the King had to receive him, and Porion's audacity, having tried to have him killed and failed, in having the young man arrested and taken to the Bastille.

Monsieur de Sartine began to frown; but it was even worse when Richelieu continued with the story of his own adventures since the morning, and told him about the visit he had just made to Messire Ulysse Carnot, the draper of the Rue de l'Hirondelle. Monsieur de Sartine had a veritable chill in his spine.

"You can see," Richelieu said, "that the situation is grave,"

"Very grave indeed," murmured the Lieutenant de Police, like an echo.

"The King is in one of his veins of honesty and repentance," said the Maréchal.

"I can see that."

"He wants to punish the guilty and do justice for the victims."

"In sum, Monsieur le Maréchal," said the Lieutenant de Police, "are you bringing me orders?"

"Yes, certainly."

"What."

"First of all, it's necessary to release the young man who is in the Bastille."

"And then?"

"To have the Tartar Prince Trespatky arrested."

"Very well."

"At the same time, you'll throw the wretch Porion into some dark dungeon, and you'll leave him there until the King settles his fate."

As the Maréchal said that, one of Monsieur de Sartine's valets came in and said: "Père Cinnamon is asking to be introduced to the presence of Monsieur le Lieutenant de Police.

Richelieu did not know Porion's soubriquet. "Who's that?" he said.

"One of my agents," said Monsieur de Sartine, feigning the most complete indifference. "Let him wait."

The valet went out.

Then Richelieu continued: "I'm going back to my house in the Rue de Hanovre for a few hours, where I'll wait for you to give me the result of the instructions I've had the honor of giving you, Monsieur."

And the Maréchal stood up.

Monsieur de Sartine had summoned up all his presence of mind. "Monsieur le Maréchal," he said, "I ask you for four hours to execute the King's orders."

"So be it, Monsieur."

The Maréchal headed for the door by which he had come in.

"This way," said Monsieur de Sartine; and he opened another door at the back of his study, which led discreetly to the main stairway of the house. The Lieutenant de Police wanted, above all, to prevent the Maréchal from encountering Porion in his antechamber.

Richelieu went out by that door, unsuspectingly. Monsieur de Sartine accompanied him, with insistent salutations, and did not want to quit him until the courtyard where the chamber-pot in which he had come was stationed. Then, when the Maréchal had gone, he went up in all haste to his study and said: "Send Père Cinnamon in."

Porion arrived.

Monsieur de Sartine had had time to put an icy mask over his face.

"Monseigneur," said Porion, as he came in, "the day has been rude, but Your Lordship will be content with me." At the same time, he looked around, and seemed to be wondering where the Maréchal had gone.

"Let's hear about the day," said Sartine, coldly.

Porion related his exploits of the night and morning, the danger he had run in the Place Royale, and concluded with the words: "It's absolutely necessary that Your Lordship gives me *carte blanche*."

"With regard to whom?"

"That wretch Mardochée."

"Monsieur Porion," Sartine said then, "you're nothing but an idiot."

Those words fell upon Porion's head like a thunderbolt. He cast a bewildered gaze at the Lieutenant de Police.

Then the latter took a cruel pleasure in relating to Porion every last detail of his conversation with the Maréchal. But while he was speaking, Porion recovered somewhat from his emotion. Porion was one of those men who grow with obstacles and rise to the sublime where others would lose their heads completely.

"Well, Monseigneur," he said, when Monsieur de Sartine had finished. "What are you going to do?"

"Throw you in prison, first."

"So be it. Then what?"

"Have Monsieur de Pierrefeu released."

"Marvelous. And then!"

"Give the order to have the Tartar arrested"

"All that's well and good," said Porion. "Except that I'll give Your Lordship one piece of advice."

"Oh, really?"

"Has Monsieur de Richelieu gone back to Versailles?"

"No, he's staying in the Rue de Hanovre until I tell him that the King's orders have been executed."

"Ah!"

"Why ask me that?"

"Because I believe Your Lordship would do well to go to Versailles."

"To do what?"

"To see Madame de Pompadour and ask her advice."

"But…"

"The Marquise hates Monsieur de Pierrefeu, is interested in the Tartar, and perhaps she has already turned the King inside out like a glove."

"Oh! Well…"

293

"In addition," Porion continued, "when one is Lieutenant de Police and one intends to keep one's employment..."

"Well?"

"One doesn't offend people who might disgrace you."

"I only fear the King," said Monsieur de Sartine.

Porion smiled insolently. "Personally," he said, "in your place, Your Lordship. I'd only fear Madame de Pompadour."

"But the Maréchal..."

"Oh, if you wish, Monseigneur," said Porion, "we can talk about him a little."

"Speak."

"Everything that the Maréchal has done this morning has been less with the aim of being agreeable to the King and Monsieur de Choiseul than that of being personally disagreeable to me."

"I can believe that."

"Your Lordship would do well, then, to go to Versailles and take orders from the Marquise."

"But that's to quarrel with the Maréchal."

"I'll reconcile you with him between then and now."

"What?"

"I have the honor of repeating to you Monseigneur, that I will take charge of bringing the Duc de Richelieu round."

"You?"

"Me."

"But how?"

"That's my secret." And as Monsieur de Sartine looked at Porion suspiciously, he said "I can divine your thought, Monseigneur."

"Ah!"

"You think I want to run away. Well, Your Lordship can have me accompanied to the Maréchal's house by two agents."

"I prefer that plan," said Monsieur de Sartine, naively, "but what will you say to the Maréchal?"

"That's my secret," Porion repeated. And he refused to explain.

"So be it," said Monsieur de Sartine. And he rang in order to give his orders.

XXXII

Richelieu had, in fact, returned home.

He was radiant, the worthy Maréchal, and he could already see Porion groaning on the damp straw of a frightful dungeon.

But there is no perfect felicity in this world, and every joyful event is almost immediately counterbalanced by a small misfortune.

The gentlemen of petty birth who cluttered the antechambers of Versailles, seeing the Maréchal pass by, said, with a sigh of envy: "There goes a fortunate man!" The Maréchal, however, sometimes had cruel anxieties. The King liked him a great deal; all the beautiful lades of the court were smitten with him, even though he was over fifty, and the courtiers envied him—but that did not prevent the Maréchal from often being annoyed, like the simplest of mortals.

The Maréchal's ennuis were, moreover, very prosaic. He was indebted. There was not one of his châteaux or lands that were not mortgaged, not one tax collector who was not his creditor, not one Jew who had not lent him money at high interest and was refusing to lend him any more, and finally, not one supplier who was not complaining loudly about unpaid bills.

The King had paid the Maréchal's debts several times, but the King did not always have money, to such an extent that he had said very recently: "The Marquise is a spendthrift who is cleaning me out; I only have a hundred pistoles in my casket."

Richelieu, who had need of a hundred thousand livres, had not dared to ask for the hundred pistoles.

However, he had, in recent times, nourished a secret hope. That hope rested on the head of a worthy provincial gentleman, a distant cousin, for whom he had obtained the reversion of an excise-farmer. That very morning, Richelieu, pressed by his creditors, he said to himself: *My cousin will be only too glad to lend me fifty thousand écus.*

He had therefore put Monsieur Lépaule on horseback, and had instructed him to run to Chartres, where his cousin lived, to lose no time en route, and to bring him back the fifty thousand écus in gold or cashable bills. He was so sure of success that he had gone into the King's apartments radiant, and we have seen him occupied with his affairs all day long like a man who has fifty thousand écus in his coffers.

So, on arriving back home, he asked urgently: "Has Lépaule arrived?"

"Yes, Monseigneur," replied the gigantic steward.

"Where is he?"

"In the billiard room."

"Has he brought the money?"

"I don't know."

Richelieu frowned. Then he headed in all haste toward the billiard room, where Monsieur Lépaule, who was a very young man, was occupied on his own in learning to play the game that Monsieur de Chamillard had made fashionable.[37]

Richelieu only pronounced one word; "Well?"

"Monseigneur," replied Lépaule, who hastened to set aside his billiard cue, "I went to Chartres, but it was a futile journey."

"Futile!"

"Yes, Monseigneur."

"The peasant dared to refuse?"

"No, Monseigneur, but Your Lordship's cousin is no longer in Chartres. He departed three days ago for Toulouse, where he has property, and he won't be back until next month."

Richelieu stamped his foot in rage, and allowed a fine collection of oaths to escape. At that moment, the steward came in. He was permitted to speak freely to his master. "Monseigneur," he said, has sent away his chamber-pot?"

"Of course."

"Monseigneur was wrong."

"What?" said Richelieu.

"And if Monseigneur wants to return to Versailles this evening..."

"Certainly I'm returning there!"

"I don't know how Monseigneur will do it."

"What about my carriage, imbecile?"

"A carriage requires horses to pull it."

"Don't I have mine?"

"Horses only trot when they've eaten."

"So what, bumpkin?" cried Richelieu, who was not in a mood to be patient. "What does all this signify?"

"It signifies, Monseigneur, that the horses haven't eaten."

"Why?"

"Because the feed-merchant refuses to extend credit any longer."

"Damn!" said Richelieu. "Which supplier still gives credit?"

"There's only the rôtisseur left, Monseigneur."

"Well," sad Richelieu, coldly, "give my horses chickens." He went into his dressing-room to rid himself of his singular costume.

Five minutes later, the steward came back.

"What is it now?" said the Maréchal.

"It's a man sent by Monsieur de Sartine."

"Ah!"

---

[37] The notoriously incompetent Minister Michel Chamillart or Chamillard (1652-1721) had remained in favor nevertheless, reputedly because he played billiards with Louis XIV.

"Who is asking to be introduced immediately."

"Send him in."

The steward stood aside to leave the way free, and the Maréchal, stupefied, saw Porion come in.

A man who has just been told that his horses have no oats, and that the money on which he was counting will not arrive, cannot be in a very good humor. On recognizing Porion, the Maréchal was seized by such a fit of wrath that he seized his cane and raised it, saying: "What are you doing here, wretch?"

Porion did not recoil. "Strike, Monsieur," he said, "if that is your pleasure; I have a solid back. Strike, but listen to me."

That composure disarmed Richelieu. "What do you want?" he said.

"Monseigneur," Porion replied, "one often has need of someone humbler than oneself, and I'm convinced that if, this very evening, I could lend even Your Lordship a bagatelle of a hundred thousand écus..." The cane escaped Richelieu's hand. Porion went on: "Your Lordship would pardon me."

The steward was still on the threshold. "Go away," said Richelieu. Then he looked at Porion. "Do you take me for the King, rogue, and do you dare to make mock of me?"

"That depends on you, Monseigneur."

"What?"

Porion had recovered all his audacity. "Will Your Lordship deign to listen to me?" he said.

"Pooh!"

"I have indeed made mock of you," said Porion.

"You admit it, wretch!"

"Yes, Monseigneur, but it was in your own interest."

"My own interest?"

"Yes," said Porion, calmly.

"Well!"

"And this is the proof," said Porion. "I deceived the King, it's true. Monsieur le Maréchal de Richelieu opposes that, and in order that I do not deceive the King any longer, he has me put in prison."

"Without prejudice to the rope that waits you, scoundrel."

"Monsieur le Maréchal is wrong," replied Porion, coldly, "for, if I can continue to deceive the King, Monsieur le Maréchal will find, this very evening, in an hour, a hundred thousand écus of which he has need."

"In truth!" said Richelieu. "And where will you get them?"

"That's my business. But, if you would care, Monseigneur, to pardon me for having distanced you in the affair of young Cécile, you'll have the hundred thousand écus, and what is more..."

Porion stopped.

"And what is more?" said the Maréchal.

"The King is beginning to suffer from ennui again," said Porion.

"So?"

"The Parc-aux-Cerfs no longer contains any but vulgar beauties."

"Hmm!"

"In order to stimulate the mind and heart of the King, it will require a marvelous beauty that I know..."

"You?"

"Yes, but I'm a man to give Your Lordship his revenge."

"How's that?"

"It will be you, Monseigneur, who will speak of that pearl to His Majesty."

"Demon!" said Richelieu. "I believe you're tempting me."

"I'm trying, Monseigneur," said Porion, with effrontery.

"Truly? And you'll let me have a hundred thousand écus?"

"Yes, Monseigneur."

"And...this girl?"

"I'll take Your Lordship to her abode."

"When?"

"Tomorrow morning."

"Well," said the Maréchal, "now the conditions."

"Your Lordship will no longer occupy yourself either with the Dumas affair, or the Tartar, or the petty gentleman."

"All right. But what shall I say to the King?"

"Nothing," said Porion.

"What! Nothing?"

"It's quite simple. Tomorrow, Your Lordship will arrive in Versailles in all haste."

"Very well."

"He will be announced to the King."

"And then?"

"The King, who will probably have forgotten already the mission with which he charged Your Lordship, will ask you what's new."

"And?"

"And you'll talk to the King, Monseigneur, about a treasure of innocence and beauty."

"Ah! She's innocent as well?"

"Like the little provincial girl she is,"

"Oho! And you think that the King..."

"When one talks to the King about a mistress, he no longer things about anything else."

"But Monsieur de Choiseul..."

"Monsieur de Choiseul has broken his leg; he'll be at Chanteloup for a long time."

"Is that true?"

"Quite true, Monseigneur."

"But...the Tartar..."

"It's the Tartar, who, on my entreaty, will lend the hundred thousand écus."

"He's very rich, then?"

"So rich," said Porion, with a hint of irony in his voice, "that to quarrel with him would be a folly that Monseigneur le Duc de Richelieu, has too much intelligence ever to do."

The Maréchal hesitated momentarily. "Well," he said, finally, "go fetch me the hundred thousand écus, and we'll see."

Porion departed triumphant. "In truth," he murmured, as he climbed back into a carriage, "it must be said that a benefit is never wasted. That child saved my life this morning; I'm going to help her win her lawsuit."

And the wretch laughed with frightful cynicism.

"What are you thinking about, Père Cinnamon?" asked one of the agents commissioned by Monsieur de Sartine to guard him.

"I'm thinking," Porion replied, "that Monsieur le Lieutenant de Police is only a poor man who can't see further than the end of his nose."

XXXIII

Porion had himself taken directly to the Rue du Pas-de-la-Mule, to the Tartar's house.

He was received by the German doctor, who said to him: "The Prince is waiting for you impatiently."

"He thought that I'd come then?"

"He wasn't sure, but he was hopeful."

"Aha!"

"He has, moreover, an extraordinary agitation, and an anger that nothing approaches."

"Why is that?"

"He's come back from Versailles; he presented himself at Madame de Pompadour's apartments and was not received."

Good, thought Porion. *Here's an adventure that will advance the Maréchal's financial affairs.*

And Porion went in to see the Prince.

"Oh, there you are, rogue, scoundrel, impudent liar!" cried the Tartar, on seeing Porion.

Porion was not disconcerted. "Monseigneur," he said, "At any other time I would allow Your Highness to insult me at his ease, but at the present moment, it would be a waste of precious time."

"What?" said the Tartar.

Porion took a large silver watch out of his fob pocket and looked at the time. "It's nearly nine o'clock, Monseigneur," he said, "it's winter and the nights are long."

"So?"

"With good horses," Porion went on, "Your Highness can put thirty leagues between himself and Paris by daybreak."

"Are you mocking me, scoundrel?"

"No, Monseigneur."

"Then what do you mean?"

"That tomorrow, at this hour, if Your Highness remains in Paris, he will be in the Bastille."

"Get away!"

"It is as I have the honor of telling Your Highness."

The Prince paled slightly. "Go on," he said. "What's the matter?"

"A reversion has taken place in the King's mind. More than ever, he believes in the murdered children."

"Really?"

"And he has given the order to let your most terrible accuser out of the Bastille."

"Monsieur de Pierrefeu?"

"The same."

"And to whom has he given that order?"

"To Monsieur de Sartine, via the intermediary of Monsieur de Richelieu."

"Him!" cried the Tartar. "But I thought he was on my side!"

Porion winked. "It's easy to see," he said "that Your Highness us unfamiliar with the ways of the Court."

"What do you mean?"

"When one is playing for high stakes, the means of having Monsieur de Richelieu on one's side is to interest him."

"In truth?"

"The Maréchal has debts, and consequently creditors, who are tormenting him."

"If he'd sent me his creditors, I would have paid them."

"That would have been all the wiser," said Porion, "as the Maréchal has a great deal of influence over the mind of the King, and is the only one capable of counterbalancing the influence of Monsieur le Duc de Choiseul."

"And the Maréchal is against me?"

"Which is to say that he went to the Rue de l'Hirondelle this morning, that he threatened that imbecile draper with the wrath of the King, and that the latter confessed everything to him."

"So the King knows everything."

"The King knows nothing yet, for Monsieur de Richelieu, who gives priority to pleasures over affairs, is remaining in Paris this evening, expecting a gallant rendezvous. But tomorrow, he will be at the King's *petit lever*, and he will obtain a *lettre de cachet* in your regard."

"Oh, that's too much!" said the Prince. "If I'd known he needed money..."

"For fifty thousand écus," Porion sighed, "he would have been ours."

"And now?"

"Now it's too late."

"Even by offering him double that sum?"

"I fear so, Monseigneur. And I repeat to Your Highness that the best thing to do is to ask for post-horses."

The Prince stamped his foot in anger. "And if I don't want to go?"

"Then, Monseigneur, you'll go to the Bastille."

"From which one emerges..."

"Yes, to go to the scaffold."

The Prince shivered. "Can't you reach the Maréchal?"

"I don't know, but I'll try."

"Do that, and tell him that I have a hundred thousand écus at his service."

"Monseigneur," said Porion, "That's not the way that it's necessary to proceed."

"Really?"

"The Maréchal would throw me out if I only brought a promise."

"And if you brought the money?"

"Well, I don't know…"

"Let's try," said the Tartar. And he took a pen and wrote:

On presentation, will Monsieur Boemer, cashier, pay the bearer, against this mandate, the sum of a hundred thousand écus, for which he will debit my account.

Paris ****,
Prince Trespatky.

"Damn!" said Porion. "He has a nice strong-box, Père Boemer. It's only German bankers who have that much gold."

"He'll pay this very evening," said the Prince.

"What! At nine o'clock in the evening?"

"If it were midnight, he'd pay it."

Porion took the mandate. "Monseigneur," he said, "I'll try; but I won't answer absolutely for success, and in my absence, Your Highness would do well to be ready or any eventuality, and ask for post-horses."

"Go!" said the Prince.

Porion picked up his greasy hat and his ivory-handled cane and walked backwards to the door.

"When will you be back?" asked the Tartar.

"Perhaps in an hour, perhaps two. For one thing, it's not certain that the Maréchal will allow himself to be tempted right away."

"Ah!"

"And then, I have one of those frightful vehicles known as chamber-pots, which go so slowly, so very slowly…"

"Take my carriage."

And the Prince struck a bell. Hermann came running.

"Have Monsieur put into my carriage," the Tartar ordered.

Porion went out, murmuring: "If I'd told the Tartar that Monsieur de Richelieu would be ours for a hundred thousand écus and that it was a done deal, he'd have offered half that sum. Whereas, he's afraid of seeing his head detached from his body, and didn't haggle. Porion, my friend, you're a diplomat of real value."

And, having paid himself that little compliment, the rogue climbed into the Prince's carriage.

"Where are you going?" asked Hermann.

"Boemer's, Rue des Lombards."

The jeweler Boemer, whose sons were to sell the famous necklace thirty years later,[38] was a rich German banker with whom Prince Trespatky had opened an unlimited credit on coming to Paris. The Prince had been right to say that Boemer would pay at any hour. In fact, the Prince had accustomed him to opening his safe, sometimes by day and sometimes by night, in accordance with his needs as a gambler and womanizer.

Like all money men, Monsieur Boemer led an orderly life. He shut his shop at nine o'clock, sent his assistants home, compiled his daily accounts, supped frugally and went to bed in the same room where his safe was lodged.

Porion arrived just as the financier was finishing his meal.

The sound of a carriage stopping outside his house had made the latter shiver, and he hastened to open the door. He recognized the Prince's carriage, and thus knew what to expect.

"Monsieur," Porion said, presenting him with the mandate, "I am the Prince's new steward, and I've come in quest of money.

Monsieur Boemer bowed to Porion and invited him in. "You'll be paid immediately," he said, "for my treasury is never closed." At the same time, he led Porion to his bedroom. He slid a curtain along a rail, and Porion perceived a monumental steel safe at the back of the alcove, in the lock of which there were three keys.

"Do you want a great deal of gold?" asked Boemer.

"The Prince has told me to take hundred thousand écus' worth."

"There," said the jeweler, placing three leather sacks on a table. Porion was too well brought-up to insult Monsieur Boemer by verifying the contents.

A quarter of an hour later, Porion, furnished with the hundred thousand écus, climbed back into the carriage and shouted to the coachman, while Boemer closed the carriage-door himself: "To the house."

But when the vehicle reached the corner of the Rue des Lombards, Porion lowered the glass, tugged the flap of the Coachman's coat and said to him: "To the Maréchal de Richelieu's house, and quickly.

Twenty minutes later, Porion entered the courtyard of the hotel in the Rue de Hanovre. As he got out of the carriage he saw a head at a window and recognized the Maréchal. *Let's go!* he thought. *I believe he's waiting for my with as much impatience as if I were a pretty young woman.* And he marched toward the perron at as brisk a pace as the weight of hundred thousand écus of gold would permit.

"Monseigneur," he said, on entering. "I have everything I promised."

"You have the hundred thousand écus?" said the Maréchal.

---

[38] In fact, the two jewelers involved in the famous affair in the 1780s, in which Cardinal Rohan was tricked into purchasing an expensive necklace, allegedly on behalf of Marie Antoinette, were the royal jewelers Charles Boehmer and Paul Bassenge.

"Yes, Monseigneur." And he set the three sacks of louis and the stack of bills before Richelieu, saying: "Count it."

The Maréchal uttered a sigh. "Ah!" he said. "It's a long time that I've found such a treat. Decidedly, the Prince is a charming man, and I'm entirely at his service."

Porion bowed.

"However," said Richelieu, who started piling up the gold and bills in a small desk placed beside the fireplace, "the young woman you mentioned to me—it's necessary that I see her if you want me to talk to the King about her."

"Nothing is easier."

"Really?"

"Your Lordship will be out of bed at eight o'clock tomorrow morning?"

"Of course."

"Well, Monsieur le Maréchal, I'll come to pick you up at that hour."

"And you'll take me to her?"

"Certainly, and you'll see that she's a pearl."

"Rogue!" said Richelieu, who finished counting his money. "Give me some advice. Is it necessary to pay my debts?"

"Monseigneur," Porion replied, "there is a proverb that says that the man who pays his debts enriches himself, but it's false."

"Oh! You think so?"

"It's better to keep one's money," Porion added.

"That's what I'll do, then," said Richelieu. And he locked the desk and put the key in his pocket.

XXXIV

While Porion was buying the good offices and the discretion of Monsieur le Maréchal de Richelieu with the Tartar's hundred thousand écus, desolation was in the house in the Rue Saint-André-des-Arts where Robert Damiens, Cécile and the young surgeon Firmin lodged.

That great despair came from the bad news that Mardochée had just brought. We have seen the gentleman painter running away from the Place Royale that morning with the conviction that Porion was no longer anything but a cadaver at the end of a rope and his pockets full of the gold that the latter had allowed to escape during the struggle. Brave as he could be, Messire Mardochée de Mardoche had too great a fear of the sergeants to look back, and he had quit the Place Royale without the slightest suspicion that Porion had been snatched from an almost-certain death. Then, in order to put the watchmen off the track, he had made multiple turns and detours in the back-streets extending around the square, reached the Rue du Temple and traversed the Place du Châtelet.

Once on the Pont au Change, Mardochée had paused for breath, but he took pleasure in palpating in his pockets the beautiful brand new louis that had escaped from Porion's pockets, and as he had an excellent heart, he had immediately thought of his friends in the Rue Saint-André-des-Arts. In his view, Hector should have returned from Versailles, and the King had doubtless given him a good welcome, and justice would be done.

He went straight to the Rue Saint-André-des-Arts and went up to the top floor humming a tune. Firmin's door was open. He went in. He saw Firmin sitting sadly at his work table. Next to Firmin, Cécile was plying her needle, her eyes full of tears. And at the very back of the mansard, Robert Damiens, his head in his hands and his elbows on his knees, was somber, mute and grim.

"What's the matter?" exclaimed Mardochée. "What's happened now?"

It was Cécile who replied: "Hector hasn't come back from Versailles."

"Since yesterday?"

"Alas, no,"

Mardochée frowned; nevertheless, he did his best to console his friends. "Well," he said, "what does that prove? The King might have given him an audience very late, and he's slept in Versailles."

Cécile shook her head. "I have ominous presentiments," she said.

"Why?"

"I don't know, but it seems to us that a new misfortune threatens us."

Mardochée did not reply, but he picked up his hat, which he had placed on Firmin's bed."

"Where are you going?" the latter asked.

"To Versailles, of course." And Mardochée ran to the door and disappeared down the stairs.

Five minutes later he was in the street, having run to the Carrefour Buci. He climbed into a chamber-pot and, fortified by his well-garnished pockets, he said to the coachman: "If you get me to Versailles in an hour and a half I'll give you a louis."

The coachman, enticed by the promise, whipped his horse hard, so frequently and so effectively that he arrived at the gate of the château within the specified time.

But one does not enter the château even when one is wearing a sword and declared that one is a gentleman. After a futile negotiation with the sentinels, Mardochée said to himself: *I'm an imbecile to persist thus. One of two things must be the case; either Hector is still at the château and he'll come out eventually, or he's gone, and it won't get me any further to get in there.*

He paced up and down in front of the gate for an hour, inspecting all the people who went in or came out. But a man as curious as the gentleman painter, who is always thirsty as well, cannot be patient. Wearing of waiting, Mardochée de Mardoche climbed back into the chamber-pot and told the coachman to take him to the Singe Vert.

When he went in, the main room was crowded. The conversation among the drinkers was very animated, and the events of the previous night were the only topic.

While drinking Mardochée lent an ear.

One gentleman said: "Poor Vicomte de Mauroy, his indemnity is paid in full; the King will keep him in the Bastille until the end of his days, taking charge of his nourishment and accommodation."

"Bah!" said another. "The King isn't immortal,"

"Nor the Marquise," said a third.

Mardochée approached the last and said: "I beg your pardon, Monsieur, but what has happened?"

"Monsieur," the latter replied, courteously, "it's a matter of two gentlemen who were sent to the Bastille his morning."

"Oh!"

"For having been found in possession of a copy of the *Gazette de Hollande*."

"Is that a crime, then?" asked Messire Mardochée de Mardoche, naively.

"Yes, for the paper insults the Marquise de Pompadour."

"Damn! And who are these gentlemen?"

"One is named Vicomte Gontran de Mauroy."

"And the other?"

"The other is a poor petty gentleman who, it's said, had an audience with the King."

Mardochée shivered. "Do you know his name?" he asked.

"Yes," said another gentleman at a nearby table. "His name is Hector de Pierrefeu."

Mardochée uttered a cry.

"Do you know him?" someone asked.

"He's my friend," said Mardochée, in a lamentable tone. And his visage suddenly expressed a veritable desolation.

The gentleman who had spoken first leaned toward him. "My young friend," he said, "would you like some good advice?"

Mardochée looked at him fearfully.

"It's not good to have friends in the Bastille," said the gentleman, "much less to boast about it. If you'll take my advice, you'll slip away from Versailles quietly. There are zealous people everywhere who meddle in what doesn't concern them. In addition, Madame de Pompadour has police that..."

Mardochée did not hear any more. He got up, extended his hand to the gentleman and went out with the tread of a drunken man, so much had the news devastated him.

He climbed back into the carriage and returned to Paris.

On seeing him return, Cécile, Firmin and Robert Damiens understood that their presentiments were well-founded.

The painter only pronounced one word: "The Bastille!"

None of the three uttered a cry of astonishment, none found that denouement implausible. It was, on the contrary, quite simple. Hector, poor and paltry, devoid of money and influence, had gone to ask for justice against powerful men. To get rid of him, he had been sent to the Bastille.

Cécile dissolved in tears. Firmin spoke about vengeance. Only Robert Damiens did not say a word—but he stood up abruptly, and went out.

"Father! Where are you going?" asked Cécile, bewildered.

Robert Damiens did not reply. He went downstairs, somber and grim, reached the street and headed at a slow and jerky pace toward the river.

When he had arrived at the Petit-Pont, he leaned on the parapet and gazed at the black and muddy water that was flowing through that narrow space. Never, at any other point in its course, does the Seine have a more sinister aspect. It attracts people who lean over to gaze at it; it seems to be saying: "Come to me, forgetfulness of the evils of earth is in my bosom."

Robert had vertigo. "Oh," he said, "I believe that I'd do better to finish it immediately, for if I persist in living, the temptation that obsesses me will eventually triumph, and I'll commit a great crime."

At that moment he was pale and grim, and an abundant sweat was trickling over his forehead. "Oh, my God," he said, "forgive me!" And he put his leg over the parapet, resolutely.

One second more and that would have been the end of Robert Damiens; the black stream would have opened and closed over him. But at that moment a vigorous arm seized him and dragged him back to the middle of the bridge, at the same time as a grave and soft voice said to him: "Are you in despair of God's bounty, then, you who want to die?"

Robert, bewildered, raised his head and found himself in the presence of an old man with a white beard. "Who are you?" he said. "By what right do you interpose yourself between destiny and me?"

"My name won't tell you much," the old man replied. "It's Patureau. I'm a poor servant, like you, if I can judge by your clothing, and I'm in the service of Mademoiselle Espérance de Beaulieu." Then, passing his arm beneath Robert's, he added: "Espérance—isn't that a beautiful name?"

"Indeed," stammered Robert, bitterly.

"If you lack bread, we'll give you some," said the old man. "If you're in despair, we'll console you. Come with me. Oh, when you see my young mistress smile, you'll understand that she merits the name Espérance, and you'll no longer want to die."

XXXV

Robert Damiens had been dragging out a miserable life for a long time. He was a man of the people, and the people, in that era, rarely had happy days. Never, perhaps, had a voice as consoling and as sympathetic resonated in his ear.

He looked at the old man. "Don't deceive me," he said, "with the sole aim of preventing me from dying. Are there really people as you say?"

The old man was still holding his arm. "My friend," he said, "God forbids taking one's own life, whatever burden weighs upon us. Do you no longer love anyone in this world, then?"

That question made Robert shudder. He covered his face with his hands. "O my daughter!" he murmured. "Forgive me!"

"Your daughter!" exclaimed Patureau. "You have a daughter!"

"Yes."

"And you wanted to die?"

"Of, if you knew!" murmured Robert. Then his face took on a grim expression. "But those things," he said, "God alone ought to know..."

Patureau drew him to the far end of the bridge. "Come," he said. "Don't remain exposed to temptation."

Robert allowed himself to be led away with the docility of a child. The old man made him traverse the Cité thus, reached the right bank of the Seine and drew him in the direction of the Rue Saint-Antoine. Robert followed him mechanically.

"Let's see," said Patureau. "You're without a place, aren't you?"

"Alas, yes."

"And you can't find one?"

"I haven't looked."

That response was at least strange; it struck Mademoiselle de Beaulieu's steward. "You have a distracted gaze," he said. "Tell me, as a friend: why do you want to die?"

Robert began to shiver. "Oh, don't ask me today," he said. "Later...later..."

"So be it," said Patureau.

And Robert, under the empire of a sudden terror, clung on to the old man's arm, and said to him: "Tale me...take me wherever you wish...but don't leave me alone, now that you've prevented me from dying...for I'm afraid of myself..."

Patureau increased his pace. He did not ask Robert any more questions, and Robert fell back into a somber silence. They marched thus to the entrance of the Place Royale. There. Robert stopped momentarily. "Ah!" he said. "Is it here that your mistress lives?"

"Yes."

"And you think she won't throw me out?"

"Mademoiselle Espérance," the old man replied, "is kindness itself. She will hold out her hand to you, and, as I've told you, she will console you."

A few minutes later, Robert penetrated, on Patureau's heels, into the house where, that same morning, Porion had returned to life.

The young woman was sitting in front of a table on which a shaded lamp was laced, devoting herself to some needlework. When Patureau came in she did not even look up. "Is that you, my friend?" she said.

"Yes, Mademoiselle."

"Well, have you seen Maître Tavernier?"

"Yes, Mademoiselle. I waited for a long time, of course. All these quibblers and procurators are overwhelmed by affairs and their antechambers are full of solicitors, but I finally had my turn."

"What did he say?"

"That he had examined the dossier in its entirety."

"Ah! What does he think."

"He believes the suit excellent…impossible to lose, in fact…"

"Oh my God!" murmured the young woman. "May he be telling the truth!"

"But he asked me whether Mademoiselle does not know anyone in Paris."

"You know very well."

"Someone highly-placed, preferably at Court, who can force the Parliament to abridge the delays and judge the affair as soon as possible."

"Alas," said the young woman, who did not see Robert, who was standing discreetly on the threshold of the room, behind Patureau, "you know that all the friends and relatives that my father had in Paris are dead or dispersed."

"I know that, Mademoiselle. He also said to me that my mistress could address a supplication to the King…"

At that name Robert shuddered, and if Patureau had turned round at that moment he would have seen him as pale as a dead man.

But Patureau did not turn round, and he continued: "Mademoiselle's father served the King loyally."

"Undoubtedly."

"And Mademoiselle might be able to take advantage of his services."

"But how? By whom?"

"Maître Tavernier also told me," Patureau continued, "that if Mademoiselle does not know anyone, he will attempt a personal step toward a great seigneur who has a considerable influence over the king, and who is his client."

"Ah!"

"Yes," the old steward concluded, "Maître Tavernier recently won an important lawsuit, which everyone had judged in advance as doomed, to the benefit of the Maréchal Duc de Richelieu."

"The Maréchal de Richelieu!" exclaimed Espérance.

"Yes, Mademoiselle."

"But he commanded the Maison-Rouge at Fontenoy."

"Exactly."

"And my father was in the Maison-Rouge, as you know."

"Yes, Mademoiselle."

While speaking, Espérance had gradually turned her head. Her eyes encountered Robert, pale, immobile and quivering. She uttered a slight cry. "Who is that man?" she asked, sharply.

"This man is a desperate unfortunate whom I've snatched from death."

"Yes?"

"Yes, Mademoiselle, I too wanted to save a man," he said, smiling at the allusion to the morning's event, "And I stopped the unfortunate fellow as he was about to throw himself into the Seine."

"Oh my God!" said the young woman, fearfully.

"Then, as he struggled with me, begging me to let him finish with life, I spoke to him about you, Mademoiselle, and I brought him here."

"You did well, my friend." And Espérance stood up, and the lamp illuminated her radiant beauty.

She extended her hand to Robert, and said to him, in a voice as soft and mild as an Aeolia harp: "You were so desperate, then, that you wanted to die, my friend?"

"Yes, Mademoiselle," relied Robert Damiens, "because I did not know that God had left one of his angels on earth." And he kissed the hand that the young woman held out to him, respectfully.

"You wanted to die?" he repeated. "You no longer love anyone in this world?"

Robert hid his face in his hands.

"He has a daughter," said Patureau.

"And he wanted to die! Oh, my friend…have you lost your reason, then?"

"Yes, Mademoiselle…but I sense that in your presence I'm returning to better sentiments. I want to live, now…to live and work..."

"How old is your daughter?" asked Espérance, then.

"Sixteen, Mademoiselle."

"She's doubtless unfortunate too. Well, you'll bring her to me, won't you?"

"Yes, Mademoiselle."

And Robert Damiens, penetrated by gratitude, fell to his knees before the young woman.

"My friend," said Mademoiselle de Beaulieu, raising him to his feet, "Patureau is the only servant I have, and his strength is beginning to betray him. "Would you like to stay with me? If you don't want to separate from your daughter, well, bring her. She can doubtless do needlework?"

"Oh, certainly, yes, Mademoiselle."

"Well, you'll share our life. And if I win my lawsuit, I'll be rich. Then I'll endow your daughter, and give you a small pension, which will permit you to live in comfort."

Robert Damiens wept hot tears.

The following morning, those who had seen Robert somber and grim would not have recognized him. What had happened in that mysterious and somber soul? No one could have said—but there had been a sudden appeasement within him.

At eight o'clock in the morning he came to salute Espérance and said to her: "Mademoiselle, you wanted to permit me to bring you my daughter."

"Certainly, my friend."

"Then I'll go to fetch her," said Damiens.

Patureau came in at the same time. Under his arm he had the familiar bag of parchments that he had been parading around Paris for nearly two months. "I'm going to see Maître Tavernier, Mademoiselle," he said.

"Go," said Espérance, "and tell the procurator that if he attempts a step toward Monsieur the Maréchal de Richelieu..."

"He will, Mademoiselle, be sure of it."

"Remind him to tell Monsieur le Maréchal that my father was in the Maison-Rouge, d'Estaing's company."

"Yes, Mademoiselle."

Patureau went out, and Robert went with him, for the simple reason that the former was going to the Carrefour Buci, where the procurator lived, while the latter was heading for the Rue Saint-André-des-Arts. They would therefore be going almost all the way together.

Espérance, leaning on her window-sill, watched them draw away and disappear under the arches. Then she resumed her needlework.

Five minutes later the bell at the door of the entrance to the apartment rang discreetly. Mademoiselle de Beaulieu never received visits, because she did not know anyone in Paris. But at that early hour suppliers came, including the baker, and the milkman, who brought a cup of milk for the young woman's breakfast. Espérance therefore got up and went to open the door.

It was not a tradesman who had rung; it was the excellent Père Cinnamon, who saluted the young woman and sad: "Excuse me for coming to disturb you so early, Mademoiselle, but when you know what I've brought, you won't be annoyed."

And the wolf entered into the sheepfold.

XXXVI

Espérance let the old man in.

Porion seemed even more decrepit than they day before, and he had put on a face radiant with kindness and gratitude. He had an appearance so respectable that Mademoiselle de Beaulieu did not express any sentiment of suspicion, and said to him: "Whatever the motive that brings you, be welcome."

Porion followed her to the room where she worked in the morning.

"Mademoiselle," he said, "I'm a poor man; I have a great deal of difficulty living, and certainly, if I've ever suffered from my poverty, it's today, for I'd like to be able to express my gratitude to you."

"You've testified it to me sufficiently," said Espérance, smiling.

"Yesterday, therefore," Porion went on, "as I went away from your home, I started racking my brains for a means to be useful to you, and I believe that I've found one."

"Really?"

"In the matter of your lawsuit."

Espérance shivered. "How do you know that I have a lawsuit?" she asked

"Your steward mentioned it in my presence."

"Ah!"

"Lawsuits, you see, Mademoiselle, can be won or lost. They are won, especially, when one has a protector."

"Alas, yes," said Espérance.

"Well, such as you see me," said Père Cinnamon, "a poor, paltry old man, I have a protector."

"In truth?"

"Can you imagine, Mademoiselle," that my late father was a steward for forty years in a great family, and that the last scion of that family, in memory of my father's good services, has given me a small pension of thirty livres a month, which I collect regularly, as you can imagine."

"Poor man!" said Espérance, smiling.

"My day was yesterday. I therefore went, when I left you, to Monseigneur's house. As you can imagine, I usually deal with the steward, but Monseigneur happened to be at the house; he saw me through a window, and made me a sign to go up.

"I did not have to be begged, as you can imagine. 'Well,' he said to me, 'how are you?'

"'Well, Monseigneur,' I replied, 'but I had a narrow escape this morning. Once again I was mistaken for my rascal of a brother.'

"'You were beaten?'

"'Worse than that, Monseigneur; they tried to hang me.'

"'Hang you?'

"'Yes, Monseigneur.'

"And I told him about my adventure, and what you had done for me.

"Then," Porion concluded, "Monseigneur said to me: 'That's a worthy young woman, and I'd like hazard to furnish me with an opportunity to be useful to her.'"

"Oh! He said that?" said Espérance, whose heart began to beat faster.

"Yes, Mademoiselle."

"Then you thought..."

"I told him immediately that you had come to Paris to sustain a lawsuit on which your entire fortune depended."

"Very nearly," said Espérance, simply.

"In that case," Monseigneur said to me, "It's necessary to send her to Tavernier, my procurator. I'll recommend her to him warmly, and..."

"Tavernier!" exclaimed Espérance.

"Yes, Mademoiselle."

Espérance heart beat even faster. "But," she said, "what is the name of this great seigneur of whom you speak, and who pays you a small pension"

Porion swelled with pride. "Mademoiselle," he said, "it's Monseigneur le Maréchal Duc de Richelieu."

Espérance paled with emotion. "Really!" she said. "And you know him?"

"Yes, Mademoiselle."

"And he's promised to take an interest in me?"

"Yes, Mademoiselle."

"Oh, my God!" said, Espérance, palpitating. "What singular good fortune!"

"Eh?" said Porion.

"The procurator charged with my case is the very same Tavernier."

"Is it possible?"

"It's true."

"In that case," said Porion, "the thing will go like clockwork."

"Oh, why isn't the good Patureau here?" exclaimed Espérance.

"He's gone out?"

"He's gone to see Maître Tavernier.

"Well," said Porion, "when he returns, he'll be content." The he took a pinch of tobacco, winked, and continued: "I haven't told you everything yet, Mademoiselle."

Espérance looked at him in astonishment.

"Don't scold me," Porion continued, "but when Monseigneur had said all that to me, I thought of something..."

"What?"

"That you'd never believe that a great seigneur like the Maréchal could be interested in a poor devil like me."

"Why wouldn't I believe it, since you say so?" said Espérance, ingenuously.

"Then," Porion went on, "I said that to the Maréchal."

"Really? And what did he say?"

"It's here that I fear being scolded, Mademoiselle."

"Speak, my friend."

Porion feigned embarrassment. "It's just that," he said, "it's perhaps not very appropriate. But excuse me…I'm a poor man ignorant of fine manners."

"Whatever you've done," said Espérance, smiling, "I forgive you in advance."

"So, I made Monsieur le Maréchal party to my dread," Porion continued.

"Good."

"He started to laugh and said to me: 'Where does your liberator live, my friend?'

"'The Place Royale, Monseigneur.'

"'Well, I'll get you out of the difficulty,' he said. 'I'm going to the Place Royale tomorrow morning to see an old friend, the Maréchal de Ph***. Go see Mademoiselle de Beaulieu and ask her to go to her window.'"

"Really?" said Espérance, blushing. "He said that?"

"Yes, Mademoiselle, and he even added: 'I'll put my head out of my litter and I'll salute her, and she'll see then that you're not boasting.'"

Espérance was a provincial young woman; she knew nothing of the terrible reputation for gallantry that the Maréchal had acquired. In any case, Porion had an expression so naïve, so respectable, that there was no great inconvenience in doing what he asked. Finally, perhaps, a sentiment of curiosity slid into the young woman's mind.

"So," she said, "the Maréchal is going to pass by?"

"Yes, Mademoiselle."

"Across the square?"

"Beneath your window."

"But how will he recognize me and salute me, since he has never seen me?"

"He'll recognize you because I'll be at your window, beside you."

"Oh that's true.,."

Porion opened the window. "My word!" he said. "I only just had time to make you my petty confidence."

"Pardon?"

"There's Monsieur le Maréchal's litter emerging on to the square over there."

Espérance came to the window. She did, indeed, see a litter bearing a coat of arms, whose four porters were clad in a red and white livery with cockades on their hats, preceded by a runner in the same colors, armed with a long cane and carrying a knot of ribbons over his arm.

At the same time, she noticed two bourgeois sitting on a bench in the garden, and heard one of them say: "Isn't that Maréchal de Richelieu's litter?"

"They're still his colors," replied the other.

Espérance could no longer have a shadow of a doubt.

The litter traversed the square and came to pass under Espérance's window.

Then a head showed itself at the side of the litter and looked up.

Espérance blushed.

The Maréchal removed his hat gallantly, and the litter continued on its way and stopped ten doors further on, at the house of the Maréchal de Ph***.

Less than an hour later, the Maréchal's litter was going back up the Rue du Faubourg Saint-Antoine, and Porion was running after it.

"Well, Monseigneur?" the wretch asked, drawing level with Richelieu.

"I'm dazzled," said the Maréchal.

"Truly?"

"She's the most beautiful woman in the realm."

"Then I've kept my promise?"

"Undoubtedly, and I'll run to Versailles to speak to the King about her."

"It's high time," said Porion, "for the King will be starting to find your absence a little long."

"My carriage is waiting for me at the Hôtel-de-Ville. I'll burn the pavement to get there more rapidly."

"One more word, Monseigneur."

"Speak."

"If everything goes well, it's necessary to use your influence."

"To do what?"

"It's necessary that Mademoiselle de Beaulieu wins her lawsuit."

"She'll be Queen of France if she wishes," said the Maréchal, enthusiastically.

"Amen!" murmured Porion. And while the Maréchal continued on his way, the police agent said to himself, with a malign smile: *And Monsieur de Sartine was trembling before the Maréchal yesterday evening! Ha ha ha!*

Then the wretch plunged into a maze of narrow streets and headed for the house of the Lieutenant de Police, whom he was about to inform that everything had worked out for the best.

Now, let us leave Porion on his way to see Monsieur de Sartine and Richelieu on the road to Versailles, and penetrate into the Bastille, where Vicomte Gontran de Mauroy and his young friend Hector de Pierrefeu were still detained.

XXXVII

The wrath of a Fleming is of short duration. When the colossus known as Gontran de Mauroy had cursed and raged extravagantly, delivered four of five kicks to the door, which did not budge, and tried to shake the bars of the window, which resisted, he calmed down.

Hector, overwhelmed and prey to a kind of prostration, neither moved nor spoke. He was sitting sadly on his bed, and, with his head in his hands, he was thinking bitterly of the happy days of his childhood.

The Vicomte came to him and took his hand. "Come on, my friend," he said. "Courage!"

"You mean resignation," murmured Hector.

"Resignation? Never!" said the Fleming

"I can't see what use our courage is going to be."

"We'll need it to get out of here."

A dubious smile came to Hector's lips. "You know full well," he said, "that no one gets out of the Bastille."

"Not if one expects mercy."

"Then…"

"But people escape."

"How?"

"I don't know, but there must be a means, and we'll find it."

"But, Monsieur," said Hector, "when we came in here you were asleep, and you didn't see what I saw."

"What did you see, damn it?"

"First of all, a broad ditch more than thirty feet deep."

"Bah!" I know that."

"Then at least a dozen doors, all of which opened and closed upon us.

"And?"

"Sentinels everywhere, in all the courtyards, under all the windows."

"Is that all?"

"Finally, they've taken away everything we had on us, including my knife and my purse."

The Fleming had recovered his spurn phlegm. "In consequence," he said, "we have no instrument with which to fabricate a saw or corrupt a jailer."

"Alas!" sighed Hector.

"Well," said the Fleming, "what does all that prove? Haven't the Abbé de Gondi and Monsieur de Beaufort escaped?"[39]

"They had collaborators outside, and we don't."

"We'll create some," said the Fleming, full of self-confidence. Then, looking at Hector: "Have you ever heard it said that anyone has ever gone to the moon?"

"Certainly not."

"Well, if I ever put my mind to it, I'll go. In consequence, have courage." As Hector continued to smile, he said: "I don't know when we'll get out of here, but we'll get out. How? I don't know—but we'll find a means." And as all those assurances were insufficient to clear Hector's face, the Vicomte added: "And justice will be done."

"By whom?"

"By me," said the colossus, coldly.

That conversation was interrupted by the sound of footsteps in the corridor. Then a key turned in the enormous lock. Three large bolts were heard sliding in their sockets, and the door opened.

A short man with a bald head and a fat belly, wearing the blue and yellow uniform of the employees of the Bastille, with an enormous bunch of keys at this waist and a small sword by his side, appeared on the threshold.

"Bonjour, Messieurs," he said. "A thousand times bonjour. I've come to see whether you're comfortable and if, by chance, you need anything. If the regulations don't oppose it, Messieurs, it will be a real pleasure for me to be agreeable and useful to you."

"It's doubtless to Monsieur the Governor that we have the honor of speaking?" said the Fleming, although he did not believe a word of what he was saying.

"Alas, no!" replied the little man. "I'm merely the senior turnkey."

"My gentleman," said Monsieur de Mauroy, politely, "you have such fine manners and a worthy appearance that I would have sworn that you were Monsieur de Launay in person."

"Alas, no!" replied the fat man. "I'm not the governor, and when the titles of nobility were revoked for a second time some ten years ago, they did not want to maintain mine—a blatant, abominable injustice, my dear Messieurs."

"From what province do you hail, my dear Monsieur Turnkey?" said Monsieur de Mauroy,

"Artois."

"That's almost my homeland, and I know the old nobility like the back of my hand."

---

[39] The escape of the Abbé de Gondi from the Bastille is cited in Alfred de Vigny's *Cinq-Mars* (1826) and Monsieur de Beaufort's in Alexandre Dumas' *La Tulipe noire* (1850). Ponson probably found the relevant data in the two novels.

"In truth?"

"What is your name?"

"Duverger de Beauverger."

"God's blood!" exclaimed Monsieur de Mauroy, with great seriousness, "the steward who revoked the titles of your province is an ass, my dear Monsieur."

"That's what I'm told."

"An ass and a pedant. The Duvergers are noble, very noble; they go back to the crusades, not to the first, the second or even the third generation."

"That's what I killed myself telling the steward, but those people only do anything for money."

"That's true...and perhaps...don't you have any?"

"It's the pure truth, Monsieur, we were ruined during the Fronde,[40] and such as you see me, my dear Monsieur, I've been obliged to accept the modest employment I occupy in order to live."

"And what does it bring you?"

"Nourishment, lodgings and two hundred livres."

"In fact, that's less than nothing."

"Which is to say, Monsieur, that I'm in poverty."

"But you have gratifications?"

"Almost none. We only have dastards in the Bastille. Excuse me, I don't have the honor of knowing you, and I'm saying nothing about you, but it's the pure truth. The time of the great seigneurs is past, we have none any longer!"

"Truly!"

"The last one left this morning, and you see me inconsolable."

"Why is that?"

Monsieur Duverger de Beauverger sighed. "That's what I can't say clearly, but suffice it for you to know that if he'd stayed for two more days, my fortune would have been made."

"Bah!"

"It's as I have the honor of telling you."

"But how?"

A thin smile came to the lips of the stout little man. "My dear Monsieur," he said, "if I added one word more and that word reached the ears of the governor, I could well change condition in the Bastille."

"How's that?"

"I've said enough; let it suffice, Messieurs."

---

[40] The Fronde was a series of civil wars in France between 1648 and 1653, occurring in the midst of the Franco-Spanish War, which had begun in 1635. The king confronted the combined opposition of the princes, the nobility, the law courts (regional parliaments), and most of the French people, and yet won out in the end.

"My dear Monsieur de Beauverger," said the Fleming, working hard to get himself into the good graces of the turnkey, and suppressing his patronymic with the sole aim of proving that he was convinced of his nobility, "I'm not a great seigneur, but you can inform yourself on my account; I'm rich."

The turnkey's eyes widened.

"Very rich," the Fleming continued, "and if my rights hadn't been compromised, I wouldn't be here."

"It appears," said the turnkey, "that you've insulted Madame la Marquise."

"That's the pretext."

"Ah!"

"I've been sent here in order not to pay me ten thousand livres that I'm owed."

"Ten thousand livres!" exclaimed Monsieur Duverger de Beauverger. "A tidy sum."

"Trivial for me."

"Are you talking seriously?"

"I'd give thirty thousand to get out of here, and I can assure you that it wouldn't inconvenience me. But I'd forfeit my right in so doing."

"Thirty thousand livres!" murmured Monsieur Duverger de Beauverger, his little eyes widening immeasurably.

"More rather than less—but," the Fleming added, "all that, as they say, is just talk, for one only gets out of the Bastille at the King's pleasure."

"That's true, Monsieur, and it rarely pleases His Majesty."

"The governor, the doorkeepers and the soldiers," Monsieur de Mauroy went on, "form an utterly incorruptible army."

"Incorruptible is the word." And Monsieur Duverger de Beauverger sighed for a second time.

"With the result," the Vicomte continued, "That I shall await the King's pleasure."

"There are examples, Monsieur."

"Of the King granting mercy?"

"Yes, as witness the great seigneur who was released this morning."

"What is his name?"

"Monsieur de Nocé, the son of the friend of Monseigneur le Régent."[41]

"He was here?"

"For having lampooned Madame de Pompadour in a song. He was even in a dungeon, in the Rat-Hole."

"What's that?"

---

[41] Several individuals by the name of de Nocé are featured in 19th century fiction, but the one most likely to have been fresh in Ponson's mind is featured in a drama by his rival feuilletoniste Xavier de Montépin, *La Magicienne du Palais-Royal*, premièred at the Ambigu-Comique in 1865.

"A dungeon hollowed out thirty feet below ground, where the obscurity is complete and the rats nibble your feet."

"Damn!"

"Well, the King granted him mercy, and that appeared extraordinary in itself."

"He didn't expect it?"

"Not at all. Monsieur the Governor uttered loud protests...and I've lost my fortune." There was a third sigh. "However," Monsieur Duverger de Beauverger went on, "let's not talk about all that; I'm talkative and I'm forgetting my duties. So you're comfortable here?"

"Quite," said the Fleming.

"The food is good, you'll see. You've been classed among the prisoners at fifteen livres a day; that's reasonable."

"Can one have wine at discretion?"

"One can buy it."

"Marvelous! Can one read and write?"

"Of course."

"And can one ever stretch one's legs?"

"Yes, twice a day, unless one's in a dungeon. So you don't need anything for the moment?"

"We'll tell you that after lunch, Monsieur. When is that?"

"In a hour."

"Very good."

"Monsieur," said Monsieur Duverger de Beauverger then, "I'll permit myself to pay you a little visit this evening and bring you my titles. You'll see that the steward of the province of Artois has done me a great injustice."

"He's an ass," said the Fleming.

Monsieur Duverger de Beauverger went away.

When he had gone, Monsieur de Mauroy looked at Hector. "There's a man," he said, "who'll be ours body and soul when we wish."

XXXVIII

Hector looked at Monsieur de Mauroy with astonishment.

"You're young, my friend, said the Fleming, "you don't know men. The one you've just seen has two passions."

"What?"

"First he has a passion to be noble. I've conquered his amity by telling him that his ancestors, who were doubtless pedants like him, went back to the crusades."

"And?" said Hector.

"In addition, he likes money."

"That's not a reason..."

"What!" said the Vicomte. "Child that you are, you haven't understood?"

"What?"

"The story is quite simple, however. If Monsieur de Nocé had remained in the Bastille two days longer, Beauverger's fortune would have been made."

"Yes, but how?"

"Because he had probably conceived and was about to carry out an escape plan."

"You think so?"

"I'm sure of it."

"All right," said Hector, "but I don't see what there is in common between Monsieur de Nocé and us."

"There might be the sum promised by Monsieur de Nocé, and which I can give him."

"You're forgetting that when we came in here, they took away our purses," Hector observed.

"My purse contained a hundred pistoles at the most, and you can imagine that I didn't come to Paris with that miserable sum alone."

"All right, but..."

"I have a correspondent in Paris, a jeweler by the name of Boemer, who has my funds."

"But how will you reclaim them?"

"Still the child," said the Fleming. "It isn't me who'll go to Boemer in search of the money, it's him."

"The turnkey?"

"Yes, of course. Don't worry, and don't despair. We'll get out of here."

Hector had no great faith in the Fleming's promises, but he did not attempt to contradict them.

The hour for the midday meal arrived. Two valets brought a table ready served.

"The rogue hasn't lied," said the Fleming, sitting down at table. "The food's passable." He took a few mouthfuls of a slice of beef and emptied his glass. "But the wine's bad," he added. Addressing one of the valets, he said: "Can't one have some other wine?"

"Yes, Monsieur," the valet replied, "by paying."

"And what does one do to get the money that was taken from me?"

"Prisoners are never allowed to have money, Monsieur" the valet said, "But Monsieur the Governor, if he has their money, pays for what they buy."

"Well," said the Vicomte, "buy me a basket of Bordeaux wine for this evening."

The valet bowed.

Hector was too depressed and distraught to have any great hunger. On the other hand, Vicomte Gontran de Mauroy ate and drank like the true Fleming that he was. Then, when his meal was finished, he stuffed his pipe as tranquilly as he had done in the dining room of the Singe Vert, and started smoking.

Hector had fallen back into a somber reverie. He was thinking about his dead brother, and about Cécile, whom he loved, and would perhaps never see again. The future appeared to him even blacker and more dismal than the present, which was already so bleak and desolate.

After smoking his pipe, the Vicomte shook out the ash, replaced it in his pocket and looked at his companion in captivity.

"My young friend," he said, "As it's beyond doubt that we'll get out of here at the first opportunity, let me talk to you a little about the future."

Hector looked up at him sadly. "I'm listening," he said.

"You have a duty to fulfill; it's necessary to avenge the death of your brother."

"Yes," said Hector.

"You love Cécile?"

"Yes," said the young man, again.

"In spite of the inequality of condition that separates you, you'd make her your wife?"

"Certainly, yes."

"In that case, your life has two goals," the Vicomte went on. "I'll help you pursue the first. As for the other…"

"Well?" said Hector.

"When we get out of here, it's necessary to go find the young woman and discover whether she'll consent to go with you."

"But where will we go?"

"You'll come to my homeland, to my château. From my windows one can see the frontier of the realm. If the constabulary pursues you—and they will pursue you when we've avenged your brother—you'll be on Brabantine soil within a quarter of an hour, where the King of France has no authority."

"Truly," said Hector, "I admire you, Monsieur."

"Why?"

"Because you speak as if we'd already got through the twelve doors of the Bastille."

"Pooh!" said the Fleming. "That, I think, is a detail of minor importance."

"So be it," said Hector, "but how can I avenge my brother?"

"Follow my reasoning carefully."

"I'm listening."

"What did you go to Versailles to do, yesterday? Demand justice from the King?"

"Of course."

"If the King had accorded you justice, what would he have done? He would have had the Tartar arrested, have sent him before the Parliament, and the Parliament would have condemned him to death, wouldn't it?"

"I hope so, at least."

"What shall you and I do? We'll assemble a veritable parliament ourselves, judge the man and condemn him to death."

"But who will execute the sentence?"

"Us, of course."

"How?"

"Don't worry about that until we get out of here, and trust me."

The phlegm, the assurance, the perfect confidence in the future and himself that the Fleming showed ended up influencing Hector.

"Oh, Monsieur," he said, "whatever happens, I shall bless the star that placed me in your path."

"I bring wellbeing," said the Fleming.

The rest of the day went by, and the last radiance of sunset disappeared from the high window that illuminated the two prisoners' cell. Shortly thereafter, the door opened and the two valets from the morning reappeared. They brought supper for Monsieur de Mauroy and his companion. One of them had a basket of six green-sealed bottles under the arm. It was the Bordeaux that the Fleming had requested.

"Has the governor paid?"

"Yes, Monsieur," the valet replied. "He even made a reflection."

"What?"

"He said that a prisoner who drinks such wine must be very rich."

"Pooh!" said the Fleming, modestly. And, as in the morning he sat down at table with an excellent appetite,

The valets withdrew, but the door opened again almost immediately and Monsieur Duverger de Beauverger appeared. He had a wad of parchments under his arm that would have made a procurator's donkey buckle under the weight,

"Damn!" said Monsieur de Mauroy. "And that imbecile steward didn't want to believe that you're noble?"

"No, Monsieur."

"Well, sit down for a moment, my dear Monsieur de Beauverger; we'll examine that in a little while. Would you accept a glass of wine?"

"Gladly," said the turnkey.

The Fleming held out his own glass, and took Hector's. "To your health," he said, "and in memory of your ancestors who died in the crusades!"

The turnkey quivered with pride.

"You ought to have martlets in your arms," the Fleming continued.

"I don't."

"You ought to have them, you have them, I tell you. All those who went to the crusades have them."

"It's quite possible."

Monsieur de Mauroy poured a glass of wine for Monsieur Duverger de Beauverger, who was careful not to refuse, and went on: "In a while," he said, "we'll examine these parchments, but for the moment..."

He winked

"Very well," said the turnkey.

"I'd like to have a word with you."

"Ah!" said Monsieur Duverger.

"Do you know Monsieur Boemer?"

"The jeweler?"

"Exactly. He's my banker. He has a great deal of my money. Simply on my signature, he'll pay anything I wish."

"Damn!" said the turnkey, his little eyes widening again.

"No," Monsieur de Mauroy went on, "suppose you were to give me pen and paper, and I wrote: *Pay the bearer the sum of a thousand livres...*"

Monsieur Boemer would pay?

"Naturally."

"Oh," said the turnkey, who became very pensive. "Perhaps you'd like to employ that means to send for money? But the regulations oppose it."

"I know. But you can't guess...I'm curious, my dear Monsieur de Beauverger, very curious."

"Ah!"

"And I'd gladly give a thousand livres to know how the precipitate release of Monsieur de Nocé lost you a fortune."

Duverger shivered. "Oh, no," he said. "It's impossible for me to tell you that."

"Bah!"

"There's my employment."

"If we were indiscreet—but believe that we're such perfect gentlemen..."

"Undoubtedly, undoubtedly...but..."

"But a thousand livres is a tidy sum."

"I don't deny it, but still...."

"I can see," said the Fleming, "that you're afraid that Monsieur Boemer won't pay. Do you know diamonds?"

"A little."

The Fleming took a ring from his finger. "Here's one," he said, "that's worth three times as much as the sum I proposed to you. I'll give it to you as a guarantee."

"But, Monsieur..."

"But I need the story of the fortune you lost because Monsieur de Nocé got out of here too soon."

"But I could lose my job."

"You won't lose anything. We're discreet men."

"But they'll throw me in a dark dungeon if they knew..."

"No one will know anything."

Then Monsieur Duverger de Beauverger, almost as fascinated by the Fleming's gaze as the gleam of the diamond, lowered his voice and said in a mysterious one: "Well, if the King hadn't granted Monsieur de Nocé mercy, I'd have helped him escape, and he'd have given me twenty thousand livres."

Ah, my lad, thought Monsieur de Mauroy, *now I have your secret, you'll have go on to the end.*

XXXIX

Scarcely had the turnkey made this confidence than he manifested a great anxiety.

"Oh, Monsieur," he said, "You appeared to me so honest that I let myself lapse into a moment of forgetfulness, but in truth my imprudence in unparalleled."

"Bah!" said the Fleming, Don't you trust me, then?"

"If I didn't trust you, would I have made you such a confidence?"

"Well, then, instead of trembling, tell us the whole story in detail."

And Monsieur de Mauroy poured a third glass of Bordeaux for Monsieur Duverger de Beauverger, knowing full well that nothing loosens the tongue like good wine.

The latter went on: "So, Monsieur de Nocé was in the Bastille, without any hope of getting out. He knew how irritated Madame de Pompadour was, and when he found himself in the rat-hole, he thought that dungeon would be his tomb. But he had friends outside.

"Like us," observed Monsieur de Mauroy.

"His friends ended up putting him in communication with a cousin of mine, a petty relation, as we say in the nobility, who had been obliged, in order to live, to go into commerce."

"Aha!"

I have three days of leave per month, usually between the fifth and the tenth."

"And you spend them with your cousin?"

"Which is to say that I do him the honor of asking him to dinner, Monsieur."

"That's what I meant. And then?"

"Monsieur de Nocé's friends met with me at my cousin's home. At first I turned a deaf ear to them, as you can imagine, but when they mentioned the figure of twenty thousand livres, I couldn't forbid myself a small calculation.

"Let's hear the calculation," said the Fleming, his elbows on the table.

"If I had twenty thousand livres," I said to myself, "I could go and live very tranquilly in my homeland, buy my family's little manor and keep a good table."

"That's sage reasoning, my dear Monsieur de Beauverger."

"But as it's necessary to foresee everything," the turnkey continued, "I said to myself that if Monsieur de Nocé escaped, I might be suspected of having favored his escape. A lot of unpleasant things might happen to me, the last of which would certainly be remaining in the Bastille, no longer as a turnkey but as a prisoner."

"Which isn't very agreeable, in fact."

"Then my cousin, who was to have his little benefit in the affair..."

"How much?"

"Five thousand livres."

"A tidy sum, Monsieur de Beauverger."

"My cousin and I searched for a means of helping Monsieur de Nocé escape without me being suspected, and the date of his escape was fixed for tomorrow, a day when I would be on leave, and in consequence out of the Bastille."

"Very good," said the Fleming. "But what was that means?"

"I forgot to tell you that my cousin's shop is facing the Bastille, at the very end of the Rue Saint-Antoine."

"Ah! Really?"

"Between the Rue Saint-Antoine and the prison, a deep subterranean conduit was hollowed out last year, which permits excess rainwater to flow into the Seine. That conduit is level with the cellars of the Rue de Saint-Antoine, and my cousin knew that it wouldn't be difficult to piece a tunnel between his own and the conduit, which is empty of water at present."

"But the conduit isn't the Bastille, my dear Monsieur de Beauverger."

"No, indeed, Monsieur. But one hasn't been a turnkey for twenty-five years without knowing the mysterious stories of the prison."

"What do you mean?"

"I possess a secret that Monsieur de Launay thinks that he alone knows."

"What?"

"You've heard it said, haven't you, that the Duc de Beaufort, the bastard of King Henri IV, was once imprisoned in the Bastille?"

"The man they called the King of Les Halles?"

"Exactly. His partisans, who were numerous, had dug a tunnel, and that tunnel was supposed to end beneath the dungeons of the Bastille. It was three-quarters finished when the Duc, impatient and not knowing exactly what his friends were doing, made the decision to escape through a window whose bars he had sawn through. Which means that the tunnel, which starts from the conduit, remained incomplete."

"And Monsieur de Launay knew about it?"

"Yes."

"Why didn't he have the tunnel filled in?"

"Because, according to him, it would have needed a month of work to finish it, and there's never been an inmate of the Bastille rich enough and well-enough served by his friends for that means of escape to be practicable for him."

At this point Monsieur de Beauverger paused to draw breath and swallow a fourth glass of wine.

"Oh," said Monsieur de Mauroy. "Monsieur de Launay had that opinion?"

"Yes, Monsieur, but he had counted without Monsieur de Nocé's friends, without my cousin and without me, who told them about the existence of the tunnel."

"What did you do, then?"

"My cousin brought together four workers of whom he was sure, and had them dig a runnel from the cellar to the conduit."

"And then?"

"Once in the conduit, we easily found the opening of the old tunnel, and the laborers set to work.

"The tunnel was only fifty feet deep then; now it's sixty-six, and if our calculations are exact, it's six or eight feet vertically underneath the rat-hole—which means that, in an hour or two, and with a hundred blows of a pick-ax, one could get as far as the floor of the dungeon. Now," Monsieur de Beauverger went on, after a further pause, "they were to do that tomorrow evening, the day when I would have been absent from the Bastille. At ten o'clock, the governor visits all the prisoners. At eleven o'clock, they're certain that they won't be disturbed until morning. The work on the junction was therefore to be commenced between eleven o'clock and midnight, and when it was concluded, the floor of the dungeon would have collapsed, and Monsieur de Nocé would have fallen into his liberators' arms. As for me, I'd have absolutely nothing to do with the escape, which wouldn't have prevented me from collecting twenty thousand livres."

"And your cousin five thousand?"

"Yes, Monsieur."

"And the four workmen?"

"A hundred and twenty-five livres each."

"Total, twenty-six thousand livres, my dear Monsieur de Beauverger."

"That's right, Monsieur. And instead of that, we'll have nothing at all." And the turnkey uttered a heart-rending sigh.

"But you haven't foreseen everything, Monsieur," said the Fleming.

"How's that?"

"The next day, Monsieur de Nocé's escape would have been perceived."

"Of course."

"A search would have been made, of the tunnel first, and then the conduit."

"Naturally."

"And they would have found the communication established between the latter and your cousin's shop."

"No, Monsieur, because that communication would have been walled up during the night, and it would have been assumed that the prisoner had followed the conduit all the way to the Seine and had bravely leapt into the water."

"So you're going out tomorrow?"

"At midday."

"For three days?"

"Yes, Monsieur."

"Well, I'll give you some advice."

Monsieur Duverger looked at the Fleming sideways,

"Go to your cousin first."

"Right."

"And tell him that nothing has changed, and that he won't lose the five thousand livres any more than you'll lose the twenty thousand livres on which you were counting."

"I believe, Monsieur," said the turnkey, "that you're mocking me."

"Not in the least."

"Who will give me that money, then, since Monsieur de Nocé no longer has need of me?"

"Those who still need you."

The turnkey shivered.

"Me, for example," said the Fleming, coolly.

Monsieur Duverger looked at the Fleming. "You?" he said

"At least, Monsieur Boemer, on my signature."

"Is that possible?"

"Give me paper and a pen...."

"I don't have a pen, but a pencil..."

And Monsieur Duverger de Beauverger took a small notebook out of his pocket, from which he ripped a sheet of paper, and from which he extracted a pencil with a silver shaft. Then he held them out, in a hand trembling with emotion, to Gontran de Mauroy.

The latter took the pencil and wrote:

My dear Boemer.

On receiving this note, please pay the bearer the sum of five thousand livres. An hour after you have given him that first sum of money, the bearer will present himself at your house again. You will then count him out twenty thousand livres, which he will put in his pocket, but instead of letting him leave, you will keep him in the safest place in your house, even if you have to watch over him night and day, until I deliver him by paying you a visit.

I am, my dear Boemer, your devoted client and friend.

Mauroy.

The Vicomte put the notes before Monsieur de Beauverger's eyes.

"There's one thing I don't understand," he said.

"I can guess, and I'll explain. When you have the five thousand livres you'll take them to your cousin."

"Very well."

"After which you'll go to constitute yourself a prisoner at Boemer's until I'm free. It's a little guarantee, which you'll find quite natural, I think?"

"Oh, certainly," said Monsieur Duverger. "But alas, Monsieur, there's one thing that neither you nor I have thought of."

"Bah! What?"

"That that escape, which was so simple for Monsieur de Nocé, is impossible for you."

"Why?"

"Because you're not in the rat-hole."

"And it's impossible to go there?"

"One only goes there in two cases."

"Which?"

"The first is by order of the King."

"And the second?"

"For a grave infraction of the regulations of the house."

"Then don't worry," said Monsieur de Mauroy. My friend and I will go,"

"What are you going to do?"

"That's my business. Don't worry, and take my note."

"But after all, if you don't succeed in getting there...and they set to work..."

"You're leaving the Bastille at midday tomorrow?"

"Yes."

"Well, we'll be there by ten o'clock. In consequence, you'll know before leaving."

"You're astonishingly calm," said the turnkey. And he put the note into his portfolio and the portfolio in his pocket. Then, taking out his watch, he said: "Oh, my God! I'm forgetting myself. The governor will visit you at ten, and it's half past nine. I must go."

"Well," said Monsieur de Mauroy to Hector, when the turnkey had gone, "do you believe now that one can get out of the Bastille?"

"But how are we going to be put in the dungeon?" he asked.

"Don't contradict me in anything I do, and speak as I do, and all will be well," said the Vicomte.

XL

Monsieur de Launay, the present governor of the Bastille, was still in his study at the moment when the turnkey left Monsieur de Mauroy and Hector.

For nearly a century, the government of the Bastille had been a kind of hereditary royalty in the de Launay family. Monsieur de Launay had succeeded his father, and raised his son with the idea that he would succeed him in his turn.

Monsieur de Launay was alone in his study, his feet on the fire-irons before a large fire, and he seemed very anxious.

"I don't understand anything," he murmured. "If anyone had told me a week ago that Monsieur de Nocé would be out of the Bastille by any other means than an escape, I'd have laughed. When one is here for having displeased Madame de Pompadour, one doesn't get out again—as witness Monsieur le Chevalier de Latude, who occupies the bats' nest, as Monsieur de Nocé occupied the rat-hole. Is something extraordinary happening at Versailles, then? The Marquise isn't dead, since I was sent two prisoners this morning arrested at her request. Nor is she in disgrace, since they wouldn't have brought me the two gentlemen. Truly, it's incomprehensible."

The sound of a bell caused Monsieur de Launay to start. The bell was the one that announced that the main door was opening, whether for a visitor, a prisoner or someone attached to the service of the prison.

Perhaps it's Monsieur Lange coming back, thought the governor. Monsieur Lange was the governor's private secretary. He was a middle-aged man, tall and thin, with blond hair, blue eyes, and a pinched face, who had always possessed Monsieur de Launay's absolute confidence.

A cross between a Jesuit and a diplomat, Monsieur Lange was discreet, prudent, exceedingly polite and possessed an exceptional flair.

On seeing the order of liberation concerning Monsieur de Nocé, Monsieur de Launay had been so astonished that he had sent Lange to Versailles, enjoining him not to come back until he had the key to the strange enigma.

Monsieur de Launay was not mistaken with regard to the ringing of the bell. It was indeed Lange returning.

"Ah!" said the governor, seeing his private secretary come in. "I've been waiting for you impatiently."

"I've been diligent, Monseigneur, but it wasn't easy to discover what very few people know, as yet."

"So, the Marquise?"

"More in favor than ever, Monseigneur."

"How has the King been able to grant Monsieur de Nocé mercy, then?"

"It wasn't the King, it was the Marquise herself."

"You're joking, Monsieur Lange?"

"Not at all, Monseigneur."

"Then explain this charade to me."

"The term is accurate, Monseigneur; it's a charade whose key is that the King is suffering ennui..."

"Speak, speak," said Monsieur de Launay, impatiently.

"I'm getting there, Monseigneur. So, the King is suffering ennui..."

"That's not news."

"At Versailles, well-informed people, such as the Marquise, recognize that the King's ennui has three symptoms."

"Go on."

"First of all, when the King yawns—but people don't worry much about that symptom. The King yawns habitually; in him, it's a nervous tic, and it doesn't prevent him from going to the Parc-aux-Cerfs every day."

"And the second symptom?"

"That's when the King summons Monsieur de Sartine and asks him to tell him lewd stories. That's more serious.

"Really?"

"Nevertheless, the King goes to the Parc-aux-Cerfs as usual, and the Marquise remains tranquil. But the third symptom is even more serious. When it manifests itself, the Marquise frowns, and understands that the hour of concessions is nigh."

"And what is it, the third symptom?"

"It's when the King meddles in politics, works with his ministers, talks about reforming abuses, repressing license and punishing the great criminals of the kingdom. Then the Marquise understands that it's absolutely necessary to distract the King."

"And the King is in one of those moments?"

"Yes, Monseigneur."

"But what connection does this have with Monsieur de Noce?"

"You shall see. For three days, the King hasn't gone to the Parc-aux-Cerfs; he claims that there's no longer anyone there except the ugly."

"Very well."

"The Marquise has therefore gone on campaign. Better than anyone she knows what can and ought to please the King, and God knows, alas, whether it's easy. Now, it appears that this morning, the Marquise received a visit. A gentleman from the provinces, a cousin of Monsieur de Noce, came to say, boldly: 'A *quid pro quo*; set Monsieur de Noce free, and I'll bring you a pearl.' With those words he brought a miniature out of his pocket, before which the Marquise was literally in ecstasy. And as she absolutely wanted to know where the original was, the gentleman said to her: 'You can send me to the Bastille too, but you won't know. Set Monsieur de Noce at liberty, and in three days, trust me, the girl will be at the Parc-aux-Cerfs.'

Madame de Pompadour didn't hesitate. Do you understand now, Monseigneur?"

"Yes, certainly. The Marquise is still the sovereign, then?"

"Absolute, Monseigneur."

"And have you asked how I should treat the two gentlemen who were brought this morning?"

"With the greatest rigor."

"Very well."

The clock on the mantelpiece chimed ten.

"Ha!" said the governor. "It's time for my round. Come with me, Monsieur Lange."

Lange bowed.

Monsieur de Launay took off his dressing-gown, put on his uniform and strapped on his épée.

"If you wish," he said, crossing the threshold of his study, we'll begin with them."

"This morning's prisoners?"

"Yes, where are they?"

"On the second floor, in cell number 17."

"Good. Let's go."

A few minutes later, Monsieur de Launay, followed by his secretary, went into the room occupied by Monsieur de Mauroy and Hector de Pierrefeu..

The governor was a very courteous man. He saluted the new inmates with a perfect grace, and said to them: "How are you finding things here, Messieurs?"

"Very good," replied the Fleming, "which is to say that the Bastille is a true paradise."

You do me great honor, in truth," replied Monsieur de Launay, flattered in his self-esteem as governor.

"For one thing, one is well-nourished..."

"Ah!"

"Then, one drinks good wine."

The governor appeared to have forgotten that the wine was at the prisoners' expense.

"Then again," the Vicomte continued, "it's very peaceful here."

"What do you mean?"

"One can't hear all the afflicting rumors from outside."

Monsieur de Launay shivered. "What do you mean by that, Monsieur?"

"Alas, Monsieur Governor," the Fleming went on, "one can see that you don't leave the Bastille and that you don't know anything about that's happening out there and what people are saying."

"What are they saying?"

"That France is in disarray..."

"Monsieur! Monsieur!" said Monsieur de Launay,

"That the King is half-mad..."

"Monsieur!"

"And they he allows himself to be governed by the worst of trollops, an abominable slut. Isn't that so, my friend?" And the Vicomte turned to Hector.

"Indeed," stammered the young man.

"Ah! That's your opinion too, Monsieur?" said Monsieur de Launay, pale with anger and looking at Hector.

"Yes, Monsieur."

"Messieurs," cried the governor, "I will not tolerate such language!"

"Have I been misinformed on your account, Monsieur Governor," asked Monsieur de Mauroy, in a mocking tone, "and instead of a gentleman, are you also one of the favorite's slaves?"

His time, Monsieur de Launay exploded. "Monsieur," he cried, "you're impudent, and I shall punish you immediately." He turned to his secretary. "Monsieur Lange," he said, "you'll put these two men in one of the unfurnished cells on the ground floor; you'll deprive them of wine and they'll be on a ration of three livres a day instead of fifteen."

And he went out, as red as a turkey-cock.

Monsieur de Mauroy burst out laughing, "In truth," he said, "that's a good beginning."

"Yes, said Hector, sadly, "but we haven't been put in the rat-hole."

"We'll be there tomorrow."

"You think so?"

"Yes, if you do everything I tell you to do."

"I'll do it," said Hector.

"And stay tranquil, and hope."

Less than a quarter of an hour after the governor had left, the door opened again. Two turnkeys with surly faces appeared and said: "It's necessary to get out of here."

"Are you going to set us free?" Monsieur de Mauroy asked, laughing.

"You'll soon see," replied one of them. "Come on. follow us."

There was a picket of soldiers in the corridor to escort the prisoners. They were taken down from the second floor to the first and from the first to the ground floor. There, after taking them along a somber corridor they were introduced into a narrow cell where there were two frightful bunks by way of beds. Then they were locked up, leaving them without light.

"Well," said the phlegmatic Vicomte, "here's a substantial step toward the rat-hole. What do you think, Hector?" And he threw himself fully-dressed on to one of the bunks, saying: "Bah! A bad night is soon past!"

XLI

The following morning, a trickle of pale daylight descended from the narrow loophole that let light into the cell in which Gontran de Mauroy was sitting on one of the beds. Hector was still asleep.

The Fleming smoked all day long. He stuffed his pipe, struck the briquette, procured fire and started launching large puffs of smoke toward the ceiling. When he smoked slowly, it was evidence that his mind was at rest, but if he smoked quickly, it was because his mind was at work.

Now, the Fleming started launching puff after puff, and, in consequence, was evidently searching for something he had not yet found. That something was the means of being put in the dungeon.

Suddenly, his face lit up, and he exclaimed: "Hector! Hector!"

Hector woke up.

"My friend, said Monsieur de Mauroy, "The visit of some turnkey or other can't be far off, and we need to have a little chat before then.

"I'm listening," said Hector.

"Let's understand one another well," the Fleming went on. "What do we want? To get out of here, isn't it?"

"Undoubtedly."

"And for that, we have to go to the rat-hole."

"Necessarily."

"And who wants the end wants the means..."

"That's incontestable."

"Of course, remember that you'll quarrel forever with the King, the Marquise and the courtiers."

"The courtiers, the Marquise and the King will certainly let me die here," Hector relied. "In consequence, I don't have anything to lose."

"Good! I like to see you with those sentiments."

"What are you going to do, then?"

"You'll see..."

Perhaps the Fleming would have explained more clearly if he had had time, but time was lacking. The door opened and the two turnkeys appeared. They seemed even surlier than the evening before.

"Let's go," said one. "Get up and take a turn around the exercise-yard."

"Already?" said the Fleming.

"The prisoners who have privileges," replied the turnkey, "stroll when they wish."

"And the others?"

"From eight to nine o'clock in the morning."

"Then we don't have privileges?"

"Certainly not. You've insulted the governor."

"Bah!" said the Fleming, "he'll hear many others."

The turnkeys looked at him askance.

The two prisoners stood up and followed them.

At the end of the dark and dank corridor in which their cell was situated one of the prison exercise yards opened. It was a small, narrow courtyard limited by high walls, a veritable draughty corridor. At the two extremities were two sentry-boxes occupied by sentinels.

"Brrr!" said the Vicomte, on entering the yard. "It's damnably cold here."

"It's very salutary, Monsieur," sniggered one of the turnkeys.

"One can see that we have no privileges, to make us go out so early in such weather."

"What would you say, then, if you were in the dungeon?" said the turnkey, in a mocking tone.

"And the soldiers—what are they doing here?"

"Watching the prisoners."

"Then we're going to give them some work. Pay attention, Hector."

And the Fleming turned on the turnkey who had spoken to him insolently exactly like a wild boar turning on the hunter that has wounded it.

"Rogue," he said to him, "I'm a gentleman, and you're only a valet, and you permit yourself to speak to me with your hat on your head."

"I'm your superior here," said the turnkey.

With the back of his hand, the Fleming sent the turnkey's hat flying through the air. The latter uttered a cry of anger, which was soon followed by a cry of pain, for the colossus had placed his large hands on his shoulders, applied slight pressure, and knocked him down.

Hector had understood the maneuver perfectly. He threw himself on the other turnkey, and before the sentinels had come running, the turnkeys had each received half a dozen punches.

The sentinels arrived, bayonets forward. Monsieur de Mauroy allowed himself to be arrested without resistance, and Hector did likewise.

"Ah!" said the turnkey with whom the Fleming had been dealing, "You're going to the dungeon! Don't worry. The governor will be able to reckon with you."

The prisoners were returned to their cell.

"In an hour," the Fleming whispered in Hector's ear, "we'll be in the rat-hole.

The Fleming was not mistaken.

Less than an hour later, the door of the cell opened again, the governor appeared in person, even redder in the face than the previous evening, his eyes ablaze. Monsieur Lange, his phlegmatic secretary, followed him.

"Messieurs!" cried Monsieur de Launay, "You're behaving in a fashion beyond all measure. I condemn you to a month in the dungeon."

"Bah!" replied the Fleming, calmly. "It's necessary to hope that in a month, La Pompadour will be dead and eaten by the worms. The putrescence of the body will follow that of the soul."

"That's my opinion," said the docile Hector.

"Ah! You're insulting Madame de Pompadour," cried the governor, "the lover of our good King!"

"Your King is an old idiot," replied the Fleming, who knew full well that Monsieur de Launay could not punish them more harshly than by putting them in the dungeon."

"Monsieur Lange," said the governor, "you'll give the orders, won't you?"

"Yes, Monseigneur."

"To the dungeon with these two wretches."

"Which one?"

"The rat-hole."

And the governor went out, saying to his secretary: "It's necessary to make sure that the Marquise knows this, my friend."

"Certainly," said the secretary.

A quarter of an hour later, Monsieur de Mauroy and Hector were taken to the rat-hole.

It was a dungeon hollowed out thirty feet underground, in the south-western corner of the edifice. There was no daylight; one lived there is complete obscurity. No table, no chairs, no bed, but a little fetid and moldy straw in a corner destined to serve as a prisoner's bed.

"Finally!" said the Fleming. "Do you believe that we'll get out now?"

"I hope so," said Hector. "But, assuming that everything succeeds and we do get out, woe betide us if we're ever caught again."

"Bah! We won't be. Let's get out first."

The day seemed long, nevertheless. The walls of the cell were sweating moisture, and Hector repressed a cry and a shudder several times. He had felt a rat pass beside him or climb up his leg.

In the depths of that tomb one could not hear the great clock of the Bastille, which chimed the hours. When taking his money, they had also taken the Fleming's watch. The watch was a repeater, and he would have been able to determine how many hours still separated them from the hour of deliverance.

The prisoners in the rat-hole ate nothing but dry bread and no longer drank anything but water. So that morning, when they had been brought, they had been left a loaf of black bread and a pitcher. By virtue of a final refinement of barbarity, Monsieur de Launay, who wanted absolutely to be agreeable to Madame de Pompadour, had had the Fleming's pipe taken away.

At about six o'clock—at least, they estimated that it ought to be about then—a little spy-hole in the cell door opened. A hand holding a taper passed through the gap, and its light was projected on to the two prisoners, who were lying side by side on the straw. At the same time they heard a voice, which said: "This time, they're quite tranquil."

The spy-hole closed again.

The Vicomte put his lips close to Hector's ear. "That's the evening visit," he said. "No one will come again now.

As time marched on, doubt took possession of Hector's soul. "Who knows," he said, "whether Duverger will keep his promise?"

"Child," said Monsieur de Mauroy. "Does a man of that sort give up on twenty thousand livres?"

Another hour went by, then two, and a third.

"It's certainly after midnight," said Hector, "and we still can't hear anything."

The Fleming did not reply. He too was beginning to find the time long.

"Perhaps," said Hector, someone suspected his projects, and Duverger has been arrested."

"Patience!" said the Fleming. But he pronounced the word is a tone that doubt was beginning to invade.

Suddenly, Hector shivered, and made an abrupt movement.

"What's the matter?" asked his companion.

"It seems to me that I heard something."

"I can't hear anything."

"Put your ear against the wall."

"It's done."

"Can't you hear anything?"

"Yes," said the Fleming, after a moment. "A dull and distant sound."

"It's our liberators."

"But those aren't strokes of a pick-ax that I can hear," said Monsieur de Mauroy.

"What is it, then?"

"Human voices."

"Ah!"

"They're beneath us…they're getting closer…"

Suddenly, the prisoners jumped on the straw of their cell. Another noise had become audible, and the ground had trembled.

"This time," said the Vicomte, "it's the stroke of a pick-ax."

It was, indeed—and it was followed by another, and another. Then the work proceeded with activity. At every blow, the ground trembled beneath the two prisoners.

"As long as no one comes from upstairs in the meantime," said the Vicomte.

Finally, after half an hour, the blows were so close that the prisoners understood that the moment of their deliverance was imminent. One might have thought that a volcano was seething beneath them.

Suddenly, the ground collapsed, an abyss opened up, and Mauroy and Hector, holding one another by the hand, were dragged into it.

"This time," the Fleming exclaimed, "we're saved, well and truly!"

And they continued to slide into the cavity, the bottom of which they could not see.

XLII

The cavity into which Gontran de Mauroy and his young friend Hector de Pierrefeu had been dragged following the collapse of the floor of their cell was, as you can imagine, not very deep.

They were both received with open arms, which deadened their fall.

Hector had closed his eyes, instinctively. When he opened them again, he saw that he was in the corridor minutely described by Monsieur Duverger de Beauverger. Five men were surrounding him and Mauroy. Four were laborers, to judge by their costume; the fifth was dressed like a well-to-do bourgeois. The fifth was holding a lantern.

"Ah!" said the Fleming, looking at the fifth man. "You must be Duverger's cousin?"

"Yes, Monsieur."

"Our liberator, in consequence."

"I have that honor," said the bourgeois. "But it's not over yet. We have to get out of here."

"Good!"

"And get away as quickly as possible."

"Show us the way; we'll follow you."

The bourgeois took the lead, lantern in hand. Mauroy and Hector followed him, and the laborers brought up the rear.

After a few minutes, the Fleming thought that he could hear splashing. "What's that?" he said.

"Monsieur," replied Duverger's cousin, "it has rained a lot in recent days."

"And?"

"There's water in the conduit."

"A lot?"

"Four or five feet, at least."

"Damn!" murmured the Fleming. "We've already spent a glacial night; I'd prefer something else to a cold bath."

"Don't worry, Monsieur," the bourgeois replied. "We have a boat."

"Aha! Where did you get it?"

"It was moored in the conduit, to which municipal workers sometimes descend in order to make repairs."

Indeed, at the end of the tunnel, the Fleming perceived a large flat boat equipped with two poles destined to steer it. Duverger's cousin climbed in first, and fixed his lantern to the prow. The Fleming and Hector took their places next, and laborers took possession of the poles.

The boat set forth and began to move up the conduit.

"Well," said Monsieur de Mauroy to Hector, "at present, the governor of the Bastille is sleeping soundly. He won't be very cheerful when he wakes up."

The conduit was exactly as Duverger de Beauverger had described it. It was a wide vaulted aqueduct, such as would later be found throughout Paris. As it had a slight slope, the current of the water was rapid, but the laborers were vigorous, and they maneuvered the boat upstream.

After a quarter of an hour, the boat stopped. At the same time, the shopkeeper directed the radiance of his lantern at a breach in the wall, which gave access to another tunnel.

"Good," said Mauroy. "That's the entranced to your cellar, I presume?"

"Yes, Monsieur."

"And you're going to block the breach once we've gone in?"

"Certainly," said the shopkeeper.

"But my dear Monsieur," the Fleming continued, while one of the laborers, leaping ashore, steadied the boat in order that the passengers could get off, "have you thought hard about what it is you're going to do?"

"Of course, Monsieur."

"You're going to close up that breach again once we've passed through?"

"Yes."

"And you say that when the governor of the Bastille perceives our escape, if he follows our tracks, he'll go up and down the channel without being able to determine which way we've gone?"

"Naturally." The shopkeeper started smiling.

"But my dear Monsieur, nothing will be easier than to recognize the closed breach, thanks to the freshness of the masonry."

"Your Lordship is mistaken," he said.

"How is that?"

"I've had soot mixed into the mortar, and the workmen will take great care to replace the stones in the order in which they were removed. I defy a skillful mason to recognize it afterwards."

"Aha! said the Vicomte, laughing. "I see that you're a careful man."

The workmen replaced the two poles in the boat and allowed it to drift downstream.

"My friends," said the Fleming, "there'll be an extra hundred livres of gratification for you."

And while they immediately set to work, in order to close the breach again as soon as possible, Hector and Mauroy followed the shopkeeper. The latter took them through several successive cellars in which he kept wine, and they finally arrived at a stairway that went up to the shop.

"I'm a widower," said Duverger's cousin, showing them the way, "and I've sent away my only maidservant. There's no fear of any feminine indiscretion."

"Very good," said the Fleming.

"One of my two assistants is in bed; the other is a reliable fellow in whom I have every confidence; he's the only one you'll see. He's at his post and holding the horses in his hand."

"What horses?"

"But," said the shopkeeper, naively, "after escaping from the Bastille, I don't suppose that..."

"We're remaining in Paris, you mean?"

"Well, Monsieur de Sartine's police would soon recapture you."

"Don't worry, the Fleming replied, "We're don't intend to remain here—but we have a few small matters of interest to take care of first, and we'll remain hidden for a few hours."

"Where?"

"Oh, don't worry," said the Fleming. "I have a safe place."

The Vicomte took out his watch.[42] "Two o'clock in the morning," he said. "It won't be light until seven; it'll be eight before they perceive our escape, so we have six hours before us." He turned to Hector. "Aren't you dying of hunger, my friend?"

"I don't know," the young man replied, distractedly.

"Well, Monsieur," said the Fleming, "Since you keep a wine-shop, one can obtain supper in your establishment?"

"Oh, certainly, Monsieur. I even anticipated that you might be very hungry and I've set up a table there, in that small room." And Duverger's cousin invited Mauroy and Hector to pass from the main room where they were into a small room, where there was indeed a table laden with cold meats and bottles of wine covered with veritable cobwebs.

"You're a worthy man," said the Fleming, "and I proclaim you the king of innkeepers—so I want to show myself the king of prisoners."

The shopkeeper did not understand.

"I'll explain," Monsieur de Mauroy continued. "I can't accept that the expenses you've just made for us should be counted in the five thousand livres agreed. When we've supped, we'll go liberate your cousin Monsieur Duverger de Beauverger, whom I left as a pledge with Monsieur Boemer, and the latter, after counting out his money, will give you a thousand livres for you and a thousand livres of gratifications for the laborers."

The dazzled shopkeeper bowed to the ground. "In truth, Monsieur," he said, "I doubt that Monsieur de Nocé would have shown himself as great a seigneur as you."

The Fleming smiled and sat down at table.

Hector imitated him. He was neither hungry nor thirsty, but he ate and drank nevertheless, to obey the Vicomte, who said to him: "We need our physi-

---

[42] The author has evidently forgotten having specifically stated that Mauroy's watch had been removed from his possession.

343

cal strength. Getting out of the Bastille is nothing. It's necessary to be able to avoid going back."

When they had eaten and drunk well, the Vicomte said to the innkeeper: "My dear Monsieur, would it be possible for you, without compromising yourself, to get a note that I will write to Monsieur de Launay?"

"Nothing easier, Monsieur. There's a letter-box at the prison into which letters are dropped that people hope will reach the prisoners, and which, most of the time, are taken to the governor."

"You'll put my letter in the box, then?"

"I'll have one of my waiters take it"

"Marvelous! Give me what I need to write."

When the innkeeper had brought a pen and paper, the Fleming wrote the following lines:

Monsieur le Gouverneur,

When this reaches you, I shall have had the dolor of separating myself from you. I have always liked the open air, and the prison regime can only cause my health, which I prize greatly, to deteriorate.

Before saying farewell to you, however—for I believe that we shall not see one another for a long time—I want to make you a confession. I knew that my friends were working for my deliverance. That deliverance was only possible on condition of being confined in the rat-hole. In order to arrive at that goal, it was necessary to irritate you and make you angry. For that reason, therefore, I spoke in your presence in inappropriate terms about Madame de Pompadour, for who, in the depths of my heart, I have always had the most profound respect.

Put in the Bastille for having had a copy of the Gazette de Hollande *in my pocket, I also ought to tell you, Monseigneur, that I found that paper on the table of the hostelry of the Singe Vert, and took it up to my room with the intention of burning it, so revolted was I by the infamies that it contained in respect of the most spiritual and most virtuous of women.*

Be assured, therefore, Monseigneur, that the Marquise has all my respect, and please believe that I am,

Your very obedient,

Mauroy

But why have you written that?" Hector asked.

"Because that letter will reach the Marquise."

"And?"

"Her anger will diminish, and from then on, no one will occupy themselves with us any longer."

With those words, the Vicomte stood up. "Now," he said, "let's go to Boemer's. I'm very ill-at-ease having no money in my pocket."

XLIII

Monsieur Boemer, the excellent jeweler of the Rue des Lombards, was of German origin, with a little Dutch blood on the distaff side. He was a calm and cool man, of absolute discretion, who was ignorant of the vice, so frequent in humankind, of curiosity. To tell the truth, Monsieur Boemer was not a man but a cash-register. He had correspondents in Dresden, Vienna, Saint Petersburg and Berlin, and he had others in Ghent and The Hague. What those correspondents asked, he did.

Prince Trespatky had arrived with a letter of credit obtained in Saint Petersburg. On the Prince's signature, Boemer paid out everything that was asked of him. He did not belong to the world of the modern financier, who has regulated habits, who closes his cash-box at five o'clock and asks anyone who has business with him to come back the next day. As the Tartar had said to Porion, Boemer paid at any hour of the day or night.

One of his correspondents in Ghent had written to him two days before:

Monsieur le Vicomte Gontran de Mauroy is coming to Paris. Give him anything he asks of you.

Boemer did not want to know any more.

On the morning of the day when the Fleming had met Hector at the Singe Vert, he had arrived in Paris, and Monsieur Boemer had opened his treasury to him. The Fleming had taken a hundred pistoles. Monsieur Boemer had not asked him what he was going to do in Paris.

The next day, between four and five o'clock in the afternoon, a man had presented himself at Monsieur Boemer's establishment. That man was none other than Monsieur Duverger de Beauverger. He was the bearer of a letter from Monsieur de Mauroy. Boemer read it. He did not express any surprise, although the letter was strange; he did not even ask where the Vicomte might be. He counted out the money destined for the innkeeper and the laborers, and simply said to Monsieur Duverger de Beauverger: "When will you return?"

"This evening," the turnkey had replied, who, as you can imagine, had refrained appearing in the uniform of a Bastille employee.

It was the same evening that Porion arrived in his turn in the Tartar's carriage with the bond of a hundred thousand écus destined for the Maréchal de Richelieu. As we know, Monsieur Boemer had paid and Porion had left, not suspecting that the jeweler had already paid out part of the price of the escape of the two gentlemen that he had taken to the Bastille.

Scarcely had Porion departed, however, and Monsieur Boemer had gone to bed, than someone knocked on the door again. It was Monsieur Duverger de Beauverger, who had come to constitute himself a prisoner.

Monsieur Boemer then said, with his Germanic phlegm: "Do you want the twenty thousand livres immediately? In that case, it will be necessary for me to open my safe again."

"It's all the same to me," replied the turnkey, who now knew perfectly well with whom he was dealing.

"It suits me too," said Boemer, without departing from his calmness. "It will take me a quarter of a hour to open my safe again. Then again," the jeweler added, "my house isn't disposed to serve as a prison; it has no bars on the windows, and if the desire took you to escape, nothing would be easier. If you don't have your money in your pocket, that desire won't grip you."

That rigorous logic made Monsieur Duverger de Beauverger smile.

The jeweler took him up to the first floor of the house, opened a door and said: "This is your room. You can sleep here. What time would you like breakfast? If Monsieur de Mauroy hasn't come to deliver you tomorrow morning, you'll do me the amity of sharing my meal."

He said all that quite simply, left a candle on the mantelpiece, and wished the turnkey goodnight. But the latter did not possess the virtue of discretion that did Monsieur Boemer such great honor.

"A word, I beg you, Monsieur," he said, as the jeweler withdrew.

"Speak," said Monsieur Boemer.

"You're a widower, are you not?"

"Yes, Monsieur."

"Do you have children?"

"I have two sons who are learning commerce, one on Germany and the other in Holland."

"And we're alone here?"

"My clerks come at eight o'clock and leave at six. My housekeeper arrives at seven and only leaves after my dinner."

"Which means that you sleep all alone here?"

"Yes, Monsieur."

"With no fear of thieves?"

Monsieur Boemer smiled. "My safe guards itself."

"It's well-locked?"

"The lock has secrets that I alone possess.

"But it might be broken..."

"Yes, but inside it there's a miniature cannon loaded with grapeshot, which would fire and kill the thieves trying to break into it."

Monsieur Duverger de Beauverger bowed. "Monsieur Boemer," he said, "You're a prudent man."

"It's necessary to be," replied the old man, with his habitual simplicity. And he left.

An hour later, that man, who had millions in his home, was sleeping as tranquilly as La Fontaine's shoemaker before acquiring his hundred écus. But

Providence begrudged the jeweler his slumber that night. At three o'clock in the morning, Monsieur Boemer, who had not finished his first sleep, was woken up with a start. Someone was knocking on the door of his shop.

He got up, rubbed his eyes and went out, without manifesting the slightest ill-humor

"It's doubtless Monsieur de Mauroy."

Nevertheless, when he had lit his candle and got dressed, instead of opening the door he opened the window and looked out into the street. He saw two men at his door.

"Who's there?" he asked.

"Mauroy," one of them replied.

Monsieur Boemer left his room and went to Duverger's.

"Hey, Monsieur," he said to him. "I believe someone's come to liberate you."

Monsieur Duverger de Beauverger was sleeping fully dressed. Furthermore, he was not asleep. Ask a man who is on the point of collecting twenty thousand livres to close his eyes and snore like anyone else!

Monsieur Duverger leapt out of bed and followed Boemer downstairs.

Three minutes later, Mauroy and Hector came into the shop.

"Ah, my dear Monsieur Boemer," said the Fleming, "perhaps you're astonished to see me?"

"I'm never astonished by anything, Monsieur le Vicomte," the jeweler replied.

"You don't know where I've come from, then?" The Fleming looked at Duverger with a surprised expression.

"No," replied Boemer, in the tone of a man who would reply: *Whether you come from Heaven or Hell, it's perfectly indifferent to me.*

"I've come from the Bastille."

"Ah!"

And without further astonishment, Monsieur Boemer headed for his safe, of which he began to study the complications and the various locks, turning a screw here, a copper handle there, juxtaposing one letter with another, and introducing a small key into each of the locks.

Monsieur Duverger de Beauverger leaned toward Monsieur de Mauroy and whispered: "Well, it all succeeded, didn't it?"

"As you see."

"Your horses are ready?"

"No, we're not leaving."

"What! You're going to stay in Paris?"

"Of course."

Duverger made no reply. In a matter of hours he had acquired something of Monsieur Boemer's character. Then, leaning toward the Fleming again, he said:

"The jeweler doesn't know anything, and there's no need to give him the details."

"So be it," said Mauroy.

Monsieur Boemer, having finally opened the safe, turned to Duverger. "Do you want gold?" he asked.

"As you wish," the turnkey replied.

"Monsieur Boemer," said the Vicomte, "be good enough to add eleven hundred livres to the twenty thousand." And he said to the turnkey: "It's a small gratification that I promised your cousin."

Monsieur Boemer counted out the twenty-one thousand one hundred livres, and Duverger pocketed them. Then the Fleming held out his hand to the latter. "Delighted to have made your acquaintance, my dear Monsieur," he said, "and it's a pleasure to see you again. Beware of thieves when you go."

Monsieur Duverger shook hands with the Vicomte, saluted Hector, and left. Monsieur Boemer made no objection, but he turned to the Fleming and said: "And you, Monsieur, would you like some money?"

"I should think so," Mauroy replied.

"How much do you need?"

"Give me ten thousand livres in cashable bonds and five thousand in gold."

"Sit down at that table, take that pen and write me a receipt."

Monsieur de Mauroy gave him the receipt and put the money in his pocket. Then Boemer said to him: "You won't need me again tonight?"

"Certainly not."

"I hope, in that case, to be able to sleep. I would only have had one visit to fear, that of Prince Trespatky, who often wakes me at night, but his stewards came this evening."

The name of Prince Trespatky made Hector go pale, and his blood rushed to his heart.

"Pardon me, Monsieur Boemer," said the Fleming, swiftly, "I know the Prince well."

"Ah!"

"He's returned to Paris then?"

"Two days ago."

"Where is he lodging, if you please? I'll go to pay my respects to him tomorrow."

"At the Duc de Clermont's house in the Rue du Pas-de-la-Mule, Monsieur."

"Thank you very much. *Bonsoir*, Monsieur Boemer."

"*Bonsoir*, Messieurs."

"Very sorry to have disturbed you."

"Oh, it was nothing."

And Monsieur de Mauroy left the jeweler's shop, drawing Hector with him, and murmuring: "We already know where to find the Tartar. That's something."

And the two of them drew away at a rapid pace, while Monsieur Boemer went back to bed.

XLIV

When they were at the corner of the Rue des Lombards, Monsieur de Mauroy stopped under a lantern to consult his watch.

"It's nearly four o'clock in the morning," he said. "We have nearly four hours. We need to make a decision immediately."

Hector looked at him.

"In four hours," he Fleming went on, "our escape will be perceived, and it won't be a good idea to show our faces in the streets of Paris. Let's talk seriously, my young friend."

"I'm listening," said Hector.

"If I only had myself to think of," the Fleming said, "I'd go to the hostelry of the Lion d'Argent in the Rue Saint-Denis, mount a good horse and gallop toward Flanders; but I'm thinking about you...and it's for you that I'm staying in Paris. What is the double goal that we proposed when we were in the Bastille, in case we got out: to collect Cécile and to avenge your unfortunate brother, wasn't it?"

"Yes," said Hector.

"Cécile loves you, and would like nothing better than to go with you."

"I believe so," murmured the young man, whom Cécile's name plunged into a veritable ecstasy.

"We know where to find the Tartar, so there's nothing more to be done there. Now we need to decide where to begin."

"Oh!" said Hector. "By now, Cécile and my friends must know that I'm in the Bastille."

"That's possible."

"It's necessary to reassure them."

"My friend," said the Fleming coldly, "a gentlemen can't be unaware of the art of hunting, and you've certainly chased more than one hare."

"Of course," said Hector.

"A hunted hare always returns to its starter."

"That's true."

"Now, at this moment you're a hare, and the people hunting you are named Monsieur de Launay, Porion and Monsieur de Sartine's sergeants. The first thing that they'll do is run to the Rue Saint-André-des-Arts, and pick up your trail there."

"But we'll have gone, taking Cécile."

"It will be necessary for that for you to be able to get into the house without being seen."

"That's easy. The door of the house opens for the tenants by touching a movable iron disk hidden behind the lock."

"Good."

"The stairway isn't illuminated."

"All right—but on seeing you, she'll utter a cry."

"What does it matter? On the top floor, where she lives, there are only two rooms: hers and my friend Firmin's."

"Can you answer for the latter's discretion?"

"As if he were my brother."

"But she has a father..."

"I'll answer for him too."

"Well," said the Fleming, "let's go. But let's hurry…time is passing."

They set forth, heading in the direction of the Pont Neuf.

"But when we have Cécile, where are we going?"

"I'll take care of that," said the Fleming, smiling. "I have a refuge for the three of us in Paris."

"Ah!"

"A former valet de chambre of mine, a worthy man who'd have himself cut into pieces to serve me, lodges in the Rue Saint-Louis-au-Marais, where he's established as a trader in hosiery. He has a large house, and we'll hide there for four or five days, time to look for the Tartar."

"Oh," said Hector, "I need all his blood for my unfortunate brother's."

"Don't worry," replied the Fleming, in a mysterious tone, "your brother will be avenged."

The night was cold and foggy. The hour of evil encounters was past, and there was no one in the streets. In less than a quarter of an hour, Hector and Monsieur de Mauroy arrived in the Rue Saint André-des-Arts.

Hector was perfectly familiar with the habits of the house. He pushed the iron disk and the little door opened without a sound. The alleyway was black and silent.

"Give me your hand," said Hector to Mauroy.

They climbed a stairway for which a greasy rope served as a rail, in which it was impossible to proceed two abreast, in the most complete obscurity, stifling their footfalls as best they could.

Having arrived on the top floor, Hector stopped. He had seen a thread of light passing under a door. "Poor Cécile," he murmured. "She's already at work."

And he knocked softly.

Cécile ran to open up. She wanted to utter an exclamation on seeing Hector, but he put a hand over her mouth and said: "Be quiet! You'll doom me!"

That threat froze Cécile's voice; she did not say another word, but she threw herself to the back of the room when she saw that Hector was not alone.

Monsieur de Mauroy, dazzled by the young woman's beauty, had stopped on the threshold.

Hector took her by the hand. "Cécile," he said, "Monsieur is my savior. We wouldn't have seen one another again, for I was condemned to eternal imprisonment in the Bastille, but, thanks to Monsieur, I've got out, and here I am."

And as Cécile joined her hands and addressed a grateful gaze to the Fleming, Hector asked: "Where is your father?"

The young woman went pale. "Oh," she said, "my poor father is no longer the same. I believe he's losing his reason, Hector. This evening, when Mardochée came back from Versailles and told us you were in the Bastille, my father had one of the fits of grim humor that you know, and he went out. We tried in vain to stop him. Where has he gone? I don't know. Will he come back? Alas, I've waited for him all night, praying and weeping, my beloved Hector, for I was afraid I'd never see you again..."

"Where is Firmin?" asked Hector, again.

"At midnight, the wife of a merchant of comestibles in the Carrefour Buci, seized by the pangs of childbirth, sent for him urgently."

"And Mardochée?"

Cécile went to her window. From that window, you will remember, one could see the painter's, on the other side of the street. It was from there, you will also remember, that Mardochée had seen Cécile for the first time, and Porion, with the aid of a plank thrown across by way of a bridge between the two casements, had abducted the young woman.

There was a light in Mardochée's room. The painter was not in bed either. He was not drunk, though; he had not even had supper. After having stayed with Cécile long into the night, trying to console her and telling her about a host of escapes in which he did not believe, but appropriate to calm her anguish, he had ended up going home. Instead of going to bed, however, he was sitting sadly, with his head in his hands. Through the curtainless windows, he could be seen in that dolorous and meditative attitude.

"There he is," said Cécile.

"Poor Mardochée," murmured Hector.

Monsieur de Mauroy, silent until then, intervened. "My children," he said, "this isn't the time for confidences. Remember, Hector, that our flight will soon be perceived, and it's necessary that we're in a place of safety when day breaks." Then, addressing the young woman, he said: "Mademoiselle, you love Hector, and Hector loves you?"

She blushed and paled by turns, and lowered her eyes, reddened by sleeplessness and tears.

Mauroy continued: "But the time of ordeals is past. In a week, Hector, a fugitive today, will be rich and free, for I have no children and I'll adopt him." Hector stifled an exclamation. "On the far side of the frontier, in Flemish country, I'm even richer than in France, and we'll live happily. You will be Hector's wife."

She stifled another cry.

The worthy gentleman added: "But today it's necessary to hurry. Do you want to go with Hector?"

"If I can!" she said, in a first impulse. But a name immediately rose from her heart to her lips: "What about my father?" she murmured

"Your father will come to join us when we're settled in Flanders."

"But how shall we tell him?"

"Wait," said Hector. He went to the casement, opened it, and whistled. The sound traversed space and caused Mardochée to shiver in his seat.

The painter was snatched from his reverie and went open the window. Suddenly, he perceived Hector, whose face was illuminated by lamplight. Hector had placed a finger over his lips, and the exclamation ready to emerge from the painter's throat remained there.

Strangely enough, the plank that had served for Cécile's abduction was still in the painter's studio. The latter remembered that, picked it up, pushed it from one roof to the other, and ventured boldly across the aerial bridge. A minute later, he threw his arms around Hector.

"Quickly," said Hector, "we only have a minute. Cécile is going with me, she'll be my wife. Wait for her father to return, and tell him that as soon as we're out of France, we'll write to you in order that Firmin, you and he can join us."

"Let's go, my children," said the Fleming. "Hurry up, and beware of that damned Porion."

Mardochée laughed "If you only fear him, he said, "you can walk in the sunlight henceforth."

"Why?"

"He's dead."

"Dead!"

"Yes he was hanged this morning."

"Where?"

"From a street-lamp in the Place Royale."

Mardochée was about to tell the story, but the Fleming stopped him. "Later, later," he said. "Day is about to break. Let's go."

And the two gentlemen shook Mardochée's hand and took Cécile away.

But Mardochée, as we shall see, was not to see Firmin or Robert Damiens. The vengeance of Porion, whom he believed to be dead, was waiting in the shadows and would soon reach him.

XLV

Let us return now to Versailles, where the King had had a great deal of trouble making Madame de Pompadour calm down.

The Prince de Bénavent had had once again made the reflection, on seeing the Marquise come in, that it was very fortunate that Monsieur de Richelieu had gone, bearing the release order concerning Hector de Pierrefeu, for, in order to get rid of the favorite's obsessions, the King would certainly have countermanded that order.

In the evening, they had learned about the accident that had befallen the Duc de Choiseul. The King had experienced a keen chagrin.

His Majesty, departing from his dream of the previous night, had found very different sentiments returning to him. He wanted to reform abuses, render his people happy and punish those who oppressed them.

That change of direction in the King's mind had impressed Madame de Pompadour so much that she had not hesitated to accept the bargain proposed to her by the provincial gentleman who was a cousin of Monsieur de Nocé. She had therefore gone back to find the King, and the King had signed the release.

The King had spent the day in a veritable state of anxiety, impatiently awaiting the return of the Maréchal. But the Maréchal did not return.

It was after midnight when Louis XV, weary of waiting, decided to go to bed—but he instructed his pages to admit the Maréchal as soon as he presented himself the flowing morning.

The following day, at ten o'clock, the Maréchal had still not returned. On the other hand, Madame de Pompadour came into the King's bedroom like a furious lioness.

"What's the matter now, my love?" said the King, stupefied.

"Sire," she said, "it's absolutely necessary that Your Majesty set an example."

"In regard to what?"

"In regard to the two wretches who introduced the *Gazette de Hollande* into Versailles."

"What!" said the King. "You're still occupied with that affair, my love?"

"Sire, it's an indignity!"

"First of all, there's only one guilty party," said the King. "Bénavent has explained that to me."

"Oh! You believe that, Sire!"

"Yes..."

"But Sire," the Marquise interrupted, violently, "I can see that Your Majesty knows absolutely nothing of what is happening in his kingdom!"

"Which is to say," said the King, calmly, "that I intend to know everything henceforth."

"Well, if Your Majesty deigns to listen to me, he will learn a great deal."

"What?" said the King.

"I'll tell you abominable things..."

"Go on," said the King, with the same phlegm.

"Sire," said the Marquise, "Monsieur Lange in is my apartments."

"Who is Monsieur Lange?"

"Monsieur de Launay's secretary."

"Oh."

"He's come from the Bastille this morning expressly to tell me what has happened there."

"Well?"

"Monsieur de Launay is revolted." The Marquise appeared to be suffocating, and had thrown herself on to a chair by the King's bedside.

The King took her hand. "Please explain, my beauty," he said.

"Well, those two wretches, while in the Bastille, have uttered infamous words against me in the presence of the governor."

"Both of them?"

"Yes, Sire."

"What! The young man too?"

"Certainly—and that's not all, Sire."

"What more is there?"

"They've revolted against the warders."

"In truth?"

"Then Monsieur de Launay had them put in a dungeon."

"Very good."

"And they've escaped..."

This time, the King jumped. "What! Escaped?" he said.

"Yes, Sire."

"From the dungeon?"

"By means of a subterranean tunnel that their friends had dug under the Bastille."

"In one night?"

"Yes, Sire. If you don't believe me, Monsieur Lange will tell you."

And she ran to the door of the royal bedchamber, which she opened. Monsieur Lange was in the antechamber.

"Come, Monsieur, come!" said the Marquise, beside herself. "Perhaps the King will believe you."

Monsieur Lange came in. He was clad in black and had the most severe expression.

"Let's see, Monsieur," said the King. "What has happened?"

Monsieur Lange recounted, point by point, the events with which we are familiar. Then he added that in the morning, at eight o'clock, when the cell was opened, it had been found empty, and the floor caved in. The turnkey who had made the discovery had called for help. Monsieur de Launay had arrived in person. Torches had been obtained and they had ventured into the tunnel leading to the conduit. There, they had lost all trace of the fugitives.

The King listened gravely to Lange' story. When the latter had finished, he said, coldly: "Monsieur de Launay wants to lose his employment as governor of the Bastille, then?"

The Marquise had a new fit of anger. "Sire," she said, "Monsieur de Launay is Your Majesty's most faithful servant."

"But people escape from the Bastille under his government," sniggered Louis XV." And he dismissed Monsieur Lange with a gesture.

When the latter had withdrawn, the Marquise said to the King: "Well, Sire, are you still thinking of protecting that young man, for whom you've conceived such a fine passion?"

The King bit his lips, and after a few minutes, he was still searching for a response when the Maréchal de Richelieu was announced.

That arrival extracted the King from his embarrassment. He turned to the Maréchal, who entered with a beaming smile, but who, at the sight of the Marquise, immediately furrowed his brow.

Fortunately, the latter stood up and said: "Sire, will you let me leave you with some good advice?"

"But what do you want me to say, my dear?" said the King. "I don't have the leisure or the means to make war on Holland."

"So be it," said the Marquise, "but Your Majesty can be punish those two gentlemen."

"I no longer have them in my power, since they've escaped."

"But you can have them arrested again."

"How, my darling?"

"Oh," said the Marquise, "if Your Majesty will give me *carte blanche...*"

"You'll take responsibility for it?"

"Yes, Sire, and within a week, they'll be back in the Bastille."

"I'd like that," said the King, in a weary tone.

The implacable Marquise continued: "But I'll only occupy myself with the matter if Your Majesty makes me a promise."

"What?"

"The promise to punish them severely when they're in our hands."

The King held out his hand to Madame de Pompadour. "I promise," he said.

The Marquise kissed his hand and said: "In that case, I'll set Monsieur de Sartine on campaign." And she went out, having no suspicion of the impatience with which the King was awaiting the Maréchal.

"Well, Duc?" said Louis XV, after the Marquise had gone. "Have you carried out my orders?"

"To the letter, Sire?"

"How is that, if you please?"

"Did not Your Majesty send me to Paris to carry out an investigation of the draper Ulysse Carnot, who claimed to be the procurator Dumas?"

"Yes, certainly. Well, what do you think of that charlatan?"

"Sire, he isn't a charlatan."

"Bah!"

"And, skeptical yesterday morning, you see me credulous today, Sire."

"Get away!"

"I've seen the man's leg, Sire, which is sturdy and robust and young in appearance.

"And...the other leg?"

"Is that of an old man, Sire."

"Then you're not far from believing the Tartar's story."

"Certainly not, Sire."

"But I suppose, Maréchal, that that conviction didn't prevent you from having the rogue arrested?"

"Who? The Tartar?"

"Yes," said the King.

"In truth, Sire, I would have, but for an event so bizarre, so singular...."

"What?"

"I have had such an adventure..."

"Gallant?"

"Yes and no, Sire?"

The King pricked up his ears. "Explain yourself, Maréchal," he said.

"Sire, I went to see my procurator, Maître Tavernier, about a lawsuit against me, and I saw in the procurator's home a woman such as I had never seen before."

"Beautiful?"

"Which is to say," said Richelieu, "that no painter amorous of the ideal ever dared to dream of her."

"How old?"

"Sixteen or seventeen."

"And you fell in love, Maréchal?"

"By procuration, Sire."

The King shuddered, and looked at his old accomplice in debauchery,

"If I were the King of France," Richelieu concluded, "I would put her on the throne."

"That girl?"

"And I would like the Marquise to be her humble servant."

"Oh, Maréchal!"

"In truth, Sire, I lost my head to such an extent that I forgot everything, even the young man you commanded me to have released from the Bastille."

"Well, don't worry about that, Maréchal, for he didn't wait for my permission. He got out of his own accord." And the King, already having forgotten the Tartar, added: "But tell me this story, then, Maréchal, Tell me!"

XLVI

The Maréchal was smiling.

"Sire," he said, "the Marquise de Pompadour herself would pale by comparison with my unknown beauty."

"Really!"

"And I'd like to be King of France!"

"Why is that, then?"

"Because I'd give that marvel a fate worthy of her."

The Maréchal had prepared his little speech during the journey from Paris to Versailles and had embroidered the story that he was about to relate to the King.

"In sum," said the latter, whose eye was beginning to glint slightly, "you encountered this incomparable beauty in the house of a procurator."

"Yes, Sire, Maître Tavernier, who recently won me a very thorny suit."

"What was she doing there?"

"She has a lawsuit herself."

"Oh, really?"

"A suit on which her entire fortune depends."

"And does she have a good case?"

"Excellent. Unfortunately, she's dealing with powerful adversaries who are putting everything to work."

"Perhaps she doesn't know anyone herself?"

"Absolutely no one, Sire."

"Poor girl!"

"So I offered her my protection."

"Ha ha, Maréchal. Damn!"

"I was thinking of my King, Sire."

"Ah," said Louis XV. "You want me to take her under my protection too."

"The King has nothing to lose by that, Sire."

"We'll see about that...or rather, we'll see the beautiful child..."

Monsieur de Richelieu sighed. "Sire," he said, "that's where the difficulty commences."

"What?"

"To conceal nothing from Your Majesty, Mademoiselle Espérance..."

"Her name is Espérance?"

"Yes, Sire."

"A pretty name, in fact."

"Mademoiselle Espérance is as fervently virtuous as she is incomparably beautiful. She's a robust provincial girl who knows nothing of the easy mores of the Court, and who, if she were taken to the Parc-aux-Cerfs, would certainly kill herself."

"Get away!" said the King, in a tone of naïve incredulity.

"It is as I have the honor of informing the King."

"Then she's an impregnable fortress, my dear Maréchal?"

"Impregnable by force, Sire, yes."

"And...by cunning?"

"If Your Majesty will deign to listen to me attentively, I shall have the honor of exposing a little plan that I've conceived."

"Speak, Maréchal."

"I've promised Mademoiselle Espérance de Beaulieu my protection for her lawsuit," the Maréchal continued.

"Good."

"If Your Majesty deigns to write two lines to the President of the Chamber, the affair, which might have been postponed indefinitely, will be judged next Thursday—which is to say, in three days' time. The case is sound, and the young woman's cause is just, according to Maître Tavernier."

"So she'll win her case."

"Evidently, for all the intrigues of her adversaries can do nothing against the protection of the King."

"And then?"

"Naturally, on Thursday evening, as soon as the verdict is rendered, Mademoiselle de Beaulieu will run to my house to thank me."

"Ah!"

"But she won't find me there, and my steward will say to her: 'Monsieur le Maréchal is at Marly, and he will be happy to receive you there, Mademoiselle.' In the enthusiasm of her gratitude, Mademoiselle Espérance will climb into the carriage that is waiting for her, ready-harnessed, in the courtyard of my house."

"And she'll go to Marly?"

"Naturally, Sire. Except then, I'll say to her, smiling: 'It isn't me that it's necessary to thank; it's an august personage who will be here in a few minutes.'"

"And that personage is me?" said the King.

"Yes, Sire. Marly is two paces from Versailles. Your Majesty goes there incognito. And as for the rest...Your Majesty need not worry about that. That's my business."

"Oh, Maréchal," said the King, smiling, "You're still the amiable rogue that I've known."

"Your Majesty is too kind."

"But it's necessary to wait three days..."

"Sire," said the Maréchal, "waiting is one more voluptuousness."

"That's sometimes true. But...the Marquise?"

"Oh, Sire, it will be a fine trick to play on her if she knows nothing about the adventure."

"She won't know anything about it, I promise you." And the King rubbed his hands joyfully. "But my dear Maréchal," he said, "three days is a long time. Can't I at least see her portrait?"

"I can't guarantee that to Your Majesty—but nothing is impossible."

"Ah! You think so?"

"And I'll return to Paris right away."

"Go, Maréchal, go! And if you can bring me that portrait this evening..."

"Sire," said the Maréchal, "I've just remembered that the word *impossible* is not French."

"How can I kill time between now and this evening?" murmured the King, looking at the clock and staring to yawn.

It was scarcely midday.

Richelieu had a slightly ironic smile. "Your Majesty," he said, "could occupy himself with affairs of State."

"In fact," said the King, "one means of killing time is as good as another...and for three days, Abbé Terray, my Minister of War, has been asking to work with me. I'll summon him. Until this evening, then, Maréchal."

"Until this evening, Sire."

And the Maréchal quit Louis XV, saying to himself: *The King's no longer thinking about either Maître Dumas, or the Tartar, or the young man whose brother's throat was cut. The King no longer has any but one obsession, the beautiful plaintiff that I've just mentioned to him. Frankly, I've earned the Muscovite's hundred thousand écus.*

Nevertheless, before leaving Versailles, the Maréchal went to dine with the Duchesse de S***, who had her apartments at the château.

When he climbed back into his carriage, he asked himself, not without emotion, the question: *How can I obtain Mademoiselle Espérance's portrait, then? For, after all, it's rather difficult to go to her and say: "I've talked about you to the King, who desires to see your portrait."*

After a few minutes of reflection, however, the Maréchal thought: *Bah! Porion is a man of resources; he'll get me out of it.*

That morning, on quitting him, Porion had said to him: "Just in case Your Lordship might have further need of me, Monseigneur, I'll present myself at the Rue de Hanovre at three o'clock."

Richelieu was, therefore, sure of finding Porion at his house in Paris. He made the journey tranquilly, without ordering his coachman to press the horses, and at a few minutes to three, he arrived in the Rue de Hanovre.

Porion was already pacing back and forth in front of the coaching entrance of the house.

"I have need of you!" Richelieu called to him, through the carriage door.

Porion came into the courtyard, and the Maréchal got down. He took the police agent by the arm and took him into his study.

"It's done," he told him. "The King is losing his head."

"Already!" said Porion, smiling.

"But he wants to have a portrait..."

"A portrait of the young woman?"

"Yes."

"Damn!" said Porion.

"And this very evening," added Richelieu.

Porion scratched his ear. Suddenly, however his face cleared and his little eyes shone. He said to Richelieu: "It's difficult, but it's not impossible, if..."

"If what?"

"Your Lordship has complete influence over Maître Tavernier."

"I believe so," said Richelieu.

"Monseigneur," Porion continued, "in order for me to answer you, I need to ask you a few questions."

"Speak."

"The King has accepted the Marly plan?"

"Of course."

"Then the King has consented to write to the president for the case to be judged on Thursday?"

"Yes."

"Well then, this is what I propose to Your Lordship...."

"Go on."

"You go to Maître Tavernier, Monseigneur. You ask him to send a message to Mademoiselle de Beaulieu immediately."

"Right."

"That will bring her in all haste, and the procurator will tell her that her case is about to be judged. Then, under the pretext of examining the dossier with her, he'll keep her with him for about an hour."

"All right—but the portrait?"

"Wait, Monseigneur. There's a glazed door in Maître Tavernier's study. It connects to another room. It's necessary, Monseigneur, that you persuade the procurator to allow two men to introduce themselves into that room while he confers with the young woman."

"I don't understand yet," said the Maréchal.

"It's quite simple, Monseigneur. One of those two men will be me."

"And the other?"

"Will be a painter that I'll bring."

"And an hour will suffice?"

"Certainly."

"And you guarantee the resemblance?"

"Perfect, Monseigneur."

"Then I'll go see Tavernier," said Richelieu.

"And I'll fetch the painter, Monseigneur."

Who was the painter on whom Porion was counting?

That is what we shall explain to you by going back in time a few hours—which is to say, to the moment when Monsieur de Mauroy and Hector had taken Cécile from the Rue Saint-André-des-Arts, charging our friend Mardochée de Mardoche with informing Robert Damiens of his daughter's departure.

XLVII

Mardochée was, therefore, installed in Cécile's room. He was familiar with the eccentricities and grim humor of Robert Damiens, and he told himself that the poor devil, after having doubtless wandered along the streets and the river bank all night, would end up returning to the lodgings, vanquished by lassitude and hunger, as a hare returns to its form at dawn.

When Mardochée was sober he was a man of his word, and one could count on him. He had promised Cécile to await her father's return. Although he had Porion's money in his pocket, although he had seen his friend Hector again, and had, in consequence, no further reason for sadness, all the wine merchants in the neighborhood could have open their doors simultaneously without Mardochée having though of quitting his post in order to go and refresh himself.

Furthermore, he was tried, and he became drowsy.

"Bah!" he thought, "if Robert finds me asleep when he comes back, he'll wake me up, and I'll tell him what's happened.

Having made that reflection, Mardochée lay down on Cécile's bed, and did not think either of closing the window or of removing the plank that put the young woman's room in communication with his own.

Mardochée was young and he was poor. It is only the old and the rich who sleep lightly. Mardochée therefore fell asleep profoundly as the first light of dawn was gliding tremulously over the roofs and chimney-pots.

Soon, however, he experienced a singular impression, doubtless produced by a nightmare, which is almost always a result of fatigue. It seemed that some-one was speaking a short distance away from him, and that voices and footsteps were audible in his own room on the other side of the street, and hence the other end of the plank.

Then it seemed to him that someone was walking over that plank, and fi-nally, that someone was approaching him and touching him. He tried to shake off the slumber that was oppressing him, but could not succeed in doing so.

Suddenly, however, it seemed to him that he was seized rudely, that some-thing cold suddenly covered his face, and that someone bound his hands and feet. He tried to cry out, but the cold thing that he could not define closed his mouth, stuck to his face and stifled him.

What a frightful dream I'm having! he said to himself. *How I wish I could wake up!*

Then he felt that he was being picked up bodily and carried away. Where? He did not know. He tried to open his eyes, as he had tried to cry out, but it was as if a mask of ice weighed upon every part of his face. He tried to struggle. An invincible force mastered his movements.

Increasingly convinced that he was still asleep, he said to himself: *Oh, what a vile dream! What a vile dream!*

The sound of footsteps going down stairs reached his ears, doubtless those of whoever was carrying him away. Then the noise ceased. There was a pause, and other sounds reached him. The door of a carriage opened, and, whether he was asleep or not, Mardochée understood that he was behind put in a vehicle, that two men got into it with him and that the carriage immediately moved off.

Then Mardochée said to himself that perhaps he was not asleep, and he remembered that policemen, thieves and all those who sometimes needed to carry out an abduction sometimes applied a waxen mask to the faces of their victims. He sensed that ropes bound his arms and legs.

I really am awake, he thought. *What are they going to do with me, then?*

Mardochée was brave, and as he had nothing to lose in this world, it did not matter to him whether he left it one way or another. Nevertheless, he asked himself the question: *What interest can they have in treating me like this?*

He made a violent somersault, trying to break his bonds. Then a voice was audible in his ear: "Don't move," it said, "Or you'll make the acquaintance of a nice dagger six inches long.

If he had been able to open his mouth, Mardochée would certainly have uttered a cry, for he knew the voice that he had just heard. It was that of Père Cinnamon—the Père Cinnamon he had seen hanged, his body inert at the end of a rope; the Père Cinnamon who was certainly dead!

And Mardochée said to himself: *I'm not mistaken. I'm not awake; since the dead are whispering in my ear, I must be asleep.*

And, convinced that he was choking under the knee of a nightmare, Mardochée resigned himself to not moving again.

The carriage rolled for about a quarter of an hour, and then stopped.

Then Père Cinnamon's voice became audible again. "Go on, my lads," he said. "Take this rogue on your shoulders and carry him you know where."

"Yes, Père Cinnamon," replied another voice, which Mardochée was hearing for the first time.

And Mardochée repeated to himself: *Since it's Père Cinnamon who's speaking and Père Cinnamon is dead, I'm still prey to a nasty dream.*

And he no longer preoccupied himself with the fact that he was picked up again and loaded on to shoulders. The men who were carrying him went into a house and the carriage drew away. Then, instead of going up a staircase, they went down one. That was easy to divine by the weight of their tread.

Mardochée said to himself: *Fortunately, all this is a dream, for they're definitely taking me down to a cellar. Are they going to bury me alive?*

Soon he felt damp air envelop him, penetrate his pores and pass through the resinous mask that he had over his face. Afterwards, he heard the noise of keys turning in locks, bolts grating over doors, and doors rotating on rusty hinges.

Finally, Père Cinnamon's voice was audible again.

"Everything's down there, isn't it?" it called, from the top of the stairs.

"Yes, Papa," replied a mocking voice.

"The bricks, the mortar, the trowel?"

"Everything."

"Wait for me, then, I'll come down."

Mardochée then felt himself being sat down against a wall on a hard surface that might have been a block of wood or a stone. At the same time, someone passed a sort of collar round his neck, closed by a catch whose dry click he heard.

And the voice of Père Cinnamon rang out again, no longer in the distance but close at hand. Porion said: "You can take off the mask now."

Suddenly, Mardochée passed from obscurity into the light, and his eyes opened abruptly. Then, to his amazement, he saw Porion in front of him.

"Ha ha ha!" he said. "Did we think Père Cinnamon was dead, then, my lad?"

This time, Mardochée was obliged to recognize that he was not dreaming and that he was wide awake. "Wretch!" he said. "If you're not dead, you're going to die!" And he tried to hurl himself upon Porion.

But while the latter burst out laughing, Mardochée uttered a cry of pain and rage and fell back on the block of stone on which he had been sat down. The collar that had been put round his neck was an iron ring fixed to the wall by a chain, and in trying to hurl himself upon Porion he had experienced that same dolorous shock as the one experienced by a dog on a leash that, launching itself outside its niche, finds itself suddenly retained by its chain.

Porion was laughing until tears came to his eyes.

Mardochée looked around dazedly. He saw two men whose faces were smeared with soot, but whose plaster-covered garments advertised the profession of mason.

Where was he? In a cellar about seven or eight feet broad, vaulted, and with no other exit than an open door. The wall in which the latter was pierced was several feet thick.

Mardochée began to shiver when he perceived in a corner of the cellar a pile of bricks, mortar and a trowel, and as he stared at him in bewilderment, Porion, who was still laughing, said to him: "No, my dear Monsieur Mardochée, in spite of the trouble that you took yesterday morning, I'm not dead, I'm doing marvelously, thanks to a young woman who released me just as I was about to die. But don't worry, the Devil won't lose anything by it."

"Wretch!" howled Mardochée, again.

"It's as well," Porion continued, "this being your abode henceforth, that you know where you are. We're in the cellar of a house that belongs to me, and believe that no one will come to disturb you here." Addressing the two masons, Père Cinnamon said: "Let's go to work, my friends, if you please!"

Mardochée was chained by the neck, and, in consequence, reduced to impotence. But there are times when terror takes possession of the bravest men, and the painter shivered from head to toe and sensed his hair suddenly standing on end. He had just understood, finally, what Porion was going to do with those bricks and the mortar. He was going to wall up the door to the cellar.

Mardochée started uttering cries.

"Oh," said Porion, sniggering, "Don't he inhibited, my gentleman, and if that soothes you, give yourself to it wholeheartedly. The house is uninhabited; no one will hear you."

The masons had set to work.

"Wretch! Murderer!" howled Mardochée. "Have you no fear of the wrath of Heaven?"

"I have more fear of men who want to hang me, and that's why I'm getting rid of one."

"Kill me then!"

"No, I prefer to let you die of starvation." Porion was still laughing.

Mardochée made vain efforts to break his chain, but he only succeeded in bruising his neck, and, as almost always happens, his fury soon gave way to a kind of prostration, and he understood that the folly of despair was taking possession of him.

When the wall was breast high, the masons passed the materials through to the other side, climbed over, and continued their sinister work.

His mouth agape and bloodied by foam, his eyes bulging, Mardochée saw the wall rise, and as the lamp illuminating that deadly work was on the other side, the unfortunate began contemplating the stream of light that passed between the lintel of the doorway and the wall that was still rising.

Finally, the light went out—which is to say that the last row of bricks had reached the lintel of the doorway.

And Mardochée uttered a cry of supreme horror, a cry that remained without echo.

He was buried alive!

XLVIII

Porion had been boasting in saying that the house belonged to him and that it was uninhabited. The cellar that was about to serve as the unfortunate Mardochée's tomb was attached to the house off the greengrocer and police agent who had, in the first part of this story, collaborated in the abduction of Cécile Robert.

The greengrocer lodged, as you know, in the Carrefour Buci, and he was still the faithful lieutenant of the malevolent Père Cinnamon. From the Rue Saint-André-des-Arts to the Carrefour Buci is only a few steps, and if the carriage that had helped to transport Mardochée had rolled for a long time it is because Porion had thought it prudent to take an indirect route, to go down to the river bank and return to the Carrefour from the opposite direction.

The greengrocer had lent himself to Porion's sinister projects with all the more complaisance because he had a grudge against Mardochée, who, for six months, had been proclaiming loudly that he belonged to the police and, in addition, because Monsieur de Sartine, understanding Porion's just resentments had given him carte blanche with regard to Mardochée. The greengrocer was one of the two masons, the other a policeman of whom Porion was equally sure.

When their frightful task was concluded, all three of them went back up to the shop. It was then half past seven.

"Well, Papa Cinnamon," said the greengrocer, laughing, "it's not good to do you a bad turn."

"You think so?"

"That poor devil's going to have a horrible death."

"If anyone ever hoists you on the end of a rope," Porion replied, coldly, "you'll see that hanging isn't exactly agreeable either."

"But he's going to die of hunger."

"And thirst," Porion added, with simplicity.

"What a horrible agony!" said the other mason.

"And long," said the greengrocer."

"How long might he live?"

"Four or five days." And Porion, doubtless bored by the conversation, took out his watch. "My children," he said, I have business on the other side of Paris, in the home of a great personage..."

"Eh?"

"A Maréchal de France, no less."

"Damn!" said the greengrocer. "Well, it's the Maréchal who has the worst acquaintance in France."

Porion had a fit of dignity. "Rogue!" he said, are you forgetting that I'm your superior?"

"Certainly not! Would you like something to drink, Boss?"

368

"I won't refuse. In the morning, when one's been working hard, a glass of white wine does one good."

"I'll go back down to the cellar, then."

The greengrocer went back the way he had come, and reappeared a few minutes later with two bottles under his arm.

"Can you hear him shouting?" asked Porion, tranquilly.

"One can't hear anything at all. We've put two rows of bricks in, and the mortar, which is very fine, has stopped up all the joints. Poor devil!"

"You're showing too much compassion for that rogue, who wanted to hang you by the neck," Porion said.

"Me!" said the greengrocer, nonplussed.

"And I'm henceforth entangled with you."

"What stupidity?"

"At least don't take it into your head to release him, for you'd lose your place over there."

"Don't worry," said the greengrocer. "As I said, it's not good to fall out with you, and I'm not going to do it."

"All the same," said Porion, "prudence is the mother of security."

"What do you mean?"

"That for four or five days. I'll come every morning and evening to make sure that the wall of the dungeon is intact." And he drank a glass of wine and left.

We know how he employed his morning introducing himself into the home of Mademoiselle Espérance de Beaulieu in order to make her hope for the protection of the Maréchal and to ask her then to place herself at the window in order for the latter to see her.

We also know what became of Monsieur de Richelieu's journey to Versailles and how, five hours later, he told Porion that the King wanted a portrait of the beautiful Espérance that evening.

On leaving the Maréchal's house, Porion said to himself: *There's only good and bad luck in this world. I gave myself the pleasant perspective of that scoundrel Mardochée dying of hunger in his tomb, and now I have need of him.* For Porion did not know any other painter than Mardochée, and he had had the opportunity to appreciate the painter's marvelous facility, the skill he possessed of seizing a perfect resemblance of his model, and his rapidity of execution, which was veritably prodigious.

In the presence of the whim the King had of possessing a portrait of Espérance that evening. Porion made the sacrifice of his hatred. He climbed into a fiacre had had himself taken immediately to the Carrefour Buci.

Sometimes, there are singular coincidences. One of those coincidences determined that Maître Tavernier, the procurator, also lived in the Carrefour Buci, next door to the greengrocer.

The latter, on seeing Porion come in, started laughing.

"Ah! he said. "You've some already to check that the wall hasn't been breached."

"It's not that," said Porion, coldly.

"What is it, then?"

"Get a log or a hammer, it doesn't matter which."

"To do what?"

"Light a lamp and follow me."

"But what are you going to do?"

"I want to liberate the prisoner, of course."

The greengrocer took a step back and looked at Porion in amazement. "Are you mad?" he said.

"No," said Porion.

"Then..."

"Then you're an imbecile, that's all."

"What?"

"Undoubtedly," said Père Cinnamon, "you're an imbecile, since you thought that I was a man to condemn one of my fellows to die of hunger."

The greengrocer opened his eyes wide. "However," he said, "we did chain him up."

"Of course."

"We walled up the door."

"Well, that was to scare him, that's all."

"All the same," said the greengrocer, arming himself with a mason's hammer, "you're a strange man." And he lifted the trapdoor that masked the stairway to the cellar.

Porion followed him.

When they arrived at the walled-up doorway, Porion placed his ear to the wall, and could not hear anything.

"All the same," he said, with a frisson of anxiety, "if he were crying out, we'd hear him. Is he already dead?" Now, a few drops of sweat began to form on Père Cinnamon's forehead.

Then the greengrocer began attacking the wall.

Suddenly, a muffled sound was audible on the other side, and Porion breathed. Mardochée was alive. Prey to a nameless prostration, the unfortunate, dominated by terror and the obscurity, had ended up falling silent. Even the sound of his own voice frightened him. For eight hours he had been buried alive in that horrible darkness, delivered to despair and the first cruel afflictions of hunger.

The insouciant painter, the Bohemian living from day to day, was nevertheless a Christian. He had understood that no mercy was to be expected from Porion. Face to face with the death that was advancing toward him slowly, Mardochée had made the sacrifice of his life, and he had prayed, asking God to forgive him for his sins, and also asking him for the courage to die like a man.

How many hours had gone by? Mardochée did not know. But suddenly, the silence that surrounded him gave way to an unknown noise. That noise, which soon grew, wrenched the unfortunate from his terror of death. He soon made out what it was. Someone was battering a breach in the wall that separated him from the rest of the world. Was he going to be freed, then?

And reason returned to his mind, where folly already reigned, and his heart began to beat violently, and he began to utter the cries that Porion had heard from the other side of the wall.

It was easier to destroy than to build. It had required an hour to erect the wall; the greengrocer only needed ten minutes to open a large breach in it, and suddenly, a ray of light penetrated the opaque darkness and struck Mardochée in the face.

A man clambered over the breach and entered the cellar. The man had a lantern in his hand, and the radiance of that lantern was projected on to his face.

Mardochée, breathless, had thought he would see a liberator. He uttered a cry of simultaneous rage and disappointment, for he recognized Porion. Père Cinnamon had sent the greengrocer away.

As Mardochée was chained by the neck, Père Cinnamon was not running any risk. Nevertheless, he was content to keep his distance, after having placed his lantern on the ground. He took a pair of fine brand new pistols out of his pocket and showed them to Mardochée. "They're loaded," he said, "and I can guarantee that they won't misfire."

Mardochée looked at the pistols indifferently. What is it to die struck by a bullet when one has the perspective of a death a hundred times more frightful?

"Let's talk," said Porion. "You're chained up, and if we don't fall into accord, I can bring back the masons, they'll reconstruct the wall, and all will be said. If I'm talking to you like this, Monsieur Mardochée, it's because I'm pressed for time. Would you like to buy back your life?"

Mardochée had recovered his courage. He covered Porion with a scornful gaze, and said: "What crime do you want to propose to me, then, wretch?"

"None."

"Then what do you want with me?"

"I would like you to make a portrait of my niece," said Porion.

But a cry of indignation emerged from Mardochée's throat. He knew what usage Porion had once made of the pastel portrait of the unfortunate Cécile."

"Wretch!" he said. "I can guess what you're up to. The niece you're talking about is some poor girl that you want to throw into the King's alcove."

"What does it matter to you?"

"Never."

Porion picked up the lantern. "Let's not talk about it anymore, then." And he headed for the breach, saying: "We'll reconstruct the wall"

And yet, Mardochée had hoped momentarily for life and liberty!

XLIX

Mardochée was stoical momentarily. He did not retain Porion by a cry or a gesture. He heard the police agent call to the greengrocer, and remained impassive. But when Porion had given his orders, when the pretended mason set tranquilly to work reconstructing the wall, anguish gripped his throat, the fear of death arrived in his heart. And he shouted: "Stop! Stop!"

"Aha!" said Porion, from the other side of the wall. "It appears that we're capitulating."

Mardochée replied with a dull groan.

Porion came back through the breach with his lantern and his pistols.

"My dear Monsieur Mardochée," he said, "I've already told you that time's pressing and it's a matter of take it or leave it. Do you accept?"

"Yes," stammered Mardochée.

"Then I'll send someone to fetch your box of colors and your brushes." And he gave new orders to the greengrocer.

When the latter had departed, he said: "It's necessary now, my young friend, that you know who you're dealing with. I'm not wicked, and I follow my métier honestly, but there's everything to lose by quarreling with me, as you've seen just now. I have a piece of paper in my pocket, signed Sartine, which can facilitate the means either of having you locked in the Bastille for the rest of your life or having you hanged tomorrow morning in the Place de Grève, but I'm prepared to renounce all of that, if you're good. Oh, of course, if, once that pretty necklace that's retaining you to the wall is unlocked, you were thinking of throwing yourself upon me, I'd blow your brains out with these toys." And Porion brought the butts of his pistols together.

Then he went on: "Also, of course, if, once out of here, you had the stupid idea of calling for help in order to get rid of me and not execute the agreement, I'd make use of Monsieur de Sartine's piece of paper. Thus, you see, I'm armed from head to toe."

The greengrocer came back. He had run to the Rue Saint-André-des-Arts, and no one had thought it extraordinary that he was going into the house, for he was known throughout the quarter to be one of Mardochée's creditors.

With a thrust of his shoulder he had broken down the door of the lodgings and had taken possession of all the utensils that Mardochée usually carried with him.

"Let's see," said Porion. "For the last time, is it agreed?"

"Yes," said Mardochée, in a strangled voice.

"You'll make the portrait?"

"Yes."

"And you'll be good?"

"Yes."

Porion turned to the greengrocer. "In that case," he said, "take off Monsieur's necklace."

The collar closed, as we have said, by means of a catch, but even though he was not tied up, Mardochée had been unable to release the catch, for it had a secret.

While the greengrocer rid Porion of his bonds, Porion still kept at a distance, pistols in hand. When the painter was free, Porion took the lead. The painter was walking unsteadily, so violent was the emotion he was experiencing.

There was no one upstairs in the shop.

"Hey," said Porion to the greengrocer, "Monsieur Mardochée might be hungry."

That single word could have held the unfortunate artist in respect more than all the pistols in the world.

"Am I hungry!" he said.

"There's a cry from the heart," said Porion, smiling. Then he took out his large silver watch again. "We ought to have an hour before us," he said. He addressed the greengrocer. "Serve us a ham, fried eggs and good wine. I'll gladly break a crust myself."

The greengrocer did not understand Porion's conduct at all, but he was accustomed to obey him. At a sign from the latter, he set up a table next to the window that overlooked the Carrefour. Then Mardochée recognized him. He realized where he was, but it was of scant importance. Mardochée was dying of hunger and he was breathing open air, intoxicating himself with light and sound, after having been nailed into his anticipated tomb. He was no longer thinking of rushing Porion in order to strangle him. The ham that appeared on the table absorbed all his attention. He did not eat; he devoured. He drank like a hole, and Porion had to stop him.

That lasted three quarters of an hour. At the end of that time, the sound of carriage-wheels was heard. Porion approached the window. The carriage had stopped outside the next door—which is to say, that of the procurator Tavernier.

Porion nudged Mardochée with his elbow and said: "Look!"

The door of the carriage opened and a young woman emerged. It was Espérance.

Dazzled, Mardochée threw himself sharply backwards. "Oh, how beautiful she is!" he said.

"Oh, you think so?"

"That's not a human creature, it's an angel."

"An angel who will serve you as a model."

"What! It's her!"

"Yes," said Porion.

At that moment, Mardochée forgot the infamous objective that Porion was proposing, and the enthusiasm of the artist stifled the scruples of the honest man.

"Now," said Porion, "you ought to have had enough to eat and drink."

"I'm ready," said Mardochée. And he swallowed a last glass of wine.

Porion said to himself: *My pistols have no further role to play; my man is a little drunk, and besides, he finds Espérance so beautiful that he'll make her portrait with passion. He won't try to resist me or escape me.*

Porion was right. Mardochée was only thinking about one thing now: of seeing that angelic face again at his ease, and fixing its features. He therefore picked up his box, his brushes and his hand-support, and followed Père Cinnamon.

"We haven't far to go," said the latter.

In fact, there was scarcely a distance of six paces between the greengrocer's door and the procurator's. The latter's house was an old one in which everything reeked of mildew and damp, as befits the lair of a quibbler. The alleyway was dark, the stairway tortuous.

On the bottom step, Porion and Mardochée encountered a sort of giant whom the former recognized immediately. It was the Maréchal's steward—the one who had accompanied Richelieu to the draper's shop in the Rue de l'Hirondelle.

"Follow me," the man said to Porion and Mardochée. He took them up the stairs, instructing them not to make any noise. Then, having arrived at the first floor, he opened a door and said to them: "Go in."

Mardochée and Porion then found themselves in a small room at the back of which they saw a glazed door. The steward went to lift a white curtain that was covering the door, and beckoned to Mardochée to approach.

The latter was then able to see, though a pane, on the other side of the door, the paper-filled study of Maître Tavernier the procurator. The latter was seated at a table, consulting a voluminous dossier. On the other side of the table was Mademoiselle Espérance de Beaulieu, fully illuminated, for she was beside a window.

"I couldn't have placed her any better myself," murmured Mardochée.

Porion thought he ought to make himself useful. He placed a table next to the glazed door and started disposing the colors and brushes.

In ecstasy, Mardochée engraved those features of an ideal purity in his memory.

Mademoiselle de Beaulieu was talking with an animation that gave her beauty a character of marvelous enthusiasm

As the door was closed, Mardochée could not hear what she was saying, but he understood that she was experiencing a great joy.

Finally, the painter set to work.

Porion had never seen him more skillful, even in the Pomme Verte tavern, where, drive by hunger, the poor devil made a portrait of a bourgeois for dinner and two six-livre écus.

It was an affair of three-quarters of an hour. Evidently, Maître Tavernier was in the Maréchal's confidence, for, several times already, the young woman had wanted to get up and the procurator had found a means of retaining her.

Finally, Mardochée turned to Porion, who, leaning over the easel, was following the work with an anxious attention.

"Now," he said, "I have no further need of her."

In fact, Mademoiselle Espérance's head stood out luminously, and with a perfect resemblance.

The young woman ended up getting to her feet and going away. The procurator escorted her to the door and Porion, who had a keener ear than Mardochée's, heard him say to her: "Until Thursday, then. The audience is at noon precisely."

"I'll be there," said the young woman.

"And don't worry about it in the meantime," said the procurator. "I consider your suit as won."

An hour later, Mardochée and Porion left the procurator's house in their turn. When they were at the door, Porion placed his hand on the painter's shoulder, who trembled.

"You'll see," he said, "what a good prince I am. I could send you to prison, but I'm setting you free."

"Is that true?" said Mardochée, suspiciously

"I'll do more," said Porion, sniggering. "I'll make you a gift of the money you stole from me yesterday morning."

And he left the stupefied painter in the middle of the Carrefour and went away, carrying the pastel that reproduced with a perfect resemblance the angelic features of Mademoiselle Espérance de Beaulieu.

L

Let us return now to the Place Royale, where the worthy Patureau, the old and faithful steward, was impatiently awaiting the return of his young mistress.

You will remember that a few minutes before Père Cinnamon had presented himself humbly at her abode that morning, to offer her the protection of Maréchal de Richelieu, Robert Damiens, the taciturn and grim man whom Patureau had turned away from suicide the previous day, had asked Espérance for permission to go and fetch his daughter and bring her to her.

Porion's visit, the sight of the Maréchal and the hope of seeing her suit finally judged thanks to such elevated protection, had caused Mademoiselle de Beaulieu to forget about Robert Damiens temporarily.

In fact, Patureau had come back and Robert Damiens had not shown himself. The old steward, on learning about Porion's step, had frowned slightly, because he knew the Maréchal's detestable reputation. Nevertheless, he had not thought that he should make Espérance party to his apprehensions.

All morning and for part of the afternoon, both of them had waited for Robert Damiens in vain. The man had not come back. At about three o'clock, the doorbell had rung. "That's doubtless him," Espérance had said. Patureau had gone to open the door.

It was not Robert; it was Master Tavernier's clerk, who had bought a letter from his employer in all haste.

The procurator had written:

Mademoiselle.

I have been notified by the Palais that your case has emerged from the rolls and that we will be judged next Thursday. There is not a minute to lose. Come and confer with me, therefore. We need to look at the dossier together.

I congratulate you, Mademoiselle, on the high protection that extends over you, and I have no doubt of the success.

Your very humble servant,

Tavernier.

It was in response to that note that Mademoiselle de Beaulieu had climbed into a fiacre and had hastened to the procurator's house, without suspecting, innocent as she was, that the rendezvous was an infamous trap.

Espérance therefore returned to the Place Royale full of joy and hope.

"I shall win! I shall win!" she said, embracing Patureau. "Tavernier is certain of it."

"Well, Mademoiselle," the old man replied, "if that is so, I'll give you some good advice."

"Speak, my friend."

"Will the suit be judged on Thursday?"

"Yes."

"Will we know the result right away."

"Undoubtedly."

"Well, if you believe me, we should leave for Blois that same evening."

"Oh, if you wish," said the young woman.

In the presence of that submission, Patureau did not insist. What was the point in casting an odious suspicion into that young soul?

In any case, the old servant said to himself: *Am I not here to protect her?*

"And Robert?" asked Espérance.

"I haven't seen him."

"That's quite extraordinary!"

"Which is to say that I fear that his idea of suicide might have gripped him again."

"Oh! Be quiet!"

"Oh, you haven't seen him as I have, Mademoiselle," Patureau said. "When I found him on the bridge, ready to throw himself in the water, he was frightening."

"But what's the matter with the poor man, then?"

"I don't know."

"What remorse is eating him away?"

Patureau did not have time to respond. The door bell rang.

"Ah! It's him," said Espérance. "He and his daughter, no doubt."

Patureau went to open the door.

It was, indeed, Robert Damiens, but he was alone. Pale, his eyes haggard, his garments in disorder, he precipitated himself rather than entered into the apartment, and came to throw himself at Espérance's knees, saying: "You, who are so good, who are so saintly, save me from myself! Save me!"

Where, then, had Robert Damiens come from?

That morning he had quit Patureau at the entrance to the Rue Saint-André-des-Arts, and while the latter went to see the procurator he had climbed the stairs in the house where he believed that he would find his daughter.

On the stairway, the unfortunate man, whose soul was appeased, almost dared to form a dream of happiness.

He was about to take his daughter by the hand, conduct her to Espérance, and say to the latter: "Protect the two of us."

He went up. No sound could be heard on the top floor.

The previous evening, when he had gone out, Robert had left Cécile with Firmin and Mardochée. He knocked; no one replied. As the key was in the door, he went in. Cécile's room was empty, the bed was not unmade. Robert thought that she was in Firmin's room, and went to knock on his door. The same silence. When he left, the surgeon had taken away the key.

Robert had not perceived, in his disturbance that the window in his daughter's room was open. In consequence, he had not seen the plank placed between her window and Mardochée's. However, all things considered, there was nothing so very extraordinary about Cécile's absence. Perhaps she had gone to take back her needlework.

Robert went downstairs to ask the neighbors for information. On the stairs however, he met Firmin. The young surgeon had just left the woman who had given birth.

"Where's Cécile," asked Robert.

"Cécile?"

"Yes—she isn't upstairs."

A vague presentiment assailed Firmin. He went up the stairs rapidly, and Robert went back up behind him.

Firmin saw the open window, and then perceived the plank. He uttered a cry. Robert Damiens began to shiver. Firmin ventured on to the bridge and ran to Mardochée's room. The room was empty. Where, then, was the painter also?

Firmin and Cécile's father went back downstairs. No one in the house had seen the young woman. One neighbor who lived underneath, however, claimed at that six o'clock in the morning, shortly before daybreak, she had heard the footsteps of men resounding overhead; then those footsteps had been audible on the staircase, so heavy that she had thought that the men, for there were several, were carrying something heavy.

The wine merchant who lodged on the ground floor remembered perfectly the sound of a carriage that had stopped at the door, and which had left again a quarter of an hour later.

Then Robert Damiens and Firmin looked at one another fearfully, and the former cried: "My daughter has been abducted!"

Then, sinister and frightening, he disengaged himself from the surgeon, who tried to retain him, and ran into the street, shouting: "This time, I shall avenge her!"

Where was he going?

He ran straight ahead, bare-headed, armed with a knife that he had taken from his pocket. He reached the water's edge and stated running along the river bank. After a quarter of an hour, he no longer had the strength to run, but he was walking at a rapid pace. He left Paris thus; he arrived in Bellevue, and then Sèvres, and as he encountered people on his path he said to them: "Am I far from Versailles?"

"Two leagues," they replied.

And Robert kept walking.

With time, however, the excitement calmed. The sky was cloudy and a few drops of rain were beginning to fall. As he went into the great woods, the rain became harder. Instinctively, the unfortunate fellow took shelter under a tree.

It rained for a long time. When it stopped, Robert got up, and wanted to continue on his way, but he was soaked, and Versailles was still a long way off. Then a reaction took place in his mind, and a secret voice roe up in the depths of his soul, crying to him: *Will you commit such a sin, then, wretch?*

And suddenly, his face lost its grim expression, to become anxious and fearful. A passer-by who looked at him frightened him. Robert Damiens thought that he had been divined. He threw away his knife and resumed walking—but instead of continuing his route, he turned round and went back toward Paris; and while he walked, he began to weep.

It was almost dark when he found himself back on the quays of the left bank. He had one hope—the hope that Cécile had come back. And he returned to the Rue Saint-André-des-Arts. But no one had seen Cécile or Mardochée.

Then the unfortunate had another access of folly. Oh, if Versailles had been no further away than the Louvre...!

Grim and silent, he returned to the bridge from which he had wanted to hurl himself into the Seine the day before. But there, courage failed him. Then a name vibrated in his heart, and a tender memory traversed his maddened brain: *Espérance!*

And the unfortunate Robert Damiens launched himself, at a run, toward the Place Royale. *She will save me!* he thought. *She will save me from myself.*

And as, a quarter of an hour later, he embraced the young woman's knees, she said to him: "But why, then, are you afraid of yourself?"

"Don't question me," he replied. "I wanted to commit a great crime."

"You!"

"Oh! Oh, save me! Save me!"

"God orders that injuries by forgiven, however bloody they are," murmured Espérance. And she lifted the poor fellow up, who was sobbing.

LI

Let us penetrate now into the Rue du Pas-de-la-Mule and go into the house that the Comte de Clermont, Prince of the Blood, had put at the disposition of his friend the Tartar.

It was a vast dwelling situated between a courtyard and a garden. The courtyard was separated from the street by a high wall, in the middle of which was the coaching entrance. The garden extended as far as a little deserted back-street, by which a little old man whom Prince Trespatky called his physician entered and left mysteriously every evening, the sight of whom always produced and effect of terror on the landlord of the Blue Dragon in the Rue des Enfants-Rouges. One might have thought that the house had been constructed expressly for a man given to bizarre habits, like the Tartar.

In fact, it was divided into two quite distinct parts, one facing the courtyard and one facing the garden; which is to say that a thick wall rise up in the middle of the edifice that separated it into two, from the cellars to the roof. That wall had only one door, which opened on the ground floor. On the side of the court-yard—in the front, that is, living in the sun—were the reception rooms, the dining room, the kitchens and the stables were sumptuous. There, the visitor found numerous lackeys in the Tartar's colors, and the latter, during the day, led the opulent life there of a great seigneur who does not know the fabulous figure of his income.

At eight o'clock in the evening, however, the mysterious door opened. It was a solid door, made or iron and lined behind in such a fashion that one could have fired a cannon on the other side of the wall without it being heard in the Rue du Pas-de-la-Mule. It was through that door that the Tartar and his physician disappeared, and they were not seen again before midnight.

At that hour only, the lackeys saw the Prince return in evening dress, fresh and rosy, so youthful that one might have thought he was no more than twenty years old.

What happened in the portion of the house that overlooked the garden? That was what no one knew, and it is there that we are going to penetrate.

It was half past eight. The night was dark and a thick fog extended over Paris, clinging to the corners of roofs and the steeples of churches like a gigantic sheet of gauze, ripped in a thousand places. Enveloped in his cloak, the Prince was walking in the garden, supported on Doctor Hermann's arm.

"You know," he said, "we've had a narrow escape, my old Hermann. The King of France had actually ordered my arrest."

"But thanks to the hundred thousand écus that he received, the Duc de Richelieu has appeased the King, has he not, Monseigneur?"

"The proof is," the Tartar replied, "that I have been invited to supper by Madame de Pompadour. So you can care for me, my old Hermann."

"I will do my best, Monseigneur."

"I want to be younger and more handsome than ever tomorrow. What do you have to serve me this evening?"

At that question Hermann shivered. "Monseigneur," he said, "I'm keeping you some true bull's blood for this evening."

"Please?"

"Oh, it's a whole story, Monseigneur."

"Go on."

"There's a street nearby called the Rue Saint-Louis."

"I know it."

"In that street there's a mercer…an imbecile who makes all possible steps every day in order to obtain your clientele."

"And it's him…?"

"Wait, Monseigneur."

"I'm listening," said the Tartar, "but speak quickly."

"That mercer has a man hiding in his house, a provincial, taller and more robust than you."

"How old?"

"Thirty-two or thirty-three. He's strong enough to fell an ox with a blow of his fist."

"Why is he hiding?"

"That's what I haven't been able to find out, but he's certainly got himself into serious trouble with the police, for he only goes out at night, enveloped in his cloak, to take a short walk through the deserted streets of the neighborhood."

"It's from the mercer that you got all this?"

"Yes, but wait a little longer, Monseigneur. In spite of his terrors, the man cannot prevent himself indulging in his penchant, drunkenness. There's a sort of tavern in the Rue Saint-Louis into which he slips sometimes, and it's there that I've extended my nets."

"How's that?"

"Vanda has dressed as a woman of the people."[43]

"Ah!"

"She has put a mask on her face and has introduced herself into the tavern, which is frequented, moreover, by women of ill repute. If he's drunk, our man is also a great lover of the fair sex, as Vanda perceived yesterday evening. He

---

[43] It is possible that the author has forgotten that the woman who lured innocent victims into the Tartar's trap in the prologue was named Woïna, and was clearly was the Prince's sister, whereas the present character is only passing for his sister. She cannot be a different woman, however, as she subsequently recognizes Hector.

hasn't seen her face, but he has admired her beautiful shoulders and her luxuriant tresses."

"Very good," said the Prince, coldly.

"This morning, he was handed an unsigned note conceived in these terms: *Dear and colossal unknown, If you are not completely ignorant of the mores of our time, you will understand that it sometimes happens that a woman of quality, weary of insipid homages, addresses herself to a robust and brave man like you. I am the pretended grisette who seemed so much to your taste yesterday evening. If the adventure does not displease you, be at the corner of the Place Royale this evening at nine o'clock precisely. My house is nearby. I invite you to supper.*"

"And what has he replied?"

"Nothing."

"Well?"

"For the simple reason that the messenger left before he had opened the letter."

"Do you think he'll go to the rendezvous?"

"I'm certain of it."

"And then?"

"Then Vanda will bring him here through the little door and take him to the room on the ground floor that you know, where supper will be served. That's why you see me dressed like this."

And Hermann opened the long overcoat that he was wearing. The Prince recognized that he was dressed as a lackey underneath it.

"Ah! You'll be serving them?"

"Yes, Monseigneur."

"But one thing worries me," said the Prince.

"What is that?"

"This man is a colossus, you say?"

"A Hercules."

"Do you hope, then, to carry it through?"

"Not me, but the wine we'll pour for him."

"Oho!" said the Prince, laughing.

"If that blood doesn't rejuvenate you," said Hermann, with his little dry, nervous laugh, "if it doesn't give your veins an unequaled force, you can treat me as an impostor and a charlatan."

The Prince took out his watch. "Quarter to nine," he said.

"It's time for you to take your bath, Monseigneur," said Hermann.

"So be it," said the Prince. "Come on, then."

They quit the garden and went into the ground floor. There, Hermann opened a little door hidden in a drapery, and the Tartar found himself on the threshold of a subterranean stairway illuminated by a lamp suspended from the vault.

The Prince went down thirty steps and found himself in the room into which we saw Porion penetrate a few days before. In the middle there was a bath full of blood—not human blood, but ox-blood—and Hermann said to the Prince: "You took a human bath yesterday; today this blood will suffice, all the more so as we'll keep the colossus asleep for two or three days and you can prick a vein or two when you come out of the bath, and do as much tomorrow morning."

"Yes," said the Tartar, whose eyes had a ferocious radiance. Then he undressed and got into the bath, after which he extended his wrist to the little old man.

The latter took a lancet and made an incision over one of the veins, which enabled the Tartar's blood to run out and mingle with the blood in the bath. Then Hermann went to pick up a flask from a table. That flask contained a sky-blue liquid, a few drops of which the old man poured into a spoon, which he presented to the Tartar.

Before drinking it, however, the Prince said: "Do you know that I'm afraid, sometimes?"

"Afraid, Monseigneur?"

"Indeed."

"And why?"

"What I'm drinking there, what I drink every day on getting into the bath, causes a paralysis throughout my body."

"That paralysis is necessary, Monseigneur, to bring about the mixture of your blood with that of the bath."

"So be it—but if, in an hour, you didn't give me a spoonful of another liquid, the paralysis would persist."

"Indefinitely, Monseigneur."

"What means that I could be murdered n my bath without my being able to put up the slightest resistance."

"Without a doubt, Monseigneur, but I'm here."

"Suppose, however..."

"What, Monseigneur?"

"Suppose that you were to die suddenly."

"Oh, Monseigneur," said the physician, laughing, "I have no desire to do that. Don't worry."

"You can guarantee that?"

"Oh, yes."

The Tartar took the spoon, and swallowed the blue liquid.

Suddenly, his limbs lost their warmth and their strength, and paralysis took possession of him. All the life of his body seemed to take refuge in his gaze, or it became impossible for him to speak.

"Now my functions as a valet will commence, Monseigneur," said Hermann. "It's nine o'clock and our lovers will be arriving."

Go, said the Prince with his gaze.

Monsieur Hermann went.

When he was at the top of the stairway and had closed the door of the subterranean room, the German doctor heard a sound. He went to the window and saw a man and a woman traversing the garden, arm in arm.

LII

The Hercules of whom Hermann, the German doctor, had spoken, as you have probably guessed, was none other than Vicomte Gontran de Mauroy, who, you will remember, had been obliged to seek a refuge in the home of his former valet de chambre, presently a mercer in the Rue Saint-Louis in the Marais.

It was to the home of that worthy man that the Fleming had taken Hector de Pierrefeu and Cécile. It was there that he had set up his mysterious batteries directed at the Tartar's house.

It was three days since the mercer had welcomed the three fugitives. Then, the Vicomte had said to Hector: "It's agreed, isn't it, that we're only staying in Paris to punish the Tartar?"

"Undoubtedly," Hector had replied, "and I need all his blood."

"How do you plan to obtain it?"

"Quite naturally, it seems to me," said the young man, naively.

"Ah!"

"I'll provoke him, get into his house, by force if necessary, and cross swords with him."

The Fleming shrugged his shoulders. "You're a child," he said.

"But..."

"Look. Let's assume for a moment that you're seriously thinking of putting your project into execution..."

"Well?"

"You reach the Tartar, I'll grant, and you provoke him—but he has an army of domestics around him who fall upon you and overwhelm you. That's the least of it."

"Oh!" said Hector, angrily.

"Or, they call the soldiers of the watch, you're recognized as an escapee from the Bastille, and you're taken back there."

"But it's necessary that I kill that man," said Hector, quivering with rage.

"It's not you who will kill him."

"Who, then?"

"Providence," pronounced the Vicomte, in a grave tone. And, as Hector did not understand, the Fleming went on: "The man must be judged and condemned."

"By whom?"

"By a tribunal."

"Where will you find the judges?"

"I'll take charge of that," said the Fleming. "Except that it's necessary that you obey me blindly."

"I'll obey you."

"Will you swear it to me?"

"On my word as a gentleman!"

And Hector held out his hand to the Fleming, who shook it, saying: "Trust me. The punishment will be terrible, and prompt."

The mercer had a large house, and he lived there alone. In accordance with the will of Monsieur de Mauroy, Cécile and Hector were, so to speak, locked away in an apartment overlooking the courtyard.

"My children," the Fleming said to them, "It's indispensable that you remain here without going out for two or three days. If it were otherwise, I could no longer answer for anything. You can be sure, my dear Hector," he added, in order to clarify his thinking, "that the Tartar and his servants know you, and that when the thunderbolt is about to strike people, it's necessary not to warn them of the impending storm."

"You have my word," said Hector.

From that moment on, the two lovers did not emerge from their room. As for the Fleming, he set out on campaign.

He went out in the evening, came back late, and went out again early in the morning. The mercer played his role cleverly and made contact with Doctor Hermann. The latter came to the shop and saw the Fleming. By the way in which he looked at him, the Fleming understood everything, and said to himself: *Aha! It appears that I too will make a fine bath of blood!*

The following evening, as he was sitting in the shop, next to the counter, he saw two faces stuck to the window outside: the face of a man and the face of a woman. He recognized the man perfectly; it was Hermann.

A quarter of an hour later, he wrapped himself in his cloak and went to the nearby tavern. Shortly thereafter, a woman came in and came to sit close by. She was wearing a mask, but the Fleming remembered the description that Hector had given him of the Tartar's pretended sister, and he was convinced that it was her.

When he went back to the mercer's house that evening, he said to him: "I believe that we'll be leaving tomorrow night. With the most absolute discretion, procure a post-chaise and horses."

The following day, he received the mysterious note that Hermann had mentioned to the Tartar. Then he said to the mercer: "It will certainly be this evening."

He went up to see Hector. "My friend," he said to him, "the hour is nigh."

"Ah!" said Hector.

"I've bought one of the Tartar's lackeys, and I have a detailed plan of the house."

"Really?"

"We'll sup there this evening."

Hector looked at him in amazement.

"My friend," the Fleming continued, "this evening, shortly before nine o'clock, be on the Place Royale."

"I'll meet you there?"

"Which is to say that you'll see me. I'll be recognizable thanks to my stature."

"And then?"

"You won't approach me, but you won't lose sight of me."

"Very well. I'll be there."

"Shortly afterwards," Mauroy continued, "you'll see a woman approach me."

All Hector's blood flowed to his heart. "Oh!" he said. "I can guess—it's the wretch's sister."

"She too will be punished," said the Fleming. Then, after a pause: "You'll see me draw away with her. Then you'll follow us, step by step. We'll probably go into a side-street, and toward the middle of that street a door will open for us. Then you'll stop a short distance away, and you'll wait."

"I wait until you come out?"

"No, I'll come to fetch you."

"And…then?"

"Then," said the Fleming, in a slow and solemn voice, "the hour of justice will not be far off."

And that evening, in fact, Monsieur de Mauroy was faithful to the rendezvous.

A man was strolling under the arcades, a hundred feet away, with a flap of his cloak pulled over his face. The Fleming recognized Hector.

Sitting on a bench, he waited, adopting the anxious attitude of a man who has an amorous rendezvous.

But the woman did not want to wait either. Monsieur de Mauroy had not been at his post for five minutes when he saw her emerge from the northern corner of the square and head straight toward him. He stood up and took off his hat.

She was enveloped in an ample pelisse and her head was covered by a hood. In addition, a black velvet mask only allowed her forehead and the lower part of her face to be seen.

She place a small gloved hand on the Fleming's shoulder and said to him: "You're a true gentleman. I was sure that you'd come. Your arm?"

And she drew him in the direction of the Rue du Pas-de-la-Mule. At the entrance of that street, however, she turned left and plunged into a side-street. It was the one that led to the rear of the house. In a matter of seconds, they reached the little door.

Then, while she introduced a key into the lock, the Fleming turned his head slightly and saw a shadow grazing the wall. It was Hector.

The door opened, and the Fleming went in, still giving his arm to the masked woman.

The garden, planted with large trees, seemed deserted. No light shone in the windows,

"I've sent all my servants away," she said, in a fresh and cheerful voice. "I've only kept an old steward, of whose discretion I'm certain."

"You're adorable, Madame," Mauroy replied. And he kissed her neck.

They reached the perron, and then the masked woman took a little whistle from her pocket, which she put to her lips. At that sound, a light suddenly shone and Dr. Hermann, dressed as a steward, came running, carrying a candlestick with two branches in his hand.

The Fleming was impassive. He had even been able to give himself the attitude and step of a soldier in luck. Still giving his arm to the masked woman, he traversed a vast drawing-room with her. Then Hermann opened a door.

Monsieur de Mauroy found himself on the threshold of a delightful boudoir, brightly illuminated, furnished with exquisite luxury, in the middle of which was a table sparkling with gilded decorations and crystal, from which escaped the delicious and penetrating perfumes of several bouquets of flowers scattered in boxes of tropical wood. The table was set for two. It had been positioned near to the fireplace, and the bitter and sensual aroma of Périgord truffles rose from each dish.

The masked woman made a sign to Hermann, and the fake steward went out, closing the door. The Vicomte seemed to be prey to an ecstatic daze. She started to laugh through her mask. "It's necessary that your happiness be complete, my sweet chevalier." And the mask fell away.

In any other circumstances, the Fleming would have deemed himself the most fortunate of men, for he had never seen a more luxuriant and more regal beauty.

She threw off her ample pelisse, and appeared with bare shoulders, dazzling with youth and voluptuousness. The Fleming enlaced her in his arms and stole another kiss. Then she filled a glass.

"Let's drink," she said, "to our amours of an hour—for tomorrow we must separate, my beloved chevalier, and we'll never see one another again."

She emptied her glass in a single draught, and the Fleming did likewise.

Then they ate supper, and she said a thousand foolish things, to which he listened, laughing loudly. He was, in appearance, the Buridan of whom that new Marguerite de Bourgogne dreamed. But there came a moment when she filled his glass with a wine as yellow as amber.

"Drink a toast with me?" she said.

"Not before you've given me a kiss," he said. He leaned over her, and she suddenly felt the sharp point of a stiletto touch her neck. At the same time, the Fleming whispered to her: "If you utter a scream, my beauty, you're dead."

LIII

The vampire's accomplice went pale, but she maintained her composure.

Mauroy had strength enough to stifle her by simply pressing with his bare hands; why, then, had he taken it into his head to make use of a stiletto?

The cold, sharp point even made a slight puncture in that neck as white as alabaster.

"A cry, a word or a mere gesture," the Fleming repeated, "and I'll kill you."

She looked at him with a gaze full of tenderness. That gaze seemed to say: "But what do you want with me?"

Still holding here beneath his dagger, the Fleming picked up the glass that she had filled. "Drink it!" he said.

She shivered, and shook her head.

"I'll give you three seconds, stealer of children, female vampire thirsty for human blood!" said the Vicomte, coldly.

She became livid, and looked at him in bewilderment.

"Think," he added, "that I simply want to get rid of you, because you're inconvenient. Choose, therefore, between this dagger and this glass, which contains a powerful narcotic that you intended for me. At least no one will open your veins to make a new bath for some wretch, and you'll be sure of returning to life."

As she still hesitated, the dagger entered into her flesh by a fraction of an inch. Fear overcame her. She took the glass and emptied it in a single draught.

"Now," said the Vicomte, "I'm tranquil. It's a matter of five minutes. Let's sup, then my dear, and tell me, pray, how you intended to accommodate me in this den of cut-throats."

She fixed her blazing eyes upon him, for life appeared to be taking refuge gradually within her, in her gaze, while a sudden chill took possession of her limbs and rose slowly toward her heart.

"Would my throat have been cut straight away, and would the Tartar have put me in a bath, or would he have given himself the pleasure of drinking a little of my blood every morning? Come on, my beauty, respond..."

But already, Vanda's tongue was beginning to suffer the effects of paralysis. That sophisticated liquor, whose effect on Hector de Pierrefeu had been almost instantaneous, had even more devastating effects on the vampire's accomplice. The dose of narcotic destined for a man of the strength and stature of the Fleming only took a few seconds to overwhelm a woman's body.

Mauroy watched that temporary death. He saw the limbs stiffen one by one, the mouth close, the eyes continue to live for about a minute, and then close in their turn.

The Fleming took Vanda in his arms and carried her to a bed that was at the back of the boudoir. Then he resumed eating, tranquilly. There was a bell on the table, Mauroy pressed the spring.

At that sound, Hermann came running.

But the Vicomte had already placed himself behind the door, and as the fake steward came in, he was seized, knocked down, and the point of the stiletto applied to his throat. Herman uttered a cry, but only one.

"My good man," the Fleming said to him, "we've arrived at the end of our little voyage. You won't be preparing any more baths of blood for anyone, for you're going to die yourself."

Hermann had had time to perceive Vanda immobile on the bed, and, not thinking about the narcotic, believed that the Fleming had killed her. The fear of death took hold of him. He put his hands together and begged for mercy.

"Have you shown mercy to others?" said Mauroy.

"My gentleman," stammered the old man, wringing his hands, "I only have a few days to live. Leave them to me…and to redeem my crimes I'll tell you everything."

"Ah!"

"I'll tell you where the Prince is, and how you can avenge yourself on him, if you've had a few victims in your family or among your friends."

"Where is he, then, the Tartar?"

"In the bath."

"Here?"

"Down below, in a cellar. Do you want me to take you there?"

But Mauroy continued to apply the stiletto to the wretch's throat.

The latter continued, in an imploring tone: "Yes, I'm culpable in your eyes, and the eyes of everyone, since I've shed blood, since I've served my master, but don't you realize that I was a slave, that he had the power of life and death over me?"

"If it only concerned me," replied Mauroy, "I'd grant you mercy, but I don't have the right to do so."

The little old man was sobbing like a woman.

"Get up!" the Fleming ordered.

The wretch had a gleam of hope in his eyes, and he got to his feet.

Then Mauroy took a gag from his pocket and forced the metal plate into his mouth. "Now," he said, "I'm sure of your silence. Hold out our hands." He took one of the napkins from the table and cut it into narrow strips. Then he bound Hermann's hands and feet with the strips, and, having reduced him to impotence, he laid him down beside the unconscious Vanda. After which he ran into the garden, murmuring: "Now let's open up to Hector."

Hector was in the back-street. In response to the Vicomte's whistle, he ran forward. "Are you armed," the latter said to him.

"I have my pistols and a dagger."

"Good. Follow me."

"What's happened, then?" asked Hector.

"Come, you'll see,"

And he led him to the little supper-room where the two wretches were, reduced to impotence.

Then he took Hermann by the arm and leaned him against the wall. He removed the gag. "Talk now," he said. "Where's the Tartar?"

Shivering, Hermann looked at Hector, whom he had recognized.

For his part, Hector had approached the bed and he contemplated the motionless Vanda. "Yes," he said, "this is the demon who caused the death of my unfortunate brother."

"To the Tartar first," said the Fleming. "She won't escape us." Brandishing his dagger, he asked Hermann: "Where is he?"

"Will you grant me my life?"

The Fleming did not reply.

"Think, my good Messieurs," said the old man, in an imploring tone, "that I'm only that wretch's instrument, that while the arm has struck, it's the head that directed it...oh, if you grant me mercy I'll offer you a means of vengeance of which you'd never have dared to dream."

"Well, speak; we'll see..."

And the Fleming looked at Hector.

"The man's right," said Hector. "He's only an instrument. Vengeance ought to rise higher."

Herman understood that if he betrayed his master completely, he would save his life. "The Tartar is in the bath," he said.

"Where?"

"Down below."

"In a bath of blood, that is?" said Hector.

"Yes, and he can't get out of it without me."

"Why?"

"He has a vein open, and he's taken a drug that paralyzes his limbs while leaving him hearing, sight and intelligence."

"Ah!" said Mauroy.

"Without me, he'll die in the bath, whatever efforts he makes to get out of it."

"Well, then," said Mauroy, coldly, "I can't see any inconvenience in sending you to the other world." And he raised his dagger—but Hector stopped his arm.

"No," he said, "the man talked because we promised him mercy. We don't have the right to kill him."

"So be it," said Mauroy. And he put his dagger back in his belt. Then, addressing Hector, he said: "Untie his feet then, and let him guide us." At the same time he picked up one of the candles from the table.

"March!" he ordered the old man, who was beginning to breathe again.

While these events were taking place up above, the Tartar, reduced to an absolute immobility in his bath, was beginning to find the time long.

What the devil in Hermann doing? he said to himself. *It seems to me that I'm losing too much blood.*

Hermann did not come down.

The Tartar tried to calm his anxiety by thinking that his faithful doctor was doubtless occupied in cutting the throat of the giant whose veins contained a burning blood endowed with great power. But he did not succeed.

His eyes were fixed on a clock suspended from the wall facing him. That clock was about to chime ten. It was, therefore, an hour since the doctor had departed, and Prince Trespatky had never taken a bath as long.

At the moment when the vibration of the clock made itself heard, the Prince's fear reached its peak. He made such a violent effort that his tongue was loosened.

"Hermann! Hermann!" he shouted.

Suddenly, he heard the sound of footsteps on the stairs—but that sound, instead of reassuring him, augmented his terror. Evidently, Hermann was not alone. Other men were coming down with him.

The stairway was facing the bath, beside the clock.

Suddenly, the Prince felt his hair standing on end. If he had had the freedom of his movements, he would have emerged precipitately from the bath and tried to take flight. He had just seen Hermann appear—but behind Hermann there were two grave, mute, sinister men. One of them was unknown to him, although, by his tall stature he deduced that it was the man who throat the doctor had been thinking of cutting an hour before. The other, he recognized immediately; it was Hector: Hector, whose blood he had once sucked; Hector, whose brother's throat he had had cut.

He succeeded, however, in uttering a further cry. "Hermann! Hermann!" he said. "Who are these men?"

The doctor roared like a wild beast caught in a trap. "Master," he replied, "they're our judges!"

LIV

Hermann was a German crossed with a Tartar—which is to say that he had been born of German parents on Muscovite soil, and that he was a slave.[44] He had told the truth in saying that the Prince had the right of life or death over him.

At that moment, his face had a satanic expression. "Master," he said, "the hour to expiate our crimes has come. We have fallen into a trap."

The Tartar uttered a roar.

"Master," Hermann continued, "this man has constrained Vanda to drink the narcotic destined for him." He pointed at the Fleming. "Vanda is as if dead," Hermann went on. "She can't come to our aid. Then this man threw himself upon me and wanted to stab me, but I ransomed my life."

The Tartar darted a gaze at him that meant: *Wretch, you've betrayed me!*

"Listen, Master," the wretch sniggered. "There's nothing as precious as life, and you know that as well as I do, you who've dreamed of being eternally young. When I saw a danger raised over me, I remembered that I'm a slave, that you've often beaten me with your noble hand, that you've had me given the knout in the past. Then, as there always comes a time when a slave is in horror of his master, I betrayed you. I brought these two men here, and now you have to deal with them."

And the wretch uttered a little cruel and dry laugh, which completed the Prince's exasperation.

Then the Fleming came forward. "Monsieur," he said, "You have heard this man?"

The Tartar tried to speak, but he could not. Only his eyes, his wide open eyes, testified that he was alive.

"You have heard this man," the Fleming continued. "Now, listen to us. You were rich and powerful an hour ago. You were able to buy consciences, close indecisive mouths, trample laws underfoot and laugh at Providence. You were so highly placed that it seemed that no justice could attain you and that your crimes would remain forever unpunished.

"Providence has decided otherwise."

He took Hector by the hand and drew him toward the bath.

"Prince Trespatky," he went on, "When it happens that judges are corrupted, that the established powers dare not punish, God sometimes permits men to come together, to constitute a supreme tribunal, to judge and condemn a criminal. We have come together, this young man and I, and we have condemned

---

[44] In the prologue when he claimed to be Hermann Schutzberg of the Faculty of Heidelberg.

you. Prince, you are going to die, and die by the same hand that was so long the instrument of your crimes."

Then the Fleming made a sign to Hermann.

The latter approached and took one of the Tartar's arms—the one in which he had made a small incision from which a trickle of blood as slowly running out.

Armed with a lancet, the doctor enlarged the incision, and the blood flowed out. Then he performed the same operation on the other arm.

This time, the Tartar uttered a new cry, a supreme cry of rage and impotence. His haggard eyes saw his blood flowing away, and mingling with the blood of the bull, which filled the bath.

At a further sign from Mauroy, Hermann activated a piston. Then the bath emptied, almost immediately, and the Tartar remained lying in it and shivering.

"Oh, you wanted a bath in human blood," said Mauroy. "Well, be satisfied."

In fact, the bath, momentarily empty, did not take long to fill up again. But it was now the blood of the Tartar that was flowing. It was flooding out, and as it did so, the monster, griped by paralysis, sensed his life ebbing away with it.

Pale and quivering, Hector could not take his eyes off that horrible spectacle. The Tartar roared, and strove to make futile efforts. His body already had the rigidity of a cadaver, and the blood was still flowing.

Finally, the roars became duller, fading away by degrees; the eyes took on a vitreous tint, and the flames that has escaped from them were gradually extinguished.

A moment came when the bath was almost full. Then the eyes closed and nothing any longer manifested life in the man who had abused the lives of so many others.

"It's finished," said Hermann.

"Yes, for that one," aid the Fleming, "but not for his accomplices." And as Hermann, frightened, fell to his knees again, he said: "I granted you the mercy of your life," he said, "but I didn't say that you wouldn't be punished." And he seized his throat with an iron hand.

Half-strangled, the old man opened his mouth, and his tongue hung out, livid and blue.

It was as rapid as the lightning that rips a cloud and is extinguished. With the blade of his dagger, the Fleming severed that tongue, which fell to the floor.

"You'll never tell this story," said Mauroy, while Hermann fell to the ground, uttering dull moans and vomiting floods of blood.

Then he took Hector by the arm.

"Now for Vanda," he said.

If you recall the first part of this story and the bizarre sensations experienced by Hector in the house to which the duenna had taken him and where, supping with Vanda, he had absorbed the strange narcotic that, paralyzing his entire body, left him the use of his hearing and the freedom of his intelligence, you will understand what the vampire's accomplice had to be experiencing.

She too was apparently dead, and her body manifested a cadaveric rigidity. The beating of her heart had stopped, or was so feeble as to be imperceptible, but she could think and hear. She heard Hermann beg for mercy before the Fleming's dagger; she heard him order to betray his master. She then heard the Fleming go away, and then come back, accompanied by another man.

Who was he?

The man spoke, and she recognized the voice.

It was the young man she had seduced, the victim who had escaped her; it was Hector de Pierrefeu.

Then Vanda understood that those men would not grant her mercy. By the last words of Hermann and the Fleming, she also understood that the hour of the Tartar's punishment had come.

She heard them draw away. But what would her fate be? Would Hector take pity on her beauty or would he condemn her to death?

An hour went by: an hour of terror and anguish.

Finally, the footsteps of the two men became audible again. Then Vanda understood that her turn had come.

In fact, the Fleming approached her and said: "Madame, your accomplice is dead. The man who bathed voluptuously in the blood of his fellows has died bathing in his own. The instrument of your crimes, Hermann, has similarly expiated his sin. I grated him the mercy of his life, but I cut out his tongue, and he'll no longer be able to give perfidious advice. Your turn has come; you must be punished too. We shall not kill you, though. A man should not shed the blood of a woman—but when one encounters a viper in one's path, if one grants it the mercy of its life, one renders it incapable of harm, and crushes its venomous dart. Your dart in your beauty. Perish, then, your perfidious weapon, with the aid of which you have de so much harm!"

And Vanda, mute, immobile, petrified, divined rather than felt a terrible mask applied to her face, destined to corrode her flesh, to tumefy her lips, to tarnish the gleam in her eyes.

"Now," said the Fleming, "no one will follow you."

And, in fact, he had put over her face a blackish paste that contained vitriol, and which burned and rendered horrible, in a matter of seconds, that visage radiant with youth and beauty.

When the mask was removed, Hector uttered a cry: "Oh, that's frightful!" he said.

"You are avenged," said the Fleming. "Now, let's go."

"Where are we going?"

"We're going to fetch Cécile," said Mauroy, "And in an hour, we'll have left Paris."

And they both ran out of the accused house where crime had reigned for such a long time. They traversed the garden at a run, reached the back-street and, a few minutes later they arrived in the Rue Saint-Louis.

The post-chaise was ready and waiting at the mercer's door.

"Run and fetch Cécile," said Monsieur de Mauroy.

"I'm ready," the young woman replied, appearing on the threshold of the shop, whose door stood ajar.

"Into the carriage, then, and let's go!" said the Fleming.

"But…my father…," said Cécile, in an emotional voice.

"He's join us later," said Hector.

"My God!" murmured the young woman. "Shall I ever see him again?"

Alas, Cécile could not foresee then in what terrible and supreme circumstances she would see Robert Damiens for the last time.

LV

The day after the one on which Monsieur de Mauroy, Cécile and Hector quit Paris, after having avenged the death of the unfortunate André, Mademoiselle Espérance de Beaulieu's lawsuit was to be judged by the Parliament.

For three days, Monsieur de Richelieu had scarcely had any rest. The old courtier had rediscovered all the activity of his stormy youth and had multiplied himself. He had gone to see the counselors and procurators furnished with the letter from the King that recommended the young woman warmly, and, as the case was good, he had had no difficulty in influencing the red robes in Espérance's favor.

On the Thursday morning, therefore, Monsieur le Maréchal got up at seven o'clock in the morning—which is to say, at daybreak—rang for his valet de chambre and said to him: "Is Porion here?"

"Monseigneur," the valet replied, "Porion arrived from Versailles at four o'clock in the morning."

"Oh! Really?"

"I wanted to wake Monseigneur, but he opposed it."

"Why?"

"He said that everything was ready, that there was, in consequence, no need to wake Monseigneur, and that it was better to let him sleep."

"Good, but where is he?"

"He left again, but he told me that he would return between eight and nine o'clock this morning.

"That's good," said Richelieu, and he finished dressing.

Eight o'clock chimed, then nine and then half past nine.

"Damn!" said the Maréchal. "That rogue is permitting himself to keep me waiting now."

In fact, Porion did not come back.

"I don't have time to waste, though," grumbled the Maréchal. "I want to attend the trial, and disappear before the end, in such a fashion that she can't thank me at the hearing, return to Versailles and go from there to Marly. Porion has told me that everything is ready, but that's not sufficient; I want to know exactly how impatient the King is."

And for the twentieth time, the Maréchal was casting an anxious glance at the clock, when the sound of the bell at the entrance door was heard.

The Maréchal ran to the window, and saw Porion traversing the courtyard in great haste. "Damn! How pale he is!" Richelieu said.

In fact, Porion was walking at an unsteady pace, and had something unusual and disordered throughout his person.

He irrupted into the Maréchal's study, and could only pronounce the words: "Oh, Monseigneur, what a misfortune!"

"A misfortune?" said the Maréchal.

"A crime, Monseigneur!"

"A crime?"

"Frightful, unprecedented! Oh, my God!" And Porion let himself fall on to a chair, sweating and distraught.

"Come on," said Richelieu, "what's the matter? Espérance..."

"It's not a matter of Espérance."

"Richelieu breathed out. "Who, then?" he said.

"The Tartar."

"He's murdered someone else?"

"No, it's him who's been murdered."

The Maréchal started. "What?" he said.

"He's been bled in his bath, and he's still there."

"Is that possible?"

"It's the truth, Monseigneur."

"But who has murdered him? How did it happen? Speak...explain yourself..."

Porion gradually pulled himself together. "Monseigneur," he said, "I'll tell you everything."

"Speak!"

Porion said: "This morning, as I was told that Monseigneur was asleep. I went home; it had been several days since I'd set foot there, and I wanted to know what was happening. From there, I went to Monsieur de Clermont's house. I was in haste to tell the Tartar Prince that I had seen Madame de Pompadour yesterday, and that she had charged me to reiterate her invitation to supper, because it's this evening that he was due to come to Versailles to see the Marquise."

"And?" said the Maréchal.

"You know that the Comte de Clermont's house had been appropriated to the Tartar's mysterious existence..."

"Yes, I've been told," said Richelieu; there's a wall that separates it into two, with only one door."

"Precisely."

"An iron door."

"Which only the Tartar and his physician go through."

"Well?"

"The domestics were prey to a great emotion. Since the previous evening the Tartar had not reappeared—which never happened before. They had held a conference. Some said that some misfortune must have overtaken him, and that it was necessary to break down the door. Others recalled the little speech their terrible master had made to them on taking possession of the house: 'I shall punish with death,' he said, 'anyone who tries to cross the threshold of that door.'

"It was then that I arrived. The Tartar had been seen to receive me with marks of consideration. It required no more for the servants to grant me all their confidence. The long disappearance of the Prince alarmed me as much as them.

"'My friends,' I said finally, 'It's necessary to break down the door; but if you fear your master's wrath, I'll go in alone.' The last means pleased them. I took all the responsibility upon myself. But one doesn't break down an iron door like a simple one. It was necessary to fetch a wooden beam from the courtyard, have several men hold it and attack the door with that battering ram.

"At every blow the house resounded like a drum, and we expected to see the Prince appear, menacingly, at any moment. There was nothing. The door finally gave way, and an empty corridor appeared to us behind it. The domestics didn't dare go any further, so I launched myself forward bravely."

"You're brave, then?" the Maréchal interrupted, in a mocking tone.

"There are days, Monseigneur. Every man has days of bravery and cowardice."

"That's true. Go on."

"At the end of the corridor it seemed to me that I could hear groaning. I hastened my steps, I opened a door that I saw before me, and I perceived a man crouching on the ground, who appeared to be prey to intolerable suffering. He had blood on his garments and his mouth as covered in it. I recognized old Hermann, the Tartar's physician."

"'What's happened to you, then?' I said to him, trying to get him to his feet.

"He didn't reply, but he opened his mouth wide, and I recoiled, horror-struck. His tongue had been cut out."

"The Tartar, no doubt?"

"No, Monseigneur, as you'll see. My presence appeared to calm his suffering and despair somewhat. He took me by the hand and dragged me to a subterranean stairway, illuminated by a lamp suspended from the vault. I followed it.

"At the end of the stairway, a new light struck my eyes, and I saw a large subterranean room, which must have been a wine-cellar that had been converted into a bathroom. A glacial cold reigned there. In the middle was a bath, and in the bath, which was full of blood, I saw the Tartar. The blood didn't frighten me at first; I knew is habits—but the physician forced me to approach, and then I realized the sinister truth. It was his own blood that filled the bath, and the Tartar was dead.

"As I uttered a cry of horror, Herman dragged me away again. He took me back up the stairs and led me to another room. There, beside a table still laden with the debris of a supper, there was a bed, and on that bed a woman, who also appeared to be dead. It was the one that the Tartar passed off as his sister.

"I recognized her by her clothes, for her disfigured face was no longer anything but an object of horror.

"'Dead too!' I cried.

"'*No*,' said the old physician, with a sign of the head. He went to take a box from a nearby cupboard, which contained his phials of poison, antidotes and surgical instruments. He opened the box and took out a bottle, which he uncorked, and which contained a yellow liquid. Then he poured a few drops of the liquid into a spoon, returned to the woman, parted her clenched lips, and introduced the spoon into her mouth.

"The effect was instantaneous. The woman stood up and opened her eyes. 'Oh, the wretch!' she said. Then, having run to a mirror, she looked at herself and started uttering frightful screams. Her despair was so great that it was only after half an hour that I was able to discover, by means of questions, what had happened."

"Go on," said the Maréchal, whose curiosity was excited by the story to the highest degree.

"Monseigneur," said Potion, "you know the petty gentleman whose brother had his throat cut by the Tartar..."

"Yes, Hector de Pierrefeu."

"And the other, the Fleming who came to claim ten thousand écus..."

"Indeed."

"They escaped from the Bastille."

"And they're the ones who committed all these atrocities?"

"Yes, Monseigneur." Porion was seized by a sudden access of fury. "Oh," he said, "I shall avenge the Tartar!"

But then Monsieur de Richelieu burst out laughing. "Porion," he said, "do you want to know my sentiment?"

"I'm listening Monseigneur."

"My sentiment is that you're an imbecile."

And the Maréchal continued to laugh wholeheartedly.

LVI

Porion could not help looking at Richelieu with a kind of bewilderment.

"I can see," said the Maréchal, "that it's necessary to explain myself."

"Monseigneur..."

"Let's see, my good friend," Richelieu went on, in a tome full of bonho-mie, "were you a relative of the Tartar?"

"No, Monseigneur."

"His friend?"

"No..."

"Does he owe you money?"

"Well," said Porion, "I had a fine bill to present to him for my actions, steps and cares."

"And how much would it have amounted too, that bill?"

"At least a thousand écus."

"My word," said the Maréchal, "as I called you an imbecile and don't take it back, I might as well pay you your thousand écus."

"Really, Monseigneur, you'd have that kindness?"

"Yes, but after tomorrow night's little affair."

"Oh, that's very just," said Porion.

"And," said the Maréchal, "on one condition."

"I'm listening, Monseigneur."

"You give me a justified receipt."

"Why?"

Richelieu winked. "The Tartar is dead," he said. "That relieves the King and myself from a great worry. The King won't have to have him hanged, and I..."

"And you, Monsieur le Maréchal," said Porion, insolently, "won't have to pay him back his hundred thousand éus."

"Naturally, but it's always necessary to mistrust rogues." And the Maréchal looked fixedly at Porion. "Rogues like you," he said.

Porion bowed, and did not take offence.

"For there's only the Tartar and you who know about it, isn't there?"

"Absolutely, Monseigneur. Monsieur Boemer, the jeweler, in handing them to me, thought that the hundred thousand écus were destined to pay a gambling debt."

"Monsieur Boemer's belief is true."

"Ah!" said Porion.

"And look," said Richelieu, "I'll even give you the thousand écus right away, if you'll make out the receipt that I'll dictate to you."

"With pleasure," said Porion, who sat down at a table where there were writing materials.

The Maréchal dictated:

I acknowledge having received from Monsieur le Maréchal Duc de Richelieu the sum of a thousand écus, for the assistance I rendered him, thanks to which he was able to collect a considerable sum that the Russian Prince Trespatky had lost playing cards with him.

"Sign," said Richelieu then.

Porion appended his signature to the bottom of his receipt.

Then the Maréchal opened the drawer in which he had placed the Tartar's money and took out a thousand écus' worth of cashable bills, which he gave to Porion.

The latter bowed again, put the bills away in his dirty portfolio, and murmured: "All the same, the Tartar's death will be avenged."

Richelieu shrugged his shoulders. "What!" he said, "even the money doesn't give you intelligence?"

"Well..." said Porion.

"Listen to me carefully," said Richelieu, "And perhaps you'll end up understanding."

Porion looked at him and waited.

"Let's suppose," the Maréchal continued, "that instead of being a Prince, instead of being rich, the Tartar had been a man of petty society."

"Well, Monseigneur..."

"And in your capacity as a police agent, you'd have done your utmost to deliver him to Monsieur de Paris, who would have broken him on the wheel on the Grève."

"That's true..."

"But he was rich, and as he wasn't stingy, you and I saved him from the King's wrath."

"That's true, Monseigneur."

"We wanted to play the role of Providence, but jealous Providence has taken possession of the situation."

"But Monseigneur, those wretches..."

"What wretches?"

"Hector de Pierrefeu..."

"A worthy gentleman who has avenged his brother."

"That Vicomte de Mauroy..."

"A faithful friend..."

"Oh, I hate them..."

Richelieu burst out laughing. "You're not a man of your métier, then?"

"Why is that, Monseigneur?"

"A policeman ought not to have any hatreds or friendships..."

"That's easy for you to say, Monseigneur."

"Otherwise," Richelieu concluded, "he's an incomplete man."

"Ah!"

"And I withdraw the little admiration I had for you." With that, the Maréchal turned on his heel and continued: "If you believe me, you'll leave those fellows tranquil, who, you see, are at least as strong as you."

"Oh!"

"You put them in the Bastille, they get out."

"That's Monsieur de Launay's fault."

"So be it. You protect the Tartar, they kill him. Is that also Monsieur de Launay's fault?"

Porion bowed his head. "No," he stammered.

"Now," Richelieu went on, "You must know the hour at which they made that Tartar take that little bath."

"Between nine o'clock and midnight—at least, that's what Vanda, the disfigured woman, told me."

"Good," said the Maréchal. "Well, between midnight and six o'clock in the morning, one can travel a long way."

"That's true."

"You can start a search for them" said the Maréchal, "but you won't find them in Paris."

"Perhaps..."

"You think they're as stupid as you are?"

"Monseigneur," said Porion, "A man in love is always more or less stupid."

"And which is the one who's in love?"

"Hector."

"With whom?"

"With the little girl...you know...with regard to whom Your Lordship bore me a grudge."

"Damn!"

"Which means that he might well, instead of getting away, have come back to prowl around the vicinity of Cécile Robert's house."

"Unless he's taken her with him..."

Porion uttered a cry of rage. "Oh, if that were the case..."

"Well?"

"I believe I'd go throw myself in the Seine."

"You can do it tomorrow, if you wish, but today, I have need of you, for we haven't yet said a word about Versailles."

"All's going well, Monseigneur."

"But what's new?"

"The King has sent Monsieur Lebel to Marly."

"And?"

"A little supper will be prepared, and the King will arrive at about eleven o'clock in the evening."

"Incognito?"

"Very nearly—which is to say that he'll traverse the forest with an escort of musketeers."

"But in an unmarked carriage?"

"Yes, Monseigneur."

"And you're quite sure that Mademoiselle Espérance will consent to accompany me to Marly."

"I'm certain of it."

"You don't fear her old steward?"

"I've found a means of getting rid of him this evening."

"How?"

"It's Maître Tavernier, with whom I have an understanding, who'll take charge of that."

"What will he do?"

"At the moment when the judgment is pronounced, he'll make a sign to the fellow."

"Good."

The old man will approach his bench. Then Maître Tavernier will say to him: 'My friend, it's not everything to have won the case, it's also necessary to have the judgment registered and complete the necessary pursuits and diligences to render its execution. I need you to come to my study.' And he'll take him home first, then to a sergeant, and make him waste part of his evening. In the meantime, I'll offer an arm to Mademoiselle Espérance, and we'll look for you everywhere in the room where you saw her at the beginning of the hearing. Not finding you, and Patureau having gone with Maître Tavernier, I'll advise the Mademoiselle to accompany me here."

"Here, she'll learn that I've just left for my country house," said Richelieu, smiling.

"And as I seem entirely respectable," said Porion, laughing, "she'll accept the guidance of a respectable old man like me"

"That's perfect," said Richelieu.

The rococo clock on the mantelpiece marked ten thirty.

"What time is the hearing?" asked the Maréchal.

"The case will be called at eleven o'clock, but it won't be judged until two, which gives us three hours of leisure, Monseigneur." And Porion picked up his hat and made as if to withdraw.

"Where are you going?" asked Richelieu.

"Monseigneur," replied Père Cinnamon, "vengeance is the pleasure of the gods and police agents.

"On whom are you going to avenge yourself?"

"That's my business."

"You're wrong. If you bump into the Fleming, he'll do you harm."

"We'll see," said Porion. And he left.

"A singular scoundrel," murmured the Maréchal. And he rang for two valets de chambre in order to dress him.

While the Maréchal was attending to his toilette. Porion headed for the Latin Quarter at a brisk pace, saying to himself: *Let's see, then, whether that handsome popinjay Hector de Pierrefeu has been stupid enough to send his news to the Rue Saint-André-des-Arts.*

It was no longer Mardochée that Porion hated, but Hector de Pierrefeu.

LVII

Before following Porion, let us see what had become of our friend Messire Mardochée de Mardoche, the gentleman painter, of whom we lost sight at the moment when Porion made him a gift of the money that he had taken from him the day before in the tavern in the Place Royale.

When he had finally found himself rid of the company of Porion, Mardochée had experienced an indefinable sensation of wellbeing. For seven or eight hours he had no longer been alive. He had almost been buried alive, and such an experience is not of a nature to rose-tint one's thoughts.

Throughout the time when he had been with Porion, even while he was making the portrait of the radiant stranger, Mardochée had considered himself a man condemned to death whose execution has been postponed. It had required nothing less than to find himself in the open air again, free and alone, for him finally to dare to breathe easily.

So, he breathed in one lungful of air after another, murmuring: "Mardochée, my friend, I believe that you've had a narrow escape. Porion can tell me all he likes that he was only joking, but I'm certain that he'd have let me die of starvation in that cellar if he hadn't needed me."

And Mardochée started striding along the streets before him, at random, not knowing where he was going, but continuing to breathe like a man resuscitated. Finally, he gradually calmed down, and experienced the need for a drink, after any emotion, Mardochée became thirsty.

He therefore went into a tavern, and, as he had money in his pocket, he asked for the best wine. Then, drinking in small sips, he remembered the events of the night and morning, one by one. Those of the morning had not been cheerful, but those of the night brought a veritable joy to his heart.

Hector had escaped from the Bastille; he had seen him; he had talked to him. Hector had taken Cécile away, and they would both be happy. Mardochée, Bohemian as he was, had an excellent heart. The happiness of his friends was his own happiness, and as he rejoiced at the thought of seeing Hector and Cécile happy, a memory crossed his mind. They had both charged him with informing Robert Damiens and tranquilizing him with regard to the disappearance of his daughter.

Mardochée, therefore, got up and left the tavern with the intention of going to the Rue Saint-André-des-Arts. While marching straight ahead, he had drawn some distance away from his quarter, and he found himself at the other extremity of the Faubourg Saint-Germain. Night was approaching, and a few drops of rain were beginning to fall.

Mardochée started walking—but he had not gone twenty paces before he stopped, and his hair stood on end. The gentleman painter had felt a terrible suspicion invade his entire being. That suspicion could be translated as:

Porion isn't a man to forgive. He needed me, and he let me go, but he'll catch me again sooner or later; perhaps he's already set assassins in ambush around my house. In consequence, I'd be an idiot and a madman to go and throw myself in the wolf's mouth.

That reflection, you will agree, was not absolutely devoid of common sense.

After having stopped, Mardochée abruptly retraced his steps. *No, no! I won't go toward danger like that. Too bad for Robert Damiens.*

He went down to the edge of the Seine, and walked along the bank as far as the Pont Royal. Then he crossed over, reached the street that passes between the Tuileries and the garden, and did not stop until he reached the Saint-Honoré quarter.

Mardochée had money in his pocket. With money, one is received everywhere. He remembered a hostelry in the Rue des Orties-Saint-Honoré that had for a sign Au Coq-qui-chante. He went directly to knock on the door. The landlord made a slight grimace as he let him in. Everywhere that Mardochée had drunk he had left a small residue of a bill, and he was considered to be what is known as a "bad payer." But the landlord was soon reassured.

"My dear Monsieur Poussegrain," Mardochée said to him, "I've come into a small inheritance and I'm in the process of paying my debts. Do I owe you anything, perchance?" At the same time, he patted his fob pocket, full of pistoles.

That music was agreeable to his host. "Oh, Monsieur Mardochée," he said, "you owe me a pittance; it's hardly worth talking about."

"How much do I owe you?"

"Three écus."

"Here they are." And Mardochée slid into the hostelry, where, for the moment, there were only a few provincial gentlemen.

"Now," he said, "I'd like supper."

He was served with alacrity.

But fear still gripped Mardochée, and he ate without appetite.

When he had finished, he summoned the landlord and said to him, with an air of mystery: "Are you a discreet man?"

"I can be trusted," replied the landlord.

"Well," said Mardochée, "this is my situation. I became entangled with a lady who had an ardent passion for me."

"There's nothing astonishing about that," observed his host, who was always more polite to people who no longer owed him anything, and who thought that a man with pockets full of gold is necessarily a handsome man."

Mardochée saluted. Then he continued: "I've broken with her, but she won't admit herself beaten and wants to catch me in her nets again. She's a woman of quality, who has a numerous domestic staff at her orders; she has me followed by her lackeys. Nevertheless, I've succeeded in shaking them off and I've come to seek refuge with you."

The landlord bowed.

"Please give me a room in your hostelry," Mardochée continued, "for a week or so, and have my meals served there. I'll gladly pay a pistole a day for the board, and even in advance." With those words he took eight pistoles out of his pocket and placed them on the table.

The landlord did not believe a word of Mardochée's story, but did not guess the truth. He thought that Mardochée was fleeing some pitiless creditor who wanted to put him in prison, and as he was no longer a creditor himself, he was interested in the debtor.

Mardochée was thus installed in the Coq-qui-chante. He spent two days shut in his room, not daring to put his nose out of the window, behind whose shutters he hid. When a man with a forbidding manner went by in the street the gentleman painter began to tremble and thought he was seeing an emissary of Porion.

Eventually, on the morning of the third day, he remembered again the promise he had made Cécile.

But how could he keep that promise? Mardochée would not have returned to the Rue Saint-André-des-Arts for all the gold in the world.

Finally, he had an idea. That idea consisted of writing a few words to Firmin, the surgeon, who could not know any more than Robert Damiens what had become of Cécile.

But to whom could he confide the letter?

The post existed then, as it does today, but instead of distributing letters four or five times a day, it only made two deliveries a week.

Nevertheless, Mardochée decided on the latter course, and his is the letter that he went to put in the post himself once night had fallen:

To Monsieur, Monsieur Firmin.
Surgeon Barber
39 Rue Saint-André-des-Arts
Paris
 My very dear friend, I am in danger of death, and any imprudence on your part might doom me.
 This letter received, I beg you to come and see me in the Rue des Orties-Saint-Honoré, at the Coq-qui-chante, and to take care not to be followed.
 Burn this letter carefully.
 One who dare not sign, but whose handwriting you will recognize.

Mardochée had fallen upon a day when letters were delivered. Four hours later, in fact, Firmin arrived. The landlord brought him in great mystery to Monsieur Mardochée de Mardoche's room.

The latter threw his arms around him.

Firmin was sad. "What's happened to you too, then?"

"Ah!" said Mardochée, "I can see that you believe in another misfortune."

"Alas, Cécile..."

"Cécile is safe."

"What are you saying?"

"With Hector, who has escaped from the Bastille."

"You're not deceiving me?"

"Certainly not."

And Mardochée recounted how he had passed from his mansard into Cécile's, the other night, making use of the plank as a bridge.

"My God!" said Firmin. "When her unfortunate father and I saw that plank, we thought she had been abducted a second time. But why didn't you inform us sooner?"

"It's easy for you to talk," said Mardochée. "Do you know that an hour later, as I was asleep, a resinous mask was put over my face?"

"And then?"

"I was tied up, carried away, thrown into a carriage, then into a cellar...?"

"My God!"

"And they wanted to wall me up alive there." And with that, Mardochée recounted his subterranean agony.

"But who liberated you?"

"Père Cinnamon

"He's not dead, then."

"Alas no, and it was him who had me buried alive."

"He took pity on you, then?"

"No," said Mardochée, "he needed a small service, that I rendered him. But he's not a man to forgive."

"Ah!"

"And that's why I'm here. You can take it for granted that he'll try to recapture me, the wretch."

"Truly!"

"I'll even wager that the Rue Saint André-des-Arts is full of his spies."

"I haven't seen anything out of the ordinary in the last two days."

"All the same," said Mardochée, who had the courage of fear, "there's no danger of my going back there. But where is Père Robert?"

"Also disappeared."

"Since when?"

"Since the day when Cécile left.

409

"Bah!" said Mardochée. "He'll turn up. He's a man of bizarre humor: he goes away and comes back on a whim."

And Mardochée, having reassured Firmin as to Cécile's fate, felt his conscience entirely settled, and no longer thought about anything but putting himself beyond the reach of the terrible vengeance of Père Cinnamon.

Firmin spent the evening with his friend Mardochée. The latter kept him to begin with in order to have the pleasure of eating supper with him, and then because he preferred Firmin to wait until after nightfall before leaving. Mardochée was not a complete and irreproachable man, it must be said. He had his hours of bravery and cowardice, as well as his days of wisdom and ignorance. He was in one of his intervals of cowardice—and that is certainly quite excusable, since he had been buried alive and, if hazard had not determined that Porion had need of him, he would have died of hunger in the cellar where he had been walled up.

So, when he was on the point of separating from Firmin, he demanded that the surgeon take a thousand precautions as he left.

"You'll examine the street before going out," he said to him.

"Yes.

"Yes," said Firmin.

"If there are too many people, you'll wait?"

"There's nothing to fear there," said Firmin, smiling, "for the Rue des Orties is virtually deserted."

"Don't go through the common room downstairs; there are always provincials there, and you know how curious provincials are."

"All right!"

"You'll take the little narrow alley at the bottom of the staircase."

"Yes," said Firmin.

"Then, if the landlord escorts you to the door, as it's necessary to anticipate everything and there might be people in the street who know you, don't forget to tell him that you're returning to see your patient tonight."

Firmin could not help smiling, so excessive did Mardochée's fear seem to him. However, as the painter extended his hand to him, he said: "But you're not going to stay here indefinitely?"

"I don't know."

"You'll need to leave some day…"

"I'll leave when I'm certain that Père Cinnamon is no longer thinking about me."

"But how will you acquire that certainty?"

"Well, I don't know…" Then, after that naïve response, Mardochée started reflecting. "Listen," he said.

"Go on."

"Every morning and every evening, examine the Rue Saint-André-des-Arts carefully."

"And then?"

"If that wretch Père Cinnamon has posted spies, you'll recognize them, I'm sure."

"Oh, certainly."

"Then you'll lie low."

"Very well. But what if I see nothing suspicious?"

"Well, you'll come to deliver me...but only after two or three weeks."

"*Adieu*, then," said Firmin, "or rather, *au revoir*. Try not to die of boredom."

"I'll paint," Mardochée replied. "It's a long time, since I've had the leisure to do a painting."

Firmin left, and took all the precautions that had been so minutely recommended to him by Mardochée. Then the latter, who, still being afraid, had drunk reasonably, felt his head growing a little heavy, threw himself down on his bed, and triumphed over the fear to the point of sleeping profoundly.

But he had a dream.

In that dream, Mardochée was rich—so rich that he had just bought the terrain of Mardoche sold by his ancestors. He had restored and furnished the château, the antechambers of which were crowded with valets in bright livery. There were thirty horses in the stable, a hundred dogs in the kennels. As far as the eye could see, he perceived farms that he owned, and the steeples of villages that were in his seigneurie.

And Mardochée, unused to that sudden luxury, saw himself seated in his huge armoried armchair, by the side of a vast fireplace in the hall of honor of the manor, wondering how, in one night, he had made such a fortune, and not finding any solution to the question he posed.

Mardochée was conscious of having slept the previous evening in Paris, in the mansard of the Coq-qui-chante.

And, although he was still there, Mardochée believed that he had woken up in the manor of Mardoche, as rich as a prince in the Thousand-and-One Nights.

Then the décor suddenly changed.

The hall whose walls were charged with family portraits was suddenly succeeded by the dining room of the manor. And in the middle of that room was a laden table buckling under the weight of the most exquisite dishes and the most generous wines.

Mardochée stopped on the threshold of that room. He looked at the table, which was surrounded by costumed waiters, and he saw two places laid.

It appears, he said to himself, *that I have a guest. Who have I invited to supper, then?*

Then the scene changed again. The lackeys and waiters vanished as if by enchantment. In their place, Mardochée no longer saw anyone before him but a little old man dressed in an embroidered coat, who was smiling at him benignly and calling him "Monseigneur" fulsomely—which did not prevent Mardochée from shivering slightly. In that little old man he had recognized Père Cinnamon.

However, in becoming rich, Mardochée had become brave again, and, his fear evaporating, he said to Père Cinnamon: "Ah, rogue! So it's you I've invited to supper?"

"Oh, Monseigneur," Porion replied, "You've never done me such an honor, and were you to do so, I wouldn't think myself worthy of it."

"What are you doing here, then?"

"Monseigneur is forgetting that I'm his steward."

"Oh! You're my steward?"

"Yes, Monseigneur."

"Then you know why I'm rich?"

"Of course. The immense fortune that has just fallen to Monseigneur comes from his wife."

"My wife! I'm married, then?"

"Of course. And from the generosity of the King," Père Cinnamon added.

"What has the King done for me, then?"

"He has endowed Madame de Mardoche."

"Why?"

Père Cinnamon smiled…and did not reply.

Then Mardochée said: "But who's going to sup here with me?"

"Your wife, Monseigneur."

And suddenly, both battens of the door opened, and the stupefied Mardochée saw entering…the beautiful and charming young woman whose portrait he had made in the study of Maître Tavernier, the procurator.

She was his wife!

It was her that the King had endowed, her that had brought him, the vagabond, enough gold to resuscitate the ancient splendor of his ancestors!

And Père Cinnamon's smile told him why the King had endowed the beautiful young woman. Mardochée made a slight grimace at first. But Mardochée was a philosopher, after all, and he lived in a century in which everything that came from the King was gladly considered as a benefit. And he started supping joyfully with his wife, holding gallant conversation with her, and planting amorous kisses on her beautiful shoulders.

However, the scene was to change again.

Suddenly, a door opened. Mardochée then saw a great seigneur come in, whom he recognized by virtue of having seen him before.

That great seigneur was the Duc de Richelieu. He advanced toward Madame de Mardoche, leaned over her, and whispered a few words in her ear.

Then Mardochée frowned, but the Maréchal Duc did not pay the slightest heed to him.

Madame de Mardoche blushed slightly, and then stood up.

Then Mardochée, furious, tried to stand up too—but a mysterious force nailed him to his seat. He saw the young woman make him a slight sign of adieu, and then take the Maréchal's arm. Mardochée tried to speak, but is voice expired in his throat. He tried again to get to his feet, but could not.

Madame de Mardoche went out slowly, on the Maréchal's arm, and the door closed again.

Then Mardochée saw Porion smile.

Making a violent effort, he found the use of speech again, and said to his steward: "Speak, rogue! What does all that signify?"

"What!" replied Père Cinnamon, "Monseigneur is asking me that?"

"Of course."

"What is happening today happens every evening, however."

"What?"

"The Maréchal comes to fetch Madame de Mardoche at the usual hour."

"To do what?"

"Well..." Porion seemed embarrassed,

"Speak, then, scoundrel!" cried Mardochée.

"But...to take her...to the King."

This tie, Mardochée uttered a loud cry, succeeded in tearing himself out of his chair, and launched himself toward the door, shouting: "I don't want it! I don't want it!"

And Mardochée woke up, his heart palpitating and his forehead bathed with sweat, and found himself in the little room in the Coq-qui-chante. The sunlight was frolicking joyfully on the curtains of his bed. His dream had lasted all night. The restored manor, lackeys, horses, princely pack, large farms and traditional steeples had all vanished, as dreams do.

Mardochée was still the gentleman painter, the vagabond painter, who would find himself as poor as before when he had spent Père Cinnamon's last écu.

Only one thing remained to him from his dream. He woke up infatuated with the ideal figure that his brushes had reproduced. Mardochée was in love with the young woman who was doubtless destined for the King's pleasures, and whom he would never see again.

And the poor artist got up with a sigh, opened his box of colors, set up his easel, and, with a feverish hand, he set about reconstituting from memory the portrait of Mademoiselle Espérance de Beaulieu.

LIX

While Mardochée was asleep and dreaming of fortune, Firmin returned to the Latin Quarter. The poor surgeon had only one preoccupation: to find François-Robert Damiens, Cécile's father, and tell him that his daughter was safe, that Monsieur de Pierrefeu was free and that both of them would be happy.

But where was he?

Firmin made scrupulous enquiries of the neighbors, from the fruiterer opposite to the tavern-keeper on the ground floor of his own house. No one had seen Cécile's father during his absence.

In addition, Firmin, remembering his friend Mardochée's recommendation's, darted an investigative glance around the street, and saw nothing suspicious there. He knew the majority of the people he perceived by sight, and did not notice any sinister figure.

I believe that Mardochée is greatly exaggerating the danger he's in, he thought.

To search for Robert in Paris was almost futile. Paris is so vast! The simplest, the wisest and the most reasonable thing was to wait. It was impossible that the poor man would not come, eventually, to wander around the house and enquire after his child, whom he believed he had lost for a second time.

Firmin spent the night at home, only sleeping with one eye, and shuddering at the slightest sound. The night went by and daylight arrived. Firmin did not leave his house, but he went downstairs to the street four or five times in order to keep his promise to Mardochée.

The street had its customary physiognomy.

Mardochée is mad, he thought. *No one is thinking about him, and he's wrong to imprison himself voluntarily in that house in the Rue des Orties.*

The entire day went by without Firmin hearing any mention of Robert Damiens.

There was a further night of insomnia, and when daylight returned, he went down to the street again. No one had seen Damiens.

On the other hand, he was told that a man wearing the long boots of a postillion, a powdered wig and a coat with three rows of yellow buttons had gone into the house opposite and had made enquiries about Messire Mardochée de Mardoche.

Firmin frowned. *Certainly*, he thought, *it's an emissary of the terrible Père Cinnamon.*

He was also told that the postillion had said that he would return at nine o'clock.

And, indeed, as nine o'clock chimed in the neighboring parishes, the postillion reappeared. He went into the tavern on the ground floor of Firmin's house, in which the latter had stayed. He approached the counter and asked again if anyone had seen Messire Mardochée.

"No," said the tavern-keeper, "but there's one of his friends here." And he pointed at Firmin, sitting at a table. The postillion went straight to him.

Firmin looked at him suspiciously. "Who are you?" he asked him.

"Monsieur," the man replied, "my name is Joseph Michelin; I'm a postillion by profession, and I do the relay between Paris and Chantilly."

"Ah!" said Firmin, taking note of his interlocutor's naïve and frank face.

"Yesterday morning," said the postillion, "I conducted in a post-chaise two young gentlemen and a young lady who paid me handsomely."

Firmin shivered.

"One of them gave me a letter for Monsieur Mardochée de Mardoche."

"Where is the letter."

"Here it is. And this purse was added to the letter." The honest postillion took out the purse, which was full of gold, from his pocket.

Firmin cast his eyes over the letter and recognized the handwriting. It was Hector de Pierrefeu's.

"My friend," he said to the postillion, "you can confide all of it to me. Monsieur Mardochée is my friend, and the letter and purse will be faithfully transmitted."

The postillion did not raise any objection.

Then Firmin opened the letter, even though it was not addressed to him, and he read:

My dear friend,

We left in such great haste this morning, Cécile, Monsieur de Mauroy and me, that we forgot the most essential thing: to leave money for you, our good Firmin, and Cécile's father. The postillion who left us at Chantilly appears to us to be an honest man, and we have not hesitated to confide this letter and a hundred pistoles to him. You will certainly have seen Cécile's father. Don't hesitate for a moment; set out, all three of you, leave Paris and take to road to Lille in Flanders. Lodge at a hostelry that has the sign Aux Arquebusiers de Brabant, and there you will certainly have news of us on the day of your arrival.

Hector.

The postillion Joseph Michelin, whom Monsieur de Mauroy, the generous Fleming, had paid handsomely, to use his own expression, refused the pistole that Firmin offered him, accepted a glass of wine, and left.

Then Firmin thought: *It's time to extract Mardochée from his voluntary prison. I'll take him this letter and assure him that no one is occupied with him in the Rue Saint-André-de-Arts.*

And Firmin left the tavern and set forth.

As he arrived at the Carrefour Buci he noticed a little old man with an amiable expression, who stepped out of his way. Firmin had never seen the little old man before, and he scarcely suspected that he had just encountered Père Cinnamon.[45]

Père Cinnamon, who knew Firmin perfectly, continued on his way, then retraced his steps in a hesitant fashion, and ended up saluting Firmin and saying to him: "Excuse me, Monsieur."

Firmin stopped and returned his salute.

"I'm a stranger in Paris," Père Cinnamon continued, adopting a strong Norman accent for the occasion, "and I can no longer find my way."

"Where are you going?" asked Firmin, in whom the amiable old man inspired no suspicion.

Père Cinnamon had divined that Firmin was preparing to go over to the right bank. "My dear Monsieur," he said, "I've been traveling the streets one after another for an hour without being able to find the Rue de l'Arbre-Sec, where I'm staying."

"Come with me, then," said Firmin. "I'll be able to show you all the more easily because it's on my way."

The amiable old man went with him, offering profuse apologies.

Firmin went down to the Pont-Neuf and traversed it, and then turned on to the Quai de l'École and took the first street on the right. "Here it is." he said.

"Oh, a thousand thanks," said Père Cinnamon. I recognize it now."

Firmin returned his salute and headed for the Rue Saint-Honoré.

Père Cinnamon waited until he had turned the corner of the Rue de l'Arbre-Sec, and then, when Firmin was out of sight, he murmured: "Either I'm mistaken, or my man is going to pay a little visit to our turtle-doves."

Porion possessed to the highest degree the marvelous art that policemen have of rendering themselves unrecognizable in a trice. He took a blond wig out of his pocket and put it on his head, taking his hat in his hand. He unbuttoned the long overcoat he was wearing and put it over his arm; he was then clad in a short blue jacket.

Then he lengthened his stride, and in three paces he was in the Rue Saint-Honoré. Porion no longer resembled the old man that had just asked the surgeon Firmin the way, any more than night resembled day.

When he was in the Rue Saint-Honoré in his turn, he perceived Firmin, who was continuing his route in the direction of the Palais Cardinal. Porion increased his pace. Firmin went past the Palais without stopping; Porion continued to follow him. Firmin arrived thus at the Rue des Frondeurs. At that moment,

---

[45] The reader will probably remember, although the author clearly does not, that not only did Firmin see Père Cinnamon during Cécile's abduction, but the narrative voice informed us then that he already knew him.

Porion overtook him, Firmin glanced at him distractedly, and did not recognize him; then he turned into the Rue des Orties.

Porion saw him arrive at the door of the Coq-qui-chante.

Good, he thought, *I'm fixed now*. And he slipped into a doorway and waited until Firmin had gone in. After that he went back at a rapid pace to the Rue Saint-Honoré, jumped into an empty chamber-pot that was passing and demanded to be taken to the Rue Saint-Sauveur.

It was then just after nine forty-five.

I have time in hand, thought Porion, who promised the coachman a good tip if he went quickly.

On great occasions, Père Cinnamon recovered the devouring activity of youth. Less than an hour after Firmin had entered the Coq-qui-chante, Master Poussegrain, the worthy hotelier, was on his doorstep when he saw a chamber-pot coming up the street laden with a large trunk and two valises.

The chamber-pot stopped outside the door of the hostelry, and a man enveloped in an ample traveling cloak got down.

Master Poussegrain approached him hurriedly.

The traveler said to him: "My dear Monsieur, my name is Corbon; I'm a lawyer in Melun and I've come to Paris to sustain an important suit. Friends have advised me to stay in your house, telling me that one finds a good table and a comfortable abode there.

And Porion, for it was him, although unrecognizable and even better made up, went into the hostelry, while the waiters hastened to unload his baggage.

"Do you desire a meal right away?" the hotelier asked the pretended traveler.

"What time is it?"

"Half past ten."

"Oh, no," he replied. "I don't have time. I need to go to the Palais. Quickly, take me to my room, so that I can change. I'll have lunch when I return.

At that moment, Messire Mardochée de Mardoche scarcely suspected that the man whose name alone gave him gooseflesh was so close to him, and we shall follow Firmin into the room where the gentleman painter had imprisoned himself voluntarily.

LX

Firmin had gone straight upstairs.

Mardochée believed that he was so unsafe that he locked his door and never opened it without asking who was knocking. Firmin therefore knocked; but he did not obtain any reply.

He put his eye to the keyhole. He saw Mardochée with his back turned o him, standing at his easel, working ardently.

Firmin knocked again, more loudly. This time, Mardochée seemed to emerge from a sort of contemplation, turned abruptly toward the door and asked in an ill-humored fashion what was wanted of him.

"It's me," said Firmin.

Mardochée recognized his voice and came to open the door.

Firmin came in, while the painter closed the door again, and took two paces toward the easel. He then found himself in the presence of a woman's portrait, and thought that Mardochée had created an imaginary head.

"Ah! A pretty face," he said.

"And I believe it's a good resemblance," said Mardochée, who came back toward the easel and started contemplating ecstatically.

"Resemblance?"

"Yes."

"It's a portrait, then?"

"Made from memory."

"Where's the model, then?"

"The model is a woman with whom I'm madly in love," murmured Mardochée, with a sigh.

"Good!" said Firmin, smiling. "You're often in love, my friend."

"Oh, this time it's for life." And at that moment, Mardochée, whose eyes were feverish and his features distraught, gave Firmin the impression of a madman.

"But who is this woman with whom you're in love?" asked the surgeon.

"The one of whom I made a first portrait."

"Through the intermediary of Père Cinnamon?"

That name brought Mardochée back down to earth, for, since he had resuscitated Mademoiselle Espérance on canvas, the gentleman painter had been living somewhat in the clouds.

"Ah!" he said. "The wretch! You've come to talk to me about him, haven't you?"

"No," said Firmin.

"You haven't seen him?"

"Not at all."

"But his spies are looking for me?"

"I don't think so."

"You have no bad news for me?"

"Absolutely none."

Mardochée breathed out.

"On the contrary," said Firmin. "I've brought you good news."

"What?"

Firmin threw the purse on the table, which clinked pleasantly.

"Gold!" exclaimed Mardochée, who was rarely charmed by that music.

"And gold that comes from our friends." At the same time, Firmin held out Hector's letter.

Mardochée read it.

"I believe," the surgeon said to him then, "that when we're in Flanders, you'll no longer tremble merely at the name of Père Cinnamon.

Mardochée darted a sad glance at the portrait, which was almost finished. "And my amour?" he said

"What?" said Firmin.

"I'm seriously in love," signed Mardochée.

"With a woman that you'll never see again."

"Who knows?"

"A woman who is destined..."

"Oh! Shut up!" cried the gentleman painter, stamping his foot. And Firmin saw his eyes blaze, and his entire visage express a violent anger. "I love her, I tell you," he repeated.

"You're mad."

"If you knew the dream that I had the other night..."

"What did you dream?"

Mardochée appeared to calm down somewhat. He sat down on the foot of his bed and started telling is friend about the bizarre dream, which we know.

Firmin listened with a sad smile.

"My poor friend," he said, "all the more reason to leave. You'll never see that woman again...and if you ever did see her again..."

Mardochée put his head in his hands.

"Oh!" he said. "I'm a wretch!"

"Why?"

"Instead of lending myself to the desires of that infamous Père Cinnamon and making the portrait that was to be set before the King's eyes, I should have opened the door, thrown myself at her feet and said: 'Flee, Mademoiselle, flee!'"

"It's too late," said Firmin.

"Who knows?" said Mardochée.

"What do you mean?"

"Perhaps the King hasn't seen the portrait yet."

"All right—but where is the young woman?"

"I don't know."

"Then how can you warn her?"

"That's true, murmured Mardochée, whom that reflection plunged into a profound dejection.

"My friend," said Firmin, "forget all that, and think about our imminent departure. I have a presentiment that I'll find Cécile's father today, and that we'll be able to set forth this evening."

"For Flanders?"

"Yes."

Mardochée darted another sorrowful glance at the portrait. "Is it necessary to renounce seeing her again?"

"I believe so," said Firmin.

Suddenly, however, Mardochée slapped his forehead. "I've got an idea," he said.

"What?"

"I know where the procurator lives."

"The one in whose house you made the portrait?"

"Yes. What if I went to see him?"

"With what objective?"

"I'll tell him about the danger the young woman is in."

"But my friend," said Firmin, "you're forgetting that if you were introduced into the procurator's house, if you were hidden in a room next to his study, and if the procurator was obliging enough to retain his pretty client for as long as possible, it was because he had an objective—that of finishing the portrait."

"Well?"

"And, in consequence, he knew what they wanted to do with it."

Mardochée uttered a sigh that resembled a groan.

"The procurator won't tell you anything," Firmin continued. "Perhaps he'll even have his clerks lock you up."

"Oh, I'd defend myself."

"And he'll warn Père Cinnamon."

At that terrible name, fear gripped Mardochée again. "Yes," he said, "you're right, Firmin. It's necessary to renounce it."

"And leave Paris as soon as possible," the young surgeon added, getting to his feet.

"You're leaving?"

"Yes, I'm going back to the Rue Saint-André-des-Arts. Something tells me that Cécile's father has returned there."

"So we're leaving this evening?"

"Yes. Shall I'll come back this evening in any case?"

"All right," said Mardochée.

421

Firmin took a step toward the door.

"And you're leaving the gold?"

"We'll need it for our journey. Keep it."

Mardochée opened the door again and the surgeon drew away, saying: "Until this evening."

"Until this evening," Mardochée repeated. And he locked the door again carefully. Then he went to sit down at the easel and fell back into a contemplative reverie.

It was not six minutes since Firmin had gone when someone knocked on the door again. Mardochée was so absorbed at that moment that he forgot his ordinary prudence. In any case, he thought that Firmin had forgotten to make him some final recommendation, and, instead of asking who was knocking, in accordance with the habit he had adopted in the last two days, he opened the door without suspicion.

Suddenly, however, Messire Mardochée de Mardoche recoiled, his hair standing on end, his throat dry and his eyes bulging. One might have thought that the head of Medusa had just surged forth in front of him.

He found himself face to face with Porion.

Père Cinnamon also seemed slightly astonished. "Oh, damn!" he said, "If I thought I'd find you…!" And he came into the room and closed the door.

Mardochée was so troubled that he did not even think of leaping on his sword, which was on the bed.

Porion had more presence of mind; he swiftly took possession of it. "That ensures," he said, "that you won't deliver yourself to any extravagance, and we can chat tranquilly." At the same time, he perceived the purse full of money on the table. "Oho!" he said. "What's this?"

And, sword in hand, he took another step toward Mardochée, who was trembling more than ever.

LXI

Porion had the eye of a police agent; what other men see in detail, he saw in a single glance, and in him, thought was at the service of that gaze; at the same time as his eye embraced the ensemble, his thought generalized everything.

He picked the purse, telling himself that if Firmin had brought that money it was because that money did not come from him, but from the Vicomte de Mauroy, who distributed gold so easily. Thus, before leaving, the Fleming had been in communication with Firmin. In order for the Fleming to have sent the gold, it was also necessary that he had brought Hector, and perhaps also Cécile. What was the destination of that gold? That was easily deducible. Hector and Cécile wanted Mardochée and Firmin to come and join them.

He made all these reflections in the time it took him to take two steps toward Mardochée. Mardochée was facing him, in the attitude of a bird fascinated by a reptile.

If Porion had been the master of his time, this is what he would have done:

He would have exchanged a few banal words with Mardochée, would have done his best to reassure him, and would have left. Then he would have lain in ambush in a nearby street and would have waited until Firmin came to collect the gentleman painter, and would have followed them when they left. That was the simplest means of discovering the secret of Hector's retreat.

But Porion did not have time to spare. He had to be at the Palais by noon at the latest, and he would only emerge again to conduct Mademoiselle Espérance to Monsieur de Richelieu's house, and then to Marly.

Therefore, in order simultaneously to obey his interests, intimately linked to those of Monsieur de Richelieu, and his animosity toward Hector and the Fleming, he had to cut the matter short and go to work rapidly.

It was therefore necessary that Mardochée talk, and for Porion to be audacious.

After having locked the door, he put the key in his pocket. Then, although he was already armed with Mardochée's sword, he took from the same pocket the pistol that he had been carrying since his adventure in the Singe Vert—an adventure that had begun so badly but had finished so well for him.

"My dear Monsieur de Mardochée," he said, the, "You can see that I'm entirely able to hold you in respect, but that's purely for form's sake, for I wish you well and not harm. God is my witness that when I came in here, I did not expect to find you."

Those words reassured Mardochée somewhat. "What?" he said. "You didn't expect to find me?"

"No."

"Who were you looking for, then?"

"People you know."

"Really?" said Mardochée. "Then it's not me that you're after?"

"Not at all."

"Well, as you can see, the people you're looking for aren't here. Give me back my sword, then, and..."

Porion stated to smile. "And you want me to go, don't you?"

"Too true!" said Mardochée, naively, "After the trick you played on me..."

"Fear's got hold of you, I can see. The proof is that you've taken refuge here, and you've told the hotelier a story, and...you don't go out by day or night, for fear of encountering me. That's it isn't it?"

Mardochée bowed his head.

"That's all the more childish on your part, my poor friend," Porion went on, beginning to address Mardochée in a familiar fashion, "because I have no rancor against you."

"You've already told me that, but..."

"But you don't believe it?"

"Well..."

"Well, let's chat, and I'll prove it to you."

Mardochée waited.

"You wanted to have my hanged, it's true and I held that against you greatly," said Porion. "Let's agree that I had some justification for that."

"I don't deny it, but..."

"But since then, there are two people who have done me a much worse turn than you."

"And those two people are...?"

"Are a Fleming you don't know and a young man you know, named Hector."

"What was the turn?" asked Mardochée, who wanted to play the innocent.

"I had both of them locked in the Bastille."

"Oh!"

"And they got out."

"Is that possible?"

"Mardochée, my friend," said Père Cinnamon, I don't have time to jabber uselessly. Don't play games with me, since you know perfectly well that they escaped three days ago."

"But I swear to you..."

"As this purse proves, which they sent to you."

"All right," said Mardochée. "What bad turn are you talking about?"

"Their escape, which dishonors me and makes me pass, in the eyes of the Lieutenant de Police, whose esteem I prize greatly, for an incompetent."

"Really?"

"Which means that the anger I sense against them has dominated that which I sensed against you, and I'm ready to pardon you entirely..."

"You're not mocking me, Père Cinnamon?"

"If you render me a little service."

"And what is that service?"

"You tell me where the two rogues are."

"I don't know."

"But that gold comes from them?"

"I don't deny it."

"And the gold was doubtless accompanied by a letter."

Mardochée shivered, and with an instinctive gesture he put his hand to his hose, in the pocket of which he had stuffed the letter.

"Good," said Porion, "I was right. Now, my friend, it's necessary to give me that letter."

"Never," said Mardochée.

"Then I'll kill you."

"You can kill me if you wish," said Mardochée, suddenly recovering his courage, "but it won't be said that I betrayed my friend." And he recoiled from the point of the sword that Porion raised toward his face.

As he stepped back, he unmasked the easel. Porion's eyes fell on the portrait, and the fellow uttered an exclamation of surprise.

"What's this?"

Mardochée, pale a moment ago, could not help blushing.

Then Porion guessed. He lowered the sword, stopped advancing toward the painter and said to him, compassionately: "Oh, my poor friend, you're in love."

"Madly in love," said Mardochée, naively.

"Poor boy!"

Mardochée had fallen back into ecstasy before the portrait, and was no longer thinking either about Hector or Porion, who had threatened to kill him a moment ago.

The latter threw the sword on to the bed, but he kept the pistol in his left hand. Then, approaching Mardochée and placing his right hand on his shoulder, he said: "You'd like to see her again, wouldn't you?"

"Oh, if it were possible..."

"Everything is possible, when I wish it/"

"And...you'd...wish it?"

"That depends."

Mardochée shivered again.

"There's more," Porion went on, "And if you'd like to be good, sit down on that chair and don't get carried away, we'll chat."

"All right," said Mardochée, and did as he was bid.

"You suspect, don't you, who I wanted to have a portrait of that lovely person?"

"Yes," stammered Mardochée. "The King..."

"Well, extraordinarily enough, the King only finds her moderately to his taste."

"That's impossible."

"The King is amorous for another woman, and I'll wager that he'll content himself with supping with the young woman and send her away afterwards with a portfolio stuffed with cashable bills."

"The King is having supper with her, then?"

"Yes."

"When?"

"This evening."

"Ah!" said Mardochée, who had a glint of jealous anger in his eyes."

"Whatever happens," Porion went on, "the girl won't have too much about which to complain. She'll have a nice dowry, and as she has absolute confidence in me, she won't refuse the husband that I propose to her."

"Oh!" said Mardochée, shivering from head to toe. "And...that husband..."

"It might well be you."

"Père Cinnamon," said Mardochée, in a strangled voice. "I believe you're mocking me."

"Would you like me to prove the contrary?"

"Speak."

"You're going to come with me."

"Where?"

"To the Palais de Justice. She has a suit that is being judged today, and you'll see her."

"I'll see her!" exclaimed Mardochée, losing his head.

"Of course—but before then, it's necessary to give me that letter."

"Hector's letter?"

"Yes."

Mardochée hesitated again.

Suddenly, he made the reflection that his friends were far away, and that, no matter what diligence he employed, Porion could not overtake them.

"Truly?" he said. "I'll see her?"

"Yes, if you give me the letter."

A cloud passed over Mardochée's brow. He looked at the portrait, was dazzled, felt his heart hammering, and, with a feverish gesture, he handed the letter to Porion.

The latter took possession of it eagerly and read it. But while reading it, the recoiled toward the bed, and, uttering a cry of rage, he took possession of Mardochée's sword again.

"Gone!" he murmured. "Gone!"

"What are you doing?" cried Mardochée, who saw him with the sword in his hand for a second time.

"My lad," said Porion, in whom reading the letter had produced a sudden change of mind, "I've just reflected, and as I want to make you party to my reflections, keep your distance."

Nonplussed, Mardochée had stopped two paces way, and was looking at Potion in amazement.

"I've promised that you'll see the demoiselle," Porion went on, calmly, "and I'll keep my word, but, all things considered, I'd prefer that it isn't today."

"Why not?" said Mardochée, his forehead bathed in swear, already repenting of his treason.

"You'll understand. You're in love, aren't you?"

"Madly in love."

"Well, you will be tomorrow as much as today, and I'd rather you didn't do anything stupid."

"What do you mean?"

"How do I know? See the demoiselle, say something stupid to her—as, for example, that in going with me she's accompanying a police agent, that Maréchal de Richelieu, whom she's going to thank for winning her lawsuit, is the King's accomplice...and a host of other things..."

Mardochée felt his hair standing on end.

"In consequence," added Porion, "I'll take my precautions."

And he retreated as far as the door, still keeping Mardochée at bay with the sword, and he opened the door, shouting: "Hey, Master Poussegrain! Come up here quickly!"

LXII

It was necessary that Porion could count on the hotelier reliably to hail him from the top of the stairs like that.

The fact is that before entering Mardochée's room, Porion had taken his petty precautions. While the inn's employees hastened to take his baggage into a room and install him there, Porion had stayed on the landing. The room he had been given was situated underneath Mardochée's. So, when Firmin came down. Porion recognized him, but, still convinced that Hector and the Fleming were in the hostelry, he limited himself to telling the waiter that he wanted to talk to the landlord.

The waiters went out, and Master Poussegrain hastened to come up to the pretended traveler's room. Porion took off his overcoat and his wig, to the great amazement of the landlord, and said to him, coldly: "Perhaps you don't know me?"

"I have the honor of seeing you for the first time," replied Poussegrain.

"Good. Have you heard mention of Monsieur de Sartine?"

At that name the landlord recoiled.

"I'm his lieutenant," said Porion, tranquilly. At the same time, he took from his pocket a green card, which he set before Master Poussegrain' eyes.

"A policeman!" the latter exclaimed.

"Who doesn't wish any harm to your establishment," Porion said, "and who will even offer you his services on occasion."

Slightly reassured, Master Poussegrain bowed.

"But who, for the moment, has need of you," Porion added. "You have suspect individuals here, and it's possible that I'll have recourse to you. Go downstairs, remain at the bottom of the staircase, and if I call you, come up with ropes and two of your sturdiest waiters."

In all times, furnished hotels, inns and all public places, have had need of the police. Master Poussegrain therefore made no objection, and went downstairs, greatly troubled.

Then, as we have seen, Porion irrupted into the room from which Firmin had emerged, and which he believed to be occupied by Hector and the Fleming.

You will understand now why Porion had called Master Poussegrain with so much confidence.

Master Poussegrain came upstairs. He was accompanied by two robust waiters, who were carrying coils of rope over their shoulders.

"Ah! Wretch!" said the hotelier, on seeing Mardochée, held prudently at sword's point. "How can you compromise an honest and tranquil house like mine?"

"My dear Monsieur Poussegrain," replied Porion, smiling, "You're exaggerating things greatly. Your establishment is not compromised."

"Oh!" said Poussegrain.

"In addition, Messire Mardochée de Mardoche here," the police agent went on, "is a friend of mine, and I beg you not to insult him."

Master Poussegrain looked at Porion with a bewildered expression. Why, then, had he been asked to come up?

"Except," Potion continued, "he's a young man, and a trifle light-headed, and as I'm particularly interested in him, you're going to render me a service—that of tying him up, hands and feet first, and then gagging him."

Mardochée uttered a roar of fury. But Master Poussegrain's two waiters rushed upon him and knocked him down immediately. He was tied up and reduced to impotence in a trice.

"Is it necessary to send for a chamber-pot?" asked the hotelier, thinking that Porion was going to take his prisoner away.

"Not at all," said Porion. "My young friend is going to stay here."

"Oh!" said Master Poussegrain, slightly astonished.

"And you'll take good care of him."

"Really?" said the landlord, his astonishment increasing.

Mardochée no longer had anything free but his gaze, for after having been tied up he had been gagged with a handkerchief, but he compensated or that by rolling his eyes furiously.

Porion took out his watch. It marked a quarter to noon. "Listen to me carefully," he said to Poussegrain.

The latter waited.

"You'll keep my friend until six o'clock this evening."

"All right," said the hotelier.

"At six o'clock, you'll take off his gag and render him the use of his limbs. If he's hungry and thirsty, you'll give him supper, and if he asks to take a stroll, you won't oppose it."

"Which is to say," said Poussegrain, "that we'll set him free?"

"The most complete liberty—but between now and then, you'll answer to me with your head."

And Porion made an amicable gesture of farewell to Mardochée, who was foaming behind his gag, and he left.

"I'm going to be late," he murmured, running downstairs. "Monsieur le Maréchal will be looking for me everywhere."

At the corner of the Rue des Orties and the Rue des Frondeurs, Porion leapt into a chamber-pot, promise the coachman a petty écu if he made haste, and indicated the Palais de Justice as his destination.

A quarter of an hour later, he arrived in the hall where Mademoiselle Espérance de Beaulieu's lawsuit was being judged.

On the way, Porion had changed his appearance again—which is to say that he had put his overcoat on again, removed his wig, resumed the attitude of an old and decrepit individual, to the extent that when he emerged from the carriage, the amazed coachman only recognized his voice.

The Duc de Richelieu had been at his post for a long time, and he was even parading an anxious gaze over the crowd that filled the enclosure of the Tribunal, searching for Porion, who was akin to his right arm in the affair.

The case had just been called, and Mademoiselle Espérance's advocate was explaining his demand to the judges. The young woman, dressed in black, in a modest and dignified attitude, was sitting next to Maître Tavernier, her procurator.

Her adversaries, who had doubtless caught wind of Mademoiselle de Beaulieu's high protections, had not appeared, and were represented by their procurator.

The gazes of the crowd were fixed on Espérance, whose sovereign beauty excited a murmur of admiration. The presence of the Maréchal had also caused a sensation. Mademoiselle de Beaulieu had to be very interesting, or be very nobly related, for a great seigneur like the Maréchal to come to witness the arguments of her suit.

Finally, the Maréchal perceived Porion.

The little old man with the debonair manner curbed himself, made himself small, offered effusive apologies to the people who blocked his path, and finally succeeded in insinuating himself close to Monsieur de Richelieu. That made the people who had begun to murmur fell silent, full of respect on seeing him in such good company.

The Maréchal leaned toward him.

"I feared that you weren't coming," he said,

"Oh, Monseigneur..."

"And I was beginning to find myself greatly embarrassed."

"I was delayed," said Porion, apologetically. "Has Mademoiselle de Beaulieu perceived Your Lordship?"

"Not yet."

"I'll try to get her to turn round," said Porion. And he slid as far as Maître Tavernier, who was consulting his dossiers while the adversaries' advocate replied.

"Mademoiselle," whispered Porion in Espérance's ear.

Espérance shivered, and turned round. "Oh, it's you, my friend," she said. Hr voice was emotional, and he understood the anguish that was gripping her soul.

"Have courage," said Porion. "But turn round a little further."

Espérance obeyed; then she saw the Maréchal, and shivered.

"You see," said Porion. "His Excellency has kept his promise. "You'll win your suit, Mademoiselle."

"May God hear you!" said the young woman.

"First of all, your case is excellent," Porion went on, in a low voice, "but the presence of Monsieur le Maréchal here has an enormous influence. Ordinarily, the judges are asleep. Today, they're listening with scrupulous attention."

Porion's words reassured the young woman somewhat. She turned to the Maréchal for a second time; he saluted her with his hand. Then, blushing, she resumed her original attitude, listening attentively to her adversaries' reply.

The affair lasted about three hours. There were replies after replies, arguments upon arguments.

Finally, the president announced that the debates were closed, and the case heard. While the judges deliberated in low voices, Maître Tavernier leaned toward Patureau, who was seated to his left, while Espérance was to his right. "I believe the case is won," he said.

"Ah!" said Patureau, in a voice strangled with emotion.

"But if so," Tavernier went on, "you need to follow me immediately."

"Where to?"

"To the clerk."

"I'll go," said Patureau, who would have gone to the end of the world provided that the case was won.

A veritable agitation reigned in the auditorium, all gazes concentrated more than ever on Espérance.

Finally, the president rang his bell and covered his head. Then complete silence was established. One could have heard a fly buzzing. From that moment on, Mademoiselle Espérance no longer saw or heard anything but the president.

The judgment, justified at length, gave victory in the case to Mademoiselle de Beaulieu.

Espérance uttered a cry.

"Come on, come on," said Tavernier to Patureau.

Espérance was so emotional that she leaned on Porion. "You see," the latter said. "The Maréchal..."

He did not finish, for Espérance seized his arm eagerly and, recovering all her energy, she said: "Take me to him! Take me, quickly...so that I can throw myself at his feet to express my gratitude."

The crowd, excited and joyful, opened spontaneously before the young woman, who had forgotten Patureau, and, giving her arm to Porion, was searching for the Maréchal in the place where he had been a little while before.

But the Maréchal had disappeared.

"Where is he?" Porion asked animatedly. "Where is he?"

"Who?" asked a member of the audience.

"Monsieur de Richelieu."

"He's just left."

"Oh!" said Espérance, uttering a new exclamation.

"He wanted to hide from your gratitude," said Porion, "but perhaps we'll catch up with him at the door of the Palais. Let's run!

"Let's run!" repeated Espérance, who did not notice that Patureau was no longer with her.

And she allowed Porion to draw her away.

LXIII

The young woman, still drawn on by Porion, traversed the Salle des Pas-Perdus and arrived at the door of the Palais. The Maréchal's carriage was no longer there. Porion spotted a man that he knew, whom he had posted there in advance.

"Have you seen the Maréchal?" he said.

"The Maréchal's just left," said the man. "He climbed into his carriage and I heard him say to the footman: 'To the house.'"

Porion turned to Espérance. "Mademoiselle," he said, "it's absolutely necessary to thank Monsieur de Richelieu."

"Yes," said Espérance, "yes, certainly."

Porion signaled to the driver of a chamber-pot that was stationed in the square. The vehicle approached. Porion helped Espérance to climb into it.

"But where's Patureau?" she said, then.

"Patureau is with your procurator, who has taken him to the clerk," said Porion. "Oh, Mademoiselle, you have time to go and thank the Maréchal and return to your apartment in the Place Royale ten times over before Patureau gets back. Monsieur Tavernier needs him or two full hours. It's not sufficient to obtain judgments—they need to be executed."

"In that case, let's go," said Espérance.

"To the Hôtel de Hanovre!" Porion shouted to the coachman.

The chamber-pot set forth with lightning rapidity. If Mademoiselle Espérance had more experience of Paris, she would have been astonished that a cab-horse could go at such a pace.

In a matter of minutes they had crossed the distance that separated the Palais from the Rue de Hanovre, and entered the Maréchal's house.

"Ah!" said the steward, who ran to open the carriage door, "you've arrived too late, my dear Porion."

"Too late!" said the latter, feigning astonishment and disappointment so well that Mademoiselle Espérance did not doubt his sincerity for an instant.

"Yes, my dear," said the steward. "Monsieur le Maréchal has gone."

"Gone!"

"Ten minutes ago."

"But where has he gone?"

"To Marly."

"But where's Marly?" asked the young woman, increasingly desolate.

"Two leagues from Paris."

"Well," said Espérance, "let's go there!"

Devil's honor! thought Porion, whose heart was swelling with an infernal joy. *One doesn't even need to push the ewe into the wolf's mouth.*

And, in order not to give Espérance time to reflect, he hastened to order the coachman to take the road to Marly. The chamber-pot resumed its rapid course.

They were soon out of Paris and traveling along the Chemin de Courbevoie.

It was not yet dark, but it was already no longer daylight, and the sun had disappeared over the horizon.

Entirely given over to the joy of having win her suit, which assured the splendor of her house, represented henceforth by the young brother whom she had brought up and whom she had served as a mother, Espérance raced along the road to Marly without the slightest dread. In any case, did not Porion, her traveling companion, with his gray hair, and his benevolent manner, inspire the most absolute confidence?

Soon, the chamber-pot had crossed the Seine and reached the hill of Courbevoie.

Then Espérance, to whom Porion had not ceased to recount a host of imaginary stories about the noble heart and good deeds of the Maréchal, put her head out of the window. She saw tall trees and a deserted countryside.

"Are we far away?" she asked, slightly troubled by that solitude.

"We're more than half way," said Porion. "Are you afraid, Mademoiselle?"

"Are the roads entirely safe?" she said.

"Oh, most certainly," he said. "One encounters people in the King's service at every moment."

That name made Espérance shiver."

"Is the King at Marly, then?" she asked.

"No, at Versailles."

"Then why does one encounter the people you mention?"

"Because it's the same road—except that, to reach Marly, one turns left."

"Ah!" said the young woman, entirely reassured.

Porion resumed his stories, and the chamber-pot continued on its way.

It went through the village of Courbevoie, then that of Nanterre, and reached Reuil. There it turned left and followed a road that rose up there flank of the hills of Bougival, passed La-Celle-Saint-Cloud at a distance, and headed toward Marly.

Half way up the hill, there was an inn. That inn, which was situated approximately half way between Versailles and Paris, near Marly, was the rendezvous of all the vehicles and all the horsemen that passed that way. They had a drink there while the horses were given oats.

At the moment when the chamber-pot reached the inn, there were two musketeers at the door. Porion called to them. "Hey, Messieurs, are you going to Paris?"

"We're coming from it," one replied.

"Then you're going to Versailles?"

"Yes."

"Passing through Marly?"

"Naturally."

"You'd be very kind, in that case, to escort us as far as Marly," said Porion.

"Gladly," said the two musketeers.

"Now," said Porion quietly to Espérance, "you're no longer afraid, are you? We're traveling under a good escort."

"No," said Espérance.

And the chamber-pot set off again, with the two musketeers to either side.

Son, they had reached the top of the hill and went into the forest, the profound obscurity of which the chamber-pot's single lantern only penetrated to a depth or two or three paces in advance. But Mademoiselle Espérance was no longer afraid.

Was she not escorted by two of the King's musketeers?

She could hear the steel scabbards of their swords beating the shiny rumps of the horses, and the hoof-beats clattering over the sonorous road.

They traversed the forest, and the château soon appeared.

Since the previous reign, Marly had been quite deserted. The King did not go there often, and when he came, it was with one or two courtiers, to go hunting in the park.

One the other hand, Monsieur de Richelieu, who was the superintendent of the petty crown buildings—which is to say, semi-royal residences—came quite often. The King had even authorized him to give fine suppers there and gallant rendezvous. There was a limited domestic staff at Marly: a steward, half a dozen footmen, two coachmen, two grooms, two cooks and the gardeners, that was all.

As the orders that had been give that morning were in the Maréchal's name, the steward had assumed that it was the latter who as giving a supper. So the château was barely illuminated, and at the gate of the park, Mademoiselle Espérance, who had just parted company with the musketeers, in thanking them for their courtesy, had put her head out of the door, saw the château at the end of the avenue and believed that she was arriving at the Maréchal's residence.

Porion get down at the end of the avenue.

Two domestics had come with torches to meet the vehicle.

"Is Monsieur the Maréchal here?" asked Porion.

"Yes, since half an hour ago," was he response.

"As long as he's willing to receive me," said Espérance.

"Here," said the valet, who knew his role, "Monsieur le Maréchal always receives." And he led Porion and the young woman to the perron, the steps of which they climbed.

Then they traversed a large vestibule whose walls were covered with paintings and hunting trophies. The young woman found herself on the threshold of an elegant little drawing-room were a good first was blazing.

"Monsieur le Maréchal will come," said the valet,

Espérance was cold after the journey. She approached the fireplace and exposed her little feet to the flames of the hearth.

In the meantime, Porion paraded a naïve gaze around him and said: "He must be a very rich and great seigneur. I'd like to be lodged like this."

The valet had retired discreetly, and a quarter of an hour went by without the Maréchal appearing. But if Mademoiselle Espérance was impatient to thank her protector, Porion was no less so to see the Maréchal arrive. Once Espérance was in the latter's hands, his responsibility ceased and he could leave.

Porion was in a hurry to get back to Paris.

Why? He had the intention of going to find Monsieur de Sartine, asking him for money, full powers and post-horses, in order to set off at top sped in pursuit of the Fleming and Hector de Pierrefeu. Porion wanted to avenge the Tartar's death.

So, as Mademoiselle Espérance was beginning to give evidence of some anxiety at not seeing Monsieur de Richelieu appear, the old wretch said to himself: *I'll go see what's happening.*

And he went out of the drawing room, leaving Espérance all alone.

In the vestibule, Porion met the Maréchal. "Come quickly, Monseigneur," he said, in a low voice. "The girl's impatient."

"Oh," said Richelieu, with a smile, "I'll persuade her to be patient. The king won't arrive until ten."

"It's scarcely eight," Porion observed.

"The essential thing is that she's here."

"Of course, but..."

"But what?"

"How are you going to keep her here for two hours, Monseigneur?"

"I have an idea," said the Maréchal.

"What?"

"The King is nervous and impressionable," Richelieu went on, "and if that skittish beauty is going to utter screams and shed tears at a first interview, the King is capable of going away in an ill humor."

"Then?"

"What do you think about a narcotic?"

"Well," said Porion. "That's your affair, Monseigneur, not mine. Perhaps it would be best. *Adieu*, Monseigneur."

"What" You're going?"

"Yes, you have no further need of me. In any case, it's necessary that all the credit for the adventure goes to you."

And while the Maréchal headed toward the door of the drawing room, Porion went into the courtyard, where the chamber-pot was still harnessed, climbed into it and said to the coachman:

"To Paris, now, and swiftly. You'll have a good tip, and if your horse breaks down, you'll have another. It's the King who'll pay!"

LXIV

When he was serving his King, Maréchal de Richelieu was full of personal abnegation, and he was able to renounce his advantages.

He had arrived an hour before Espérance's chamber-pot, and that hour had been sufficient for him to prepare his little comedy.

Richelieu had an apartment in the château, and he found a valet de chambre there specifically attached to his person. That valet de chambre, who had taken the Maréchal to the wardrobe where he usually put on his evening dress, had hastened to set out pomades, cosmetics and perfumes while Richelieu took off his traveling clothes.

But the Maréchal began to smile. "My poor Lafleur," he said, "I'm fifty-nine years old today." Lafleur, not understanding, had stared at the Maréchal. "Which is to say," Richelieu continued, "that I want to be as respectable as possible."

Then the Maréchal had put on a simple and severe costume, kept his graying hair, devoid of powder, neglected to wax and tint his moustache, and had given himself the appearance of a very respectable old seigneur who has renounced all the pleasures of youth.

Lafleur was amazed.

"Go fetch me Madame Canizou," the Maréchal had added,

Madame Canizou was a lady of fifty in charge of the château sewing-room, who put on great airs and had an exceedingly elastic conscience. She had played a role more than once in the Maréchal's suppers and the King's amours. The dowry-less daughter of a petty gentleman, she had married some thirty years before, by courtesy of the Maréchal's protection, a certain Monsieur Canizou, a valet de chambre of the late King, who had died shortly hereafter, leaving her his lowly name and a few possessions. Monsieur de Richelieu had placed Madame Canizou at Marly, and had nothing but praise for the services of every kind that he asked of her.

However, Madame Canizou was not completely satisfied. She had a secret ambition that was eating her—an ambition, what is more, that the Maréchal had divined. She would have liked to be the superintendant of the royal house of the Parc-des-Cerfs.

Lafleur, therefore, went in search of Madame Canizou, who hastened to come.

"My dear beauty," the Maréchal said to her, "it's probable that in a few minutes we'll see the prettiest creature in the world arrive."

"Ah!" said Madame Canizou, darting a mocking gaze at the Maréchal.

"A little provincial girl, a lily, fresh and wild."

"Very good," said Madame Canizou.

"It's a matter of domesticating the lovely bird," the Maréchal went on, "all the more so as the girl, in coming here, thinks she's arriving at a château that belongs to me, and that she has no other objective but to thank me. I enabled her to win a lawsuit today on which her entire fortune depends."

"Oh, the dear child," said Madame Canizou, whose smile was still mocking.

"So, in order to domesticate her, "it's necessary that she finds someone respectable here."

Madame Canizou made a slight grimace. She carefully hid her age and still had a few pretensions.

"As she's provincial," the Maréchal went on, and she doesn't know anyone at Court, she'll mistake you for the Maréchale."

Madame Canizou quivered with pride.

"Go and dress yourself, my dear beauty," Richelieu continued. "Put on your diamonds and give yourself a venerable air."

"But isn't Your Lordship also going to dress up a little?" said Madame Canizou, looking at Richelieu.

"No. I want her to take me for a patriarch."

"Then I no longer understand," said the duenna.

The Maréchal smiled. "That beautiful fruit is too green for me," he said.

"Ah!"

"And we're expecting, from Versailles..."

"The King!" exclaimed Madame Canizou.

"And if we're content with you, my dear beauty," the Maréchal added, "it's probable that your wishes will be accomplished."

Madame Canizou reddened with pleasure.

"You'll change residence and go to the Parc-aux-Cerfs."

The duenna did not want to hear any more. She ran to her apartment, palpitating, and put on a costume extravagant in luxury and bad taste.

In the meantime, Espérance's chamber-pot had stopped at the perron. Then, as we know, the young woman waited for a full quarter of an hour, after which Porion had left her alone.

Finally, the door of the drawing room opened and Monsieur de Richelieu came in.

Espérance rose to her feet, very emotional, and wanted to throw herself at his knees.

But the Maréchal stopped her, and led her to the armchair she had just quit.

"My lovely child," he said, "I'm glad you had the kind thought of coming here. Madame la Maréchale will be charmed to see you."

And almost immediately, the door opened again, and Madame Canizou came in. She ran to Espérance and took her in her arms.

"Dear beauty," she said, "how glad I am that the judges have found in your favor."

"Oh, Madame," stammered Espérance, who mistook Madame Canizou for the Maréchale, "I know everything that I owe to Monseigneur le Maréchal."

Also thank the Maréchale, my dear child," said Richelieu. "She is very interested in you."

"Without knowing me?" said Espérance, blushing.

"I divined you, my child; and then, the worthy Porion had told us so much about you. But...where is he?"

And the pretended Maréchale pretended to search for Porion with her eyes.

"In the servants' parlor," said Richelieu. "The poor devil was dying of hunger."

"My beautiful child," said the pretended Maréchale de Richelieu, "You'll have supper with us, won't you? And you'll stay with us until tomorrow. I'm going to Paris anyway, and I'll take you in my carriage."

"Oh, Madame," said Espérance, "that's quite impossible."

"And why is that, my darling?"

"But Madame," said the young woman, "I have an old servant, or rather, a friend, a poor old man who served my father, and who, if he doesn't see me return, will be prey to a mortal anxiety."

"Don't let that worry you," said the fake Maréchale. "We'll send a domestic on horseback to inform him."

The Duc had such a paternal air, and the pretended Duchesse was so respectable at first glance, and they both insisted with so much kindness, that poor Espérance thought she ought not to refuse. How could she, in any case, bearing in mind how much she owed the Maréchal.

Madame Canizou sat her down at a small writing-desk that was in the drawing-room. Espérance wrote a long letter to Patureau, in which she announced her return for the following day.

Scarcely had the letter been written than a door opened at the back and the steward, in gala livery, announced loudly that Madame la Maréchale was served.

The Maréchal offered his hand to the young woman, and all three went into the dining room, where supper was served.

My God, Espérance said to herself, *I was right to have faith in you; you have had pity on an orphan and you have placed protectors in her route.* The poor child now had a blind faith in the good Maréchal and the pretended Duchesse de Richelieu.

They made her tell her story.

She told them naively how she had been left an orphan with a very young brother; how she had been despoiled of the fortune that, thanks to them, she had just recovered, and Madame Canizou, continuing her role, interrupted her to embrace her.

Then the pretended Maréchale addressed Richelieu. "I hope, my friend, that we won't stop on this fine road. You'll have Mademoiselle's brother admitted to the École des Cadets, and we'll make him a fine officer."

"Oh, Madame," said Espérance, "that's too much generosity. How could I ever repay you?"

"By loving us," said the pretended Maréchale.

Espérance ate very little. She scarcely moistened he lips in a glass filled with old Bordeaux wine. However, toward the end of the supper, her head suddenly grew heavy, and an excessive weight took possession of her entire body.

She had spent so many sleepless nights in recent times, and had experienced such great emotion, that that sudden lassitude appeared to her to be the result of the agitations to which she had been subjected. She tried to get up, but her limbs were numb.

The pretended Maréchale continued to smile at her. Richelieu's smile had broadened, and one might have thought, at first glance, that Espérance was with her father and mother.

The heaviness rose from her limbs to her heart and descended from her head to the rest of her body. Espérance's eyelids became increasingly heavy; her eyes closed. She succeeded in opening them again, but that final effort was the last act of will that she manifested. Her head slumped on to her shoulder, and soon her entire body was slumped in the armchair in which she was sitting.

Then Madame Canezou and the Maréchal exchanged glances.

"Help me to carry her to the chaise-longue," said the latter.

And Madame Canezou obeyed.

Mademoiselle Espérance, half lying-down, her beautiful head place on a pile of cushions, appeared to be sleeping as peacefully as the angels that God permits repose.

"How beautiful she is!" murmured the Maréchal.

The clock on the mantelpiece chimed nine-thirty.

"La la!" he said. "The King will be here in twenty minutes. I'm rendering you your liberty, dear beauty. You're no longer the Maréchale."

Madame Canezou bowed and went out.

Richelieu darted one last glance at the unconscious young woman, doubtless a glance of regret. Then he went out in his turn.

Espérance was deeply asleep; the narcotic had produced its effect.

And while she slept, there was a sound of footfalls in the garden, and two shadows appeared behind the curtains of the windows. Then a pane shattered, one of the casements opened violently, the two shadows took on substance, and two men leapt into the room.

One of them was armed with a dagger. The other was brandishing a long sword.

The first was Firmin the surgeon; the second, Messire Mardochée de Mardoche, painter and gentleman.

"Ah!" cried the latter. "We've arrived in time to save her."

What had happened, then, and how had that unexpected help reached the young woman? That is what we are about to tell you.

LXV

If Mardochée and Firmin arrived to rescue Mademoiselle Espérance, it was Cécile's father who was the cause of it, and this is how:

Robert Damiens had spent three days in Espérance's house without going out. Still prey to the baleful thoughts that assailed him, the unfortunate fellow dared not go back into the streets or pass over a bridge—in brief, put himself at grips once again with the temptations of suicide from which the worthy Patureau had snatched him

At the end of the three days, however, as he was calmer, and that was the day when Mademoiselle Espérance was to quit her lodgings in order to go to the Palais, Robert Damiens thought about his daughter again, and returned to the Latin Quarter.

Perhaps Cécile had returned.

As he approached the Rue Saint-André-des-Arts an increasing emotion overcame him, and perhaps he would not have had the strength to climb the stairs of Firmin had not suddenly appeared.

The young surgeon, who spent his days at the window, had perceived Cécile's father turning into the street. He ran down the stairs and ran to meet him. He threw his arms around him, saying: "Where have you come from?"

His tone was joyful. Robert Damiens felt his knees buckling.

"My daughter!" he said. "Where's my daughter?"

Firmin's exclamations did not take long. He told Francois-Robert Damiens in a matter of minutes that Hector de Pierrefeu had escaped from the Bastille and had departed for Flanders with Cécile.

"She's waiting for all three of us," he said.

"All three?"

"Yes, you, me and Mardochée."

"But where is he?" asked Robert, weeping with joy.

"We'll go to get him at nightfall, for he's terrified of Père Cinnamon."

That name did not make Robert tremble. Cécile's father had encountered Porion several times while he had been in Espérance's house, but he had never suspected that the seemingly-inoffensive old man might be the abductor of his daughter, the man who had thrown her into the King's arms.

Thinking about Espérance, who had rendered him calm, and had snatched him from suicide, Robert Damiens said to Firmin: "It's necessary that I'm not ingrate. A woman—an angel, rather—has saved me. At this moment, great interests are battling for her, and her entire fortune is at stake. Let me go to see her. Where will we find Mardochée?"

"Can you be at the corner of the Rue Saint-Honoré and the Rue des Frondeurs at six o'clock?"

"I'll be there," replied Cécile's father. And without giving the surgeon any further explanations, Robert, joyful to know that his daughter was safe, but full of anguish relative to Espérance's lawsuit, went back over the Seine and went to the Palais.

As he arrived at the door, he saw an immense, noisy crowd applauding. That crowd was forming a escort for Mademoiselle Espérance de Beaulieu, who was giving her hand to old Porion..

Robert tried to reach them, but the crowd was compact and the young woman had already climbed into a carriage in the company of Porion while Robert was still some distance away. He heard it said, however, that the case was won, thanks to Monsieur de Richelieu, and that Mademoiselle Espérance was going to the latter's house to thank him.

Then he made his decision. *I'll wait for her at the door*, he said to himself. And, gradually disengaging himself from the crowd, he started walking rapidly, heading for the Rue de Hanovre, where he arrived a fall half-hour after the vehicle that had conveyed Espérance. The two battens of the coaching-entrance were open and the street was empty of any carriage.

In the middle, the gigantic steward the Maréchal had taken with him when he had gone to see the draper who claimed to be the procurator Dumas resuscitated was pacing gravely back and forth. Robert did not hesitate to approach him and say to him that he was in the service of Mademoiselle de Beaulieu and ask whether she had come.

The steward replied: "Mademoiselle de Beaulieu is on the road to Marly, where Monsieur le Maréchal is."

Robert went away. How would he get to Marly, from which, in any case, the young woman could not take long to return?

So much had been said to him, in the previous three days, in the Place Royale, about the Maréchal's protection, that Cécile's father thought it quite natural that Mademoiselle Espérance had gone to thank him. He therefore thought about the rendezvous that Firmin had given him, and he headed for the Rue Saint-Honoré.

Firmin was already at the corner of the Rue des Frondeurs, and six o'clock was chiming at Saint-Roch. They both headed for the Rue des Orties and presented themselves at the door of the Coq-qui-chante. The landlord, Master Poussegrain, recognized Firmin.

"Ah!" he said. "Have you come for your friend?"

"Yes. Has he gone out?"

"No, he's upstairs, but you'll find him in a singular state. As six o'clock has just chimed, we were about to free him."

"What do you mean?"

"He's bound and gagged, and I had orders to keep him that way until six o'clock. You can go up now and set him free."

"But who gave you that order?" demanded Firmin.

"A man sent by the Lieutenant de Police."

Firmin deduced that Père Cinnamon had passed that way. He went up rapidly, followed by Robert and the landlord.

Mardochée, reduced to complete impotence, his gag covered with foam, was leaping about like a carp on the floor. Firmin hastened to cut his bonds and remove the gag, but as Mardochée got up, furious, leapt upon his sword and swore that he was going to kill the wretched hotelier, Robert uttered a cry of surprise. He had perceived the easel, and on the easel, the portrait of Mademoiselle Espérance.

The landlord, menaced by Mardochée's cabbage-cleaver had prudently run out of the door.

Mardochée wanted to run after him, but Cécile's father took him by the arm and stopped him, saying: "Who is that woman?" And he pointed at the portrait.

You can imagine the scene that followed.

Mardochée did not know Espérance's name, but he knew that the young woman was to be taken to the King that very day. By the description that Robert gave of Porion, who had taken the young woman to Marly, Mardochée recognized Père Cinnamon.

Then Robert Damiens cried, in an inspired and fatal voice: "The time for great expiations has come!"

An hour later, three men, in a carriage, were flying along the road to Marly. Mardochée had give orders to the coachman, who was whipping his horses and going at a rapid trot along the road on the hillside in the middle of which there was an inn. While Mardochée's carriage was climbing up from one direction, Porion's carriage, returning from Marly, was coming down in the other.

The innkeeper had emerged on to his doorstep, a lantern in his hand.

By the light of the lantern, Mardochée recognized Porion, who stepped down to the ground, for he had given the chamber-pot's coachman permission to give his horse a bag of oats.

Porion paid no attention to the other vehicle that was coming up the hill, and he went into the inn. But scarcely had he sat down at a table in the presence of a bottle of wine and a piece of bread than three men appeared before him: Mardochée, Firmin and Robert Damiens.

After having served Porion, the landlord had gone to attend to the horses. There was no one in the ground-floor room of the inn but a maidservant, who, at the sight of Mardochée's naked sword, ran away screaming.

Then Firmin closed the door and bolted it, leaving the two coachmen and the innkeeper outside.

As for Porion, he understood why the three men were there.

Mardochée raised the point of the sword to his face, saying: "This time, wretch, no one will come to your aid. If you know a prayer, say it, because you're about to die."

At the same time, Firmin and Damiens had seized him, and thrown him to the ground

But at the moment when Mardochée's sword was about to plunge into his breast, the wretch had an infernal presence of mind.

"If you kill me," he said, "you won't know anything."

And Mardochée's blade remained suspended over his breast, but did not strike.

Porion understood that his minutes were centuries. "I know who you're running after," he said.

"After the young woman who saved you and whom you've betrayed, blackguard!" exclaimed Robert Damiens.

"And who will be dishonored in an hour if you kill me," said Porion. "Now do as you wish."

Firmin had conserved more sang-froid than his companions.

"If you help us to save Mademoiselle Espérance," he said, "your life will be saved." And he retained Mardochée's arm, which was ready to strike.

The hotelier had come back to the door and, on finding it closed, he had not knocked. He had even made the maidservant shut up, who had run outside screaming.

"We don't interfere with quarrels between swordsmen," he told her. "That's the means of living tranquilly and making one's fortune."

Then Porion, who sensed that he could expect no mercy if he did not deliver his secret entirely, decided to betray the Maréchal and the King. He told the three men who wanted to save Espérance that the young woman was at Marly, in the hands of Monsieur de Richelieu, that the King was leaving Versailles between nine and ten o'clock in an unmarked carriage, and that he was coming to Marly. He confessed everything, and gave the most minute details.

And the three men listened.

When he had finished his confession, Mardochée sad to him: You're going to come with us, and if we arrive too late, you'll die."

Porion had showed Mardochée how one got rid of a man by binding him and gagging him. They did not gag him because they needed his information, but they tied his hands and feet. Then they carried him to the carriage.

Firmin sat beside him and held a dagger to his throat, telling him that if he uttered the slightest cry, he would kill him.

Faithful to his maxim of never getting mixed up in the affairs of swordsmen, the hotelier watched that departure impassively, and the carriage rolled toward Marly.

Porion understood now that his life depended on the salvation of Espérance. He knew the Château de Marly marvelously. He indicated a little

door to the park where the carriage stopped, and the road that it was necessary to follow to get into the gardens. Firmin and Mardochée gagged him then, and left him in the carriage. Then they went through the little door, which was open.

Mardochée turned round thereafter, and saw Robert Damiens, who had remained with the vehicle. He thought that the latter had stated to guard Porion.

But when the two young men had disappeared under the large trees of the park, Robert Damiens climbed on to the seat beside the coachman and said: "Take me to Versailles."

And his feverish hand caressed the hilt of a double-bladed pen-knife, which he always carried in his pocket.

And as the coachman obeyed, and whipped his horses, Robert Damiens murmured, dully: "The time is nigh…and this is the hour of great expiations...!"

LXVI

A certain mystery reigned that evening over the Château de Versailles. Contrary to his habit, the King had not gone out for two days. He had not gone to the Parc-aux-Cerfs, and the Marquise de Pompadour was looking worried.

The previous evening, it was said in the antechambers, the King had asked for Monsieur le Maréchal de Richelieu ten times, who had gone to Paris and had not returned.

Finally, it had been learned that the king had ordered a carriage devoid or armories and an escort of eight musketeers. Where was the King going with such a meager entourage?

In the times of the first First Mistress, the Duchesse de Châteauroux, the King, who was young, had often made such excursions, He had gone to his gallant rendezvous, about which the Duchesse, intelligent woman as she was, had feigned ignorance.

But Madame de Pompadour, who tolerated the Parc-aux-Cerfs, evidenced more jealousy than Madame de Châteauroux, and the King had no intrigue that she did not know by heart. It had, therefore, been a long time that the famous unmarked carriage had gone out, and even though the King had given the orders in great secrecy, the entire château knew what was afoot two hours later.

The Marquise had gone to see the King.

The King had told her nothing.

She had questioned her august lover, and the august lover had had the face of a sphinx.

Then, drunk on chagrin. The Marquise had gone back to her apartments, locked herself in, and appeared to be sulking.

In the depths of hr apartments however, she had drawn up an entire plan of treason, of which the King, according to her, was to be the victim.

If the King was going to a gallant rendezvous and had not breathed a word of it to the Marquise, it was because the woman concerned was a dangerous rival. The Marquise had no objection to the King having his temporary amours, but on condition that she knew in advance who her rivals were.

People were certainly preoccupied, at Versailles, in pleasing the King, but they were even more preoccupied with pleasing the Marquise. So, that evening, the King's secret was as poorly guarded as possible.

The King had wanted to leave the château incognito, but an hour in advance, the entire château knew that the King was going out.

Lebel alone was in the absolute confidence of the monarch and knew where he was going. But Lebel was the only man that the Marquise could not win over. Lebel kept his secret.

Then the people devoted to the Marquise ran around the hostelries and the most frequented quarters of the city, and, on her orders, spread the news that the carriage without armories would leave by the main gate a nine o'clock.

The people of all countries and all times have always been and always will be eager to see sovereigns pass by. At eight o'clock in the evening, the environs of the palace were filled by a compact crowd avid to see the King.

Sheltered behind her blinds, Madame de Pompadour watched that crowd growing by the minute, and said to herself: *The King will be furious, but when he sees that crowd, he won't go out and will postpone his excursion until tomorrow. But between now and then, I'll find out what I want to know.*

The Marquise was mistaken.

The King got dressed without even asking the reason for the vague murmurs that were resounding outside. He put on a coat of a dark color, ornamented by a simple ribbon of the Order of Saint Louis, and gave himself, thanks to Lebel, who was to accompany him, the appearance of an ordinary courtier.

Then with his legs crossed, he waited for nine o'clock to chime.

In spite of his impatience, he smiled and said to Lebel: "That poor Marquise...she's enraged, I'm sure of it.

"Oh, Your Majesty can believe it," replied Lebel, "and if Your Majesty didn't cover me with his protection, I'd be a doomed man."

"Why is that?" said the King.

"Because the Marquise has questioned me, Sire."

"And you have been mute?"

"Naturally."

"Well, don't worry; the Marquise won't lose you either your employment or my good graces. Go and see if the carriage is ready."

Lebel went out and came back a few minutes later.

"Sire," he said, "there's treason."

"Treason!" exclaimed the King.

"There are two thousand people around the château..."

"Uh oh!"

"Who are awaiting the appearance of Your Majesty, who wants to go out incognito."

"Damn!"

"And who are shouting 'Vive le Roi!' as loudly as they can."

"It's one of the Marquise's tricks. I recognize that!"

"Your Majesty will go out alone?"

"Of course."

"And...will go to Marly?"

"Flat out. Tell the coachman to harness fast horses, and the squadron to gallop."

"Yes, Sire."

And the King, haughty and frowning, demanded his cloak and went out of is apartments with his head held high.

The courtyard was crowded with people.

The gates had been opened and the crowd, pushing the guards, had driven them back in such a fashion that they had entered in a tumultuous flood.

"Vive le Roi! Vive le Roi!" they cried.

The King had a moment of hesitation; for a moment he thought about going back in and giving the musketeers orders to charge the people and drive them back outside.

But then he thought that the Marquise would triumph, and, obedient to an impulse of chagrin, he marched straight toward the carriage, leaning on Lebel.

But as the footplate came down and the King got ready to climb into the carriage, a man emerged from the crowd, approached the King swiftly, and struck him.

The King uttered a cry, put his hand to his breast and took it away again bloodied.

The man had not budged, and he was still holding his knife.

The two guards who are at the carriage door threw themselves upon him, at the same time as an immense clamor went up.

"Who is that man?" said the King, pale and trembling.

"My name is François-Robert Damiens, and I have no accomplices," he replied, calmly.

The King was only slightly wounded.

"Arrest that man," said Louis XV, "But don't do him any harm."

And the King's guards interposed themselves between the assassin and the crowd, whose members wanted to tear him to pieces.

"Mademoiselle Espérance is saved!" murmured Damiens, who did not put up any resistance.

MYSTERIES & THRILLERS

M. Allain & P. Souvestre. *The Daughter of Fantômas*

A. Anicet-Bourgeois & Lucien Dabril. *Rocambole* (stage plays)

Guy d'Armen. *Doc Ardan: The City of Gold and Lepers; The Troglodytes of Mount Everest/The Giants of Black Lake; Doc Ardan: The Abominable Snowman*

Cyprien Bérard. *The Vampire Lord Ruthwen*

A. Bernède. *Belphegor; Judex* (w/Louis Feuillade); *The Return of Judex* (w/Louis Feuillade); *The Shadow of Judex* (anthology)

A. Bisson & G. Livet. *Nick Carter vs. Fantômas* (stage play)

André Caroff. *The Terror of Madame Atomos; Miss Atomos; The Return of Madame Atomos; The Mistake of Madame Atomos; The Monsters of Madame Atomos; The Revenge of Madame Atomos; The Resurrection of Madame Atomos; The Mark of Madame Atomos; The Spheres of Madame Atomos; The Wrath of Madame Atomos* (w/M. & Sylvie Stéphan)

Félicien Champsaur. *Homo-Deus; Nora, The Ape-Woman; Ouha, King of the Apes*

Jules Clarétie. *Obsession*

V. Darlay & H. de Gorsse. *Arsène Lupin vs. Sherlock Holmes: The Stage Play* (stage play)

Harry Dickson. *Harry Dickson vs. The Heir of Dracula; Harry Dickson vs. The Spider*

Séamas Duffy. *Sherlock Holmes in Paris*

Alexandre Dumas. *The Return of Lord Ruthven* (stage play)

Paul Féval. *The Black Coats (The Parisian Jungle; Heart of Steel; The Sword-Swallower; 'Salem Street; The Invisible Weapon; The Companions of the Treasure; The Cadet Gang); Gentlemen of the Night; John Devil*

Paul Féval, *fils. Felifax, the Tiger-Man*

Louis Forest. *Someone is Stealing Children in Paris*

Émile Gaboriau. *Monsieur Lecoq; The Casebook of Monsieur Lecoq*

Arnould Galopin: *Harry Dickson: The Man in Grey; Harry Dickson: Tenebras*

Goron & Émile Gautier. *Spawn of the Penitentiary*

G.L. Gick. *Harry Dickson and The Werewolf of Rutherford Grange*

Léon Gozlan. *The Vampire of the Val-de-Grâce*

Georges Grison. *The Heads that fell in Paris*

Paul d'Ivoi. *Around the World on Five Sous* (w/Henri Chabrillat)

Paul Lacroix. *Danse Macabre*

Jean de La Hire. *Enter the Nyctalope; The Nyctalope on Mars; The Nyctalope vs. Lucifer; The Nyctalope Steps In; Night of the Nyctalope; Return of the Nyctalope*

Rick Lai. *Shadows of the Opera: Retribution in Blood; Sisters of the Shadows: The Curse of Cagliostro*
Etienne-Léon de Lamothe-Langon. *The Virgin Vampire*
Steve Leadley. *Sherlock Holmes and The Circle of Blood*
Maurice Leblanc. *Arsène Lupin vs. Countess Cagliostro; Arsène Lupin vs. Sherlock Holmes (1. The Blonde Phantom; 2. The Hollow Needle); The Island of the Thirty Coffin; 813; The Many Faces of Arsène Lupin* (anthology)
Gustave Lerouge: *The Mysterious Doctor Cornelius* (3 vols.)
Gaston Leroux. *Chéri-Bibi* (stage play); *The Phantom of the Opera; Rouletabille & the Mystery of the Yellow Room; Rouletabille at Krupp's*
Maurice Limat. *Mephista*
Jean-Marc & Randy Lofficier. *The Katrina Protocol;* (anthologists) *Tales of the Shadowmen 1-13; The Vampire Almanac* (2 vols.)
Richard Marsh. *The Complete Adventures of Judith Lee*
William Patrick Maynard. *The Terror of Fu Manchu; The Destiny of Fu Manchu*
Frank J. Morlok. *Sherlock Holmes: The Grand Horizontals* (stage play); *Sherlock Holmes vs Jack the Ripper* (stage play); *Sherlock Holmes, Fantômas, Lupin, Raffles and More: The Spanish Plays* (stage plays)
Jean Petithuguenin. *The Adventures of Ethel King, The Female Nick Carter*
P.-A. Ponson du Terrail. *The Immortal Woman; The Vampire and the Devil's Son*
Georges Price. *The Missing Men of the* Sirius
Charles Rabou: *The Secret Bureau 1; The secret Bureau 2: The Brothers of Death*
Antonin Reschal. *The Adventures of Miss Boston, The First Female Detective*
Norbert Sevestre. *Sâr Dubnotal vs. Jack the Ripper; The Astral Trail*
Eugène Thébault. *Radio-Terror*
P. de Wattyne & Y. Walter. *Sherlock Holmes vs. Fantômas* (stage play)
David White. *Fantômas in America*
Pierre Yrondy. *The Adventures of Thérèse Arnaud of the French Secret Service*

NON-FICTION

Stephen R. Bissette. *Blur 1-5. Green Mountain Cinema 1; Teen Angels*
Win Scott Eckert. *Crossovers* (2 vols.)
Georges Grison. *The Heads that Fell in Paris*
Jean-Marc & Randy Lofficier. *Shadowmen* (2 vols.)
Randy Lofficier. *Over Here*
Brian Stableford. *The Plurality of Imaginary Worlds*

www.ingramcontent.com/pod-product-compliance
Lightning Source LLC
Chambersburg PA
CBHW030749030726
47497CB00001B/208